toxic

Part One

Celestra Series
Book 7

ADDISON MOORE

Books by Addison Moore:

New Adult Romance

Celestra Forever After (Celestra Forever After 1)
The Dragon and the Rose (Celestra Forever After 2)
The Serpentine Butterfly (Celestra Forever After 3)
Perfect Love (A Celestra Novella)

Someone to Love (Someone to Love 1)
Someone Like You (Someone to Love 2)
Someone For Me (Someone to Love 3)

3:AM Kisses (3:AM Kisses 1)
Winter Kisses (3:AM Kisses 2)
Sugar Kisses (3:AM Kisses 3)
Whiskey Kisses (3:AM Kisses 4)
Rock Candy Kisses (3:AM Kisses 5)
Velvet Kisses (3:AM Kisses 6)
Wild Kisses (3:AM Kisses 7)

Beautiful Oblivion (Beautiful Oblivion 1)
Beautiful Illusions (Beautiful Oblivion 2)
Beautiful Elixir (Beautiful Oblivion 3)
Beautiful Submission (2016)

The Solitude of Passion

Burning Through Gravity (Burning Through Gravity 1)
A Thousand Starry Nights (Burning Through Gravity 2)
Fire in an Amber Sky (Burning Through Gravity 3)

To my family,
thank you for letting me live in my imagination.

Preface

Love can play host to rich delusions. It stifles reality and skews the truth to meet our insatiable desire to be wanted, longed for, needed. It waxes poetic on destiny and soul mates with thoughts of forever and happily ever after pinned high on its wings. Love affords you the luxury of a unique brand of trust, an intimate level of confidence that solidifies two souls as one. It unifies them under the false banner of all things holy and right.

I gave my heart away in exchange for beauty and a song. I put a hook through my nose and leashed it, handed the reins to the one who held my affections and gave him permission to lead me astray. It was the scourge of my youth that bore a thousand different sorrows.

Deceit. The grey clouds of deceit clotted my world. The battlefield moved from heaven to my heart. It came at me from all directions at once—an entire landscape of smoke and mirrors. Deception in acres spawned heartache for miles. This was no ordinary illusion. This was the severing of a lover's cord. The death of a pure and righteous love I believed in.

I bought into the calm still waters that surrounded the one that I loved and entered in, but the current pulled me under and swept me away—dangerous—inescapable.

A rainbow of truths finally emerged. It pushed the darkness away and thrust us back into the light.

We held our faces to the sun only for a moment before death clapped over us like a bridegroom snatching away his betrothed.

Death is a promise incapable of deception.

It tells the truth. You were destined to die from the moment you were born. It makes no promises, holds no delusions. Your corporal form was never meant to linger—

only love, in theory, is capable of withstanding time and memoriam.

Love promises happily ever after, it boldly professes forever—but delivers only one thing—a reckless brand of hope.

1

After the Fall

Chloe spears us together in one svelte move—the spirit sword's blade as sharp and deadly as her beauty. She bleeds venomous hatred as she drills the elongated razor into Logan's back. Her necrotic laughter bubbles to the surface like a demon's choir.

Logan and I illuminate from the inside a perfect sterile blue. My body trembles, a warm buzz vibrates throughout my veins and carbonates my blood. I look past Logan's shoulder at my beautiful Gage—my helper, my everything, my deceiver—and mouth the words, *help me—my forever.*

Chloe lights up the fog between us with her anxious breath. "Here's to happily ever after."

The stone opens up, swallows Logan and I—the blade still skewering us together, holding us secure.

"*Skyla!*" Gage's voice goes off like a gong, reverberating through this timeless tunnel of embers in one desperate cry.

Logan wraps his arms around me, pulls me in until his lips crash against mine.

We fall forever.

We search for happily ever after, but it never comes.

The darkest night—unimaginable sorrow. Searing pain blooms throughout my abdomen. It livens me with a white-hot jab that tempers the shock, the magnitude of the heartache Gage bestowed upon me. I would rather Chloe skin me alive ten thousand different ways than live through a deception so cruel.

Logan whispers something soft, soothing. His words come in spasms, a rhythm all their own. He's chanting, praying, petitioning a higher power as we continue to plummet with the sword still needled through our bellies. Logan and I are one, unified in every way. Captured by the Counts, our every nightmare finally realized.

I coil myself around him tight—my body locking up at the joints. This is my forever—one with Logan and the Counts. Wherever we land, whatever torment Demetri and the rest of those bastards have for us, I won't leave Logan for a minute. I'll die before they separate us. I'd run through a fire for the ones I love if I knew it would save them. As long as Logan is by my side the Counts haven't taken everything.

Falling in this dismal abyss, my new reality sets in and pierces me with a pain greater than the one delivered by the sword itself—Gage is the enemy.

This is the hour of the Counts. Everything is lost, covered in sorrow and mourning. I had little faith this time would come—that this moment ever had the power to exist. There was no anticipation, fear, or agony in preparation. This was the unthinkable, the impossible unfolding, every microsecond as unbelievable as the next.

A bloom of light sharpens at our feet as we pick up speed.

"Skyla." Logan's voice claps like thunder.

His body twists. He lays his strong hands over my shoulders and bears down on me with insurmountable pressure. The thick cords on his neck morph into cables of aggressive affection—painful and erotic. His beautiful face, knife-sharp cheeks, and eyes that glow like embers lie over me. They study the landscape of my features as gravity wraps its arms around us—pulling us down, heavy as lead.

The light below races to greet us. I brace myself before landing hard on my back with a jolt, and my head reverberates off the ground like a melon. A cry gets trapped in my throat, as the breath is crushed from my lungs.

The bloodied sword jumps from Logan's back and lands rather unceremoniously by our side.

Logan heaves over me, panting loud, searing breaths directly in my ear. "Skyla?" He rolls off. "Skyla, open your eyes."

I struggle to breathe, to think, to feel.

I give a few unsettled blinks before the world fades to a comfortable shade of pitch.

I'm falling again, this time in my dreams. It feels safe in this netherworld, locked in slumber, and for a moment, I wonder if this is what death feels like—if I've discovered it like some invisible horizon I've been chasing all along.

A familiar face appears from the nothingness—ruddy and tall, so gallant and strong—my father.

"Daddy!"

"Skyla." He shouts my name like a reprimand. His brows knit in horror as I take a bold step forward.

A large field emerges, alive with color. The shade is an incomprehensible emerald I'm not sure exists in the natural order of things. Flowers dot the field in exotic pinks and purples. They sing a hymn—buzz their choir of praise for all to hear.

"You need to leave," he barks at my celestial infraction.

"No." Running to my father is a pleasure—a treasure. This isn't a dream. This is real. This is more real than anything I've ever experienced before.

"You can't stay." A younger woman with her hair twisted up in a chignon appears beside him. She wears a smile perfumed with peace. Her features look strikingly familiar—I know that face, those mysterious sky-washed eyes.

"It's you!" I marvel at my grandmother in all her eternal glory. "You're so beautiful," I say it breathless, lost in her unblemished features. Both she and my father hold the gift of youth, neither older than thirty.

"Please, don't stay," my father begs. His loving eyes bow in sorrow, his voice wrapped in all of the pity he can muster.

"You can't stop me." I land safe in his comforting arms. His entire being emits a vibration, so soothing and calm, it rivals anything Marshall is capable of producing. This is love. It pours from him, saturating my soul with his ceaseless affection. I take in his familiar scent—hold the frame of his body, strong as a tower. "I love you so much."

His voice drips with grief. "You need to do something for me."

"Anything."

"Go home." He bores the words into me. "Write this down and remember it. Each day I want you to look in the mirror and say, 'I'm as pure as gold.'"

"I'm as pure as gold?" I look up at his sun-drenched features kissed by the strange light that ignites this new world.

"Pure as gold—I promise." He drops a kiss on the tip of my nose.

"Take me somewhere." My entire body yearns to run free and explore this alien mural come to life. "I want to see everything."

"You mustn't stay." My grandmother touches my hair. "It's not your time." Her eyes reflect silver pools much like my own. I've never seen her look so beautiful, so regal—elegant as royalty.

"You still have work to do, Skyla." Dad nods with a grieving smile. "I'm going to scare you now. I want you to wake up. Do you hear me?" He holds me back by the shoulders as he morphs into a thing of horror.

I let out a viral scream that rattles through every existence I've ever known.

A sharp quiver runs through me, and I bolt up in bed. A cold sweat trickles down my cleavage.

"Hey—" A hand smooths over my bare stomach. "It was just a bad dream." A seam of blue moonlight falls over the man lying next to me. I recognize those infectious dimples, that ebony-glossed hair—Gage.

He pulls me down toward him and drops a soft kiss on my cheek.

"It was my dad." I pant. "He had this giant eye on his forehead. It was just blinking out into nothing. Scared the hell out me." The image of my father, the Cyclops, brands itself into my memory, deep into my subconscious as a tool of torment for later.

A soft rumble of laughter thunders from his chest. My leg washes over his, and I'm all too aware of his hot flesh, the soft hair on his shin—his bare thigh. It's not until he pulls me in and covers my body with his that a slight rail of panic spirals through me. I seem to be just as unclothed as he is.

"Where are we?" I flex up my elbows, trying to adjust to the dark.

The walls, the bed—it's all in the wrong configuration. I don't recognize this bedroom, and it disorients me.

"Come here." He jostles me by the knee as if to wake me up from my slumbering stupor. "I'll remind you." Gage lands a searing kiss over my lips—wet kisses that stream forever. His body arches over mine, his stomach relaxing against me.

"What are you doing?" I slap my hands against his chest in an effort to keep him from sticking the landing.

A peaceable smile comes over him. His dimples dig in deep, turning into twin black pools under the anemic stream of moonlight.

"You're my wife, Skyla." He dips a quick kiss to the tender skin below my ear. "We do this all the time." He pushes my knees apart with his and nestles his body over my hips with his weight. The singe of his skin against mine sets me ablaze, and every inch of me detonates with pleasure.

A light explodes over me. I'm in another room—another dream.

Blinding light, white-hot pain.

"You can do this." A male voice pants in my ear. He sounds familiar, but a fire gnaws at my insides like a train derailing at a million miles an hour. I cry out in pain, and the room fades to grey.

The gentle roll of the ocean fills my ears, as the scenery changes again. My feet sink into warm sand as the beach greets me with its wide-open arms. A tiny hand squirms in mine. A blond head bobs beside me. A beautiful little girl stands level with my hip. I look up to find Logan holding the other small hand. He smiles over me and winces into my confusion.

"Another perfect day." His voice swims with a melody all its own.

A clap of darkness overcomes me as the scenery morphs.

I'm in bed with Gage again. He writhes over me, plunging a passionate kiss on my lips. He has me surrendering all of my formidable anger—all of the charges against him are dropped in an instant. I would worship at his feet all night long for him to love me like this under the cover of darkness with all of his smoldering affection, his heated skin over mine.

"Skyla," a voice whispers tender in my ear.

My eyes grit like sandpaper as they struggle to open.

The room takes shape, altogether different than before and I'm fully awake.

A warm leg hinges around mine.

I look up and see a bare chest, then follow the contour of his neck to his face. It's not Gage lying beside me this time—it's Logan.

2

Room for Two

The lights are on. Logan and I lie side by side on a bed smaller than my twin. My body glides over the sheets, slick and cold, devoid of any clothing. I pull the covers to my chin and scoot against wall in a feeble attempt at modesty.

I peek beneath the velvet cloth that acts as a blanket and affirm my theory.

"I had to take off your dress." He offers a threadbare smile. "You were bleeding, but the wounds healed. Are you in pain? Do you feel weak?"

"No. I feel..." I reach to the back of my head. "I feel fine."

"Good." Logan lets out a sigh. "I'll give her one thing, she managed to miss vital organs and spinal cords—we have that to be thankful for."

The idea of a laugh rumbles in my chest. I can't find it in my heart to be thankful for anything having to do with Chloe. She'll forever be the vindictive witch who linked Logan and I together with Demetri's haunted blade.

"I had these weird dreams." I reach up and pat my fingers along the high ridge of his cheek. Logan is weathered, older—noble like his light-driving self. "You're so handsome," I whisper. I stop shy of mentioning Gage, the way he defiled me as his wife. "Are you OK?"

"Don't worry about me. You're the one with an egg the size of a softball back there." He adjusts the pillow under my neck.

The room forms around him. It comes into focus with its black-and-white checkered floors, cathedral stained-glass window emblazoned with two fighting lions, and a ceiling that rises eternally to the sky. A bookshelf lines the back wall of this tiny cloistered space, smaller than my room back on Paragon. Dozens of novels and board games sit unattended, watching over us in stacks.

A water globe the size of a cantaloupe sits proud in the middle. A tiny black serpent glides along the inside, slithering from end to end as if looking for a way out—probably Demetri's dick.

"Where are we?" The words reverberate in my skull like a cymbal.

"I'm guessing the Celestra tunnels." Logan secures the blanket between us like a barrier, runs his hand over my thigh before relaxing in the divot of my hip. "I've heard Barron mention them. He was glad that at least our parents weren't dragged off here."

"Oh great." I groan. "So basically you're saying this is a fate worse than burning alive." Not the outlook I was hoping for.

I take in the fairytale-inspired room. It hardly seems capable of delivering such a grizzly fate.

"I tried to break down the door and shatter the window." He shakes his head with futility. "They've got the mother of all binding spirits guarding this place." He slides his hand up over mine and presses out a wry smile. *Can you hear me now?*

Yes, I say.

"That's all we've got left. No other powers work down here. Other than telepathy, we're practically human." He twitches his brows as if this amuses him on some level.

"What happens now?" It comes out with far more child-like innocence than warranted.

The light from above shines off Logan's shoulders and dusts his skin with an otherworldly illumination.

"I think we should expect someone soon." He leans in. "I'm pretty sure they're listening—watching. I wouldn't be surprised if there were an entire army of invisible Fems in the room right now."

His last sentence provokes me to draw up the covers tight around my neck.

The tiny worm trapped in the water globe stops abruptly—it leers at the two of us as if observing from afar.

Logan reaches up and brushes my cheek, my mouth with his warm fingertips.

"I love you, Skyla Messenger." It escapes from him like a prayer. He seals a kiss over my lips as one final act of worship. "I'm sorry you're down here with me, but I would be lying if I didn't say that I'm glad to see your beautiful face. I could conquer anything with you by my side—even death."

"I love you, too." I pull him in by the back of his neck. "And I hope I have a face by the time they're through with me." Logan and the ways he loves me are a thing of beauty all their own. He could conquer anything with me by his side and I sure hope the tunnels are on the short list.

Gage impresses himself in my thoughts uninvited. His invisible skin electrifies over mine. I fall back against the pillow and take a quick breath as a pang of fire rips through my skull.

I let out a groan that sounds more mating call than it does apocalyptic headache.

"It's OK," Logan whispers as if trying to soothe an infant.

"Brielle had her baby," I lament.

"I know." He pulls back the blanket and nestles into me, warm and inviting.

My eyes widen at the sheer acreage of flesh pressed against mine.

"Why aren't you wearing any clothes?" I ask slightly alarmed by where this might not so accidentally lead us.

"They were bloody." The beginning of a naughty smile curves on his lips. "I promise I have on boxers."

"Nice." I close my eyes and try to decipher whether or not the idea of Logan in nothing but his boxers is a sexual disaster in the making. "Logan?"

He groans in lieu of a reply, burrowing his face into my neck.

Logan and I are like injured children trying to comfort one another while pinned in the wreckage. Two trapped rabbits waiting for the hunter to break our necks—shoot us if he's merciful.

"Why do you think Gage did it?" A moan rattles deep in my chest at the thought of Gage being the well-placed boyfriend—that Chloe Bishop could have orchestrated our love seems every bit wrong, an entire black ocean of poison— an unfathomable deceit.

Logan brushes the side of my neck with his lips before twisting onto his back. He picks up my hand and bounces it on the bed between us three times before letting out a breath.

"It's Gage, Skyla." He says it flat as though I should give into the idea that Gage would never hurt me. Even if deep down inside I want that to be true, it's not at this very moment. The revelation is still fresh with its offense.

"I know it's Gage," I whisper. "That's why it hurts so damn much."

At regular intervals, the lights go out for what feels like a solid span of hours. They come on slowly, glowing like embers as if to rouse us naturally from our slumber. We've had no food for weeks, save for the water in the bathroom, and oddly, we don't crave fluids either.

The useless board games provided by Demetri's incompetent staff are rife with missing pieces. Box after box of well-worn boards, marbles, plastic houses, and paper money as worthless as our powers within these foreign walls. Then there are the books. Each of them written in some foreign script with fonts that run in dizzying patterns, the characters round and shapely like the figure of a robust woman—it's almost obscene to try to make them out—calligraphy bordering on pornographic.

The tiny serpent in the water globe amuses us. It quickly becomes our demented little pet. Logan and I track our fingers over the hollowed out glass, and it follows dutifully wherever we lead. It holds a menacing appeal, but there's a desperation it emits when we try to pull away that says, "play—stay a little longer, don't leave." Now and again it bears its silver, pointed teeth. It dares us to think we have power— that we are anything but impotent. It lets us know that it would kill us and eat us if given half a chance.

I drape the velvet blanket over myself like an evening gown, while Logan remains shirtless with the black pants he was wearing at prom.

The bathroom comes complete with a gold toilet. It erects itself from the stone floor like a monument to stupidity, as crass and egotistical as the Counts themselves.

"You think my mom and Tad are looking for us?" I peer over my cards at Logan. We're embroiled in a heated game with no stakes and loose rules. Really we're just going through the motions, so we don't succumb to insanity like they want us to.

"I think everyone's looking for us." He lays out a pair of cards with twin symbols printed on them, birds with talons three times the size of their bodies—probably some kind of flying Fem we've yet to encounter.

"OK, you win." I go over and lie on my stomach, pointing at my shoulders. "That means you get to massage me."

"Very funny." He moves in next to me, depressing the mattress as he takes a seat. Logan kneads his hands into my back, gently moving in a circular motion. He leans in and brushes his lips over the rim of my ear. "If you're the prize, I always plan on winning." He seals the sentiment with a searing kiss, high over my cheek.

Fighting off Logan's advances has been the real challenge, not that he hasn't tried to be a perfect gentlemen. Thankfully, he's no Holden Kragger. Logan wouldn't breathe in my direction if I asked him not to.

"Tell me something I don't know about you." He scratches my back in a series of lethargic circles.

"You know everything about me." I purr as his assault over my shoulder blades picks up pace. If Chloe the Frankenstiened cheer-bot didn't snap my back in half, Logan just might. "Slow down, please."

He reduces the tension by half. "What do you love?"

"You for doing this—you in general. Chocolate, sushi, malt shakes. All things I'm highly deficient in at the moment. Well, other than you."

"What do you hate?"

"Chloe and clowns. Come to think of it, Chloe is a clown."

"Other than Chloe. What do you dislike? I want to know you—know everything about you."

I twist around and study him from this angle. There's a sweet innocence about him, and Gage wanted me to believe Logan was nothing but a womanizing panty snatcher before I came to town. Gage spoon fed me lies right from the beginning.

I land my cheek back on the pillow. Just thinking about Gage sends me reeling with resentment and sorrow as wide as the sea.

"I hate caramel," I announce.

"Nobody hates caramel, Skyla," Logan teases, dropping his hands down my back.

"*I* do. I also can't stand humming or whistling. It's annoying as hell. It grates on me like nails on a chalkboard. In fact, I'd rather listen to a chalkboard being clawed than someone's oral cavity spinning a tune."

A sharp knock erupts at the door and startles us to attention.

I bounce into Logan's arms and cover myself in his protective shelter.

It's happening. They're here, and now everything is going to change.

Soon we'll wish we were on fire—dead—anything but alive and in the Counts incapable hands.

The door creaks open. The shadowed figure of a man fills the interim of light. He takes a step inside and brims with a wicked smile.

It's him.

Knew it.

3

Elysian

Demetri Edinger is not a handsome man by modern day standards, nor ancient standards for that matter.

His smile diminishes as he glowers at the two of us before shutting the door.

A thick wave of hair swoops neatly to the side, his large hooked nose lies prominent over his face, and yet he still manages to hold a debonair charm reserved for vampires and super villains alike. I can see how my mother might be swayed by his illicit advances, especially since her husband, Tad the moron seems incapable of giving her the attention she yearns for, like fire craves oxygen.

"I see you're comfortable," he says through a false smile. Demetri hasn't quite honed the fine art of acting human. He walks over to the bookshelf and taps the globe that houses the tiny worm behind a buffer of glass.

"You've met Isis," he says, running his finger over the sphere in one smooth stroke.

I decide to ignore his amphibious introduction. "How is my mother faring without me?" I say the word *mother* extra slow, trying to needle him with the guilt of my captivity. "I bet she hired you to scour the island clean, looking for the two of us."

"You flatter yourself." It comes out a tranquil hiss. "She's done nothing of the sort. In fact, I've yet to bump into her. I've been busy here myself." He reaches behind his hip and produces a thin silver blade in the shape of an elongated diamond, at least a foot in length. "Logan," he says, bowing slightly. "I have an offer for you." The sword ignites electric blue.

ADDISON MOORE

"More cutlery from the spirit sword collection?" I don't know why I bother to fear Demetri. Gage once said both Logan and I would live a nice long life. Not that he's batting a thousand with those visions, but still, you've got to believe in something, especially with a spirit sword staring you in the face.

"That's what I like best about you, Skyla." He extends the S in my name like the hiss from a cobra. "Your wonderful sense of humor. That, and the fact your perfect Celestra being is gracing my tower. Countenance is so pleased with my latest capture. They've initiated a festival in the honor of your blood. Does that make you feel like a celebrity? It should."

"No. Oddly, it makes me feel like choking the life out of you, which I'm certain will happen sooner than later."

Don't go there. Logan's chastisement comes out more of a lament.

"Nevertheless," he says, shifting his gaze to Logan, "you've sworn allegiance as a brother to Countenance. This is your opportunity to be promoted to council should you accept the challenge."

You get a promotion, and I get the blood siphoned from my body? Nice, I say.

"Skyla is in need of an Elysian." Demetri wands a hand over the sword, and it returns to its alloy luster. "A guardian, if you will—someone to watch over her mortal body and escort her to the tunnels whenever her blood is needed."

"You're letting me go?" I hang onto the one thread of mercy I can find in his words.

"Yes, but there are spiritual strings attached—a spiritual leash if you will—or noose." His eyes widen with malevolence. "I've no intention to cause emotional stress to the mother you speak so glib of." He gives a long blink. "Ordinarily, I would have you reside here. People disappear from the planet every day, Skyla. You would be missed, but you would most

24

certainly be mine. These four walls would be your new home."
His fingers strum through the air trying to entice me to the
mythical surroundings. "In your case, you wouldn't be alone.
You would have the companionship of the one you love by
your side. So many here in the tower are isolated—dare I say
all." He points to the wall just past the bed and it becomes
transparent. A window bleeds into the next room, then the
next, and the next until the rectangles compact in on
themselves. Each room houses but one person, and each one
looks bored to tears, grievously alone—one at the desk,
another on the bed, a third flat on the floor in utter despair.
Their pale, gaunt faces are lost in a hollow gaze. They have
been stolen by the Counts in every capacity, baptized with
cruelty in both body and soul.

Demetri snaps his finger and the wall restores itself like
switching off a remote. "We house the children with their
mothers." He nods as though it were perfectly sane. "And, of
course, the final destination—the Tenebrous Woods—that, my
friends, is—how would you say it? Where the action takes
place." He gives a curt nod and the wall ignites into a big
screen again. An overwhelming darkness appears, then a sea
of tree limbs form before our eyes, gnarled and twisted. The
hint of a dark navy sky glimmers between the branches.
Squared-off units—cages, emerge with a sickly glow and in
each one are people pinned to the walls, held hostage within
these cells, strapped with their arms spread wide, their legs
secured in a harness. It looks satanic, something just this side
of sexual, illegal and corrupt on every level. In another cell,
people are roaming about then pause to look up at us. They
move their arms toward us and in true 3-D fashion they
extend into the room.

I touch my fingers to one, and a jolt of fear so viral
lurches through me, it sends me deeper into Logan's arms. I
reach out and touch another.

Help, he cries. *Kill us. The only way out is death.* I pull my hand back like snatching it out of a fire.

"Logan." I bury my head in his chest.

"Yes, it can be quite disturbing." Demetri straightens as if my fright invigorates him. "The Countenance view the treatment chambers as nothing more than a factory with unruly employees. But how those Celestra souls cry out for people—how they hunger for the touch of another. It's the constant ignorant thread of hope that gives them something to look forward to all those long dreaded weeks while replenishing their vital fluids. Of course, they don't last long." He shakes his head in mock pity.

Dear God. I let out a breath in lieu of words. *He's got this entire dungeon filled with Celestra blood dispensers. That's so sick.*

I wouldn't go off just yet. Maybe wait until he's out of the room, Logan gives a slight squeeze as he says it.

As if.

"They're not as interested in companionship as you think," I say. "You know what they want more than an ice cream social?" I bark into Demetri's crooked nose. "To get the hell *out*."

Logan steps in front of me and clears his throat. "So, I'll be Skyla's Elysian?"

I can tell he's trying to defuse Demetri's temper, but in doing so, he's riled up mine. I'm not so hot on discussing spiritual leashes either.

"You will—should you choose to accept the offer." His dark eyes bear into Logan with the challenge. "You must do all that is asked. You, yourself, will be the purveyor of her torment. It's you who's to secure her body once the treble is initiated, if need be, to choose the celebrant who will be blessed to partake in the nectar of her marrow."

"No. I won't do it." Logan doesn't wait for him to finish.

Demetri tilts his head thoughtfully to the side.

A flash of lightning ignites through the window and fills the room with a dull rainbow of color. Rain pelts the stained glass, first slow and methodical then hard and biting. It's as though Demetri's anger has successfully channeled the weather phenomenon brewing outside.

"Then you die." Demetri nods into his revelation. "You'll be inflicted with a choice new body piercing." He briefly holds up the knife. "If you're still living by nightfall, I'll have you siphoned by a brood of thirsty Counts—an especially rabid group—they have an all-out carnal desire for the taste of human blood. They seem partial to the cry of a Celestra." He drills his eyes into me, burning through to the deepest part of who I am—the part where I stow my father and all of our best memories while we were still able to build them. He reverts back to Logan. "Robbing you of your lifeblood would bring them a profound sense of joy and accomplishment."

Tell him you changed your mind, I say.

I won't let them gain pleasure from watching me torture you. I would never hurt you.

But they would, and they will. Even if you die, you won't stop what's coming. Logan, please. They're going to do this to me anyway. I beg of you don't leave me.

"Are negotiations underway?" Demetri lowers his chin.

"They're done," I say, straightening. "He'll do it."

"Logan?" He looks over my shoulder at him.

Logan tightens his grip around my waist, touches his temple to mine. *Forgive me, Skyla.*

"Your answer?" Demetri broadens his shoulders with a sense of false accomplishment.

"Consider it done. I'll be her Elysian."

27

4

Tenebrous Woods

"Come." Demetri offers me his hand, but I refuse.

Demetri is complicated, like a puzzle with too many pieces—none of them interlocking. He wants every part of my mother, while he aspires to kill her daughter. There is no rhyme or reason to the things he does. Love and hate are one and the same to a monster like him.

Logan and I rise to follow him out of the room, but Demetri pauses, touches the water globe with a swift stroke of his finger, igniting the creature inside into a spasm of fear.

Figures. Not even an attention-deprived worm welcomes his affection.

"Isis," he whispers, the soft sound of the S reverberates unnaturally.

Demetri leads us out into an ornate hall, black-and-white checkered floors stretch for miles in either direction. Long mahogany doors line the corridor. Probably a Celestra soul locked in each one. If there wasn't a binding spirit dousing this place with its ironclad vice, Logan and I could do something—we could *help*.

"You've traveled two years into the past." Demetri says it causal as if it were common for small talk to center around time travel. "Or, what is it you kids are calling it these days? Light driving?"

I make a face.

Chloe originally called it light driving. Chloe is the one who should be down here. Her wickedness should be repaid in full measure by becoming the sole resident of these haunted halls. God knows she's got enough Celestra in her to qualify.

"What's with the time delay?" Logan squeezes my hand as he asks. I shoot him a look for fraternizing with the enemy, even though I was sort of curious myself.

"Reserves are terribly low," Demetri is quick to spill. "The faction has instated a treble until each year's needs have been met, and here we are, two years later, thirsty as ever. I'm afraid we'll need to devise a clever scheme to replenish the supplies."

He expels a wicked grin when he says the words "clever scheme" and it incites me to believe he's already mastermind one.

A blond man with a pale face, dressed in black from head to toe, comes upon us in the hall, and Demetri takes a clipboard from him. "Wonderful. It will be youth council then."

I recognize the man with silver colored spectacles hovering over his notes as Ellis's father, Morley Harrison.

"Hello—Skyla, Logan." He gives a polite nod to the two of us before dipping back to his work, banal as if he had passed us on the streets of Paragon.

"Shit." Logan seethes as he sweeps on by.

Demetri continues to lead us through the tunnel of my discontent. Gilded carvings of long vines slither over the walls, assaulting our vision from above as they take over the crown molding. It reminds me of the body art Emily inflicted on me during ski week. Gage was supposed to be the vine, the one constant that traced all over my frame, bleeding into my future with the promise of forever. And now here I am, a prisoner locked in this hellish vineyard—my blood the wine.

We walk for miles down the elaborate hall before hitting a set of black double doors with large gnarled fingers that protrude as handles. God—I bet they're the petrified hands of some poor Celestra. I can just imagine Demetri dipping them

29

into molten iron with glee while they were still very much attached to their unwilling donor.

"Logan," Demetri says, giving a slight bow, "you're to do what is asked of you. I've assigned a principality who will lead you through the procedures." He lowers his gaze to me. "Mr. Harrison informed me there were enough captures to bring the supplies to somewhat sufficient levels. I'm going easy on you, Skyla." He bears his teeth. "I'm gifting you to a youth pledge. I'll let the Elysian decide which one." He glances back at Logan and something wicked flickers in his eyes as if there were sexual implications involved for me.

My heart picks up pace as Demetri reaches for the handle. A panic quickens in me like a bull at the gate. My entire body is numb from shock and my limbs lock up at the joints.

"Please don't do this." I plead for one final act of mercy from the purveyor of this affliction, but he doesn't flinch, doesn't acknowledge my cry for help.

The door opens. A cool breeze licks against my face, my lips. It tastes my fear, taunts me with its icy tongue, lets me know I'm no longer my own.

An expansive darkness greets us on the other side. An owl cries out—a bloom of fog filters through the arid space before revealing a forest dipped in midnight. Another cry erupts, then another.

Dear God—those aren't animals howling into the night, they're people—Celestra—my people.

"No," I cry out in a panic.

"I tried to send you home." Demetri sharpens his features. He gave me the option at the stone and I refused to leave Logan. "You chose to be here." He widens the entry apathetically. "Bring her in," he instructs.

Logan picks me up and cradles me in his arms. *I'll die before I let them hurt you.*

He bounces a soft kiss onto my head before walking us through the door.

🦋 🦋 🦋

An overwhelming darkness, a blackness you can feel and taste, embraces us. A cool mist baptizes our flesh. It holds the hint of a peculiar scent, something metallic and bitter that I've never been exposed to before.

"I've left instructions with your principality, Ingram. Pay careful attention to whatever he tells you. Follow his commands, or it will cost you everything," Demetri says, laying his icy hand over my forehead as if he were offering some sort of satanic blessing. His cold palm has me recoiling from his touch and burrowing deeper into Logan's chest. "I'll see you both on Paragon." And with that he evaporates.

I jump out of Logan's arms and land with a thud on the soil of this wicked forest. A primal howl comes from the abyss of darkness. Screams, moans, and wails go off at regular intervals like a heartbeat. This is no room, no architecture of man holding us within its haunted walls. This is an evil thicket, a dimension of terror all its own.

"Let's get out of here." I try to pull Logan out the way we came, but the doorway—the walls—they're gone.

A glowing creature appears from nowhere, a man with grey skin that illuminates a dull phosphorescent. "Ingram." His lips spread into the idea of a smile. "Death will come to the Elysian if you escape," he says without moving his lips. His sodden eyes reflect an eerie yellow like that of an animal. He has a quiet way about him that neither alarms nor charms me. The translucent clipboard in his hand lights up like a laptop with a strange font visible from both front and back. "Both humiliation and torture are dispensed. I know this as a fact," he assures. "I'm in charge of doling out the two." He pulls his lips into a bleak line and points down a dim lit path. "Seventh chamber to your left."

"Chamber?" I gasp at the thought. There are only two kinds of chambers I'm even vaguely familiar with: one has to do with shacking up with Marshall under the sheets, and the other has the word "torture" associated with it. Right about now I'd opt for Marshall a thousand times over. It would be heaven to gift myself to Marshall in lieu of this insanity. I close my eyes and will him to be here, to touch me. I'd wrap my naked limbs around him and let him have me in a dozen animalistic ways if he wanted so long as I was free from this nightmare. Marshall corrupts my thoughts as I imagine his tongue burning a line of fire straight down my chest, his fingers kneading into my bare thighs as he dives down below my belly with a rash of heated kisses.

Logan rattles my hand. *Skyla?*

Sorry. I give a desolate smile. *I can't help it. I'm stressed.*

Logan moves us at a decent clip through thick-robed darkness. Walls open up to our left, rooms without doors, just large expansive clearings lined with cages. I slow down and observe the incomprehensible sight.

"Oh my God." I breathe the words. A wave of nausea fills me, and passing out would be a welcome reprieve.

People in every shape and size imaginable fill those oversized gorilla cages. Men sitting on the floor, women bustling against the bars with their hands held out in despair.

Farther down, a little girl sits alone. She springs to her feet when she sees me and presses her tiny body against the bars. Her pale stone eyes gaze out at me, her lips an ashen blue, skin the color of plaster. With everything in me, I want to take her back where she belongs—volunteer to die in her place. I slip away from Logan and bolt toward the chamber they hold her hostage in and her face enlivens with hope.

"Help me," she calls, reaching out for me in haste.

I snatch up her hand and press her tiny fingers to my lips in a kiss.

"What's your name?" I ask, uncertain of how I could ever help her.

"Lacey." Her little hand trembles in mine. "My mom is out there, but they always bring her back."

I glance down at her neck for signs of bruising, or puncture wounds but I see neither.

"Elysian," Ingram barks. "Retrieve her immediately."

I give a quick glance behind my shoulder at the irate old fool.

"I've gotta go." This is the part where I should promise to rescue her, to free her and her mother from the horror of this evil den. But I'm not sure I can keep that promise.

"Skyla." Logan wraps his arm around my waist. *I'm sorry, Skyla. We'll do what we can for her.*

"I'll come back," I whisper, unsure if I ever will.

Her serious eyes ingrain themselves in my mind. Her desperate face, her frail body tattoos itself over my heart. It's as if she's willing it to happen to ensure I never forget about her, imprisoned here in misery.

"Come back for me," she says. It comes with a hiss, but it's not until I see the tears swelling in her eyes do I realize she pushed those words out from a dam of grief.

I press my gaze into her and resolute the only way I know how without making a clear promise to this sweet innocent child. "I will try my best to come back for you, Lacey. You and your mother."

"Now," Ingram barks.

Logan pulls me from the cell and back onto the blackened pathway.

I glance back at Lacey as she wipes tears from her eyes.

33

ADDISON MOORE

Shit. If I didn't hate this hellhole enough before, I despise it now. I'll get Lacey out if it costs me every drop of blood in my body. I hope it doesn't, but I'm pretty sure it will.

"Logan," I hiss at his eagerness to deposit me into some youth council's waiting arms.

"No, no." The guide temporarily disrupts our journey. "You must never again address the Elysian by his proper name. He is to be referred to as Master at all times." His gaze shifts to Logan. "You must either punish or humiliate your subject in the event she refuses to address you properly. You must be prompt with your consequence. Should you forgo chastisement of such behavior, you'll receive a demerit." He leans in. "Three demerits and you, my friend, are out—in a rather slow yet violent manner. If it's one thing the Countenance takes seriously, it's the ritual in which they carry out their ceremonies. The proper exaltation of their being is of utmost importance."

"Good to know," I seethe. I'll be sure to spit in Demetri's eye the next time I'm within striking distance. Obviously, my bodily fluids were wasted on Marshall. It was Demetri I should have been going after all along. Master my ass.

"Be glad, Skyla darling." It comes out cold, like a reprimand. "And do not forget—he is your Master, and there is no other." Ingram's face illuminates a little brighter. It reminds me of the sickly glow you get from a flashlight just before the batteries expire.

We proceed down the torture trail, and another chamber opens up to our left. The glint of metal catches my attention. A rope hangs from a lone bar in the center of the room as a blue fog penetrates the baron space. The next chamber stretches wide like a mouth, expansive and cavernous, ready to swallow me whole. It hardly qualifies as a room. Evil pulses from its skeletal frame as alive as Demetri himself.

A lone chain hangs from a crossbar with opened metal cuffs.

"Strap her in," he instructs. "I'll retrieve the council."

I look to Logan with a biting pain in my heart. I asked him to stay, to do this to me willingly, and now we were both regretting my decision.

He looks to the bar, then back to me. He presses a lifeless kiss against my lips before scooping me in his arms and running like hell.

5

Pain in the Offering

We move swift as shadows through the ever-increasing darkness. Logan jostles us through a murky fog, thick as grief, before a large bearlike creature blocks our path.

Logan lowers me to my feet without taking his eyes off the beast. Its head has been badly burned, and beneath the scars, lie the faint features of a man with fangs that dip down to its chin.

"Run," he says, getting down on his knees and bowing in defeat to the misshapen Fem.

"No." I pull at his shoulder. "I'm not going anywhere without you."

Ingram materializes like an apparition before Logan can get on board with the run-like-hell-from-the-Fem plan.

"There is no escape, Skyla." Ingram steps into me. "Logan, your council status will be denied, and your prisoner status invoked, should you choose to rebel once more. I'm feeling rather soft this evening. Don't test me again." Ingram places his hand on my shoulder, and within a moment I'm in the chamber again with a lone chain hanging from the bar up above and Logan nowhere in sight.

"Where is he?" I ask the bastard who dared to separate Logan and me.

"I'm afraid he's detained at the moment." His grey skin wrinkles into the idea of a smile.

A million versions of what that might mean pulsate through my mind.

"You're a Levatio." I say it as fact. Levatio are the only ones I know capable of teleportation.

"You show me yours, I'll show you mine," he says nonplused as he glosses over his clipboard. "Wrists in the manacles, please. Drag this out another ten seconds and I'll replace the junior council with a Count so perverse you'd rather lick vomit off my feet than be subject to his touch."

"There was a little girl back there," I say, cinching the makeshift dress tight around my body and securing it at the top. So help me God if this velvet toga falls off—although I suppose my dignity is low on the priority list compared to what Logan is up against. I raise my arms voluntarily to the cool metal and the bracelets automatically latch over my wrists.

"Many children reside in the tunnels." Ingram doesn't look up from his clipboard. "There's nothing you or I can do about it. Tragic, isn't it?"

"So are you a prisoner here, too?"

He glares over at me, his finger frozen midflight above the razor thin device. "None of your business."

Curious.

The last thing I want to do is piss him off. He's already invoked his supposed mercy once, and personally, I'm hoping for a replay.

"Is this going to hurt?" I ask, changing the subject.

"Most certainly. Although on the rare occasion it evokes pleasure. Let's hope for the latter." He scans me with his unearthly yellow eyes. "That boy—he loves you." It comes out as fact. "I believed in love once." A sour smile plays on his lips. "Tell you what—seeing that your master is presently occupied, I'll bring in the junior council and let you choose the celebrant who'll drain you. Fair?"

I find it amusing he managed to follow up the words *drain me* with the word *fair* with a straight face. But in truth my arms are already killing me in this exaggerated position, so I go along with it.

"Fair." A thin film of fog expels as I say it.

A hard groan—a scream from a distinctly familiar voice emits from the bowels of this hellhole.

"Logan," I shout his name in one agonizing cry. I struggle to break free, but the bracelets lock over my wrists tighter than before, cutting off the circulation on my right.

I still my breathing as I try to listen for him. God, what if they've killed him? My chest heaves with a dry sob at the thought of losing Logan. The idea of him suffering because of me is too much to bear.

Ingram reappears with four boys about my age; two darker looking souls with nefarious grins that lend me to believe they might actually run around in the world with Kragger as their surname, a frail-looking boy with a shock of red hair, who openly sneers at me, and an open-faced boy with dark hair—eyes like brilliant peridots. He looks eerily similar to Gage, like he could be a brother, a twin, right down to the dimples.

"You," I say, accusingly.

His eyes widen. For whatever reason, he wasn't expecting to make the cut, and he nods as if to thank me.

"You've chosen Wesley." Ingram waves the other boys away. A necrotic blue fog wafts over them, and they disappear quick as they came.

The boy comes forward, steady in his gait. His broad shoulders and muscular arms remind me in every way of my former love, the boy who fashioned a knife out of Chloe and pummeled my heart with her.

Ingram secures a pair of shackles over my ankles, foiling any plans I might have had of introducing my knee to my new suitor's balls. He pulls down on a metal chain from behind, and my arms and legs separate a good two feet. It feels vulnerable like this, altogether wrong and perverse.

I glance behind him in the navy forest for any sign of Logan, the sound of his voice, of his footsteps, but there's nothing.

"Wesley." The boy reiterates his name instead of hello. "I won't hurt you. I promise." His eyes soften as he dusts me with his gaze. "I'm sorry," he offers before licking his lips. He blinks a depleted smile and steps in close, nuzzles his face into my neck without any further sentiment or ceremony. His arms encircle my waist as a soft moan escapes him. If we were anywhere but here, if my limbs weren't stretched taut until my bones were on fire, you would think he was my boyfriend, that he was about to shower me with his lingual affection— that I wanted it.

His black hair catches the light, and for a brief heartbreaking moment, I fool myself into believing its Gage— the one I thought I knew, but it's not. It's some twisted nightmare devised by the Counts. I wish that this were nothing but a dream. That I could open my eyes and my father would still be alive—that Paragon and all of its inhabitants were nothing but a figment of my imagination.

Logan's voice rips through the night. He's fighting for his life because of me, and here I am, inadvertently wishing he never existed.

Wesley's teeth graze along the left side of my neck just under my jaw. I can feel the puncture, feel the first slow pull, and I take a breath and hold it—forget to let go.

This demon—this boy, takes in my blood with a greedy fervor.

Logan lets out a horrific growl every few seconds. I can't bear his torment. I wish he were home, at the bowling alley— coiled around Lexy Bakova's body, anywhere but here suffering because of his love for me.

A strangled silence settles over the chamber—nothing but the quickened pace of Wesley's breathing fills the interim.

"Logan," I whisper. As unbearable as it was to hear him, not hearing him feels a hell of a lot worse. I'll make this up to him. I'll spend my life trying to do just that.

A sob quivers from my chest. I try to focus in on Wesley, so I don't lose it. A caramel-haired girl fills his thoughts. At first I'm afraid to venture any deeper, in fear this is about to morph into some fornicating bonanza, but he doesn't go there. Wesley envisions himself dropping to his knees, holding a small velvet box between the two of them like an offering. She nods, ecstatic at the proposal, prompting him to his feet. He takes her face in his hands, cradles her with a kiss that's almost chaste. Every cell in his body radiates his love for her.

Laken. He whispers her name over and over, and I latch onto it like a song. It sounds hauntingly familiar, like I've heard it somewhere before, but can't pinpoint where.

Gage passes through my mind and I try to evict him swift as he came, but he lingers. He stains my thoughts like an indelible inkblot I can never be rid of. Gage scarred the landscape of my soul. I rearranged my relationship with Logan for him and he, in turn, rearranged my heart in pieces. Gage appears behind my lids and falls to his knees. He holds a small velvet box between us like an offering. It's empty inside, no ring, no promise of forever in the form of a shiny gold band. He rises and takes up my face in his gentle hands, drains me from the inside with a smoldering kiss without my permission.

I riffle through the junk drawer of my mind for every moment we once shared—the first time we met, the day he told me I would be his wife, the day he gave me Nev.

I swim in the memory of who we once were until the world beneath my lids ceases to exist.

Barely breathing. A cool breeze. A moan prods me to open my eyes.

Logan lies beside me on the bed.

"Oh my God." It takes all of my effort to breathe those words.

A series of crimson welts lay across his back in thick cordlike stripes. Inflamed pillows of flesh rise in long, striated lines, like claw marks from very sharp nails.

"Logan." I brush against his shoulder. My arm hardly shifts at my command, too weak, too heavy to move in concert with my mind. "Logan?" It comes out a hoarse whisper.

His eyes flutter open, first in slits, then enough to expose a thousand broken blood vessels.

"Oh, God!" My chest heaves from the effort. I might pass out at the sight of his battered body. They've destroyed him. And it's all because of me.

"I'm OK." He takes a shallow breath and sits up slowly, wincing from the shock of pain. "Skyla." My name gravels out of him. Logan pulls me into his arms and cradles me, despite his injuries. I melt into him, mourning the two of us tangled in pain and sorrow. We've fallen so far from who we thought we were last summer. Our affection for one another was proving lethal whether or not we took down the Counts. There's no doubt in my mind they planned to drain us both, right from the beginning. It's only a matter of time before they take him, too. Our days are numbered, and soon, we'll both be with my father in Paradise. Gage was wrong regarding the measure of our years. He was nothing short of a liar—a traitor in the worst capacity.

A blast ignites from above as the window shatters.

A rainbow of colored glass explodes across the room like a sheet of crystallized confetti. I pull the blanket over the two of us and the tiny shards press against the velvet with their knife-sharp fingers.

We look back up to see a madman wielding a baseball bat, trashing the window until every last piece of the framework is destroyed. He jumps into the room and smashes the bookshelves with a violent force. The mirror that once hung proud explodes under the supervision of his weapon. He pounds large walloping holes into the walls with a fierce level of anger.

I take him in from the side—that shock of black hair, the alabaster skin, the structure of his body, I recognize him intimately.

He turns and spears Logan with his insolence.

"Gage." I meant to scream it, to *hear* it, but it comes out less than a whisper.

He lifts Logan up and tosses him against the wall inspiring the water globe to nosedive off the shelf.

"You touch her?" He roars it out with a viral aggression.

"No." Logan moans from the spontaneous jostling.

A shadow slithers across the floor and catches my attention. The water globe lays shattered, and the strange worm that once took up residence in it begins to augment in size. It inflates into a fully formed snake, then unrepentantly continues to grow in both girth and stature.

"Skyla—" Gage appears before me. "We have to get out of here," he says it low, almost loving in nature. He scoops me in his arms and brushes his lips over mine. "I know you hate me." He squints into his words. They gutted him on a primal level, but it probably has more to do with his ego than genuine devotion. "I just need you safe." I fold limp as wet paper as he maneuvers us through the room. "Move," he barks at Logan.

Gage climbs out of the window with me tucked in his arms. He lands us safe on a strange glass surface.

"Give me your hand," he instructs Logan as he hoists him out. A wound stretches open over Logan's shoulder and a river of blood baptizes his chest. "What the hell did they do to you?"

"I'm all right." Logan takes a quick breath.

The serpent continues to fill the room with its ever-growing body until its grotesque head protrudes out the window with odd teeth, long as steak knives.

"Shit!" I try to snatch at his shirt in a panic, but the energy it requires has left me.

A vaporous wall warbles in front of us like steam lifting from a sidewalk on a hot July day. It radiates a layer of warmth in smooth, inviting ripples.

"Hold your breath," Gage shouts at the two of us.

"Can't breathe," I whisper. I'm so weak, so depleted to begin with, that all of this excitement might actually finish me off.

Gage seals his lips over mine, and we fall backward into a pool of icy water. He presses in a sweet kiss as he swims us to the top.

It's bliss like this with Gage, if only for a moment.

6

Gage in a Rage

Gage places me in his truck as the evening sky rotates above with a summer storm to greet us.

He lands a soft kiss over my cheek. "I love you with everything in me, Skyla," He whispers as his eyes sear me with their pain.

He heads over to Logan and helps him into the back of the truck. I watch as Logan collapses onto his stomach, the rain pelting over his wounds, soft as tears.

I take a deep breath at the surroundings—the crystalline pool, the long rolling lawns, the mansion the size of a warehouse—a replica to the one in the Transfer. I recognize this place as Demetri's paradise-like backyard, complete with ornate fountains—a rose garden that stretches out for miles.

"Paragon," I whisper.

Gage jumps in next to me and starts up the engine.

"Are you in pain?" His eyes dart over me, wild with concern.

I shake my head. "Just weak."

He buckles me and speeds us the hell away from Demetri Edinger's estate.

The familiar roadway opens up as Paragon extends its loving arms to greet us. Trees wave wild as the sky gives birth to a torrent. I forget all about the weirdness between Gage and me and relax into his seat, praying Logan doesn't drown in the back.

"How long were we gone?" I ask, as the scenery picks up to a more familiar structure. The property lines begin to narrow in comparison to Demetri's sprawling lair.

Gage pulls into the Oliver's driveway, reaches over and takes off my seatbelt with the upmost care.

"One night," he says, appearing on the passenger's side without missing a beat. Gage cradles me in his arms as he extricates me from the truck.

"One night?" I whisper. We were gone for weeks.

"You were in a treble." Gage teleports us to the back of the truck, touches Logan's shoulder and we blip out of existence.

It's been a good long while since I've been to the morgue—and for good reason. Dead bodies and I don't always get along.

Logan appears lying prone on a metal gurney. He groans into his pain, his back covered in bloodied streams and beads of rain.

"Dear Lord God almighty." Barron's voice booms like a fire and brimstone preacher as he approaches. He looks aged. Deep lines crease his forehead at the sight of his brother slash nephew. He lifts his gaze to me lying limp in his son's protective arms. "Lay her there." He points behind my shoulder before handing him a neatly folded sheet. "Heat this in the microwave. Pull it out before it catches fire."

Gage places me down on a mat laid over the metal bed where the autopsies are routinely performed and presses out a smile. Just the thought of him siding with Chloe makes me want to vomit all over him.

He disappears and plays with the microwave, returning a few minutes later with the sheet and lays it over me—oven hot—and I seize, greedy for its warmth.

"Ms. Messenger." A familiar voice strums over me smooth and inviting.

Marshall.

I would pay in flesh to have him cover me with his body—reconstitute my blood back to life-giving levels.

"What happened?" Barron inquires while spraying down Logan's back with an aerosol bottle, and the room lights up with the antiseptic odor.

Logan lets out a roar before sitting up and batting away Barron's efforts.

"Counts had us nearly three weeks." The words knife out of him, still in pain from having his wounds cleansed. "Demetri came in last night and decided to conduct the blood draw—said we were back in time two years. They're desperate." He goes on to explain about the Elysian and the beating he received at the hands of a Fem. "I don't know what happened to Skyla." He gives a forlorn look in my direction, the sum total of every apology man has ever known, rolled into one.

"What happened?" Gage leans in and brushes the loose hairs from my forehead with a tenderness you would think one could never fake and it makes my heart break all over again.

"She's been tormented, you dolt." Marshall speeds over and presses a luscious kiss over the top of my head. His feel good vibrations radiate from my forehead like a symphony. "The fresh bruising on her neck should have alerted you." He takes up my hand, sends a pleasant reverberation through me, and I hold on tight, begging for him to never let go.

"Skyla—" Barron appears beside Gage. "You must undergo a transfusion. There's no doubt in my mind that your organs are grinding. You could have scarring, permanent damage could occur—but I don't have the blood of a Celestra on hand."

"Logan." My lips hardly move when I say his name.

"No, love." Marshall sharpens his gorgeous features over me. "The Counts will turn him into a ball of yarn for the celestial cats running wild in the tunnels. Not a drop of his blood can enter your body. He's one of them now, and they take treason quite seriously." He pauses. "If Logan dies, it's final. Once a Count is resurrected, they're as mortal as the rest of you. They will know if his blood enters your body, and they will kill him."

"Logan." It comes with tears this time. I can't bear the thought of losing him. I've already lost Gage. Although he's physically hovering above me, he's merely a shell of who he used to be. This is an imposter—Gage has been one all along.

"Marshall?" His name quivers from my lips. "Give me your blood."

"I would be more than happy to comply, but it would kill you with efficiency," he whispers as his golden hair catches the light like a flame. "There is a way. I've instructed Dr. Oliver to prepare an elixir that will force your body to restore your blood to normal levels within hours. I won't lie—it's quite painful. However, in order to correctly boost the levels in time to stop an internal meltdown, your body needs to undergo a powerful irritant." He says it matter of fact like he were reading something banal off the back of a cereal box.

"No thanks." The thought of irritating my body in order to boost my levels sounds about as appealing as road kill stew. In fact I'd rather eat road kill stew and die in peace.

I relax in the false bedding beneath me and reconcile the fact that soon I'll be reduced to nothing more than casket decor.

"Nice try." Marshall refutes my efforts. "But the faction war needs you. The entire human race is in need of your supernatural services. I'm afraid death is not an option and neither is convalescing until the next time the Counts pull you under for an involuntary donation."

I open my mouth to protest, then realize for the first time Marshall is actually standing here and he just mentioned the faction war and the Counts in front of all three Olivers.

"Everyone knows you're a Sector?" It's the first thing that springs from my lips with vigor.

"No point in lurking in the shadows now that you've been captured." He glides in and out of a smile. "I'm not advertising my celestial status outside of this small circle and neither should you."

I shake my head, not admitting to the fact I may have let a few other people in on his secret, like Dr. Booth and Chloe. Chloe is just like that worm back at Demetri's hall of horrors. Once you unleash her into the world she becomes nothing but a big, fat nuisance.

"So what's the plan? How are you going to heal me?" I'm hoping this involves Marshall's body, his feel-good vibrations, and very little else.

Marshall dips his chin down to his chest and gives the gleam of a wicked grin. "I'm going to poison you," he says with unrequited calm.

Exactly what I was afraid of.

7

Stranger Danger

The idea of Marshall poisoning me swills through my mind.

Gage blips Logan back to the house, so he can get some much-needed rest and takes Dr. O with him to get Logan settled. It's a relief having Gage out of the vicinity. I'm far too weak and tired to bleed out my emotions for another minute.

Marshall sits me up and I recline against his blessed-by-God body. I could spend an eternity resting in his pleasurable embrace. I watch the rain press into the glass as it spreads into sheets against the window. Every now and again, the world lights up with an electrical charge so violent you could swear the end was near. That's how I envision the great apocalypse, all hellfire and rain, nonstop thunder and earthquakes—Gage with Chloe in his heart.

Marshall heads over to the sink, and I lie back on my side and observe him as though every move he made were imperative for my survival, my sanity as a whole. He washes an entire batch of apricots before smashing them to bits and pieces with a small wooden mallet. The mortuary in general isn't the best place to whip up a fruit salad, but who am I to school a Sector on culinary hygiene?

"What are you doing?" I inquire.

"I'm attempting to prepare the right ratio of cyanogenetic glycosides. Just enough to kill you—no point in going overboard."

Sorry I asked.

Gage pops back into the room.

"Hey." His dimples go off, and I look away. Their obvious powers of seduction are still in play even in this sorry state of being. "My dad needs a few minutes. Are you feeling better?"

He pulls up a chair. Gage doesn't hesitate picking up my hand and kissing it. I'd slap him silly, but I'm all about breathing at the moment with no reserves for anything else.

"Marshall is preparing a dish for me. But don't worry, it's just enough to kill me," I manage just above a whisper.

Gage pulls a bleak smile, averts his eyes toward the exterminator in question for a brief second. "I won't let him kill you."

"Marshall doesn't have to worry about killing me," I seethe, holding his serious gaze hostage. "You beat him to it."

"Skyla." He pulls my name out in a mournful sigh.

"I *forbid* you to speak to me." I pull my fingers free, and my hand falls limp to my side.

"Lover's spat?" Marshall appears holding a glass of milky brown liquid.

I shoot him a look. Marshall is relishing this "lover's spat." I can tell. Anything that lends me distance from the Oliver boys and sweeps me in his Sector arms is more than a welcome change of pace.

I nod for him to continue with the toxin concoction he plans on inflicting me with.

"Never fear, love." Marshall helps prop me up and holds the elixir to my lips. "I wouldn't dream of letting the reaper make haste with my bride-to-be."

I smile at Gage when Marshall says the words *bride-to-be*. I hope he chokes on those words at dinner, hears them over and over on a loop until he's dizzy and wants to vomit.

Marshall taps the glass. "I promise you the effects of the cyanide will simply shut down your kidneys and force your blood to mass-produce hemoglobin in an effort to push it through the liver and rid the destruction through your digestive tract. Nothing a little one-on-one with the porcelain throne won't cure."

Crap. Not only am I going to die after chugging down the suicide solution, but I'm going to have a rabid bout of explosive diarrhea as my last living memory.

"As your future bride-to-be, I appreciate your honesty." I nod at Marshall and reluctantly take the dark liquid from him. I glare at Gage for a moment. Honesty is something he's allergic to.

"It's soda with an apricot seed reduction," Marshall asserts.

"A cyanide smoothie." I smile at him lovingly. "I can't wait until our honeymoon," I say with the last bit of energy my body is able to dispense. I have high hopes of Gage having a coronary episode while envisioning my post marital vacay with our math teacher, and how apropos for him to succumb to his demise in the morgue of all places. And with no Dr. O around to save him—tsk, tsk.

I push the drink to my lips and knock it back in one giant gulp.

Shit!

A bitter jolt corrodes my taste buds, viral as battery acid. My tongue inflames before swelling like a balloon. It arrests my ability to swallow and throws my gag reflex into overdrive.

Poison! It finally hits me. Marshall really is trying to freaking *poison* me.

With an animated level of panic I no longer thought possible, I toss the glass clear across the room and flail in a fit of retching histrionics.

Dry heaves bubble to the surface. An entire string of inglorious belching discharges from my body until finally I manage to hurl food I didn't even know existed inside me all over the toga I have strapped on.

Gage swishes around like a blur, producing a glass of water from a beaker, and I swill the liquid in my mouth. The thought occurs to me the beaker probably has the chief function of housing eyeballs, extracted dental fillings that Dr. Oliver might be selling for gold on the side, or God forbid, strange bodily fluids that ooze from the deceased, and I puke like a fountain.

Gage glances at his phone. "I'll be back." He no sooner evaporates then he reappears with his father.

"Good God, child." Dr. Oliver's face is white with shock.

"I've already converted the oil base." Marshall strides up with a hypodermic needle. "The smoothie wasn't to her liking."

Gage helps douse the vomit fire out of my lap with a dozen tiny towels.

"I'll get you some clothes." He looks up at me, his face veiled in pain. "I never wanted to hurt you." He disappears before I have the chance to properly hurl on him.

I never wanted him to hurt me either.

"Her complexion is ashen, and her pulse is weak," Barron says, replacing my wrist in my lap. "If the shot doesn't work, I've no choice but to run her to the emergency room."

Marshall flicks at a tiny vial with his finger and a squirt of liquid jumps from the needle.

I hold my arm out and look away. I hate shots but if it'll let me spin on this planet just a little bit longer, it's totally worth it.

"Oh, dear Skyla." Marshall swims with glee. "That's not where I'm making the deposit."

I dart a quick look to Barron, and he shakes his head.

Marshall gives a lewd smile as he trails his hand down my body and lifts the back of my makeshift dress well past my thigh.

Crap.

Just Crap.

Once he administers the horrifically humiliating and equally painful septic dose, Marshall rights me and cloaks his body around mine for a brief second.

"I'm afraid my soothing effects will negate the results we're looking for." He presses a sweet kiss into my ear as his pleasurable sensations course through me. "I must leave at once." Marshall tenderly sweeps his thumb over my cheek. "I can't bear to witness my beloved in pain." He pulls back, exposing Gage standing there holding a pair of my jeans and a sweater. "I bid you take her home at once." He glances over at him. "Don't leave her side. Though she loathes the very sight of you and wishes you seeped in a vat of boiling oil—she needs you more than ever." And with that, Marshall explodes out of the room in a thunderclap.

"Why would Skyla loathe you?" Dr. Oliver creases his brow at his son, perfectly stymied how a love like ours could ever go wrong. "Skyla, you have less than a minute to get dressed before the full effect takes place. I'll call later to see how you're doing." He nods before leaving the room.

Great. It's just Gage and me and my body, the ticking time bomb.

I make Gage turn around while I pull on my jeans and sweater. I muster the energy to glance in the mirror just above the hand sink.

Gah!

I'm hideous!

Raccoon eyes have invaded my face courtesy of faulty mascara, and my hair is balled up in a giant bird's nest, big enough to house an eagle.

"I look horrible," I announce mostly to myself.

"You look beautiful." Gage turns his head just enough when he says it.

"Wow, Chloe must have paid you a bundle."

ADDISON MOORE

Gage turns around once he's surmised I'm fully dressed, like he didn't strip me clean the first chance he got last year after I passed out in his truck—pervert.

"Chloe didn't pay me a penny," he says, tucking his cheek back in frustration.

"Nice to know you'd stab me in the back for free."

"You know I wouldn't do that." It comes out sweet, like an elongated song that reverberates its tragedy.

"I don't know you at all. You're worse than a stranger." I'm quick to correct.

The room sways. I grip the side of the stainless sink as my stomach seizes in painful knots.

I let out a childlike cry that burns as it razors out of my throat.

Gage picks me up in one fell swoop.

A horrible, biting pain rips through my abdomen.

"I've got you," he soothes. "It's going to be OK."

My body starts in on a series of violent convulsions.

Gage is wrong.

Nothing will ever be OK again.

8

Livin' on a Prayer

The sky over the Landon house spins in a color palette of grey, as Gage rotates us in the direction of the front door.

Fat cumulous clouds dusted in soot hibernate above, their lining embalmed in a fairytale blue. They hold a covenant with the heavens to pour down their blessings over the island within minutes. They make promises and know how to keep them.

An uncontrollable shiver runs through me. My teeth chatter with such violent force I'm convinced I'm chipping them in the process.

"Let's get you to bed." Gage runs me up the porch. The front door sits slightly ajar, and we find Tad sorting through a pile of sleeping bags in the entry.

"Aha!" He straightens. With his hair graying on the sides, and the severe spare tire around his waist, he doesn't look like he has a whole lot to *aha* about at the moment. "Mia and Melissa said you haven't been home all night. I knew you were off in some seedy motel room. I have news for the two of you. Prom is not some fornicating bonanza that lets you forgo your morals. Just because you spent seven or eight hours groping each other on the dance floor does not make it OK to lock yourselves in a room and let loose."

It takes a heroic effort for me not to hurl some serious projectile vomit in his direction—and I'm completely capable, I can feel it.

"Sorry," Gage offers. "We were watching the sunrise at Rockaway. It's sort of a tradition around here. We must have fallen asleep." Gage looks down at me, warms me with his eyes.

"By the way," Tad says, barreling past Gage and his excuse with his own verbose agenda, "Melissa said that crazy teacher of yours came storming in this morning looking for some brochures your mother promised, and he broke the mirror I gave her for our anniversary. Who the hell goes into someone else's bedroom looking for marketing material?"

"He's a complete idiot." Gage affirms with a nod.

"Finally," Tad shouts, "someone who sees him the way I do. You'd think he has everyone else under some kind of spell the way the entire island yields to his charm."

I hate to interrupt this precious bonding session between Tad and Gage over, of all things, their shared disinterest in Marshall, but everything in me feels as though it's going to pop from the unearthly amount of pressure brewing in my belly.

I let out a harrowing moan.

"Skyla's not feeling so good." Gage starts toward the stairs.

My stomach sears with a flash of pain, and I bury my face in Gage's chest. He smells good, familiar—and strangely safe. He tries to make a break for my bedroom, but Tad blocks his path.

"Oh, she's sick is she?" Tad snickers. "A little too much booze filtering through the liver, hey? I'll have you know Drake had his baby last night while the two of you were off cavorting. If my guess is right, we'll be hitting the maternity ward once again in about nine months' time—and it won't be for me." He mutters something about missing his wallet and continues to riffle through the camping discards splayed out all over the entry.

"Congratulations." Gage speeds past him. "You enjoy that new grandbaby. I'll hang out with Skyla and make sure she's OK."

"I bet you will." Tad's voice bellows up after us.

Gage lands us inside my room at superhuman speeds, pushes my dresser over the door with his shoe, easy as sliding a book.

He doesn't say anything—simply wraps me in my comforter and grabs the tiny trashcan under my desk before teleporting us up to the butterfly room.

The soft swish of tissue paper wings greets us as I double over in agony and let out an anguished cry.

For a brief moment, I thought maybe he was bringing me up here to draw on serendipity, that the romantic implications of it all would somehow bring me back to him. But now I see the practicality involved as well as the puke bucket I'm sure to put to good use.

He pulls me onto his lap and drags his lips from my cheek to my ear. I can feel the heat emanating off his body, his heart beating up against me with its smooth percussion. I thought we'd grow old like this—that his lust for me would hold out for ages.

"Throw up if you need to. Don't hold back."

Not quite the words I was hoping he'd say—then again, he's not quite the person I thought he was.

Strong, grinding pain gnarls my insides, incapacitating my ability to think or speak. My mouth opens, and I try to scream or breathe. It's all too much to bear—such blinding hot pain—nothing but a violent rush of excruciating agony.

Gage rocks me in his arms, prays over me with fervent whispers—invokes the name of the Father, the Son, and the Holy Spirit as if he were performing an exorcism. Gage begs for a divine mercy that never comes.

I thrash and writhe, land my lips on the flesh of his neck and linger for a moment. Something about his being offers me respite in the midst of this incomprehensible storm.

A flash of pain ignites through my skull, and I buck uncontrollably until Gage—the butterfly room—it all fades to nothing.

🦋 🦋 🦋

My lids flutter as a pale blur warbles in and out of focus from above. I give several hard blinks and find Gage gazing down at me. His dimples dig in and assure me I've survived the mortal assault Marshall commandeered against my body. I wrap my arms around him and inhale his scent. I miss the perfume of his skin. I miss everything about Gage with a terrible ache.

"How do you feel?" He outlines my jaw with his thumb.

"Like killing you." It comes out maudlin, and sad, and only a tiny bit true. I sit up and marvel at what little effort it takes. "Hey, I do feel better." A strange tingling sensation filters through to the ends of my fingers all the way to my toes. Something's different. Something's all together off about this new me. "Looks like you shot those prayers off in the right direction."

I take in a smooth breath and feel my energy level rise.

"Here." Gage produces a soda that I keep as a part of my stash and extends it to me like an olive branch.

I hesitate before taking it from him, then down it like I haven't had a drink in ages. I let the carbonation burn through my esophagus and fill my stomach with the tepid liquid as I pour it down my throat.

"Thank you," I pant.

Gage and I stare at one another a very long time. We drip with honey-sweet sadness. You could spill us out over the black, sparkling floor of the butterfly room, we were spent, not one emotion left in us—broken beyond our years.

"I can't bear that I've hurt you, Skyla."

"I can't bear that you've hurt me, Gage." I say it soft, just this side of tears. I've hurt Gage before—badly wounded him, but this was a betrayal that swept us off our feet. It sailed us further apart than any grievance could ever have had the power to do.

"Let me tell you everything." He gives it in a heated whisper directly into my ear. It brings back that dream I had the first night in the tunnels—Gage and me interlaced beneath the sheets—his sweltering body pressed against mine.

"Not now." Not ever is what I really should have said. The last thing in the world I want to hear is how Gage and Chloe converged in a union to deceive me. "Can I ask you something?" I turn to face him fully.

"Anything." His eyes widen with hope. Gage looks as if he would trade the world for another chance at what we had.

"You gave me this ring." I look down at the tiny silver band, the sapphire cut into a heart set in the middle. It glistens underneath the light, happy in its ignorance. It spells out his deception with every sparkle. "You said you'd love me forever." I shake my head. "You loved me, Gage. I could feel it, but you let everything we built that love upon lay over a foundation of some pact you made with Chloe—*Chloe.*"

Gage closes his eyes. Remorse pours from him, heavy and smothering.

"I don't want you to say anything." A knot the size of a fist locks up my throat. "Right now I'd just really like for you to leave."

Gage takes in a breath and gives a reluctant nod.

"Just know that I love you. I would die for you." He leans in. "To die for you would be an honor, Skyla." He brings my hand up to his lips and brushes it with a kiss.

Gage evaporates slower than I ever thought possible, makes me wonder if he's left a part of himself behind.

I sort of wish he did.

9

Baby Phat

In the morning, I stare out at the dark, prominent shield draped over Paragon. I search for signs of Nevermore, his thick ebony plumes glossed to perfection from the swirling fog. It would be a pleasure to see him stretched out in full wingspan, but there's not one sign of my fine-feathered friend.

I shower and dress. The bruise that wrapped around my neck like a bright green ring has already dissipated. I feel renewed, refreshed at the thought of heading over to the hospital to visit Brielle and Drake's love child, baby Beau.

I still can't believe my best friend had my stepbrother's baby at prom, in the parking lot no less, with Gage at the helm of the delivery.

It brings the curve of a smile to my face, and I'm almost happy at the thought of being an aunt. Almost. Gage pummeled my heart and now it seems impossible to soar with joy ever again.

I drive downtown just missing the oncoming storm and purchase flowers from the gift shop before taking the elevator up.

On the maternity ward, a large glass window stretches out for an infinite expanse, shielding a row of tiny newborns nestled tight in white flannel blankets.

Logan stands in the center of the hall with his hand pressed against the window.

"Hey you." I brush my lips just beneath his ear and take him in. Logan is a testament to all that's true and right in this world—plus he's hotter than a bonfire.

"Skyla." He offers a brief hug and winces.

"You're in pain. Your blood should've healed you." I lament, rubbing my fingers against his perfect jaw.

"It did, for the most part."

I wrap my arms gingerly around him again and refuse to let go. "I love you so much. I'm sorry they hurt you."

"Skyla, it's you they hurt, not me." The line down his cheek inverts and magnifies my attraction to him. It's from the cut I gave him with a root beer bottle so many months ago. Who knew by trying to injure him, I'd only inflict him with more sexiness? "I'm the one who's sorry." He punctuates it with a kiss over my temple.

"We'll get through this," I say, pulling back and taking in his Adonis-like perfection. "We can make it through anything this life throws at us as long as we stick together."

He clouds over with the slight look of agony. "And we will be—together." He offers without remorse. Logan looks back at the tiny sleeping bundles with their wrinkled faces, each with its own button nose. "They're so beautiful." He warms my back with his hand. "Can you imagine something so perfect coming from two people who love each other? I want that one day," he rasps the words out, "with you, Skyla."

My heart thumps unnaturally.

Tears come to me unexpected as we observe the sea of glowing faces. One of the tiny beings blinks to life, and his gaze wanders.

"I want that, too." I press my lips into Logan's cheek and mean every word.

"You look terrific, by the way," he says, dusting my neck with his thumb while observing my injuries. "Was it bad?"

"A little worse than that." I swallow hard trying to deflect thoughts of Gage holding me through the night. "You see Brielle yet?"

"Yeah, I was just taking off for the bowling alley. I gotta see for myself what carnage Kragger may have caused—see what level of damage control I'm in for." He leans in. "Those tunnels—we can't let that happen again. I won't take you down there."

"They'll kill you if you don't."

"They *are* killing you," he says it sharp, angry. "Talk to Dudley, see if there's a way out of this. I'll see what I can do on my own." He drops a kiss on the top of my head and starts heading out.

"Wait, what do you mean on your own?"

"Never mind. I'll catch you later."

"Logan!"

"I promise we'll figure this out. Nothing's impossible."

I shake my head at his words. I'm pretty sure the Counts have figured out a way to swallow the impossible.

Inside Brielle's hospital room, there's a party-like atmosphere.

Brielle sits on the bed with her copper hair gnarled up in a ball reminiscent of the do I was sporting just last night. Mom sits beside her while Drake, Tad, and Ethan sit on the tiny sofa facing a giant flat screen, soaking in a basketball game.

"Congratulations!" I spring over to the bed and offer her one long, rocking hug. "Are you OK? Is the baby OK?"

"We're both fine," she says, plucking the blanket off her chest. "I'm nursing."

"Oh my God! I almost killed it!" I gasp.

"Relax, Drake already dropped him." She tries to yank him away from her body and her nipple stretches elastic like a gummy bear. "Lizbeth, get this critter some food, my boobs are on fucking fire," she snipes. "Sorry," she whispers. "I'm a little cranky, what with no sleep and all."

"Right, hon." Mom jumps up and offers me a brief hug. "How was prom?"

"So overrated." I roll my eyes without meaning to.

"Oh, don't say that." Mom sags with disappointment. "You'll get to college and wish they had those special boy-girl get-togethers."

"They do, Lizbeth." Tad belches. "It's called 'the weekend.'"

"He's right," Brielle chimes in. "Every weekend is a freaking party. My sister's not even coming home for summer vacation."

I keep forgetting Brielle has relations other than her mom.

The door whooshes open and, speaking of her mom, Darla enters on cue with her undesirable, not-so-human other half—Demetri.

She breezes by and plucks the baby out of Brielle's hands.

"Beau Geste." Darla coos into the tiny bundle. "That's a big name for a little bugger." Her short pixie hair spikes him in the face every now and again, and he starts in on the world's softest cry.

"Here, let me." Mom hitches a crimson lock behind her ear and pries the infant right from Darla's unwilling hands. She bounces him up over her shoulder gently, and he quiets down to the bleating of a lamb. Meanwhile, Mom is totally missing the uber pissed off expression on Darla's face.

"Skyla." Demetri has the nerve to breathe my name as he nods hello. As if he didn't just make a withdrawal from my blood bank and deposit it straight into some hungry Count's stomach.

I don't respond. I refuse to look at him or acknowledge his existence. He killed my father, and now he wants me in the grave next door. Well, it ain't happening.

Mom tap dances with the infant in her arms. "I'm throwing a big graduation party at my house next weekend for Ethan." She exaggerates a whisper while patting away at the baby's back. "You're all invited. We're family now." She adds that last part in a trancelike state while gazing into Demetri as though it were their infant she were slapping into oblivion.

I wish my mother would lose her obsession with the demon that stands before her, and yet, her fascination with the blunder from down under continues to fester. I bet she'd like nothing more than to have a big, giant, family with that hook-nosed rat.

"We've always been family, Lizbeth," he says, relaxing his arm around her waist as she cradles the newborn babe.

"My turn," I declare, holding out my hands. I've never held an infant, but I won't let my reluctance stop me from breaking up the love fest between my mother and the malignant spirit nestled up beside her.

Mom comes over and places the tiny bundle into my waiting arms.

"He's so light!" It's like holding air. I swear he weighs less than the blanket.

"Eight pounds six ounces," Brielle scoffs. "I have the stretch marks on my ass to prove it. And by the way, Gage did fantastic."

I hear Brielle's voice on the periphery, but I'm spellbound by this beautiful, tiny creature—his dot of a nose, perfect bowtie lips that purse for no reason.

"He's so sweet," I whisper, amazed at the sight of him.

"He's a prince I tell you," Mom sings. "By the way, Gage is a hero. He's truly amazing. You are one lucky girl, Skyla. That boy is a keeper."

I turn just enough so my mother doesn't see the sorrow in my face.

Baby Beau fidgets and squirms to life. His lips twitch, and he presses his face into my chest.

"He's a boob man," Darla says it proud while taking him back.

"Just like his daddy." Brielle is quick to point out.

Lovely.

Demetri steps toward me. His ebony hair is swept back in a series of coarse waves.

"Better already?" His dark eyes try to hide their mocking laughter.

"You better watch your back," I whisper. "I plan on telling my mother every little horrific detail of your den of terror and what that meant for yours truly."

"Your mother?" His lips curve on the sides. "Which one?"

"Both," I seethe.

"What if I told you they already knew?"

I don't say anything—just pass a glance at my mother who is openly denying something to Darla—probably the fact Demetri is an asshole.

He gives a hard sniff. "Regardless of what you believe, I don't desire to harm you."

"Liar."

10

Tactical Alert

Bitterness descends from the sky in heavy sheets. I drive through a torrent of black rain on my way to Marshall's house. Long, striated spears fall from the sky and create a blinding barrier, leaving the windshield wipers pulsing over the glass just enough to glaze it.

I run out, holding my jacket above my head, and manage to saturate myself by the time I hit the door. I give three brisk knocks, and Marshall answers with his alarming good looks. He should be outlawed for showing off his flawless features, for pressing up against the landscape and out bidding the beauty that God afforded around him.

"I need you," I say, barreling past him and dropping my sopping coat on the floor.

"Love in the afternoon? I'm more than happy to oblige." He's quick to descend upon me, locking his arms around my waist. "I can't imagine a better way to pass the time."

"That's not what I need you for."

He burrows his head into my neck, my hair. "One day that's all you'll ever need me for, and I'll feel rather used." He gives a sly smile.

"Oh, stop." I push him away with the flat of my hands. I let him in on the crap house that is the "Celestra tunnels" and before I'm through, I spot that magic mirror of Demetri's, haunting his residence.

"Tad was less than impressed that you broke in and took it." Although it doesn't look broken at all.

"Breaking and entering is hardly how I operate." He leers at me suggestively. "All of the entering I'm involved in is mutually consensual," he whispers it low and my stomach ignites with heat. "I come invited."

Marshall drips with lust for me and I have to look away before I buckle to his advances. This entire nightmare with Gage and the Counts has my resistance at an all-time low.

"Back to the mirror." I speed over to it in an effort to hide the color in my face.

He cuts a venomous look at the contraption. "I've broken it twice already, and each time, it's morphed back into shape."

"Get rid of it." I pull him in tight as if it might morph into a clown, or Ezrina, or, God forbid, Demetri himself. "Bury the damn thing."

"I shan't." He lets out a breath. "Finders keepers and all those good-for-nothing euphemisms. Besides, it has properties. I merely haven't discovered them yet. I've been throwing things in it all day. I've loosed two squirrels and a jackrabbit into the black hole, and they've yet to return." He strokes the side of his face. "I'm guessing I'll need to send in the reserves—a raven to be exact."

"Discover whatever the hell you need to discover then get it the F out of dodge," I say. "Marshall..." I cup his face with my hands and pant into him. "I can't go to that prison again." I try to control my agitation. "As your future wife, I absolutely forbid you to let them take me again." I have no problem pulling the wife card with Marshall. Hell, I might just need every weapon in the matrimonial arsenal to prevail against the Counts.

"Dear girl, count your blessings they released you at all. You are aware the other Celestra prisoners are denied their weekend fun pass. You, my dear, have invoked a peculiar vein of mercy from the purveyor of your grief."

"Are you freaking kidding me? So what? You want me to write Demetri a thank you?" I'm shocked Marshall isn't livid— breaking the piano in a fit of rage or setting the barn on fire, better yet, the entire freaking forest. "Do you know what's it's like down there? It's a hellhole! People were screaming. They were *afraid*. There was a child down there for Pete's sake, who by the way, I won't rest until I rescue. Speaking of children, does my mother know I was down there?" And I'm not talking, Lizbeth.

"The woman knows everything. Of course she knows."

"Oh my God." I grip my fingers to my chest. "She's a monster. How could she ever find that acceptable? She didn't come. She didn't help—she *let* those horrible things happen to me—to others." I shake my head in disbelief.

"She didn't come to your rescue, did she?" Marshall reels me in again. "She wanted you to see it, feel it, taste all of its displeasure, and swill it in your mouth like rancid fat."

"She could have taken me there and given me the tour, thank you very much. I *lived* it," I hiss.

"Perhaps she wants you to do something about it." His cheek twitches as he withholds a smile.

"Me? What is wrong with you people? First you want me to fight a war so *you* can stay in power, and now she wants me to concoct some lame idea on how I'm going to open the tunnels and set my people free?"

Shit.

Having your mother in charge of your destiny has got to be the worst idea ever. If only she would have had more children, she could have spread the misery around.

"Yes, I believe it's finally sunk in." Marshall warms my back with his hands. "We need you."

"I'm a useless human!" I totally don't mean that. I just want to get the celestial superiors off my effing back.

"A Celestra, my dear, is far from human. Nevertheless, you were chosen. The Master insists that humans have free will, free reign, free charge over just about everything. The war cannot be fought without flesh and blood. Divine officers have only so much say—it is you who holds the power."

"But the tunnels—my mother has the power to free those people. You probably do, too."

"No, Skyla. We're not to interfere in that manner. We can assist, guide, comfort." He squeezes my waist when he says it. "Intervening when evil prospers is not our lot. Justice comes at the end of the day and not a moment sooner."

"At the end of the day, we'll all be dead."

"Observant of you to note." Marshall gently lifts my chin with his finger. "You, Ms. Messenger, are not like the rest. Your mother has purposed a legacy for you. The challenge is yours should you accept it. It is a generous lot, but it's yours for the taking. Be strong. I can help you do this."

"Free me from Demetri. I beg of you. Don't let him take me again."

"Skyla," he says, glancing down with a look of agony, "there are rules."

"And I've been captured." I circle a nod in disbelief. "There must be a way. A protective hedge like Chloe has or a spirit that can guard over me."

"No, love. Once the capture has been engaged, it is a binding covenant. You're at their disposal." He bites hard on his lip until it loses all color. "The only way to break the covenant is to invoke the mercy of your captor—and already you've tasted a portion. I'm afraid you'll have to tread lightly with your father's killer."

"He loves my mother." I can't believe I'm entertaining the thought of selling my mom out to that maniac. "Marshall," I shout, shaking him by the shoulders, "how am I going to have a life? How am I ever going to marry you, if the Counts keep draining me like some magical drinking fountain?"

"There is one remote possibility." Marshall casts a glance out the window. "Let me consult with others. I'll see what I can do."

"Thank you!" I bounce my forehead off his chest and let his feel good vibrations hum through my body like a song. "So what happened with Gage?"

"I'm afraid Jock Strap is hopelessly in love with my future bride." He tilts his head. "Should I do away with him?"

"Swiftly," I say, only half-teasing. "What did he say?"

Marshall leads me to the couch, and I lean my head over his shoulder as if he were about to tell me some haunted bedtime story—more like haunted love story, the kind without a happy ending.

"He found me just after midnight and told me about the stone, how the Pretty One and you were pinned with a blade. When I informed him there wasn't a single thing I could do to alleviate your discomfort, he dropped to his knees. The look of grief on the poor boy's face alerted me to something."

"What's that?" I stare up at Marshall's fiery eyes. Each their own unique shade of burgundy.

"He feels just as strongly for you as I do." Marshall focuses his gaze straight ahead. The fireplace roars to life without provocation. It brands the room in colors pink and gold. "I thought I understood love, knew the lay of the land— all of its inroads." He sighs hard, landing a soft kiss to my temple. "I knew nothing of it until I met you, Skyla. You've redefined love for me. It's sacred—anointed with the highest regard and blessing."

I've never heard words like that from Marshall. His placating sexuality, his wry wit and humor are all gone, nothing but the naked form of a man underneath, declaring his love for me. Our eyes lock. A strong magnetic pull lures me to his lips, and everything in me longs for a kiss.

"Yeah, well," I say, shaking the idea away, "turns out Gage is Chloe's pawn," I inform.

"Is he?" Marshall raises a brow. "Or is she his?"

11

The Party

Days bleed by. I tell Mom I'm not feeling well and miss the last two days of school, letting the rest of the week drip down to nothing without returning any calls to my newfound traitor—the boy who stole my heart then stomped all over it while I had a sword thrust in my chest. May as well have been him delivering the fatal blow.

The Saturday morning of the big graduation party, I trot downstairs to find the house alive with an assortment of unappreciated scents. An entire bouquet of vomit-like odors assaults my senses.

"What's going on?" I ask, peering over Mom's shoulder at a bubbling brew in what, honest to God, could double as a witch's cauldron. Witchcraft, poison cuisine, her insatiable lust for Demetri the Celestra hunter—all clear evidence that my mother ditched her sanity once my father died. Her union with Tad should have tipped me off that permanent placement in a psychiatric facility is completely necessary.

"Steel cut oats and spinach—Swiss Chard. I'm trying to make enough for the whole family." She makes a face. "You know," she whispers, looking past my shoulder briefly, "I have to say, I'm not appreciating the way Brielle and her mother are keeping the baby from us."

"They are?" I've been lost in the bubble of betrayal and haven't really noticed. It seems like Drake is gone all the time, so I assume he's next door pulling daddy duty.

"Every time I go over, they say the baby's napping and that I shouldn't interrupt." A clear look of hurt clouds her features. It seems lately her diaper dreams are being dashed from every angle.

Maybe it's a good thing that she doesn't spend that much time with baby Beau. It might inspire her to kick Operation Procreate back into high gear and get her mind off demented Demetri. Although, who knows what sexual shenanigans will ensue—and with who.

"I'm sure they'll bring the baby tonight," I say, trying to offer her a pick me up. Half the town is coming, including the Oliver of my discontent.

"You're right." She pulls me in and inhales deeply. *And so will Demetri.* She squeals with a smile.

There it is. Proof positive she's totally ready to dive into some serious philandering with my least favorite Fem.

Mia and Melissa bound into the kitchen and groan at the savorless offerings.

"All you ever cook is crap," Melissa quips.

"Melissa!" Mom snaps.

"The child speaks the truth, Lizbeth." Tad appears and plucks a bright green banana from the counter and attempts to peel it, but it's sealed itself successfully from being digested by humans and Tad alike.

"Excuse me?" Mom's eyes enlarge with a tempered rage. "This whole family is embracing a new healthy lifestyle, and I would appreciate it if you wouldn't let *our* daughter speak to me in such an outright rude manner."

"I'm not embracing anything that smells like crap." Mia is quick to join the dissension in the ranks.

"The barf mobile called." Melissa cackles. "It wants its puke back."

"You're such a dumbass," Mia hisses into her.

"Shut up. You're the dumbass," Melissa snipes back.

"Girls!" Tad claps his hands. "Get dressed and clean up around here. Your mother invited an infantry to suckle off her feast."

Tad has an annoying way of making everything sound disgustingly inappropriate. Mostly sane people are coming, so that crosses suckling off the list, and my mother is preparing the meal, so for sure there will be no feast.

Ethan wanders in with his hair sticking up in the back and yanks open the fridge without the proper Landon morning greeting, which consists of a bodily function salute— an offense they don't mind dispensing all day long. Chloe saunters in after him in a barely-there silk nighty that dips just below her bottom.

Speaking of the offense.

"Morning, everyone." Chloe bursts with uncalled for energy as she stretches to the ceiling, leaving her bottom exposed just long enough for it to sear itself in my nightmares. She stops short at the sight of me and scuttles on over. "Are you still breathing on the planet?" she whispers. "Aren't you the lucky little captive running around Paragon like you might live to see another day?"

"Gage rescued me." I hold out my ring. The sad blue stone may as well be filled with tears. Of course I'll be yanking it off permanently once I get upstairs and then quite possibly scalding my finger as a punishment for donning the lie to begin with.

"Must hurt like hell to have him fool you. I think he went way too far with it all." She breathes the words out. "We should team up. Let the bastard have it." Chloe brands the words in my ear.

Right. Like I'd ever fall into that bear trap again. The last time we teamed up, I had a starring role in a DVD loosely entitled, *Skyla Does Paragon*. I hear it's still a big hit with the track team.

"So what are you thinking?" I follow her over to the coffee machine. I don't mind mollifying Chloe's need to bridge the gap in our non-existent friendship. I'm sure she'd pay to see me mutilate Gage's reproductive organs—on second thought maybe not. I'm sure she dreams of desecrating those herself with a little help from her own reproductive organs.

"I was thinking maybe a stabbing." She pours herself a full cup of coffee, black as her heart.

"Invoking your specialty, I see."

"Maybe you'd like to defer to yours and lop off a body part—one you haven't seen before." Chloe glows with delight at my lack of carnal knowledge.

"Like you have," I hiss.

She needles me with her aggressive hatred. A dark smile blooms across her face.

"Why, yes, Skyla. I have."

✹ 🦋 ✹

The evening comes wrapped in a foreboding grey fog. I dread the festivities that are about to descend upon us like some celebratory plague. I'm feeling lots of things and celebratory isn't one of them.

"Skyla." Mom snatches me by the shoulder as I make my way down the hall. "The party started an hour ago. Why are you being so rude?"

"I fell asleep—I'm still shaking off that flu. I didn't want to get the baby sick."

"He's not here." She twists her lips with disappointment. "It's like they're purposefully keeping him away from us. They said he's fussy and hates people."

"Genetically identical to Drake. Who knew?"

"You're a real comedian." She spins me toward the crowd. "Now get out there. Your fiancé has been asking for you since he got here. And eat something, would you? There's tons of millet bread and quinoa." She pauses before continuing down the hall to greet an entire bevy of unsuspecting souls who she plans on accosting with her progressive cooking regime—and to think all this culinary madness has ensued just to enhance her ovaries. "And there are five full batches of wheat germ chili that nobody's even touched."

I'm pretty sure adding the word "germ" doesn't do a whole lot to enhance its appeal. In fact, I'm betting that lands it an automatic expulsion from every appetite in a twenty-mile radius.

She scrunches her nose playfully. "And I even threw in some Kohlrabi."

"Are you choking?" That or speaking in tongues—all things seem possible tonight.

"It's a vegetable." She rolls her eyes. "You should have some. I hear it's used in love potions worldwide." She gives a wink. "Then again you and Gage don't need it."

God help us. She's lacing the food with aphrodisiacs—by night's end, she might unwittingly have all of Paragon both procreating and running to the bathroom with an urgency to flush out their bowels. We'll be on the news from the bizarre baby slash incontinence boom—Gage could deliver them all since he's vying for superhero status. We could call him Gynecological Gage or Assman—Ass*hole*—take your pick.

"Looks like a real feast," I say to myself as I enter the family room.

Bodies mill around—loose laughter congests the air. Contrary to what Mom desires, nary a soul has ventured over to the buffet. In fact, there appears to be a six-foot barrier between the food and any living thing, including Sprinkles the dog.

I spot Logan and Gage near the back door and everything in me freezes.

For a second, I consider rescuing Logan from whatever deceit is misfiring from Gage's sparse brain cells, but change my mind. Instead, I head over and observe a pile of bird seed stacked higher than God ever intended on platter designed to hold something of nutritional value that humans may actually want to ingest. Mom's menu mishap is proving to be a spectacular dinner fail.

Both Logan and Gage stop their conversation midflight and turn to look at me.

I pivot on my feet and head over to Ellis who's talking to some girl I've never seen before.

"Messenger." He bumps into me with his hip and continues to espouse the finer points of hemp and its many contemporary humanitarian uses.

It takes five seconds for the skank he's trying to bag to belt out a yawn and pull a disappearing act.

"You really know how to slay 'em," I say. Ellis is cute. He wouldn't have to try so hard to herd unsuspecting girls into his bedroom, if he just behaved like a gentlemen—not some oversexed primate. In fact, if Ellis were a monkey, he'd be the one with the bright red ass who struts around loud and proud when, unbeknownst to him, his crimson-colored bottom is a total turn off to the opposite banana-hungry gender.

"I need to coach you." I nod.

"For what? Cheer?" His sandy hair reflects the light. Ellis certainly has it down in the looks department. He's just a little rough around the manwhore edges.

"No, not *cheer*. Girls 101. You could have every skirt on the island worshiping at your feet if you let me polish you up a bit."

"I already have every skirt on the island worshiping at my feet—missionary position accomplished." He expands the girth of his chest.

"You're not funny. Besides, they're the wrong girls." I dart a quick glance around the room. "And, by the way, I saw your father in the tunnel of terror last week. He is so not a nice guy."

"Gage told me what happened." He scans over me, heavy with concern. "You OK?"

"Barely. They almost killed me," I hiss. "Please, Ellis, any way you can, I beg of you to help. Get me out of this mess. I'll do anything, I swear." I hold up two fingers in earnest.

"I'll see what I can find out from my dad." He makes a face that assures me it's a futile effort.

"Are you guys close?" Somehow I doubt Ellis and his dad have logged too many hours around the campfire, unless of course, it included grilling a Celestra.

"We used to be. But I don't like the idea of him hurting my friends."

"That makes two of us."

"Hello, beautiful," a husky male voice rasps from behind.

I spin to find Logan, resplendent per usual. His long dimple penetrates the five o'clock shadow dusting his skin.

"I gotta run." Ellis darts out back as a multitude of FM's wander outside.

"Hello yourself," I say to Logan. "Do me a favor—you see your conniving evil cousin slithering in my direction, give me the heads up, will you?"

"Heads." He nods behind me.

"Skyla." Gage smiles. He punctuates his happiness with those vindictive twin darts set into his cheeks, and I melt at the sight of him.

"So, Logan," I start, "you think we'll have classes together next year? I mean you don't think a certain someone will break into the main computer at West and manipulate the situation in his favor again, do you?" I so obviously should have seen his twisted mastermind skills at work. "And lunch, too. I mean didn't you think it was odd that you had to hang out with the freshman and sophomores? It reeked of evil-handed deception."

"OK, I may have had a little something to do with that." Gage fesses up with a patina of an apology.

"You bastard." I shake my head at him. He made sure he was a roadblock for Logan and me every chance he got.

"Maybe I should return the favor this year?" Logan steps into me. "You prefer A lunch or B, Skyla?"

"I'll dine with the seniors, thank you." I cross my arms, annunciating the fact I'm expressly pissed. "You know what I really like about you, Logan? You don't feel the need to control my every move—my every emotion while you yourself are being manipulated by Paragon's resident dragon." Come to think of it, I shouldn't insult overgrown reptiles by lumping them in with Chloe.

"Thank you, Skyla." Logan pinches a smile at Gage. "Not that I didn't get the offer. She did let me know she was casting for the part of 'boy who pretends to love the new girl,' but I declined. I told her that the well-placed boyfriend thing wasn't going to work out for me. I had a feeling I'd be the real deal."

I catch my breath and hold it. What the hell had Chloe so up in arms about me anyway?

"Well, then." My chest heaves. "That's another thing I like about you." I press a kiss into Logan's cheek. "You, unlike some people, have undeniably big balls."

I turn around and head toward the backyard.

That barb of Chloe's from this morning comes back to me and my stomach sours. She claims to have seen Gage in all his clothing-deficient glory—and I know for a fact she slept with Logan. God, what if she slept with them both?

The thought of Chloe Bishop knowing both Gage and Logan's bodies so intimately kills me.

12

Walk This Way

I dart outside to where most of the guests from Ethan's graduation party have congregated and cast a forlorn look into the milky night sky. I wish Nev would swoop down and take me away, let me ride his wings like a time machine, back to before any of this madness began. Maybe Nev and I can simply run away? He could buffer me from all of this lunacy.

I spot Chloe and Ethan hanging out with Nat and Emily by the overgrown eucalyptus. The tree bark is bucking and corrugated, shedding in patches, which gives it an overall balding effect. It's as though Chloe herself had the power to strip the landscape of its beauty. I plan on avoiding the bitch squad at all costs tonight so I head in the opposite direction. No sense in adding any more misery to this evening than I have to.

"Alone?" Marshall steps in next to me and we observe the multitude of bodies milling around. "Have the Pretty One and Jock Strap grown immune to your seductive scent, or are they wrestling it out to see which one will have your hand for the evening?"

"None of the above. For all I know they're comparing the size of their non-vital organs." I shrug. "Anyways, I could care less about *Jock Strap*." I try to buy into the lie, but it bites through me as it rolls off my tongue and signals otherwise.

"Aren't you in a cordial mood? If I knew his aligning with Chloe would set you so far off the deep end, I would have alerted you to the situation far sooner."

I swat him in the stomach. "You knew?"

"Of course I knew. Ms. Bishop's pornographic ramblings entail many a deep dark secret."

toxic ~ part one

"Dear God." The harsh reality slaps me in the face all over again. He really is in this with Chloe, and come to think of it, she probably *has* seen parts of his body I thought were strictly off limits to anyone but me.

"Skyla," Marshall says, giving me a quizzical look, "he hasn't filled you in on the details yet, has he?" It comes out more fact, less question.

"Oh, I know all the important ones. I'm not interested in any more of his colorful dishonesty."

Tad squawks in the distance, inspiring Marshall and I to revert our attention.

"I spent four hundred dollars on organic fare and streamers!" Tad snatches up a fistful of curled ribbon and shakes it in Ethan's face. "And you choose *this* moment to alert me to the fact you're not walking at graduation?" He takes in a sharp breath. "I told you, Lizbeth!" He turns and bellows at my mother. "Having a graduation party a week before the actual event was going to put a hex on the situation."

A circle of gasps and titters erupt.

"Relax," Ethan says, hitting the air brakes. "I'll be taking some time off to think about my options."

A burst of murmurs erupts in the crowd.

"Options? That's the stay-home-and-watch-TV degree!" Tad continues his tirade. "You're over eighteen. It's about time you start contributing to this family. I'm not going to coddle you anymore in hopes you won't take off with the next band of hippies you come across." He wiggles his fingers for effect. "In fact, you keep up these backward life moves, and I'm going to encourage you to take a drastic course of action to straighten you out. Join the Army, the Navy—wait they won't even take you if you don't have a high school diploma. Hell—you'll be lucky to join the circus!"

"I don't need to join the circus." Ethan stretches his arms to the sky, bored with the entire situation. "I live with you, don't I?"

"He so got Tad there," I whisper.

Mom goes over to try and douse the fire otherwise known as the moron she's conjoined herself to legally.

"Skyla." Barron and Emma pop up beside me.

"Hi." I offer them both a brief hug. Just because I have a seething hatred toward their only offspring doesn't mean I don't like them. They're the nicest people on the planet even if Emma does seem to dislike me at times—most of the time.

"We heard what happened with Gage," Emma whispers secretively. Her tangerine lips twist into a frown before corking up to a smile again. "It's not so bad being single," she quips. "You'll find someone new—Logan perhaps."

God, if I ever thought for a moment this woman liked me, her eagerness to push me in Logan's direction should clarify everything. If I'm not good enough for her son, who is?

Chloe struts by on cue and gives a brief wave to the Olivers.

Figures.

"I'm sure it was nothing but a horrible misunderstanding," Barron assures in vain.

I find this doubtful. In fact, I find it doubtful Gage filled them in on the terms of his agreement with the python of Paragon. Although, I'm sure the princess of death had a few undisclosed clauses that Gage, himself, was unaware of while signing his body and soul over. I'm sure once she bared her chest at him, his critical thinking skills went right out the window.

Marshall engages the Olivers in small talk as the party guests dwindle. After Tad's animated tirade, an entire parade of partygoers streamed for the exit.

Logan should redirect them toward the bowling alley for some edible fare that can be described in words other than palatable or fibrous. But I'm too pissed off at Gage to even go near him to suggest the idea. Gage is ruining everything, right down to the dinner rush at the bowling alley.

"OK!" Mom claps like a trained seal—the one trick she's picked up from Tad. "We've got a special hero with us here tonight." She waves her hand toward the patio, where my least favorite heartbreaker darkens the doorway. "Skyla, why don't you get the cake and bring it outside. I had the bakery whip up something special just for Gage—carob and barley— it's to die for! Can I get a round of applause for the young man who delivered my grandbaby—and who will one day bless me with lots and lots of grandchildren himself!"

I gasp at my mother's audacity. Everything in me freezes as a spear of heat bisects my stomach. And, sadly, for this one moment, under a clear bed of stars, I actually wish my mother's words would come true.

I stagger inside and spot the round cake with "We Love You Gage" scrawled across the top in powder-blue icing. I pick it up and it wobbles unsteady in my hands. It's heavy—like my heart, and knowing my mother, there most likely is a heart buried beneath this innocent coat of frosting. Carob and barley—could there be a more twisted combination? Chloe and Gage. That's pretty twisted.

I'm so angry at him for ruining our forever—for cheating my mother out of her future grandchildren—I want to spit at him, slap him, eviscerate him with a cake knife.

I hobble back out, trying to balance the ode to the perfect douchebag, and hold it out in front of him.

A small crowd gathers around, and my mother appears with a camera at the ready.

Gage looks down with a soft expression of gratitude as though I had taken time out of my busy schedule from captivity and poisoning myself back to health to bake the organic, vegan, cardiac concoction because I love taking whatever the hell he dishes for me while he gets it on with Chloe on the side.

"Gage." I pause to steady my breathing. "I just want you to know that I think nobody deserves this more than you." The words vibrate with anger as they make their way from my lips.

"Thank you," he says, trying to decode my spontaneous turnabout.

"I hope it taste as good as it looks," I start, "but try not to be too disappointed if it doesn't. Looks can be deceiving. You of all people should know that."

In one swift move I shove the cake high up in his face and squish it around for good measure. I'd hate for him to miss out on all those beneficial barley greens and carobs that smell like feet.

For a moment everything stands still. It's just Gage and me, his cobalt spheres illuminate in my direction while cake and frosting drip from his face. Once upon a time we held a future that promised to spool out into eternity, and now here we are reduced to nothing more than anger and fits of public humiliation. I may have tossed a cake in his face, but he drew first blood with a sword from Chloe's personal cutlery collection.

"Aha!" Tad laughs. "You owe me ten dollars, Lizbeth. Told you she'd desecrate the confection before the night was through."

What little guests are left, bypass the new blemish on the festivities and show themselves out.

"Skyla!" Mom scuttles up and helps dust vanilla frosting off Gage's shirt. "I'm so sorry," she gasps to Emma and Barron.

Demetri crops up and the tension in our small circle rises like heat through a magnifying glass. Of course, in my fantasy, Demetri would be the ant. My anger alone has the capability to incinerate him.

"I'm having a get together tomorrow." The words slither from him, thick and wicked. "My first annual kickoff to summer, and I'd love for all of you to join me," he purrs.

Gage excuses himself into the house. A foolish part of me yearns to go with him and yet the wiser part chooses to stay out here with the people who are way more honest with me, like Demetri.

"Of course we'll come!" Mom beams. "I haven't worn a bathing suit in ages. I'm sure the only one I'll fit into is my *birthday* suit!" She titters.

"You're such a tomcat, Lizbeth." He cajoles right back. "Just like the old days."

What's like the old days? The tomcat or the birthday suit? And by the way, eww. There's an image I did not ever need.

"Anything we can bring?" Marshall bows to the invitation. "A salad, a casserole, perhaps a bloody Mary? I hear you're partial to plasma-based cocktails."

"Just your loved ones." Demetri squints out a grin. "Isis, my niece, is in town. She's eager to make new friends. She just finished up her doctorate, so if you could humor me by calling her Dr. Edinger, it would please me 'til kingdom come."

"The Kingdom will come." Marshall sharpens his tone. "And all of the travesties of justice will revert themselves. Oh, how I'd loathe to be in the judgment seat."

"I'd love to meet your niece." Mom dips her knees at the thought while ruining the perfect cadence of hatred between Demetri and Marshall.

"She's wonderful." His eyes sparkle with laughter. "Just ask Skyla. They've already met."

Isis?

In the tunnels—that's what he called the worm in the globe.

I pull bleak smile.

The only Isis I know has turned into a big, giant snake—much like Gage.

13

Love Me

After saying good night to both Logan and Marshall, I head up to my bedroom to decompress for the evening.

The sound of running water in my bathroom catches me off guard—probably just Chloe scouring the toilet with my toothbrush.

A shadowed figure emerges with a far bigger frame than the janitorial jackass I thought it was. It's not Chloe at all. It's her not-so-better half—Gage. His hair is freshly slicked with beads from the shower still clinging to the tips. He's wearing a T-shirt and old sweats I had borrowed from him a while back.

"Lucky for me, half my closet migrated over." His dimples push in without the benefit of a smile.

"Sounds unlucky for me," I say, shutting the door and locking it in the event I feel like committing a felony.

"Hope you don't mind—I cleaned up." He says it low, pulling up his T-shirt as if threatening to pluck it off.

"I mind everything about you these days," I say, taking off my sweater revealing my tank top underneath. I step out of my boots and unbutton my jeans slow and methodical, peeling them off until I step right out. "OK, you got the show. Now get the hell out." I head into the bathroom and rake a brush through my hair.

The very distinct sound of the dresser gliding across the floor echoes off the walls, and I rush back into the bedroom.

"Excuse me?" I say, posturing in my boy-shorts in the event his gaze should wander south of my chin. I hope Gage Oliver dies a slow and painful death while thinking about what he lost. I hope he dreams of touching me every single night only to wake up and discover it's nothing more than wishful thinking. The idea that Chloe is the nightmare that waits for him should make him want to hang himself off the nearest bough.

"Skyla." He depresses out my name like a song full of sorrow.

"No words." I cut the air with the underlying threat.

He gives a nod and lifts a finger toward the ceiling and the lights go out.

How'd he do that?

An anemic stream of moonlight filters in from an abnormally clear night on Paragon. Gage comes over and brushes my lips with his. My entire body sizzles with heat at his command. And here I wanted him to die a slow death by way of never touching me again. Sadly, I can't seem to invoke that punishment on him just yet.

My heart picks up pace, my breathing grows erratic. I want to tell him to leave, to go to hell—to Chloe's, but I invoke my own stupid maxim and ban my vocal cords from leaking a sound.

Gage dips in again with a gentle kiss that lingers.

My entire person goes rigid, stiff as a statue. I know what's coming, and I can't control it. No matter how hard my head shouts no, my heart and hormones out roar its efforts.

He runs his hands over my hips, rabid and hot like an out-of-control brushfire, and I pull my neck back from the pleasure of it all.

A burst of rapid kisses assault my neck before adhering to my lips like a cold drink of water in the vast thirsty desert of my newfound anger. I plunge my tongue into his mouth like diving into the ocean and reintroduce myself to his lingual landscape fast and furious as if we've only minutes to live.

God, I miss Gage. I miss the old Gage who I thought really loved me, who I believed cared and whose heart I shred to pieces with my own deception.

I pull off his shirt, run my open palms against his chest and feel the hard ridges of perfection that striate across his flesh. My thumbs circle the inside of his sweats. I open the elastic wide and send them sailing to the floor with minimal effort.

Gage pulls off my tank top, unhitches my bra in an Olympic-worthy maneuver and lands me on the bed in one heated kiss.

It is all out passion—kisses that sear through time and an entire hotbed of lies—right past the hornet nest Chloe pushed us into a very long time ago before either of us understood who we were.

An inferno ignites over the sheets. His bare stomach touches mine, and I press him in, digging my fingers into his back. I want Gage covering me, loving me—inside of me.

I ride my hands up his thighs, bristle the hair on his legs as I round out to the front of his boxers, and feel him grow.

He lets out a jagged hot breath in my ear and sighs over me.

"Not like this, Skyla." He dots the tip of my nose with a kiss. "I'm sorry. I'm sorry for everything." He nuzzles his face into my neck, then disappears.

The morning of Demetri's kickoff to summer party is suspiciously bright and sunny. I'm still reeling from those hotter-than-hell kisses, that entire heated exchange that took place in my room last night with my mortal enemy, Gage.

I open my window to cool myself off and call for Nevermore, my favorite human trapped in a Raven. Well, he's the only human trapped in a Raven's body that I know of, but still.

Nev swoops down from the top bough of a pine. He darkens the sky with the batting of his wings, spastic and furtive as he lands, then hops inside my window rather unceremoniously.

I touch my palm to his back, take in the cool of his feathers and pet him gently. Nev is enormous for a bird—the size of a small toddler.

"Guess who's a big fat traitor?" I assault him with my pent up rage before uttering a simple hello.

Ezrina?

"Nope, my mother agreed to give you guys a new trial after the faction war. Isn't that great?" So much has happened since prom, I hadn't had a chance to tell Nev about his upcoming reprieve.

Great, but I doubt the Justice Alliance will magically yield different results. He shivers, stretching out his wings before retracting them. *You do realize they would have to admit they were wrong the first time they handed down the sentence. This can only result in a harsher punishment. You know not what you've brought upon us.*

"And what if it works and you're both free?"

We won't be free. These are lasting covenants—binding agreements were made. This is far more than eternal—well, on her part at least. One faulty arrow and I cease to exist forever.

"So what are you saying? My mother is going to host a fake trial to get me off her back, and the two of you will be worse for it?" Knowing my mother, the most diabolical plan possible is the most believable and true.

Precisely that. Now back to the subject at hand, who is the 'big fat traitor' in question?

"Gage." I sit down on the bed next to him and sulk openly at the thought.

Master Oliver?

"More like Disaster Oliver." I fill him in on the heartache Gage inflicted upon me. "Can you believe he snowed me over like that?"

No, Skyla, I can't. Nev jerks his head back and opens his beak. *I smell a rat. That boy loves you. I've never seen a love so pure since...*

"Since that of your own?" Boy, Gage had him snowed, too. "I bet just before he decided to gift me his bird, he subjected you to a ton of 'spontaneous' verbal proclamations of his false affection for me. He's nothing but a first class bullshitter."

There's bull being tossed about, all right, and it's not coming from Master Oliver.

"Nev! You're supposed to side with *me*." OK, so he's not obligated but geez, it would be nice.

A harsh knock explodes over the door as Mia yells for me to get downstairs. Something about opening a café.

"One more thing before I go," I say. "Just thought you might like to know, as of last week, I've officially been captured by the Counts."

Nev lets out an ear-piercing cry, so loud, so viral, it can be heard for miles.

14

The Menu

As I make my way downstairs on this, the cursed morning of Demetri's summer soirée, I'm pleasantly surprised to find my olfactory senses filled with the familiar scent of deep fried pig flesh, which I mostly associate with Brielle's house next door. It's a nice change of pace since Tad tends to stray from cannibalistic tendencies and thus has declared all pork products off limits to the entire Landon clan and me.

I trot into the kitchen to find Mia and Melissa at the helm, working shoulder to shoulder to rescue this family from its artery blocking deficiencies.

A piece of paper has been hastily adhered to the fridge, it reads *Mia's café* all food $1.50.

A bevy of mouthwatering dishes are listed that I'd gladly surrender my entire paycheck for, including grilled cheese sandwiches with three slices of premium cheddar, peanut butter and jelly with no crusts, turkey and Swiss with pesto.

"If you want to see a real menu, look on the counter." Melissa snipes from over her shoulder.

A neatly laminated piece of blue parchment is printed up in a fancy script. *Landon Bistro*. Figures. The only thing my sisters have in common these days is the fact they're competitive.

"So who gets to cook for you, Skyla?" Mia glares at me accusingly.

"Well, it looks like you're almost done." I shrug.

"Knew it." Melissa seethes as she turns to Ethan. "It's us against them. Eat my food or die."

"If I eat your food, I *will* die." He belches before reaching in the fridge for a soda. "Yeah, whatever. Gimme something to commit a slow suicide with."

I speed over to him and resist the urge to wrap my hands around his neck for housing the enemy.

"Where's the demon you slither around the sheets with?"

"Getting a Brazilian." His lids close halfway as though he were witnessing the epilation of her pubic region firsthand.

"Why are you still with her?" Obviously he's mental. "Never mind." I acquiesce to the hopelessness of trying to drill logic into a Landon's brain.

"Morning!" Mom waltzes in, chirping like a bird. The smile melts off her face as soon as she spies the debauchery taking place in the kitchen. "Girls, I don't want you to make a habit out of this."

Tad comes up behind her and sniffs like a basset hound.

"You're ordering from me, Daddy." Melissa evokes her I'm-a-two-year-old-princess voice that sounds decidedly like Carly Foster.

Mom looks past my shoulder, and her face brightens. "Look who's here!" She belts it out so jubilantly, I half expect to see Demetri materialize in the room, but it's not the malignancy I thought it was. It's a rather benign apparition of Drake and Brielle.

"I spent the night." Brielle plops down at the table and accepts the orange juice my mother offers. I suspect Mom is going to turn up the volume on the brown-nosing routine now that things with baby Beau have entered hostage negotiation status.

"Is the baby here?" Mom grapples for hints of all things infant, even goes as far as peering down Bree's top and for good reason—she's hidden him there before, case in point— the hospital.

"Are you kidding?" Brielle bleats. "I need some freaking sleep. That kid thinks the entire world revolves around his stomach."

"Well, he *is* a boy." Mom tries to make light of the fact.

"And he is Drake's spawn," I chime in.

Mom shoots me a dirty look. "I wouldn't mind taking the nightshift." She manufactures an apprehensive smile. "I could even go over to your house if you like."

"No thanks." Brielle eyes her suspiciously as if my mother were fully capable of conducting a baby heist. "My mom and I have it all under control."

Mia hands me a plate of food that looks and smells like heaven.

Mom twitches her lips, like maybe a baby heist really is in her future. "So, have you brushed up on what parenting techniques you're going to implement?" Mom is insistent on grinding down Brielle's last nerve with her special brand of crazy.

"Parenting?" Brielle looks genuinely confused at the concept in general.

"You know," Drake interjects, "bedtimes and shit. The kid's up all night because you don't put it to sleep at a decent hour."

"No." My mother closes her eyes. "Beau Geste is an infant. He needs a schedule, not a bedtime. Infants eat all through the night, Brielle." She nods into her assuredly. "You've done nothing wrong."

"Thank you." Bree glowers at Drake.

It's sort of a miracle they can stand to be in the same room, let alone spend the night together and both wake up alive.

"If you haven't found a decent diaper service yet, I happened to stumble upon one the other day." Mom plucks a coupon from the counter. "First month is half off." She marvels as she hands the paper to Brielle.

"Cool." Brielle straightens. "So they'll come out and change him whenever? They should erect a statue to whoever thought of this."

I lean in and inspect the tiny square. "No, it's for cloth diapers," I say. "But I bet you'd make a gazillion dollars if you started a baby changing service." Just saying.

"Are you freaking kidding me?" She drops the coupon as if it were on fire. "That kid needs to wear two diapers at once just to keep the bodily fluids in."

"I could change him." Mom masks her desperation by feigning a look of indifference.

Dear God almighty. I'm about to suggest Tad haul her to the bedroom and knock her up just to get her the heck off Brielle's back. But somehow my vocal cords can't produce those impossible words—nor can the cursed visual leave my mind.

"Oh, I've been meaning to ask." Mom wrinkles her nose, forewarning us of the absurdity to come. "Did you happen to save the placenta?"

"The pla-what?" Brielle cocks her head at my mother as if she's speaking another language.

"You know, the afterbirth," Mom whispers the last word and for good reason. "It looks like a giant liver."

I suck in a breath at my mother's viral insanity.

Figures. The one single meal I've looked forward to wolfing down in this house in a good long while sits patiently before me, and yet, I suddenly want no part of it.

"Gross!" Brielle manages to look more than mildly offended.

"It's not gross." Mia is quick to defend her mother's psychosis. "My friend's mom just had a baby, and they planted it in the ground along with a tree."

"The baby?" Brielle bounces back in her seat at the thought of a live infant burial.

"No, stupid," Mia barks. "The gross liver thingy."

"Oh, I wouldn't waste it like that." Mom is quick to rebuke the idea of reducing it to compost. "I'd turn it into a smoothie or jerky."

"Holy Joseph and Mary!" Tad sends pieces of his breakfast shooting across the table like a missile. "You don't eat human baby parts. You just don't." His face explodes with color. "Your obsession with infants and digesting their body parts has come to an end."

Mom doesn't look amused by his non-supportive outburst and fries him with lasers of hatred. "The human placenta is filled with nutritious benefits, one of which is creating a fertile environment. At my age, I'm going to need all the help I can to have a baby, and if having a placenta smoothie or two helps—I won't count it out."

"That's like some pretty satanic shit." Ethan is quick to observe. "Like voodoo or something."

"Anyway, I'll ask my mom." Brielle shrugs. "But I'm pretty sure all I had was the baby. Maybe it's just older people like you who have their livers come out after?"

Mom crimps a smile. "On the bright side"—she doesn't let us out of her batshit belfry just yet—"we're all going to be at Demetri's estate today." She's quick to segue into yet another dimension of her delirium—her crush on the violent Fem himself. "I can watch the baby while the two of you enjoy some fun in the sun." Her head drops a notch at her latest attempt to infiltrate Brielle and Darla's well-secured diaper garrison.

"Are you kidding? He's coming with." Brielle insists. "He's whiter than Drake's bare ass. That boy needs some s-u-n."

"Oh, hon, he's going to burn." Mom tries to hide her newfound horror. "Well, anyway, I'll be looking forward to seeing him."

I'm pretty sure he's not the only male she's looking forward to seeing.

"Speaking of this afternoon," Tad says, stabbing his fork in the air, "there is going to be a lot of F-R-E-E food floating around that place, and I expect all of you to do your part. Load up like there's no tomorrow—I'm especially counting on you boys to really pack it in. This will be great training for the hot dog competition on the Fourth. That leaves us with two weeks left to get our digestive tracks in optimal condition. It's going to be the highlight of our summer."

"Does Paragon really host something so stupid?" Mia balks.

"Rockaway Point." Tad nods.

Rockaway? That's my special place with Gage—was anyway. Now it'll "forever" be marred with gluttony and vomit—sounds about right.

"For sure that's not the highlight of our summer." Mom waves Tad off dismissively. "The highlight of our summer is spending time with that new grandbaby of ours. Speaking of which, are you girls taking your multiples every day?" She spears Mia, Melissa, and me with her baby-making venom.

"What the hell are you talking about?" Tad snatches her by the elbow before she has a chance to open a human manufacturing plant right here in Landon central.

Mom frowns at him. "Folic acid is necessary to a young girl's body to keep the follicles in prime condition. You need to start years in advance to avoid any reproductive difficulties that might crop up later. And no," she says, turning to the three of us, "I don't want any new grandbabies in the near future." She reaches over and tousles my hair. "You and Gage are still on the five year plan, right? Of course, that's just for marriage. You could always wait to have kids."

Every pair of eyes in the room settles over me and suddenly I don't have the heart to burst Mom's matrimonial bubble.

"Yeah, that's what we're thinking." It comes out weak, deceptive.

"You know, it's never too early to start wedding planning. Some of the best locales are booked years in advance." She leans in with excitement. "We have tons of things to discuss. We'll do lunch."

Oh, do we ever have things to discuss. Like the fact her boy toy is the sole proprietor of my newfound misery. I plan on telling Lizbeth Landon every single detail of Demetri's blood-sucking arrangement. Then I'll regale her with Gage's newly demoted status in our lives—break her heart just like he broke mine.

Something tells me this is going to be the worst summer of our lives—if I live long enough to see it.

15

The Estate

The sun rides high overhead, hovering like some alien vessel intent on devouring us. The glare provides its own distinct haze, clouds up my vision with the gloss of happiness it so arrogantly displays.

I'm late—two hours to be exact, to the summer kickoff hosted by the monster who killed my father.

My father. I miss him with an indescribable ache.

I park and head over toward Demetri's estate. This is the summer I'm supposed to close out my community service by rummaging through his dead grandfather's belongings as an "I'm sorry for hoarding a boatload of pot that was never mine to begin with." I wonder what my mother will think once I clue her in on *Demetri's* illegal deviant behavior. Maybe she'll lose it—lop off his privates and throw them in a ditch. Or maybe she'll tap into her inner psychotic and marry him—revenge ala Ethan. Honest to God, whatever happened to a little street justice by way of a sawed-off shotgun?

I follow the walkway to the backyard and find the who's who of Paragon proper. A ton of people from school litter the landscape, along with a bunch of girls from East.

Carson Armistead is already drooling at Logan's feet with that over-processed haystack that sits on top of her head, paired not so well with her orange tie-die tan from a can. God, it looks like she spread Cheese Whiz all over her skin.

I start heading over and freeze in my tracks.

Chloe has Gage tucked under the gazebo, and she's yapping into him, spastic like a wind up Chihuahua. His dark head is lowered. He looks bored, angry, and actively looking for an out.

I try to turn away, to force myself to look at the row of swaying willows just behind the gazebo or the rose garden with each bloom turning its face toward the sun, but I can't move. A train wreck is unfolding, and I'm already very much a part of the wreckage.

I loved him once. He seared himself over my soul, and a part of me still belongs to his wicked heart.

Gage walks past Chloe. She tries to spin him by the elbow, but he keeps on moving until he joins Logan and a motley crew of girls from East, who are busy openly engaging in public worship.

I can't blame them. Logan is a god.

Marshall materializes in a brilliant burst of sunshine, first as a shadow, then his exceptionally gorgeous self. "He stomped off rather angry. Was that the resolution you were looking for?" He's wearing a T-shirt and shorts. His arms are immaculately cut as if he spends all his spare time pumping some serious iron.

"I don't really care how Gage and Chloe end their conversations." With a shotgun blast would be nice or maybe a butcher knife.

"You could have fooled half a dozen of your cohorts, who stood around and gawked while you froze solid, drooling over his eminence. Really, he's removed himself from the picture. Don't you think you should extricate him from your emotional radar?"

"Easier said than done," I say, following Marshall over to a shade tree where we watch the festivities unfold without risk of skin cancer and equally deadly ex-boyfriends.

"Should you need a salve for that broken heart, look no further. The panacea, which you desire, is right here." He picks up my hand and places it over his heart.

I twitch my lips to let some sarcastic remark fly out, then retract. I'm so broken, so utterly humiliated over what I've allowed to happen, especially last night, that I might just take Marshall up on the offer.

"OK, it's a date," I say, retracting my hand.

"What's a date?" Mom pops up from behind.

"We were just speaking of an upcoming engagement." Marshall lays a heavy emphasis on the word *engagement* and sends Mom into a hyperventilating tizzy.

"Can you believe it?" she squeals. "I know they're young, but they're so perfect for each other! Oh, look, Emma just arrived. Excuse me." She hops off, shouting for Emma and waving.

"She's still propagating rumors of my fake nuptials. I don't have it in me to break her heart."

"Sure you do," Marshall quips. "The heart you're trying to protect is your own. The more people who become aware of the fact you no longer have a relationship with Jock Strap, the more real it becomes, and the more real it becomes, the more it sinks in that things are over between the two of you. It's a quite painful process that could easily lead to depression, hysteria—a felony or two."

"Gee—glad I signed up for more of that. Remind me to drink a gallon of gasoline beforehand and to bring a match."

"My grievance is duly noted. Come, let's change the subject." He nods as a group of girls in bikinis strut by with their boobs bouncing high, their G-string clad bottoms winking with every step. "I did some celestial digging and found out a fascinating fact regarding your people that might interest you."

"My people? Celestra?" Although he could mean humans since he fits in neither category himself.

"Those eighty-nine slaughtered in the faction war by the Pretty One's hand are nowhere near Paradise."

I take in a sharp breath. "Are they in the Transfer?" I'd go down right now and get them myself. And, technically Holden killed them, not Logan.

Marshall shakes his head. "Close—it starts with a T."

"Transport."

"No, love, you either go up or down in the Transport, no milling around in hopes to alleviate your soul of its carnal ills as others have been prone to rationalize."

"Starts with T..." I cut my gaze across the yard and let the crystalline pool draw me in with its inviting blue sparkle. "Oh my God." I breathe out in a whisper. It feels like a knife just exploded through my abdomen. "The tunnels."

"The tunnels indeed." Marshall gives a dark look over to Demetri. "Do you realize what this suggests?"

"They're alive, and we can get them." I pant out the words as though we could leave right now. God knows I'd deliver every single Celestra soul from the Counts' twisted hands if I were able, but I'd rescue Lacey first.

"It means they're alive and *you* can get them."

"Why can't you come with me? Is there some bionic binding spirit down there or something?"

"Something." He twists into a frown. "I'm going to try and pull some strings. Your mother is involved, so already you should know where this is headed."

"Nowhere fast," I'm quick to reply. "Look, I want to speak with her myself. Please tell her I said so. I'm getting a little tired of the hurry up and wait routine from someone who professes to be 'oh so accessible.'"

"She can hear you. Rest assured, if you invoke her name, she's with you in spirit. Whether or not she responds is another matter entirely."

A flash of the brief stay in that den of horror sweeps through me like a rancid memory—that inky, unbearable darkness, the palpable fog. I can still feel it crawling all over me, encasing me in its hopeless languor.

"Marshall," I whisper, taking a hold of him by the elbow. "I beg of you, find a way to rescue those people. It's agonizing, excruciatingly painful, and they're locked up for good. They've been kidnapped—and little kids are down there for God's sake."

"There is a way." He says it low. A sadness blooms in Marshall's crimson eyes that I've never seen before. Grief clouds his features and tempers the feel good sensations flowing from his being.

"What is it?"

"It's you."

16

Confrontation Station

A slight breeze picks up and rattles the trees lining Demetri's haunted property like bones in a coffin. The sun sprays out its foreign beams, dousing us with blazing tongues of fire.

Marshall declares he has business with Barron and excuses himself, so I meander over to the buffet that Demetri's drones set out. A small army of waitresses hustle and bustle in tiny black skirts, carrying out dish after exotic dish, fussing over the ornate fruit arrangements in this magical culinary display. I wish my mother would note that both edible and beautiful can get along on the dinner plate.

I head to a table with a row of miniature palm trees set upon it with overgrown strawberries speared into their trunks by way of colorful toothpicks. A giant chocolate fountain rains dark sheets of heaven down at the other end. It's calling me, luring me over with its glossy perfection. Usually, I'd think twice before loading up on carbs, but without Gage in my life, it all seems rather pointless. In fact, I plan on dunking my head under that chocolate river before the day is through and drinking down its offerings as a part of my huge kiss off to both Gage and my skinny jeans. I'll eat a freaking carb when I want to. Gage may have taken my heart, but I'll be damned if he's taking my calories.

Mia catches my eye wearing a barely there swimsuit. Her hair is almost to her waist, and she looks far hotter than she's allowed. I couldn't wear a two-piece until like the tenth grade.

Maybe my mother really is hoping all female Landon slash Messengers will take over the maternity ward in the very near future. Weird.

A pair of prepubescent boys sits on either side of Mia like pimpled bookends. They laugh every time she opens her mouth like a pair of barking seals. I recognize the beady-eyed one on the left as Gabriel Armistead, the dolt she and Melissa keep fighting over. She shakes out her flowing hair, and he rakes over her with his eyes when he thinks she's not looking—pig.

"Hey." A low husky voice emanates from over my shoulder. Speaking of pigs...

"Hello, Gage." I pluck three giant strawberries off the miniature tree in front of me and violently jab the toothpicks back into the trunk.

"About last night." His hot breath warms my bare shoulder. I'm suddenly regretting wearing anything but a tank top and cutoffs. I wish I could wrap myself in a blanket while I'm near Gage. The last thing I want are his eyes feasting over my flesh. He's the last person on Earth who deserves said feast, and unfortunately I was too weak to prove that point last night.

A part of me wants to tell him that I would have done that with any boy that happened to be in my room—that he wasn't special, that he never was—but that's one lie I don't think I could pull off. When all is said and done, and I look back on my life, Gage Oliver will be the most devastating heartache I have ever known.

"It won't happen again," I whisper.

He presses up from behind and warms me with his body. His cologne enwreathes me, creates an ache in me to touch him as deep as the ocean.

"I was sort of hoping it would happen again." He blows it hot in my ear.

I reach over and run my finger under the warm chocolate fountain before glancing back at him with a look of mischief.

I push the chocolate covered digit into my mouth and extract it slowly.

"Need help?" His lips part at the sight.

"Who's going to help, Gage? You?" I dot his nose with the moist pad of my finger.

"Yes," he says in a hypnotic voice, "let me help you, Skyla." His breathing becomes erratic. It's nice to know his penis is in working order even if his brain and heart are clearly defunct.

I turn to face him fully. "Why are you continuing to waste my time?" I spear him with all of the hatred I can muster, but it comes out weak, just this side of tears.

"Skyla." He presses it out in a broken whisper. "Let's go somewhere and talk." His entire being radiates an apology.

"So what happened? Did you have to force yourself to kiss me? I bet pretending to be my boyfriend felt like a prison sentence. Did you and Chloe have a good laugh every night at what an idiot I was?"

"No, I swear to you it was never like that." He gives a long, tortured blink. "I beg of you, let's get out of here." He picks up my hand and massages it with his warm fingers. "I'll take you to Paris." The curve of a smile plays on his lips.

"Skyla." A male voice booms to my left. Demetri heads in this direction at a quickened clip.

"Looks like I just found someone I'd rather hang out with," I say, abandoning the strawberries and walking away.

"What?" I hiss at Demetri while watching Gage twist and writhe from my peripheral vision.

"I believe this belongs to you." He holds up a large metal disc with a filigree edge, the one I had tucked in my garter belt at prom just before I was taken.

I snatch it back from him.

God—I almost lost this. And to think it was in the wrong hands entirely. These discs were a precious gift from

Marshall. Each one had the ability to stop the faction war cold, and too bad for me, this is the last get-out-of-the-ethereal-plane-free card.

"Aren't you going to thank me?" He ticks his head. His almond eyes reduce to slits.

"Most definitely not."

"You have plenty to be thankful for."

"I assume you're talking about the treble." Like he's capable of kindness.

"It's a limited offer for the sake of the war. Of course, when the time comes I'll allow you to say good-bye to your mother—tell her you're leaving the country and never coming back. I'm sure you won't have a problem bending the truth a little."

"I don't plan on bending anything." I seethe. "In fact, I'm sure she'd be very interested in knowing the whole truth and nothing but the truth."

"That's where you're wrong." He lifts his head and sucks all the residual pride out of the air. "And even if you were to tell her the truth, who's to say she'd believe you?"

"*Me*—I say she'd believe me." I'm totally lying. Lizbeth Landon doesn't believe good morning when it sails from my lips.

"I'm betting otherwise."

I guess he's done pretending that she's a part of the scheme team.

Mom drifts over with Tad, lingering helpless by her side. He carries an overloaded plate of food with at least a dozen hot dogs that I'm guessing are all reserved to take down his colon.

"Lizbeth, we were just talking about you." Demetri collapses an arm around her shoulders. "I was just telling Skyla how stunning you look in a bathing suit. You haven't aged a day in twenty years."

Tad lifts a brow and observes his bride while stuffing a sausage in his mouth.

I needle him with a look.

That's right, Taddy dearest, he's checking out your wife in her next-to-nothings. Well, actually, it's a rather involved bathing suit that can double as a dress, but still, way more skin is exposed than this idiot deserves to see.

"Isis!" Demetri beckons a beautiful blonde with over-processed hair that shags out around her face. She's wearing a low cut V-neck, ten sizes too small, and her chest balloons out like she's hiding a pair of basketballs under her skin-tight attire. There's something odd about her. Her chest is completely disproportionate to the rest of her waifish body, much like the mutated doll version put out by toy manufacturers the world over. Barbie aside, there's something decidedly not human about her.

"Tad Landon." Tad sticks his hand out without waiting for the proper introduction and shakes her into a jiggle fest.

Dear God. He's openly ogling her. If ever a woman could say the words "my eyes are up here," she can.

"Isis Edinger, you can call me Izzy." A high-pitched squeal pinches past her lips. She leans into him and nearly spills the girls onto his hot dog-laden tray, inspiring Tad's tongue to lap out of his mouth.

"Isis, this is Lizbeth." Demetri pans his hand over my mother like a prize.

"Dr. Edinger." She holds out a rigid hand and offers a fake shake to Mom. Funny how she went from Izzy to cold as Isis in zero to five.

"Doctor?" Mom is tantalized by yet another lying Fem.

"Isis here is a psychiatrist." Demetri acts as liaison to the deceit. "She's just returned from a rather lengthy trip—studying overseas." He extends his false grin in my direction.

Isis? Overseas? She so *is* the worm from the water globe! It wouldn't surprise me one bit if Demetri had her locked up for centuries on some minor blood-related offense.

"A psychiatrist—that's fascinating." Tad leans in and dips his gaze back to her bosom and stays there.

"Marriage counseling is my specialty—"

Tad is quick to cut her off. "We were just talking about counseling this morning." The hot dogs on his plate almost topple as he enthusiastically enlightens the crowd with his marital discord.

"The counseling we were talking about was between Skyla and Dr. Booth," Mom corrects slightly mortified by his awkward declaration. "Skyla, we're thinking about reducing your visits."

"Thank you!" I love Dr. Booth, but seriously, it's been a total waste of time.

"I would love to counsel the two of you." Isis and Tad continue to nurture their budding adultery. "I don't have an office, but—"

"You can come to my place." Tad is lightning quick with the offer. And what's this "my place" business? He's sure in a hurry to scratch my mother off the deed to the house.

"I can't wait!" She giggles into him as if he had just asked her to prom. "Hey?" She sighs, plucking a bottle of suntan oil out of her bag and waves it at Tad. "Would you mind getting my back?" A sting of laughter bubbles out. It's like she can't go three words without cackling like a hyena.

"Hold this." Tad shoves his hotdog pyramid in my direction and takes off with Dr. Kiss-Your-Marriage-Good-bye Edinger.

"She seems nice." Mom isn't the slightest bit worried that Tad is busy molesting her baby-smooth skin at this very moment—and holy freaking shit! Her bowling balls are barely covered with a bright pink nipple suit that could double as eye patches.

"That girl is a true angel." Demetri glosses over me with a rancid smile.

Something tells me she's nothing but a skanky snake. I have a feeling Tad and Lizbeth Landon are going to need more than a marriage counselor when she's through with them—more along the lines of a divorce attorney.

It looks like all of the pieces are falling into place for my least favorite Fem. Too bad for him I won't let them stay there. I'm going to move heaven and Earth to make sure things don't work out for Demetri.

In fact, I plan on giving him hell long before he ever gets there.

17

The Gods of Sunday

Demetri's estate boils under the white-hot spotlight that the planets revolve around like an overt act of worship. The fiery orb makes a rare appearance for Demetri's ode to summer, but I know it's just another lame party trick he's pulled out of his enchanted ass. Manipulating the weather is simply the sleight of hand he's resorted to in order to further his efforts with my mother. After all, it was the synthetic rise in mercury he organized that got her to strip down to her skivvies.

Today is all about the Fems. I watch as they walk on their manufactured sunshine and work their black magic, trying to tear my family apart.

Brielle and Drake finally show, sans baby Beau, who thankfully averted a third degree burn, in this, his second week of life. Considering he's already survived fourteen days with Drake and Brielle as his primary caregivers, I think the kid is off to a damn lucky start.

"You look fantastic," I say, hugging Bree.

"Are you kidding? I still can't fit into my jeans. And I have all this extra skin on my stomach. I'm going to need a tummy tuck or a body transplant. I'm disgusting. And hello?" She plucks at her copper hair. "I'm freaking balding at seventeen. Don't have kids, Skyla. It's so not worth it."

I watch as Gage takes off his shirt across the pool and stretches like a bear into the sky. My stomach cycles at the sight of him. Just knowing he was mine, that it all felt so perfect, so right, kills me on a primal level. What I wouldn't give to have it all back, for it to have all been real.

"I'm not having kids," I whisper, taking off my T-shirt, exposing a very barely there, I hope-you-die-of-blue-balls-

Gage-Oliver white bikini top. It's see-through when it's wet. I made sure of it just before I put it on. Then again Gage probably isn't going to die of blue balls. I'm sure Chloe will see to that. Just the thought nauseates the hell out of me.

"Hey." Brielle throws a hot arm over my shoulder. "You OK? You and Gage still fighting? I heard you tell him off at prom."

"Yup, still fighting." Only now it's a little more genuine. "He turned out to be a real ass. Why didn't you warn me about him?"

"What are you talking about?" She pulls out a yellow bin of margarine the size of a small bucket and proceeds to scoop a pile of yellow goo with her fingers. "Gage Oliver is one of the most down-to-earth, nicest guys on the face of this planet. In fact, Drake could learn a thing or two from him." She takes a seat on a lounge chair and slathers her thighs with the milky yellow gloss.

"Yeah," I balk, "like how to be absolutely full of shit at any given time." By the way, I totally think Drake, much like Gage, has already mastered that.

"Skyla!" Brielle stops midflight from smearing the goop onto her chest. "What the hell?"

"I'll explain later."

"Look at this crap." She gives her thighs a good greasy pinch. "Sumo wrestlers have a better ass than I do."

"Oh, stop." I dip my finger in the bucket.

"Messenger!" Ellis shouts from the giant sprawling lawn. He's waving at me from behind Gage and his perfect rippling abs, his black hair shines reflectively under the alien sun—those sweet lips press out a smile in my direction, and I melt faster than the butter in between Brielle's cleavage. It's going to be hell living on the same island with him—just being on the same rock floating through space is far too close for comfort. I'll have to face the fact he broke my heart, and now

I'm going to die because living in this new world with a fake Gage Oliver is worse than being a permanent resident of the Celestra tunnels, worse than any torment Ezrina could ever dole out in the Transfer.

"Looks like a football game's about to break out," Drake says, heading over, and I follow.

Logan and Chloe, Gage the traitor, Emily, Nat and Pierce. Gah! *Pierce!* That's impossible. He's supposed to be doing loads of time in juvy this summer. This was going to be a Holden-free, three-month vacay for me. I'm so sick of Holden and his revolving door bodies. It's getting difficult to keep track of how much I hate him with each new incarnation.

"What's up, sis?" Holden crosses his arms over his chest.

"Aren't you supposed to be paying my debt to society?" I snark. He really is serving an undeserved sentence dressed up in Pierce's unlucky flesh. It's not my fault the legal system is corrupt and unjust.

"Got a weekend pass. Thanks for the new digs, by the way." He holds out his arms for me to observe his cut physique.

"It's your brother," I say disgusted. "He's staying dead, by the way." Those crazy Kraggers can get a little demanding when they lose their birthday suit.

"Sounds like I owe you."

I pause just shy of heading over to Logan. "What did you say?"

"I owe you." He gives a light sock to my shoulder. "I'm back in the game, and I'm not talking this one," he says, tossing the football into the air.

"OK!" Chloe claps her way to the center as if she's in charge. "Logan and I are team captains. Logan, go first." I bet she barks out orders to Gage in bed. Just the thought makes me want to nail them both in the head with some pigskin. And I just might.

"Skyla." Logan gives a sly smile.

Before I can head over, Chloe yelps out for Gage, and he happily complies. OK, not so happily, but all this pissed off energy he's funneling in Chloe's direction is probably just a ruse.

I lean over and give Logan a quick kiss on the cheek.

"What was that for?" There's a look of longing in his eyes as though he wanted it to linger right here on the field in front of East and West.

"It's because I really do love you, Logan." It comes out sad, honest.

Logan and Chloe call out names until two even rows of less than a dozen people square off.

Ellis calls for everyone to get into position—Ellis, who isn't even on the football team at West. I'm betting he developed a sudden interest in the sport as soon as girls in bikinis became involved at an intimate level.

"Skyla, you're a wide receiver." Logan motions me over to where Ellis is stooped, so I fall in line next to him and mimic his position. I know less than zero about football. Cheering for West has taught me squat about the game in general. It so damn foggy when they play, it's impossible to see what's going on. Anyway, it doesn't matter. What better excuse than a violent game of pig ball to kick some serious Chloe and Gage ass? Now the real dilemma is—whose face to grind into the dirt first.

The players line up and Logan keeps shouting incoherent things I can't decipher.

I expect nothing short of an exceptional performance, Marshall sneers from the sidelines. He's the only one I can hear without him touching me. I suppose it has something to do with his Sector status. *Your earthly mother is cheering you on. Do refrain from tearing your competitor's limb from limb. I'd join in on the fun myself, but it would be incredibly inappropriate to fondle your flesh and sack you right here in full-public view.*

I look back and frown at the content of his inner monologue.

I'll save the sacking for later, he continues. *We can mimic the plays of our conjugal union in the privacy of my backyard. We can roll around on the lawn like animals and invent our own naughty games—Naked Leap Frog—Marshall May I—Hide the Peak—Red Light, Green Light District—Obstacle Intercourse—Hot Lava—Capture the Sector—Skyla Says—the possibilities are endless. Our throbbing loins will reap the victory. The entire scenario is, as you would say—made of win.*

I motion for him to knock it off. Marshall and his hypersexual taunting is going to throw me off the only game that counts—the one in which I accidentally on purpose castrate Gage Oliver. He and his baby blues are going down. There is not one ounce of mercy left for him in my little black heart.

Gage looks over at me, his eyes glazed with lust. There's a sly smile on his face that suggests he might be planning a physical take down of his own. It really does beg the question, who's the hunter and who's the prey.

"Down," Logan shouts, "on two."

Bodies break like balls on a pool table, running every which way. Gage eyes me with the hint of a lascivious smile. His arrogance—his audacity to linger his gaze in my direction aggravates me to no end.

I charge at him with an unnatural fury, dissention rising in my bones, my blood. I knock into his chest, and he falls back voluntarily as his dimples taunt me with their blessed perfection. This is what he wanted; this is precisely what he hoped would happen, me sitting on his chest, panting like some foolish schoolgirl.

"Feel better?" He squints into me.

"I'll never feel better, Gage. I hope that makes you happy."

Gage Oliver lays out the trap, and I fall in every single time. I wanted to be his wife, his sex slave, and now, all I want is to see him lying at the bottom of a freshly dug grave—the open mouth of the earth ready to swallow him whole as payment for the bruise he laid over our so-called love.

The play stops, and everyone gets back into position a little farther down the field.

"Skyla, get up," Ellis shouts. "You're not tackling. You're a receiver. Run after the ball next time."

I go to push off, and Gage secures me by the wrist. Gage glows against the dark luster of the grass, as his eyes reflect the sky. They radiate an undying affection that one might mistake as genuine—so heartbreakingly right.

"Let go," I whisper.

He releases his hold and presses out a dull smile. "I'm in love with you, Skyla Messenger. You hold my entire world in your heart."

A strangled moment passes. For a second, it's just the two of us alone in the universe, all sight and sound dissipates as the world erodes under the guise of his questionable affection.

"Bullshit." I spit it in his face and jog back over to the lineup.

"Focus, Messenger!" Ellis reprimands as I fall in next to him.

Geez, he's like the female version of Bishop the Cheer Monster.

"Two," Logan shouts.

I don't pay attention to the ball or the direction Ellis tries to herd me. Instead, I go after Chloe this time, land on her back, and push her face down in a bald patch of mud—the moist soil of Paragon ready to suck her in.

"You bitch!" She comes up, gulping for air, and spins me around so fast, all I see is the sky rotating, the skirts of the evergreens shifting position. Chloe's dirty face is locked in a snarl. She lifts me a foot off the ground and slams me to Earth with a bionic aggression.

My head hits so hard it makes the world vibrate. Chloe's features repeat themselves in triplicate as her mouth swims over me in an expletive-riddled tirade.

Skyla, Marshall calls my name low and deep like a demon.

"Skyla." Gage pushes Chloe off and straddles me—the look of worry rife on his beautiful face.

The sky collapses on itself. It rolls up like a scroll, and a darkness so dense you can take a bite out of swallows up the world and all of those in it.

"Help." The word swims from me slow and lethargic.

"Skyla," Gage shouts, his voice reverberating off my skin. "Stay with me."

But I don't.

18

Black Hole

"I'm with you." Logan moans into my ear as we sail down Demetri's demonic rabbit hole on the way to the Celestra tunnels.

I wrap my legs around him—coil my arms around his waist so tight I fear for the safety of his bones.

An ever-growing darkness, one long, cloying night robes itself around our bodies, pressing in on us until we're barely able to breathe.

Logan pushes my head into his neck, cradles the back of my skull like a catcher's mitt, hoping to soften the blow upon impact.

Logan and I free-fall into nothing, lighter than air. It hardly feels like we're moving, then with an abrupt force, gravity pulls us down like the descent of a very steep roller coaster. We've become lead—a comet barreling toward Earth, wishing to burn before ever hitting the surface. This is too far, too fast. Nothing could survive the fall. I hope Logan and I are launched right into Paradise, far away from Demetri and the Counts, away from Gage and my broken heart. It would all end, and I could smile again with Logan by my side for the rest of eternity.

Logan twists over me as we smack into the floor. A brilliant pain surges through my body from the violent impact. The darkness continues to linger, thick as a blanket dipped in oil. This strange night has become a person, a thing. It caresses our flesh, blows through our hair, taunts us, and reassures us it is in every way alive.

Logan lets out a hard groan.

"Are you OK?" I pat the ground of this demented forest like a blind man until he takes up my hand and helps me to my feet.

"Hurt my elbow. I'll be fine."

A sickly light approaches in our direction.

"Welcome to the Tenebrous Woods." Ingram slathers the greeting with sarcasm.

"I can't do this, Skyla." Logan pulls me in and whispers. "I can't live with myself knowing I'm in some way responsible."

I drop to my knees, run the pads of my hands down over his stomach, his legs, and clamp onto the bottom of his jeans.

"I beg of you with everything in me, don't leave me, Logan. I will never forgive you if you do."

"Stand." Ingram clicks his heels together, and I do as I'm told. "Your proper name was invoked." He tilts his head toward Logan. "Carry out the punishment," he instructs before referring to his lucent clipboard.

"Go out with me tomorrow night." In this dim light, I can make out Logan giving the curve of a smile.

"Do I have to?" I stretch each word out with disdain in an effort to put on the best show possible for the deluded demon in our midst.

"Try again." Ingram doesn't bother looking up. "Seconds remain."

"Kiss my shoe." Logan closes his eyes with an immediate sense of remorse.

"Kiss your shoe?" It's difficult to gauge how pissed I should be. Obviously, Logan and I will have to go over a strategy of what types of punishments I might find acceptable.

I get back on my knees and press my palms to the ground, bringing my lips to the tip of his sneaker. I would much rather be bent in this humiliating position forever then have to get up and face what comes next. I would worship at

Logan's feet months at a time, if he could get me out of the stronghold the Counts have me in.

Logan helps me up and we follow Ingram down the disorganized maze of these twisted back woods, each strange looking tree cloaked in pitch.

That will never happen again, Logan assures.

Don't ever say you'll leave, I say. *I don't care what they have you do.*

I won't leave, he says, resigned to the fact. *I promise I'll die before I do that.*

A choir of screams, an entire series of muffled groans, and a sea of horrific cries fill my ears. A palpable fear penetrates the atmosphere. It soaks in my bones and settles there. I don't think the horror of this place will ever dissipate from my memory. I want to drink this madness down and take it with me to Paragon so I can do something about it—get the bastards who ever thought it was a good idea to hole up Celestra like cattle.

The chambers open up to the left, each one emitting a dull glow. A man lounges in one. He looks emaciated, depleted of both the will to live and strength. A few women linger in the next, then an entire wall of individual cells. But it's the little girl I look for. Her spirit haunts me even though she's locked in this nightmare along with her mother. Since I've made it my new mission to save these souls, I'd like to start with hers.

Ingram stops abruptly and points to an illuminated chamber that stands empty save for a large wooden beam. Twin chains hang from it about five feet apart with a rope dripping down between them like some necrotic promise.

I glance around looking for a way to break free from this lamp-lit Levatio. Vines line the forest floor, thick as snakes, which means making a run for it could pose a problem of the broken neck variety. I glance back and give a depleted smile at Logan. We'll have to think of a plan another time.

"The Elysian will do the honors." He glances down at the lights dancing on his clipboard.

Logan takes me over to the primitive-looking contraption and secures my wrists, then stretches my arms out in the shape of a cross and ties the rope loose around my waist.

He touches his cheek to mine. *I hate myself more than I could ever tell you.*

"Don't." It comes out an anguished cry. *If our hatred should be directed anywhere, it's toward the Counts.*

"Instruct her not to speak." Ingram peruses his notes as if looking at me would be cause of some gross violation.

"Don't speak." Logan says it sharp and commanding then dots my lips with a kiss. *I'm so sorry. I don't know how, but I'll make this up to you.*

Ingram barks at him to step aside. Logan leaves his hand gently cupped over my cheek until he's forced to remove it.

The dark-haired boy with the wide, serious eyes appears. Wesley. He gives a placid smile as he approaches, ignoring both Logan and Ingram. Wesley just has eyes for me and the blood boiling in my body.

What's your name? he asks as he rubs over my neck with his lips.

I close my eyes, ignoring him like he chose to ignore Logan, and block the world out of view. I can feel his bite, then the hard suction of the first pull. Wesley takes in long, slow drags, sending a dull ache vibrating from the puncture.

His thoughts revert to Laken, his girlfriend: her long glassy hair, her enthusiastic smile. He tells her he loves her, that he would never hurt her. He wishes she would just wake up, realize who she is and the promise the future holds for her, for both of them.

The world shifts and spins until the darkness bleeds to red.

Wesley, you're hurting me.

Just a little bit more. He groans.

You're a bastard—you know that? Every one of you. I gasp for breath. *I hope Laken finds a better man. I hope she leaves you and never looks back.*

A thought bounces through his mind—a football player with a shy smile. Laken has her arms strapped around his waist, and he's whispering in her ear. He has a comely face and enough lust in his eyes to set the field on fire.

That's who she'll choose, I taunt. *She'd never want you— not like this.*

Wesley pulls away abruptly.

I open my eyes and glare at this cheap replica of the boy I once loved, and the world explodes around me.

19

Bad Romance

A trickle of light penetrates my eyelids as familiar voices boom all around—nothing but shouting and laughter intermingled with my name given in heated whispers from above.

"Skyla," Gage pants. I can feel his breath pulse in and out of my ear, his rapid breathing agitating the side of my face. "Skyla, wake up."

My lids flutter open to Demetri's emerald lawn, the football game still underway as legs swish back and forth farther down the field. Chloe spits repeatedly on the sidelines, washing her face down with a water bottle as Em supervises.

"What happened?" Gage picks me up and sits me on his lap. I'd resist the effort, struggle to get away if I could, but my muscles don't respond—my entire body feels incapable of functioning on a rudimentary level.

"Can't move," I mouth.

"That bastard took you again," he seethes.

It takes all of my effort to look up at him. For a moment, I lose myself in the intense blue flame brewing in his eyes. How can he feel so much hatred toward my enemy, if he's one of them himself?

"Skyla!" Logan runs over and falls to his knees. He extricates me free from Gage just as a hammer of darkness falls over the world.

❤ 🦋 ❤

The ground shakes.

A purple film lines the sky, and it takes a moment for me to realize round four of the faction war is well under way.

"No," I breathe it.

I find myself lying supine on soggy soil, staring up at the unnatural velveteen sky. I try to clutch at the balding grass, but my fingers slip, limp and useless as the rest of my drained body.

"Mother," I rasp. Honest to God, she is not an ally in this campaign if she thinks sending me into the faction war after having my blood sucked dry is a winning idea.

The ground gives a violent jolt.

"Shit," I hiss.

It takes more than a concerted effort to lift my head and peer out at my surroundings. A hillside sits off in the distance. The thick cover of evergreens carpets the majority of the landscape. Grunts and cries of agony echo throughout the ethereal plane as I struggle to my elbows.

The thick metallic disc protrudes from my pocket, taunting me with the lack of energy to retrieve it, should the need arise.

An explosion of light goes off in the distance, as I sink my head back onto the damp soil. I'm helpless. Death can certainly come for me here. What enemy is death when everything seems to be falling to crap anyway? With a celestial mother like mine, who only seems to initiate trouble, a boyfriend who swore forever then proved nothing but a liar, and no blood left to run this Celestra machine God saw fit to gift me with—why is life important to me? Why do I find it so worth living? Why does a ray of hope flicker, despite this constant curtain of darkness that's enveloped my existence?

A flash of all those Celestra crying out in anguish down in the tunnels filters through my mind. Lacey's face brands itself over my heart. If I do one good thing in my life, it'll be freeing those souls and stopping the Counts from taking any more prisoners. Losing my life would be an honor, if I died fighting for my people. God—I hate the Counts.

"Skyla!" Logan's voice booms like a riot.

I muster the strength to get up on all fours, then fall down again.

"We need to get you somewhere safe." Logan lands by my side. His hot breath streaks across my face like a nuclear winter as he sits me in his arms.

The ground thumps as a couple of people run over. I can only assume it's Ellis and Gage, but when I look up, I'm horrified to find it's not. A boy with a broad chest and a familiar-looking face crouches next to Logan. He's holding a huge black rifle with a menacing series of barrels. His friend stays a good distance away as if keeping watch over the situation.

"What's going on?" Logan says it calm, but I can tell he's ready to snatch the monstrosity of a weapon from him and use it against the two of them.

"Who are you fighting for?" He looks from me to Logan.

I hesitate. And for a pathetic moment, I think of lying and saying the Counts. But I'll be damned if I'm going down that way.

"Celestra." It huffs out of me.

He gives a sly smile. "I knew that. And I know you." He presses his gaze into me and his face sparks a fire in my memory bank as I frantically try to place him. "Cooper Flanders." He holds a hand out to Logan and they shake. "There's a hostile battle just north of here. The Counts have assault weaponry—some kind of alien equipment." He holds up the missile launcher strapped to his chest.

"How?" It's all I can push out thanks to Wesley the weasel and his sudden urge to hydrate himself.

"I don't know," Cooper answers, assuming I'm talking about his gun. "But all they've outfitted Celestra with are primitive bows—broken arrows."

"If you're fighting with Celestra, how'd you get your hands on that?" Logan is slow to embrace this new ally and I've yet to figure out how Cooper "knows" me.

"Flynn's a Count." He glances back at the tall sandy-haired boy with a friendly face.

A roar of voices, a cacophony of gunfire erupts from the ridge.

"We'll keep them at bay," Cooper says, panning the vicinity. "Get her somewhere safe."

We watch as they take off toward a thicket in the distance. A barrage of bullets explode in the dirt just shy of their path, bringing home the fact those boys could lose everything today for a war declared in my honor. Really, it's the Sectors and the Fems, but nevertheless, they've landed us here in the heart of mortar-based danger.

I turn to tell Logan how much I hate this and all I accomplish is brushing my lips over his cheek.

Logan's face contorts with heartbreak. He touches his hand to my neck, crestfallen at what he sees.

"I can't do this." He shakes his head in grief. "I need to kill them all, Skyla."

"They'll kill you before you can off a second Count. It's futile. I don't want them to touch you."

He sets his eyes over mine. Logan feels as limp and helpless as my own body.

"You have sacrificed and loved beyond measure," I say, gathering the strength to pull his head in close to mine. His concern for my well-being has magnified to unimaginable levels. The allowances he'd make for me know no bounds. "I'll be damned if I let you make the ultimate sacrifice and lose your life."

"If it meant you'd be safe." He shakes his head. "There's nothing you could do to stop me."

"You wouldn't be helping me." Uninvited tears blur my vision. Another explosion lights up the sky like the Fourth of July. Smoke congests the area, penetrates it with a milky white fog. "Logan, if you die, I die. I would let them have me—*kill* me—I would beg them to. You're the only good thing in my life, and if you let them take that away, they win."

The ethereal plane rattles, violent screams ignite nearby—but for Logan and I, the world stands still as we lock onto one another, sunk with the prospect of death smothering us in every realm.

"Love me, Logan," I whisper. "Live for me."

He presses a kiss over my lips, and a warm tear glides from his cheek to mine.

"I'll keep fighting for us, Skyla. I'll find a way to end the misery the Counts keep inflicting."

Something quickens in me for Logan, and my heart picks up pace.

He runs his arm around my waist, slow and methodical. "How I wish we could go back to the start." A sweet smile plays on his lips.

A round of detonations goes off in the distance—followed by a choir of screams, then smoke like a furnace.

"I love you, Logan." It sounds more like a desperate plea from a child than a declaration of love from a girl hell bent on becoming a woman. "I can feel how much you care for me. I'm desperately afraid, but you calm me. Thank you for that."

Logan tilts his head as the smoke circles around us, stings our eyes with its penetrative bite. He touches his forehead to mine, warms my chest with his. I can feel him aching for me. Logan wants to fix things, but can't figure out how.

"I love you too, Skyla."

His lips brush against mine. Logan jerks before he's knocked away by a giant blur of limbs and I fall to my elbows, barely able to sustain my weight.

A dark head looms ahead—a wall of shoulders—I recognize them as belonging to Gage.

"What the fuck are you doing?" Logan roars as he wrestles Gage away from his person. He touches the back of his arm to his split lip and examines the stain of crimson.

Gage pants beside him, his chest pumping with adrenaline, a look of bitterness and contempt locked on his features. He lunges at Logan with the ferocity of a lion, and they rotate in a ball of fists, nothing but a tangle of arms and legs as the battle rages on around us.

"Gage! Stop." I struggle to my knees and falter, landing back on the ground, kissing the dirt like I mean it.

I command my body, my partial Caelestis being, my unearthly Celestra strength to rile up, but it doesn't. I crawl up on my knees, my hands shake trying to hold up my body. Something slips from my pocket and lands on the dirt with a solid thump.

"Oh God." I breathe as the shiny flat disc of failure stares up at me. I've done it. I've accidentally forfeited the region to the Counts.

The enemy gives a wild shout of victory as the ethereal plane claps into darkness.

Fuck.

Just fuck.

20

Divine Intervention

"I'm going to beat the shit out you!" Logan roars at Gage as he picks me up off the makeshift football field.

Demetri's backyard expands around us as a sea of darkness rolls overhead. A veil of grey clouds submerges the sunshine, scolding it for recklessly shining down over Paragon.

"Take her to my home at once," Marshall says in passing. I track him with my gaze as Logan picks me up in his arms and jostles me over to the side yard. Marshall walks past the hedges, and I see him dissipate easy as a vapor.

"He's going to poison me again," I whisper, mostly to myself. It's difficult to embrace the fact the only thing that can make me feel better is a good dose of cyanide, not to mention the horrid effects it had on me last time. "I don't want it." I gasp for breath. I'm so light-headed, it takes everything in me to keep myself breathing. If I stop, I swear my lungs won't continue the effort. This is all too hard.

Demetri appears from nowhere as we round out the side gate. "Leaving so soon?"

Logan doesn't bother to play his head games. He simply goes around him and darts us across the street where his truck is parked.

"I have something of yours, Skyla," he calls, but we don't turn around and give him the pleasure.

"Wait!" Gage booms from the side of the Edinger estate, just as Logan opens the passenger door. Gage appears by my side, looking at me with a deep sense of sorrow. His beautiful lips hold a smile all their own. "I'll take you." He puts a hand over my mine, clasps onto Logan's shoulder, and blinks us away.

"I have had *enough!*" Marshall roars in a dark, horrible voice I have never heard him evoke before and it inspires an echo throughout his cavernous estate. He picks up a metallic vase from off the sofa table and hurls it into the fireplace, igniting a wall of flames in its cavity that lick up to the ceiling.

Quite frankly, I'm not entirely certain about whatever the hell has Marshall up in inferno-inducing arms. It could just as easily be the fact I've squandered the last lifesaving disc, as it could be the fact Demetri let some guy who looks suspiciously like Gage suckle off an artery. I'd rather he be pissed off about the latter, since dropping the disc was a total freak accident.

"Lay her on the couch." Marshall speeds over and collects me with a sharp breath. "You!" He darts a finger at Gage. "Extricate your father from his poolside lounging and return at once."

Gage disintegrates slowly, his ghostly frame whispers *I love you* as his words wash over me with heartbreak.

"*You*, my friend, are useless." Logan belts it out at Marshall with aggressive sarcasm, and apparently, without any regard for his own personal safety.

"That you, of all people, should question my capabilities astounds me." Marshall broadens his chest as he rises. "Stand clear of Skyla so I might dispense the proper amount of retribution for such a foolish remark."

"No." I try to shield my hand over Logan's person, but it sinks back to the couch with a thud. "He's right. You are useless." I pant from the effort.

"Skyla!" Marshall sounds stupefied by my accusation, as his features dim to pitch. I can see his frustration building like a wave that's about to crest.

Gage and Dr. Oliver blink into the room.

"Let me see her." Dr. Oliver speeds over and places his hand over the tender area of my neck. "Looks like they've taken more than last time."

"It's a punishment." Marshall stands over me with his finger to his lips.

"For what?" Gage looks wild with fury.

"For flaunting the fact we've the ability to build her up so quickly." Marshall snaps. "And really? Football? Could you have chosen a more subtle way to rub it in their face? Just because we've harnessed the power to reconstitute your levels doesn't mean you should slit your wrist and hose down every Count in the vicinity with a spray of your bloody affection." He turns to Barron. "Where's the antidote?"

"I haven't had the chance to replenish the supply. I had no idea they'd come after her so soon." Dr. Oliver's glasses slide to the tip of his nose. His salt and pepper hair reflects a strange orange hue from the inferno raging out of control.

"Get used to it." Marshall reduces the flames in the fireplace with the flick of his finger. "We'll need to have three vials ready at any given time. Logan"—he pauses—"I'd banish you from her side, but seeing that you are the Elysian, I assume that's torment enough." Marshall speeds toward the kitchen.

"What's an Elysian?" Gage falls to his knees beside me and picks up my hand. I try to squirm out of his grasp, but I'm so weak he thinks I've just given him an affirming squeeze of affection.

"The Counts are using me," Logan begins. "I'm overseeing her blood withdrawals."

"How are they taking it?" Gage leans into me as Dr. Oliver and Barron grapple over something in the distance.

"Some guy comes in." Logan brushes the loose hairs from my face. "He takes it right from her neck the way Kragger used to."

"Shit." Gage looks good and pissed.

"Why do you care?" I ask in a broken whisper.

Gage pauses and darts a look into me that holds a patina of rage. "I love you, Skyla. I know how it looks and I know you can't stand the sight of me..." He bites down on his lip to keep from choking up. "When you're better, I think we should talk."

Chloe's face stains me from the inside, her effigy a permanent fixture in the back of my mind. I see her all over again at the stone of sacrifice with that look of glee on her face after letting their little secret slip on prom night. A slow, brewing rage heats through my bones, stealing all of my healing energy by singeing me with hatred.

"Marshall," I whisper, and he appears without hesitation.

"Barron is working on the formula now." He strums from above. "It should only be a few minutes before we can administer it."

"Oh, that's good." Shit. "Can you do me a favor?"

"Anything." He implores me to continue with a brief nod.

"Get rid of Gage." I cast my gaze to the ground when I say it. It's taking too much out of me to deal with this heartache. It removes all of my will to get better—to live. He's cursed me with the desire to have him, and now he's killing me softly with his presence.

"Poor dear Jock Strap." Marshall glows with delight. "It seems you've fallen *forever* out of her good graces. I gather your appeal hasn't been met with open arms. Tsk, tsk."

"There's no way in hell you're getting rid of me. Go ahead and try." Gage gets up and taps Marshall in the chest. "You sack of celestial shit." He pushes into him with a violent force. "If you love Skyla the way you claim to, you wouldn't let any of this go on for another fucking second. Makes me wonder whose side you're really on."

"We all know whose side you're on," Marshall says, picking him up and launching him toward the window. The explosive sound of glass shattering fills the room. The walls tremble from the sheer heft of his violent exit.

"What the hell?" Barron rushes in with a needle at the ready.

"I've removed your son from the premises per Skyla's wishes." Marshall straightens like a good little soldier. "He's out back if you wish to tend to his injuries. Do have him teleport you elsewhere. I'll administer the dose myself."

Dr. Oliver disappears from view, shouting for Gage as he heads out back.

"Logan?" I wiggle my fingers in his direction.

"I'm here." He pinches a smile. "I'm not going anywhere." He says it sharp as if to alert Marshall to the fact.

"Very well." Marshall lifts my shorts just enough and the needle gives a hard bite over my bottom. A deep burn settles in as the fruit-based venom seeps into my system. "I apologize once again, love." Marshall nods. "I'm unable to comfort you."

"Please," I beg. I would sell my soul for his soothing vibrations right about now.

"The toxin would never take. Your vital organs would sustain substantial damage." His eyes close a moment. "I've doubled the dose. It should take half the time. You'll be better in minutes. I'll be upstairs should you need me." Marshall presses in a full kiss over my lips before disappearing in a clap of dust.

Logan and I glance at each other as the first convulsion bucks me off the couch.

Logan is quick to scoop me up and cradle me in his arms. *I'm going to make this better, Skyla. I swear on all that is holy.* Logan increases his grip over me as my body writhes in a spastic rhythm.

Suffocating pain.

Kill me.

A hot poker of torment spears through my insides— blinding, searing explosions.

My body jerks in a quick series of convulsions and extricates me from out of Logan's grasp. A seizure powers through my body, swift as an electrical current. I hit my head on the coffee table before Logan lies over me, heavy as a lead blanket.

"I got you," he assures. He soothes me with the sound of his voice as I gyrate out of control. Logan whispers *I love you* warm in my ear until I pass out into a welcome oblivion.

21

Marshall and Me

My lids grate over my eyes like pumice before finally opening to reveal the fact I'm still firmly planted on Marshall's couch—pressed against the flesh of another. Only it's not Logan this time, it's Marshall.

"Where'd he go?" I lift my head and pan the vicinity. Logan wouldn't leave me unless Marshall, himself, managed to banish him.

"How about 'thank God it's you'—or 'praise high heavens that I'm locked in your strong arms?' Or—'how long must I wait for you to satiate me with your flesh?'" He glowers as if he's actually pissed that I let the moment pass without any of the aforementioned sentiments.

"Logan?" I call out, refusing to play into his cry for attention. Honestly, he's like a child sometimes.

"Your first instinct was correct. I banished him." He flexes a dry smile. "Nevertheless, you're better. And, yes, he stayed until the bitter end."

I spring up next to him on the couch and take a deep lungful of air.

"I feel fantastic." I marvel. "Like better than last time and well—" I wiggle my fingers and toes. "Better than ever in my entire life."

"Your blood is powerful," he muses.

"And apparently *you* are not." I meet his gaze with great intensity. "Why can't you stop this misery?"

Marshall's jaw sharpens with frustration. "Could I—I would. There is a barrier set in place designed to allow for such grievances. If there were not, the faction war wouldn't be necessary—good would always prosper over evil. But, alas, it lives, and evil thrives under its guise."

"Why? Why does it even exist? Why not stomp evil out like the cockroach it so obviously is?"

"Shh..." He cradles me in a warm embrace. "It is the price of freedom. Rest assured, this reckless brand of freedom only lasts a lifetime. The consequences of one's actions however, echo throughout eternity."

I don't really get what freedom has to do with anything. The entire concept is mindboggling, so I don't bother beating a dead horse trying to wrap my head around any of this.

"I need to rescue those souls and win the war. Help me do that."

"Sectors and Fems cannot engage in battle." He pinches his lips as though deep in thought. "I can, however, try to quell the effects of your capture."

"Yes!" I glom onto any ray of hope. "I beg of you, do whatever you can. I swear I will win this war for you, and I'll free those Celestra in the tunnels."

"I won't allow you to swear to me." His cheek slides into a depleted smile.

"In any case," I continue, "I knew you were powerful enough, smart enough to put Demetri in his place. How are you going to get the Counts to back the hell off?"

Marshall glances out the window briefly before answering. There's a far off look in his eyes as though he's wagering something significant.

"What's wrong?" I shudder unnaturally. Something has Marshall rattled and that's never a good sign.

"Let's change the subject for now."

"No." I flatten my palms against his chest. "You know something, and it's going to help me." I pick up his hand and interlace our fingers. "Tell me."

"Very well." He lands a gentle kiss over my knuckles and smolders me with a look of undying passion. To be Marshall's wife, girlfriend, one night stand would be something altogether incredible. He knows how to bring the intensity to the table, in a naughty, X-rated, only-in-your-fantasies sort of way. "I want you to know I would sacrifice my standing in the Holy of Holies if I were able to remove this blight from your life." A warm charge pulses from his hand. "I would cast myself willingly into eternal darkness to rid you of this grievous pain." His gaze dips for a moment. "I have never fully understood the human condition—the complete heartbreak this world is capable of imparting. You, Skyla, have taught me much." He tugs at my fingers. "And for this I am forever grateful."

Marshall latches onto me with his magnetic gaze. His affection for me stops up the air, creates a covenant all its own, asserting his devotion for me. I can feel him fashioning his love, lassoing my heart with his open wanting.

"Thank you for always being so kind to me." I lean in and nuzzle into his chest. "For being there whenever I need you." What I really want to add is, for not lying to me, but I loathe dragging Gage in on the conversation, even if it is by proxy.

"I plan on being here for you the rest of your natural life and beyond. I promise to be the constant, the one you can rely on. My door is forever open." He gives the curve of a lewd smile. "My bed is forever available should you need a warm place to stay the night. And, when the time is right, you'll be my bride." He says that last part so matter of fact, I almost believe him.

"What's the plan?" I refocus him on the task at hand. "How do we get Demetri off my back?"

"By dangling what he desires most in front of him."

"The ethereal kingdom?"

"Your mother."

I sink back into the couch. "Absolutely not."

"Why? He's prone to making foolish errors in the name of love. He's practically human in that respect."

"Very funny—again, no."

"I've the sneaking suspicion your mother would be a willing accomplice."

"Yeah, well, I'm not so sure what good it would do." She seems to be headed in that direction on her own.

"Simply divulge the grizzly details of your capture to her. I guarantee she'll have him reversing the order in minutes."

"Demetri can reverse my capture?"

"He and he alone."

"I don't know if she'll believe me. My mother's been going to all the Count round tables…" My heart picks up pace. "She's been seeing him behind Tad's back."

"You suspect something more is brewing?"

"God, I hope not. Even though Tad isn't ranking as stepfather of the year, I'd be horribly disappointed if my mother were doing anything like that."

"That's because marriage is sacred, Skyla. It's innate in people to understand the basic precepts—doesn't stop them from acting otherwise, but deep down inside they know."

"It's a covenant." I nod.

"It is indeed." Marshall bows his head. "One I long to enter into with you."

I give a placid smile. "So what do you think my mother would do if I told her about the bloodlet Demetri is responsible for? I bet he's even housing babies down there. Nothing would make my mother more batshit than the thought of Demetri being directly responsible for the imprisonment of an infant. Then again, if he can't have my mother, he probably wouldn't bother letting me go."

"That's where you're wrong. He thinks very highly of her. Disappointing the woman who holds his heart would wound him grievously."

"Really? Perfect," I say stunned. "Then I'll just tell my mother."

"Yes. Do tell." He taps the tip of my nose with his finger. "Now back to the topic of us. I have a vision to share." He licks his lips in anticipation.

"No."

"Fine—then look at me." He secures his arms around my waist and presses into me with his garnet colored eyes. It feels intimate, far more involved than kissing. I can't shake the feeling we're getting it on Sector style and I'm just not aware of the sexual parameters.

A vision comes to me. It's Marshall and I standing in the center of a crowd. Someone chants over us, and everyone cheers.

I watch as Marshall bends to my ear and whispers, "You and I, Skyla, have entered into a sealed and lasting covenant." He confirms the sentiment with a kiss that makes my entire person sing.

"No," I say, snapping out of the matrimonial visual.

"Oh yes, Skyla." Marshall picks up my ring finger and presses it to his lips. "Oh yes."

22

Hack Attack

An ordinary Wednesday in summer has an uncanny way of feeling just like the weekend. I open my window and call out for Nev on this fog-laden morn, which is far more traditional for Paragon then that burst of nuclear sunshine Demetri had arranged last week.

The sky stays unchanged. Not a single dark blemish, not a stroke of glossed wings gracing the arid expanse with their beauty. A stillness clots the atmosphere. It's as if the world is holding its breath in anticipation of something monumental.

Nev doesn't come.

Strange.

My phone vibrates over the nightstand. It's a text from Logan.

Falls tonight? Me and you around 6?

I text him back. **It's a date. ~S**

Truth is, he's been asking every day since Demetri's war-inspired kickoff to summer, and I've artfully said no. I've also managed to cleverly avoid Gage for the simple reason he's an ass, and Marshall because I'm half afraid I might accidently marry him.

Evading Gage has been the toughest. I've been ignoring him in all electronic forms, and I've even gone as far as getting Brielle to cover my shift, so I won't have to face him physically. Well, actually, she volunteered. Brielle is under the impression Drake's mini me is allergic to her. Every time she steps into the room, he explodes in hysterics and hives. There might be something to the allergy theory, but I doubt Brielle herself is a part of the equation.

A shrill cry comes from the next room, followed by the trampling of footsteps descending downstairs.

I run down after them to see what the ruckus is all about.

"You freaking bitch!" Mia screams at the top of her lungs. Her voice curls the last word out like an opera singer. She's shakes something furry at Melissa, causing an all-out slap fight to ensue.

Drake and Ethan jump in to break it up.

Something about Mia looks different: her hair is in a weird bun or clipped over her head or, oh freaking shit! It's *gone.*

"Look what she did." Mia thrusts a fistful of her golden locks in Mom and Tad's direction. "She hacked off my fucking *hair!*" She bursts into a ball of tears and I head over and wrap my arms around my newly crop-haired sister.

"Melissa," Mom gasps, "how could you?"

Melissa sucks back tears—her chest heaves in a panic. "She started it."

"I was sleeping!" It drills out of Mia like a whistle.

"You're lucky that's all I hacked off!" Melissa's face turns a violent shade of purple, and for the first time, I see the resemblance between her and her father.

"That's e-*nough!*" Tad barks so loud that even the dog freezes in his tracks. "I can't believe you would hack your sister's hair off like that!" His eyes bug out. I'm actually a little proud of him for sticking up for a Messenger for once. Well, former Messenger anyway, since she decided to get her name changed and switched teams. "Mia!" He growls at her as if this were somehow her fault. "What did you do to provoke this level of insanity?"

Never mind. He's still the ass I always knew he was.

"I didn't do anything!" She fills the room with a consistent level of drama.

"This is over that stupid boy, isn't it?" I step between them. I'm so sick of this fighting. The island is rife with plenty of adolescent males to go around, Gage being one of them.

Neither of them says a word. They just cross their arms and glower at one another, certifying the fact I hit the Armistead nail on the arrogant blond head.

"Neither of you is allowed to look at a boy all summer," Tad crows.

"*Oh.*" Mom averts her eyes. "Now there's a viable punishment. Why don't you just give them a pocketful of cash and drop them off at the mall and tell them shopping's off limits, too."

My heart thumps.

I hate that Mom and Tad are starting to fight in front of us with an alarming level of frequency. Sure, the occasional squabble was exciting to bear witness to, and sure the idea of Mom divorcing Tad and moving to greener financial pastures seemed lucrative at the time, but now with Demetri in the picture, all of this verbal scrimmaging seems like nothing but a bad omen.

"What kind of punishment do you see fit—*honey?*" He says the cute moniker with an aggressive amount of sarcasm reserved for future ex-husbands the world over.

"I say we let Mia decide." Mom gives a defiant nod.

Sure—put a hormonal, and might I add, very pissed off, thirteen-year-old in charge of punitive damages where her evil step sister is concerned. Melissa just took a bad hair day to a whole new level. I'm not sure Mia can come up with anything crazy enough to compensate.

"Mia?" Mom nods. "Take your time and think up an equitable punishment to give your sister. I'm sure once you kids realize the punishment is going to be doled out by the one you decide to pick on, things are really going to change around here."

Things are going to change all right, starting with hairstyles.

"OK." Mia circles Melissa, eyeing her long flowing tresses. "I get to cut Melissa's hair."

"No way!" Melissa jumps back as if Mia's fistful of follicles has magically morphed into a thousand blond garden snakes.

"Yes," Mia says it sweetly. "I promise to do a nice, neat trim. I'll get a bowl and everything."

"Daddy, you're not going to let her do this, are you?" Melissa's widows peak engages in perfect V formation as her forehead creases with concern.

Tad cuts a quick look to Mom. "If your mother here deems it a fit punishment, then I'm on board!" He shouts it at Mom. It comes out more of a threat than an alliance.

"Well, I do!" Mom shouts back.

"Nice to see everyone getting along so famously." Ethan heads to the fridge. "By the way, Chloe's parents are heading off to Europe for a few weeks. She'll be crashing here for a while."

"What?" I speed over and snatch him by the wrist before he has a chance to mine the fridge of its anemic offerings. "She will not crash here. You crash there. Are you a dolt? She'll have an empty house. Think of all the promiscuous possibilities!"

He considers this a moment. "Empty is the problem." He pulls his wrist free and swoops a soda out. "Who's going to buy all the food? Cook? And what about fresh boxers? I only got about a week's worth, tops. Besides, she's forking over a cool grand as rent."

Tad clears his throat. "Chloe is more than welcome to seek room and board in our home." He espouses with a reserved calm. The idea of Chloe as a revenue of income pleases him to no end. Obviously the fornicating arrangement is overlooked when hard cold cash is forked over, not that Tad ever blinked at the copulating palooza.

I open my mouth to refute the idea, and nothing but a series of choking sounds emit.

"Relax." Ethan leans in. "I'm using her. I'm still really pissed she gutted me like a fish. She's worth more to me in my bed than dead." He walks off after making his moronic sexual proclamation.

"OK, girls." Tad claps at Mia and Melissa. "Make up six or seven dozen hot dogs. Your brothers and I have a training session this afternoon."

Mom brings her hand to her mouth in disgust.

I'm right there with her, ready to puke at the thought of Chloe, my own little Frankenstein, sharing downtime with me like a real live legal relation. Looks like Mia and Melissa won't be the only fake sisters trying to off each other this summer.

And God knows Chloe has more to fear than losing her tresses.

Chloe shows up while the 'rents are still hammering out the finer details of the hair affair.

"With all of this bitching and moaning, I'm beginning to feel right at home," she says it low, for my ears only.

"Soon, you'll be the one bitching and I'll be the one moaning," I quip, eyeing an entire row of bright red suitcases behind her.

"Correction, you'll be the one bitching about how you lost all trust in Gage, and I'll be the one moaning. And believe me, it won't be you evoking that pleasure-filled response in me. Would you like to guess who that certain someone might be?"

Ethan walks by and belches for effect.

"I hope he gives you rabies," I hiss.

"More like scabies, and you're wrong again. Think Oliver." She glides into a smile of faux sexual satisfaction. "The feelings I have for Gage are mutual. Does that scare you, Skyla? Does it frighten you to think it could be me wrapped in his arms *forever*?"

My stomach cinches when she says the buzzword. Have I shared that with her before? Good God, had he?

"The only thing that frightens me, Chloe, is that you keep lessening the six degrees of separation in our lives." And something tells me she won't stop until she takes over my body. Knowing Chloe, that concept is very much on the table.

"Don't flatter yourself, Skyla. I happen to hate living alone, and I do enjoy your family. Too bad you're in it."

"The nice thing about you shacking up with Ethan is..." I sharpen my gaze on her. "Oh wait, there isn't anything nice about it. I don't appreciate you using any member of my family. Get your own damn family, Chloe. For that matter, why don't you just shack up with the Olivers?" Immediate regret sets in before the words have a chance to settle in the air.

Crap. With my luck, Emma would welcome Chloe with open arms. I seriously hate this backward version of my former life, a.k.a my new reality.

"Well..." She sighs. "I'd better get settled in." She motions behind her at the army of angry suitcases as if she expects me to schlep them to Ethan's room for her.

"Good luck." I blink an irritated smile. "Hope you break a leg."

"You say that to actors, stupid."

"You're so fake, I think you qualify."

She pulls her head back and barks out a laugh.

Mom sweeps by on her way upstairs and cuts us an approving look. "It's so nice that you girls get along."

Chloe steps in as my mother drifts down the hall and shouts, "Oh, Skyla and I get along infamously."

Infamously is right.

I lean into Chloe once my mother is out of sight. "I bet that's how this relationships ends—infamously."

She turns and gives the curve of a wicked smile. "You can bet your foolish little ass that's exactly how it'll end it. I'll take you down so horrifically they'll chant about it in the schoolyard while skipping rope. People everywhere will shudder when they hear your name. I'll be sure to off you so grotesquely the entire Western Hemisphere will gawk at your misfortune on the Internet news between checking their emails and hopping on Facebook. Isn't that exciting, Skyla? You'll get your fifteen minutes. You'll be the star your father always knew you'd be."

I connect the open palm of my hand with her cheek in one swift blow, and my flesh stings from the sheer velocity.

She draws her fingers to her face, stunned that I had the balls to slap her, on this, the first night she's a paying guest in our home. Chloe reaches for a suitcase behind her and starts wheeling it toward her new living quarters.

She pauses and turns back. "Chloe Bishop took an ax and gave Skanky Skyla forty whacks. And when she saw what she had done, she gave her family forty-one."

A tingle of fear rises through my spine as Chloe cackles her way into Ethan's bedroom.

Chloe Bishop is certifiably insane.

And dear God almighty—I do believe she's going to kill us all.

Not one to waste time where revenge is concerned, Mia quickly pulls a chair into the middle of the kitchen where

Mom suggests the "mane" atrocity take place. Both Mom and Tad run upstairs to avoid the carnage, and I'm left to supervise my scissor-wielding sister while Chloe gleefully watches from the sidelines.

"Just a trim," Melissa snaps. Her fingers are pressed to her forehead from the stress of it all.

She should have thought about how shitty the payback was going to be while she was busy hacking off my sister's beautiful golden locks. All Mia is left with is a bunch of fuzz in the back and a few long strands framing her face. Come to think of it, she might be able to get away with a bastardized ponytail. She should totally replicate the effort on Melissa and they could both wear lopsided "retribution ponies" for the next few months. Before I can make the suggestion, Mia scoops up Melissa's dark hair and starts in with a quick cutting motion until it disconnects in a jagged line at the neck.

"Crap, Mia," I hiss. "It looks like a rat gnawed her hair off in her sleep."

"What?" Melissa shrieks.

"Relax!" Mia barks, "I'm going to fix it. It'll be cute. I'm sure by the time summer is over, every girl at Paragon Intermediate will be wearing the same stupid look."

I doubt entitling Melissa's new, slightly unbecoming hairstyle as a *stupid look* is the best idea while her victim is still patiently waiting for the torment to end. Call me crazy, but I'm not entirely sure spitting out the phrase *I'm going to fix it* while seething with anger is a selling point either.

"Sit still," Mia instructs as she circles around to the front.

"No bangs." Melissa yelps. "Not fair, I didn't give you bangs."

"Shut up, would you?" Mia pinches up her hair in the front and holds the scissors even with her eyes. "I've told you a million times you need to hide that hook that hangs halfway down your forehead. "I'm doing you a favor."

147

I'm with Mia on this one. Bangs would totally be a good look for Melissa—in theory.

Mia continues snipping and cutting until Melissa sports the most geometrical haircut known to man—if only it were straight. It's so damn choppy, Melissa's going to have to run, not walk, to the nearest beauty salon to rectify this catastrophe.

"Cleopatra called." Chloe snipes to the helpless Landon. "She wants her haircut back."

Melissa's mouth drops open and she runs upstairs with one long wail expelling from her lungs. Mia runs after her with the scissors still firmly planted in her hand. Obviously, safety rules such as running with scissors have been overlooked in this household, as were the dangers of running with your sister's boyfriend, who, by the way, I really blame for this entire hairy mess.

I swat Chloe on the arm. "Didn't your mother ever teach you that if you don't have anything nice to say, you should keep your mouth shut?"

Chloe would be vying for the world record in silence if she ever implemented that rule. I should have kept her *coffin* shut. That would have saved a whole lot of heartache.

Chloe scoffs. "My mother wouldn't waste her time on stupid maxims like that. She focused on much more honest truths, like, if you see something you want, go out and get it. That's what I do, Skyla. I get what I want."

Gage fills the silence between us like a ghost.

That might be the first truth to ever come from Chloe Bishop's mouth.

23

The World at Your Feet

In the cool of the evening, as I audition high heels for my date with Logan, I get a text from the other, much less tolerable yet, disturbingly desirable Oliver—Gage.

I had a dream about you. A vision. I would really like to share it. Can I see you tonight?

I stare at the words an inordinate amount of time.

My heart yearns to see Gage, to know what his dream was, what it might mean, but I don't answer. I'm just not ready to listen to whatever excuses he's come up with. I can see it now, Gage opening his mouth and an entire stream of lies pouring from him like water from a fire hydrant knocked off its base. And yet, something in my soul leans toward Gage like a wilted flower begging for light. My entire being misses his attention. I wish I didn't. I wish he and Chloe would hook up for good and get the final phase of this spectacular heartbreak over with. I just need to get over Gage once and for all and put this misery behind me.

Logan texts that he's downstairs, so I head in that direction.

Mom and Tad and a bouncy blonde congest the entry.

Isis, the slithering niece of Detective-I-don't-solve-crimes-I-mastermind-them Edinger, has arrived. Her boobs look like they're allergic to her body because I swear they're swelling right out of their casing, and eww? Why is she wearing Daisy Dukes and barefoot?

Mom clears her throat. "Izzy here is conducting an informal couple's survey tonight." She blinks at me with a note of disdain. "It's casual." She nods as if answering my question.

"It's Dr. Edinger." Isis is quick to correct before drilling her finger into Tad's belly button. "But it's Izzy for you!" She titters with an animated, slightly orgasmic spasm of delight.

Holy shit. She is freaking insane. And judging by the look on Mom's face, she's arrived at the same conclusion.

"I'm going to step out for a while." I jump out onto the porch. "Have fun."

"You have fun—for all of us," Mom whispers before shutting the door.

I will.

Right after I stop wallowing in all of this misery.

Logan and I drive for what seems like all eternity before we finally arrive at the Falls of Virtue. We pull into the parking lot and take in the glassy black lake with a sliver of moonlight dancing over the surface. A precipitous fog closes and opens over the expanse like a curtain.

I take up Logan's hand as we make our way down to the distal end of the reservoir, away from the chaotic rush of the falls.

I have my bathing suit on underneath should the need arise to dive into a freezing body of water. If Logan wanted me to, I'd dive off a cliff—naked. I'm so happy he's still around, still my Elysian, even if it does bring him pain.

"I can't believe it's been so even keeled, no rain in weeks," I say. "Just white milky clouds, mist in the morning and at night. I like Paragon's version of summer."

"Right after the Fourth of July, it takes a turn for the worse." He gives my hand a squeeze as though it were an analogy of what's about to happen to the two of us.

We stop just shy of the tiny marsh that connects to the lake and take a seat on a nearby boulder. I kick my heels against the rock, and the sound echoes for what feels like miles. A few people are shouting and laughing over by the falls, but not a sign of anyone I recognize.

"Ellis is having a party," Logan says, straddling my legs. He sweeps his hands around my waist, but there's a distant look in his eye with hurt layered underneath.

"And in other non-news." I pull him in by the T-shirt. "Ellis is always having a party." I whisper it sultry right over his lips.

"Ellis is a party." Logan blows the words over me as if he were going to finish his thought with a kiss, then retracts.

"No, it's OK." I pull him in soft by the neck. "I want to be close to you." I almost added, "again." The truth is, I crave Logan. I crave the pure blossoming love we had before Gage was injected into the picture.

"Skyla." He looks down as if he were mourning. Something is off. Maybe Logan Oliver has finally lost his desire for me.

"Logan." I pick him up by the chin. The reserve of moonlight captures his features, holds them hostage like the carving of a brilliant work of art. "I want everything we had back."

"It will come back. I promise you this," he assures. He takes in a breath that goes for miles before relaxing into me. "Just not now." He puts it out there in a mournful whisper. "Not for a while anyway." He comes in close, so close I can feel the heat radiating off his face.

"Kiss me." I breathe the words like a song. I'd pull him in and press all of the starvation I feel into him with wild abandon, but I need for him to want it too.

He shakes his head, barely noticeable.

"Yes." I'm startled by his reluctance.

"You're not over him."

"Are you going to make me beg?" I laugh and the sound of my voice ripples across the water. It ricochets off the hillside just south of the lake—sounds like a frightening cackle when it returns.

"Never beg me for anything, Skyla. I'd give the moon if you wanted it. I'd shred it in a blender and drink it for you if it would make you happy." His eyes glint a burnt sienna. Logan is sublime in every way, a prince, a lover, my earthly savior.

"I beg of you to kiss me, Logan Oliver, so now you'll have to comply." I lean forward and pucker.

"Comply, I will." His elongated dimple inverts where I sliced him. "But before I do—I want you to know, I really think you should hear Gage out. You love him, and he loves you. I know your feelings didn't just up and disappear. I'm still in this for your heart, Skyla, but not like this, not when I know you and Gage are long from over—that the faction war still rages." The theoretical end of the war is the cap of my relationship with Gage according to Logan, or at least his tolerance of it.

I open my mouth to refute what he's said, tell him that I hate Gage with everything in me and that I could never love him again, but I can't bring my tongue to carry out the treason.

"Kiss me, damn it." I pull a bleak smile.

His chest rumbles with laughter. "One day, I'm going to love you until you're delirious." He caresses me at the waist, and an explosion of lust goes off like a bomb through every cell of my body. "When it's just you and me, there will be fire in the air. Forget the moon. The ocean will pull to our magnetism. We'll control the tides with our love. Do you believe me?" He winces as if my answer has the power to hurt him on the most intimate level.

"Of course, I believe you. But why wait for someday when what we both want is staring us in the face?" I lean in farther, trying to seduce him with my words, with my cleavage.

Logan drops to his knees and looks up at me with a reverence reserved for deities.

"I'm going to kiss you now, Skyla." He plucks off my heel and holds it in the air. He gives a wicked grin before dropping it behind him and plucking off the other one. He picks up my right foot and kisses the tip of my toes, picks up my left and repeats the effort. He looks up with a long expression. "The Counts have it all backward. You're my everything. I'm *your* slave, your servant in every way." He scoops my feet into his hands and settles his lips over my ankles a very long time. Logan remains still—lost in his worship. The thought of interrupting him frightens me. He pushes back with a sigh. "I'm going to love you—every part of you. It's just not my time."

I hop off the rock, fall to the ground, and hold Logan as if the entire world were disbanding around us. I wish he weren't right. I hope he's not. I don't think it's fair that Gage steals anymore of my life than he already has.

The night settles its dew over us as we embrace each other near the still end of the lake.

I wish I were over Gage.

I wish today was the start of a tangible future with the first boy I ever loved.

"It comes," he whispers.

"I can guarantee you it will." I'm quick to assure.

I can also guarantee Gage will prove to be a tremendous obstacle despite the fact he swallowed my heart and vomited it out all over Chloe Bishop's feet.

24

Party with the Lights Off

Logan and I decide to head to Ellis's after all.

We walk hand in hand past the overgrown fountain with the lazy lions that lend themselves as the climax of Ellis's opulent circular drive.

Fog presses down over Paragon, cool and welcoming. Three days in a row of seventy-degree weather and it feels downright balmy.

Dream. A voice echoes from the forest in triplicate, and I jump into Logan's chest as if he were my own protective hedge.

"That's you-know-who," I hiss. There is no way in hell I'm going to call Ezrina to myself by forming the letters of her name on my lips.

"Ezrina!" Logan shouts as if he's about to flag her down and invite her into Ellis's hotbed of carnal infections. I swear at any given time, there are at least thirteen different STD's mutating into new exotic strains that are undoubtedly resistant to the most potent elixirs modern medicine has to offer. Not even the scientific community can keep up with the contagions brewing in those bedroom laboratories.

"What the hell are you calling her for?" I yank him by the elbow when all I really want to do is rattle his skull.

"I've got some business to take care of." He washes over me with those citrine lenses. There's a painful smile on his lips as if he's about to make a supreme sacrifice. "If I'm not back, maybe Gage can give you a ride home," he says it sweetly, forlorn, as he takes up my hand.

"No thanks. I'll catch a ride with Bree, Drake or Ethan." I'd walk before I graced that lunatic's truck with my presence.

Heck, I'd hitch a ride on a train bound for the tunnels and give an artery or two at the office, or leave all four limbs with Ezrina before I get within spitting distance of that abnormally gorgeous abomination.

My stomach cycles with a bite of heat, at the thought of seeing Gage tonight.

Logan holds our conjoined hands up, amused at my psychotic ramblings, and I shake my head as an apology.

I lean up on my toes and peck a slow lingering kiss over his lips. I plan on overriding his decision to abstain from me until I iron out this bullshit with Gage. I need Logan to love me in the most intimate way possible. Logan is the balm my body desires to escape all of the madness that follows us like a plague.

Logan earned a kiss. He is due one each second of the day for his willingness to sacrifice everything for my wellbeing, right down to our love.

"I'd better go." He rasps the words out in a heated rush.

"Be careful," I whisper. "Flying objects are most certainly sharper than they appear." I nod toward the woods in which Ezrina lumbers about.

"There's a chance I might pop into your dreams tonight. You mind?" He tilts his head. His entire body aches as if there were another question he longed to ask.

"I totally don't mind." I offer a brief hug. "Guess it's official. You're the man of my dreams."

He gives a gentle moan. "Get in there and talk to Gage. He's turned into a walking corpse these last few weeks." He presses out a frown as if he didn't approve but found it necessary to arbitrate peace talks nevertheless.

I look back at Ellis's house with the music booming out of it, the windows vibrating in tune, and I try to envision Gage as a disheveled zombie. Imagining Gage as anything other than how I knew him, how I thought of him before prom is a sheer impossibility. He embodied perfection. He sold me the rights to our forever brand of love like some conman flashing the wares from inside his trench coat, and I bought everything he was willing to give me without suspecting for a minute he was running a counterfeit ring. And now, the only memory I have is a shell of who we were, smothered in the stench of Chloe's once upon a death.

"See you in your dreams, Skyla Laurel Messenger." Logan kisses my hair, my cheek, and the tip of my nose before taking off into the forest where I once killed Gage's apparent main squeeze.

"See you in my dreams," I shout after him, but he's already been swallowed alive by the somber thicket.

Why in the hell is Logan running *toward* Ezrina?

I see Ellis's smiling face as soon as I cross the threshold into the house.

"So where's your dad?" I ask. Not that I expect him to be passed out on the couch with a bright red Solo cup tucked between his legs. Although that might inspire me to do my best impersonation of Ezrina—she is in the vicinity, and hatchets are prone to happen.

"Out of town."

Code for trekking in the tunnels I suppose.

"So when's this life-coaching thing going to start?" Ellis slides his shoulder up against mine as he looks out at a sea of girls rocking to the music.

I survey the crowd and spot Chloe stationed next to Gage and quickly twist my neck in the other direction.

Shit. I knew this was a crappy idea. If Ezrina doesn't hurt Logan, I might have to for pushing me into the lion's den.

"I've reconsidered the whole coaching thing." I try not to sound so desperately grieved over what I just witnessed. "You're slaying them pretty well on your own."

"No, I think you're right." Ellis folds his arms and examines the estrogen-based offerings. "I need to go bigger, bolder—better."

"Are we talking IQ points or bra sizes?"

"You're a funny girl." He cuts a sideways glance at Michelle who, for impractical purposes, is counting matches near the fireplace. "You think she's stoned?" Ellis looks perplexed by her bizarre behavior, as she plucks a long-stem match from the mess in front of her and tries to apply it as lipstick.

"See that necklace she's wearing?" The wicked rose pendant lets off a necrotic flicker as if winking in our direction—knowing Marshall, it probably is. "It's boot camp for Fems. They invade her mind and turn it into a big gelatinous puddle of crap."

"That's effing sick." Ellis recoils at my masterful descriptive.

"I know this because I swallowed it once, and it really effed with my mind." I borrow his doctored expletive to prove my point. "You were in my hallucination. You were an ox with a body of a man. You were kind of hot if I do say so myself."

"Cool." Ellis expands his chest to annunciate said hotness.

"So, what's the word around town? You find anything out from your dad that might save my neck?" Literally.

"The Counts are really pissed." He pauses to knuckle bump some guys from East.

"Pissed? They do know they're winning the war, right? Not to mention they have me as a private contributor to their unethical blood drives, and the fact Logan is not only a soldier in their hypocritical army, but they've amassed my mother as

157

their newest doe-eyed convert. What else do these people want? World domination? OK, well, that."

"Nope." Ellis twists his lips carefully examining a group of girls clad in wet T-shirts as if we were standing in front of a buffet. "Not one of those things was on their shit list. In fact, if I remember correctly, they were only ticked about one thing."

"What's that?"

"You."

25

He Said, She Said

"What do you mean *me*?" I gawk at Ellis as the flames crackle and pop from the fireplace. An entire rainbow of sunset colors bloom across the vicinity. They dance in his eyes as if he were lit up from the inside like a ball of molten rage.

"You've got a treble." He shrugs. "A lot of it was over my head. I've never been to a meeting before, but my dad thought it'd be good for me. You know, father-son bonding."

"You went to a Count round table? And are you even allowed since you're fighting with Celestra?"

"Yeah, about that. My dad told me to knock that shit off."

"*What*? I need you. I can't lose you." I've already lost Logan to the Counts, sort of, and Gage to Chloe. "I can't fight this war on my own."

"You're not on your own. There are approximately five hundred people with you at any given time, but, of course, we've got more." I'm sure by "we" he's referring to his newfound alliance with wickedness.

"Ellis," I say, swatting him not so playfully in the stomach, "what about Celestra?"

"You'll be fine. I'm totally neutral. I don't really care who wins."

"You have to care! The Counts are kidnappers—they're *murderers*. They're going to drain me of my blood and kill me." Ellis's blasé attitude has me in a full-blown tizzy.

"OK, I care. I want Celestra to win and for you to take over—for the Counts to go to hell, but I'll be the last person to admit that to my dad. He's sort of a hard ass."

"So I gathered." I try to take it all in, but the noise booming from the speakers disrupts the process. "Thanks for letting me know about the treble."

"They want you contained." Ellis looks morbidly serious. "They're looking into whether or not they can fight the war with you bound in the tunnels."

"Crap." This cannot possibly get any worse.

"I gotta go. There's my ride." Ellis latches his arm around a girl with long raven hair, eyes cut like diamonds, and legs that give the illusion they go all the way to her shoulders. Something about her reminds me of Emerson. I shudder at the thought of another rogue Kragger eating up my brain waves. "Wait," I shout after him. "You don't need a ride. You live here!"

He gives a thumbs up, affirming my deductive reasoning skills are still intact as he leads her down the hall.

Oh, I get it. He so needs a twelve-step program to detox from tramps.

And is that really all guys ever think about? Constantly reducing women to body parts and referencing us as vehicles, units, and packages? It's so insanely inhuman. It makes me want to shake every male in here.

"So, where's Logan?" a female voice pipes up from behind.

I spin to find Brielle in full-swing party mode. Her body is awkwardly stuffed into a pair of ill-fitted jeans, and she's wearing a skin-tight T-shirt with the remnants of her stomach spilling out the front.

"Wow, you look great!" Sort of.

"I'm a cow. These are my maternity clothes. I can't get rid of my gut." She slaps her midsection, which oddly looks like the bread dough my mother was beating into submission the other afternoon. "So are you planning his party?"

"Whose party?"

"Logan's—he's turning eighteen in a couple weeks. I just thought since you guys went to prom, and Gage said..." She shrugs it off without finishing. I yank her over to the corner away from the jet engine trying to rumble its way out of the speakers.

"What did Gage say?"

Brielle gapes at me. "He said you were really upset with him."

"Did he say *why* I was really upset with him?" I bet Brielle is bound by some Count blood oath to keep at least ten different secrets from a Celestra at any given time. Gage is probably a Count by proxy, much like Chloe herself.

She leans into the crowd and scans the bobbing heads for signs of a tall, dark, and handsome linebacker before relaxing into me once her effort proves futile.

"He may have mentioned the fact you think he's somehow involved with Chloe." Her eyes expand with worry. "Really, Skyla? Gage and Chloe?" Brielle seems to be genuinely perplexed with the strange pairing.

"Guess opposites attract. I mean, didn't they sort of have a thing for each other way before I came to Paragon?"

She straightens a moment, scanning the ceiling for clues that might help propagate this theory.

"You know," she starts, "it's always been pretty apparent Chloe had the hots for him. She never hid it. I do distinctly remember her telling me she was going to drive him insane by dating Logan. That sort of backfired." She shakes her head in disgust. "Then I remember she said she was going to give him some pet of hers and that, for sure, it would seal the deal." She squints in an effort to shake more details out of the past.

Obviously, the pet was Nevermore. God, I hope Chloe isn't the reason Nev didn't show up when I called for him this morning.

161

"Anyway..." She shakes her head. "He was never into her. He could have had her. They could have easily been one of West Paragon's power couples by now, had they been together, but well, face it, you were the only one Gage wanted to fill that position with." She waves at someone from behind my shoulder. "Speaking of the devil, or should I say angel." She giggles.

I turn and catch a quick glimpse of the said celestial, football playing, heart-breaking being.

"I think you had it right the first time, although I'd hate to insult the devil like that."

She makes a face. "You're a riot. I'll take off so you guys can talk." She spins to go then pivots back into me. "Hey, before I forget, I'll be dropping off the baby sometime this week when I get a chance. I've got like three shifts between now and Saturday. It's so crazy."

"Oh, good! My mom is going to love that. She's dying to visit with him, and so am I."

"Perfect. I'll bring his coffin and have Drake drag all the rest of his crap over sometime this weekend. You guys will totally have a blast with him. He's a little cutie." She bops off to the rhythm of the music.

All his crap? His coffin? Sounds like a rather permanent arrangement is about to take place, but I won't dare say anything to Mom lest Brielle flake out again and leave us up a creek without a casket, or a baby for that matter.

Gage swoops in. His cologne reduces me to cinders without even trying. Every fiber of my being cries foul. This is mutiny on a cellular level. I forbid my body to act so viscerally toward someone whom I willfully despise on a *cerebral* level.

Back off hormones, I reprimand. *I will go Celestra all over your estrogen ass if you even think of surging with excitement.*

I've just threatened to kick my own ass, and yet somehow this doesn't alarm me. With the scope of insanity that's gripped my life as of late, providing myself with a substantial beating seems both mandatory and necessary at this point.

Gage blocks my path with a hint of a smile, those apologetic eyes drip with liquid cobalt.

He opens his mouth and hesitates. "Please," he says, just below the acoustics blaring in the room, "can we talk?"

I want to say yes. I want to press my lips against him because we've moved past that horrible DVD that shed a spotlight on my every indiscretion, and the fact that Chloe is no longer keeping us apart by way of blackmail—but then I remember what really happened, and it makes me want to run fast in Ezrina's direction much like Logan. Hey? Maybe Logan is committing some sort of assisted suicide by landing in her not-so-good graces. That makes total sense and not in a good way.

"Skyla?" He bows into me as if he were going to kiss me. "Let's go across the street so we can hear each other." I'm sure his bedroom is involved.

"Some other time." I swallow hard, glancing at the wall behind him just to get my bearings. I want to add, like never, but I think we both know that's not true. I'm caving. I can feel it. A part of me very much wants to hear what he has to say. "I have a date in an hour, so I'd better get going." More like trying to talk someone off a razor's edge—namely Logan.

His dimples depress on and off and I speed out the front door before I fall victim to their spell. The second the fresh night air hits me, I realize I have no way of getting home.

"You need a ride?" He's quick to pick up on my vehicular dilemma once I hit the bottom of the driveway.

Chloe and the bitch squad are on the sidewalk, busy with mock cheers, lighting up the night with their wicked cackles.

"Hey, Em?" I step over to their private huddle. "Do you think I could catch a ride?" I doubt this is going to pan out for me, but considering my other options lie in Michelle I'm-freaking-hallucinating-Miller, or Nat you-shipped-my-douchebag-of-a-boyfriend-off-to-juvy, I'd say my odds, although slim, are best with Emily.

"No," she says it flat and without the pretense of covering it up with some lie of how she's doesn't have enough gas or she's not allowed to drive blondes around per a stipulation on her insurance policy. I've always appreciated Emily's honesty.

"I'll do it." Chloe rattles out the offer like a snake in the grass—a venom-filled pit viper to be exact. She gives a quick glance behind me at Gage before trying to con me into joining her on a death plunge off Devil's Peak.

Just as I'm about to say "no thanks," my lips make a U-turn.

"Sure," I say, surprising even myself. What's the worst that can happen? She actually succeeds at offing me? Now wouldn't that be a shame—no faction war to lose, no heartbreak, humiliation from said heartbreak, and probably one very happy family reunion with my dearly departed father. In all honesty, death isn't looking like such a bad prospect—that is, until the Celestra tunnels whistle through my mind like a scorching nuclear wind. Souls—people—*my* people are locked in that wicked den of horrors. And what about little Lacey? She's practically counting on me. I need get them out or die trying. Face it, they're not fortunate enough to have an almighty Fem infatuated with their mothers and thus promoting them to treble status. They're locked in, twenty-four seven, damned to a life of plasma-based servitude.

"Hello?" Chloe wands her hand over my face. "I'd like to think you're zoning out and not ignoring me. I'm taking off now, if you want to come."

"Skyla, no," Gage pleads. "Let me drive you. I swear I won't say a single word. Let me do this."

A moment thumps by. For a second, it's just Gage and me. His sad expression etches itself over my soul, and for some mysterious reason I'm drawn to comfort him—*him* of all people.

"No thanks." I try to mimic Emily's nonchalant attitude while holding back tears.

His stare never wavers. Gage presses into me with those clear sapphire lenses and puts on the best show in town with his undying remorse.

"Let's get out here, Chloe," I say, following her across the street.

At least with Chloe I expect the lies.

In every way I fully expected Chloe Bishop to grind my world to pieces. I just never envisioned she'd use Gage as the weapon.

Damn it all to hell—Chloe won.

26

Shut Up and Drive

Chloe glides her hand over the wheel with an erotic display of affection.

The night lights up in an electrical blaze as a storm begins to rage overhead. I haven't seen this kind of climactic action in weeks. I'm not sure if this is a natural phenomenon, or perhaps Chloe and Gage have harnessed the power to dictate the weather much like Marshall and Demetri. After all, who knows what cash and prizes they were awarded once they shipped Logan and me off to the fluid factory? This snazzy new sedan Chloe seems to have scored recently might have been just the incentive she was looking for to lure me over to the stone of sacrifice. I'd like to think I was worth more than a mid-sized luxury vehicle that doesn't even have the modern day boast of hybrid slapped on its rear fender. I'd like to think I was worth more than the sum total of scrap metal on Earth to Gage, but then I would have never pegged him for a set up to begin with. I would have bet my life on the fact I could trust Gage Oliver, and in a way, I did.

"Come on, Skyla. Entertain me." Chloe stares out the windshield in a daze as the rain surges its aggressive assault over Paragon. "Why don't you dish about how you can't believe Gage put a spear through your gut."

I glance out the passenger window as we pass the familiar streets en route to the Landon asylum for lunatics and killers alike—myself included since I'm riding in a car with Chloe, who I might very much like to kill again.

Driving in a car with Chloe.

Honestly? I've abandoned any morsel of good sense I might have had. But in my defense, I was forced to choose between the lesser of two evils. Besides, I need to get home ASAP to begin my dream date with Logan.

"By the way," I start, "I'm totally unaffected. You and Gage can live happily ever after for all I care." The lie jags from my lips, thick and unnatural like talking though a mouthful of peanut butter. "And, technically speaking, it was you who speared me." Literally.

"You're always so black and white," she snarks.

"I'm being sarcastic, Chloe. Maybe you're the one who can't see past the analogy in the room."

"I can look past a lot of things thanks to this Noster eyeball your Sector friend was kind enough to gift me. Why do you think he gave me such a spectacular specimen?"

"Because he was trying to please me." Marshall would do anything in the world I asked as long as he were able. "Again, you can't see past the deeper meaning of things."

"And, again, Skyla—you can't see past yourself." She pulls in high on the driveway, right behind Tad's free ride from Althorpe, the establishment at which he is a modern day indentured servant. "But then," she says, shaking her head, "for some bizarre reason, Dudley, too seems beyond smitten with you." She sticks her finger down her throat. "Fill me in on the powers of your persuasion. Do tell. I mean, we're practically sisters now that we're living together. And, one day, I might even become your sister-in-law just to piss you off."

"What about Gage?" I'm stunned to hear she'd choose a Landon over an Oliver, especially the shady Oliver in question.

Chloe presses into her seat for a moment. Her face flashes with surprise as though she had just caught herself off guard.

Strange.

Chloe Bishop is a fully devout follower in the church of all things Gage. How she could possibly forget the first commandment—to worship ad nauseam and commit herself to full-throttle obsessive behavior is beyond me.

"What's the matter, Chloe?" I revel in the taunt. "Gage still locking you out physically? You running a little short on cash to buy his affections? That is how you got Brielle to befriend me, right? A thousand cool, crisp bills?"

Her dark hair coils around her face, her sharp features gleam with pride under the glimmer of the porch light.

"You know..." I tilt my head into the vibrating glass of the window as I feel the rain drum its rhythm through my temples like a cheap replica of Marshall's special brand of oscillating love. "I thought all I felt for you was hatred, but to be honest, you're not worth the energy."

"The feeling's mutual." She's quick to add.

"In fact, I feel nothing but pity. You spend all of your energy destroying others so you can steal the good things from their lives and claim them as your own. You played so well into Demetri's plan of killing my father, Ethan, bringing me to Paragon. Why have a well-placed boyfriend at all? Why the big ruse of the diary? Why pretend he hated you? Why put him on your shit list in the back of your diary and not Logan? Why have Gage by my side twenty-four seven whispering his profession of love to me, outfitting me with tokens of his affection? Touching me like he meant it. What were you so afraid of? Was it Logan and me you were trying to keep apart all along? The Counts did that without your foolish aid. I really don't get you, Chloe. I don't get your stupid games or why the hell you've invited yourself to live at my house and date my stepbrother. Why are you so richly invested in taking me down? Obviously, I missed something because nothing about you makes any sense."

"You killed me."

"Only after a long list of grievances you imparted on me and my family. Killing my father tops off the list." I fire back. "I'm onto you, Chloe. I know for a fact there is a bigger picture brewing. I will find out whatever the hell has you so riled up against me. And even though I haven't a clue what you have planned next on your make-Skyla-miserable to-do list, I can tell you with confidence that you will not prosper. You will never take me down. I will not lie under your feet, not now, not ever. I will win. I'll have love and happiness and the very last word on any lame-ass decision the Faction Council tries to make after the war. You and the rest of the Counts will be beneath Celestra. I will stamp out your wickedness once and for all."

"Are you done?" She flips her hair bored with the conversation.

"Not by a long shot. When I'm done, you will wish you never knew me—that you ran in the opposite direction once you heard the whisper of my name." I pause and take her in. "All you're good for is manufacturing drama and manipulating people. I guess that's the sort of thing Gage is into. I wish you a very unhappy life together."

I open the door, and Chloe snatches me back by the wrist.

"I *will* have a very happy life, Skyla. For the record, I have never once paid Gage for his time or affections." Her chest heaves into her words. "I paid him for yours."

I kick the door wide open and run like hell inside the house.

27

Dreamer

I speed up to my room and shut the door. I wish I could say that Chloe's words had no effect on me—that the idea of her paying Gage to be my anything was so entirely absurd that I could laugh it off, brush it off my shoulder, insignificant as dandruff, but I can't. Gage told me Chloe never paid him. It was one of the first things I asked him—accused him of, that day in the morgue. So who do I believe?

I kick off my shoes and get ready for bed. Brush my teeth like I'm trying to scour both Chloe and Gage off my person right along with my enamel. I turn the lights out and crawl under the covers, listening as Mia and Melissa argue on the other side of the wall. Their voices rumble in competition with the thunder outside. It feels as though Paragon, and the people on it, have become a nothing but a fortress of hatred.

Gage and his impenetrable love for me, all of it evaporated like smoke. Chloe held the mirror to this illusion. She worked me like a puppet, told me what emotions to feel, how far to let them seep into my soul, and I complied like an obedient child. Turns out I'm not just Demetri's, Marshall's, or even my biological mother's pawn. I was very much subject to the queen bitch herself. None of it makes sense—especially anything to do with Gage.

I close my eyes and try to pretend that the last few weeks were all a bad dream, some nightmare that engulfed me so completely it felt nothing short of real. I've had those kinds of dreams before, the kind that tap you emotionally, and then you wake up relieved that it was simply a nocturnal hallucination, the byproduct of a bad midnight snack.

What I wouldn't give to wake up from this nightmare, to have Gage back with all of his genuine affection, his undying forever love. But I can't.

I squeeze my eyes shut and marinate in the Gage I believed in. He heals this incredible ache and tells me it will all be OK. I reflect on that strange dream I had when I fell into the tunnels, Gage wrapped around me with his warm limbs. His legs hooked around mine, his hot hands riding over my hips. The sweet, tender way he told me I was his wife and kissed me on the neck like he had done it a thousand times before. He was loving me in the most intimate way possible, and I hate that it was just a dream.

I let it burn through me like a memory, like a premonition, a vision. But it was none of those things. It was nothing more than a hopeless wish that will never come true.

I don't know how I'll ever get over Gage Oliver.

But I'm damn well going to try.

A field emerges in this dreamscape. A lavender sky dips to navy with a smattering of crystalline stars. Soft rolling hills stretch out infinitely, covered with a field of weeping willows as far as the eye can see.

"Very romantic," I say, walking over to Logan, who's resting nearby.

"I try." He sits up and pats the grass beside him. "What's going on? You look upset."

"I had a horrible encounter with Chloe," I say, scooting in next to him.

Logan slips his arm around my waist and draws me in. "Every encounter with Chloe is awful."

"You got that right."

"You have a chance to talk with Gage?" He tempers his words with an apprehensive look. I'm not sure what Logan's motivation is. Maybe he wants me to solidify the fact Gage is an asshole before we dive back into a relationship together. I can't believe I ever let Gage pull us apart.

"Nope. Well, he tried, but I shut him down." I tell him all about my psychotic conversation with Chloe in the car. The idea of her paying him is enough fodder to sponsor my insanity for a lifetime. No matter how much I don't want to admit it, Chloe Bishop really has won.

"She hasn't won anything, Skyla." Logan squeezes my hand. "And paying Gage? She's lying. Look, I'm not going to defend his actions, but I really encourage you to hear him out."

"Have you?"

"Yes." He looks wild-eyed at the prospect that he wouldn't. "He's dying, Skyla. This has literally taken his existence and stomped all over it. He loves you. It's real. You have to know that."

"Whose side are you on anyway? And by the way—what about *us*?" I lie down and land my head in his lap so I could gaze up at his divinely anointed features. "You are a thing of beauty, you know that?" I whisper, captivated by Logan. "It was you in the vision I had—the one of the groom waiting for me at the end of the aisle. Never Gage." My stomach tightens at the thought.

Logan sags in defeat. He offers a depleted smile while combing his fingers through my hair. "I won't deny the fact we're going to happen."

"You're not still clinging to that 'after the faction war' maxim, right? I mean, the playing field has been cleared— Gage is no longer a contender. It was you for me from the beginning. So, obviously, it's you for me in the end. I want it to be. I never stopped having feelings for you." A writhing ache churns in my belly. I wish it was like a faucet, and I could shut off all thoughts of Gage, destroy the valve from ever pouring out a drop of affection for him ever again.

"I know," he whispers, tangling his fingers in my hair.

Everything I say in here is fair game for Logan's mind.

"I'm sorry. I wish I never knew him."

Logan clenches his jaw. "But you do and so do I." His gaze darts off across the way. "Our future happens, Skyla, just not right away."

"Wow." I give a hard blink. "You're still into that whole get-Gage-out-of-your-system thing. Well, I swear, he's out. Him and his venomous fake love." Our relationship was fraudulent on every level. I should sue him.

Logan shakes his head just barely. "It's not fake," he whispers, "never that."

A violent fit of giggles erupts from across the hillside.

"What the hell was that?" I spike up and try to discern their origin. God, what if Fems have figured out a way to penetrate Logan's dreams—worse yet, Chloe.

"That's sort of the surprise I had for you." He gives a gentle massage to my shoulders and nods out toward a curtain of trees across the expanse.

A young woman emerges. She darts around the trunk of a willow wearing a white, flowing dress. A man appears. He chases and snatches at her until he reels her in victoriously. They engage in a long heated kiss, nothing but grunts and moans expel from them as if they haven't shared a lip-lock in centuries.

"This isn't about to morph into some porn fantasy, is it?" I shoot Logan a look. I'm not entirely sure how much of his dreamscape Logan can really control.

"Maybe—maybe not." His brows furrow as he continues to gaze out at the viral display of mouth to mouth. Their hands begin to rove over one another with a heated rush as they drop to their knees.

The man pulls her back by the shoulders and murmurs something. She shakes her head and tries unsuccessfully to drag him off to the forest, but he rises and pulls her in our direction instead.

"Is this going to be trouble? Because I so wouldn't mind waking up if it is. I'm totally not into action flicks." I get enough of that in real life.

"I doubt this is trouble. He probably just wants to say hello." Logan helps me to my feet. "Besides," he leans in and whispers, "you already know him."

"I do?" I squint into him as he approaches. He doesn't even look vaguely familiar. He's tall with dark wavy hair— pretty, light blue eyes like my own. He sort of leans in when he walks as though he were perennially ready to descend a staircase, and he's grinning at the two of us. I should be creeped out, but something about him resonates a calm feeling in me.

"Dear young, Skyla, you've done another foolish thing." He pants through a smile. "I gather you have no clue who I am." He gives a slight bow. "Forgive me, I'm without my plumage at the moment." He picks up my hand and places a gentle kiss over the back.

"*Nev?*" My mouth falls open.

"The one and only." His brows bounce with delight.

"Who's that woman?" No sooner do I get the words out than the beautiful brunette races to his side. "Oh God," I mouth the words.

"Skyla," Logan intercedes, "meet Nevermore and Ezrina."

28

True Love Never Dies

I swallow hard. There are so many problems with this scenario I don't even know where to begin.

Ezrina stands next to Nev—*Heathcliff*—both of them look amazing, dare I even say Ezrina is drop-dead gorgeous.

"Am I hallucinating?" I turn to Logan. Maybe I accidentally wandered into the wrong dream and this is some Fem-inspired nightmare that's about to take a serious fucking turn for the worse. I have a sneaking suspicion that "elegant Ezrina" here is about to morph back into the hatchet princess that I know and love.

"No, I swear, this is real." Logan presses out a dull smile. He knows he's in serious hot water on some level, and mostly it has to do with me.

"Logan offered to extend his dream world to the two of us," Nev says, filling me in, "so we could spend some much needed alone time together." He takes up both Ezrina's hands, careful as if they were each their own dove, and looks lovingly into her eyes.

"Why are you letting them into your dreams?" I gasp. I happen to know for a fact that my mother, the chief celestial justice, appointed them an eternal punishment in opposite realms and dimensions for their heinous crime of defending Celestra. Stupid as it sounds, I'm pretty damn sure breaking said punishment is not going to prove to be a brilliant idea.

"It's a bargaining tool," Nev answers for him. "In exchange for Logan's unconventional request, we spend time here in our own personal Eden." He gazes dreamily at Ezrina once again. I can't get over how gorgeous she is. It's alarming on some level to think that's really her. "Although I don't quite agree with any of this," Nev continues, "nevertheless, I'm party to it now, and I can't say I regret a thing." He smiles down at Ezrina with undying affection. "Skyla, would you be so kind to join us in a binding union before we continue our foray of affection?"

"Would I what?" This is really starting to mess with my head. This is some serious rabbit hole action, and it has me taking a mental inventory of everything I may have accidentally ingested in the past twenty-four hours. I knew nothing good would come from hitching a ride home with Chloe. She probably had the seat laced with hallucinogenics.

"Declare us husband and wife, before Logan and God." Nev stretches his neck with a quick jerk just the way he does while locked in the body of a raven. "Perhaps say some kind words first."

"Oh, um, Nev? Do you take Ezrina to love and to hold, and to spend the rest of your lives together—no wait—do you love each other enough to spend all of eternity bound together by a holy covenant under God?" Marshall would be so proud. Or not.

They look at one another forlorn as though my words could never be.

"Unfortunately"—Nev sighs without ever wavering from her eyes—"the curse we've acquired forbids such a prosperous future." He depresses a kiss on her forehead.

"We have now." Ezrina sounds normal in every way, not a word echoes in triplicate or spews out like gravel. "Come." She tries to steal him away.

"Skyla?" Nev bids me to continue.

"Do you, Heathcliff..." I pause in the event he explodes. Nev has a tendency to go batshit when I invoke his real name, but in this instant, he doesn't, he just continues to smile like a lunatic who's about to get laid. "Take Ezrina"—she offers a warm smile—"to be your..." This wouldn't really be lawful or eternal, nor would any of that death do you part crap apply. "Wife?" Keep it simple.

"I do." He swims with joy. "I most certainly do."

"And Ezrina," I pause. She takes me in with those serious brown eyes. The slight curve of a smile plays on her lips. "Do you swear never to sever a limb from my body again as well as love Heathcliff as your very own husband?" I thought it wise to toss in that first part in the event once we all wake up from this psychotic stupor she's moved to rearrange body parts.

She turns to Nev. "I will love you with my every mortal instrument both physical and spiritual that the Master has provided."

They don't wait for me to officiate any further or instruct them to conjoin at the lips. They simply fall into a natural, lingering kiss that exudes a romantic magic all its own.

They begin to wander off hand in hand, and Ezrina turns around.

"Skyla?" She pegs me with a stern expression. "If you don't win this war, your body parts will very much be subject to the heft of my blade."

Nev's ears peak in slight horror before he ushers her swiftly under the cover of night.

There's the Ezrina I know—all threats and knives, filled with her special brand of I'll-cut-you aggression.

She breaks into a fit of giggles and fills Logan's strange universe with the bubbling brook from her mouth. Nev rumbles something to her, as they disappear behind the curtain of a willow and its long, green tendrils. His shadowed figure lays her gently on the grass.

"You don't think they're going to—?"

"Consummate their union?" Logan interjects, pulling me down to the earth and wrapping his loving arms around me.

I slip my hands up his shirt and his rock hard abs quiver for me. Maybe Logan and I should consummate *our* union.

Why wait another moment to experience what we've waited so long for? I want nothing more than his fevered body pressed against mine. My hand drops to his jeans and my fingers bypass the formality of the button, the zipper, and dip to the heated skin on the inside of his boxers. Logan snatches my wrist and lifts my hand up to his mouth and kisses it.

"We can't do this here, not with Nev and Ezrina as a potential audience." He raises his brows. "Not with unfinished business—"

I cut him off before he can bring up Gage. "Have it your way, but it will happen." I slide into Logan's lap and brush a quiet kiss against his cheek. "That was really nice of you to allow them to borrow your world. I'm sure Ezrina would have done anything for the opportunity." Nev is far more careful than his sword-wielding counterpart.

"She is about to do something," Logan whispers.

I snap at attention. "What?" Nev did say Logan had an unconventional request.

"The next time the Counts pull you into that treble, you'll find out."

"Logan." I press a hand into his chest. "I'm done with secrets. Tell me now."

He flexes a smile. "Only if you promise no hitting or yelling."

"Logan!" I'm petrified at what he might reveal. "I promise, no hitting or yelling." I brush the pads of my fingers along his jaw line. I can easily spend an eternity like this with Logan in his perfect dreams. Well, they're usually perfect. Tonight they're a bit scattered and X-rated in nature.

"Are all your dreams this explicit?" I reel him in by the lip of his jeans.

"Mostly." He breathes into my neck and dots a trail of kisses up to my ear.

"I bet you look forward to this every single night."

"What I look forward to"—he pauses to graze over my earlobe with his teeth—"is turning this into reality—with you—every single night."

"Just at night?" I give a flirtatious smile.

A dark laughs rumbles through him. "It sounds like we're going to have an impressive happily ever after."

"It will be most impressive," I say, running my finger up his chest and dipping it into his mouth for a moment. "OK, now spill your secret."

"I might have bartered a little with Ezrina."

"Oh my gosh, you're just like me. You have to learn everything the hard way." I'm terrified and breathless at what he might say next.

"Skyla, I can't bear the thought of the Counts torturing you. I don't want to see you afraid or in pain, ever." His eyes glitter with moisture. "In exchange for letting them into my dreams, Ezrina agreed to accept your torment."

"How? Because she's Celestra?" I'm puzzled.

"Not really. She agreed to enter your body when the treble hits, and you'll be returned safe and sound once it's over. Unfortunately, she's not allowed to undergo anything outside the treble. That's not her domain. You'll still have to endure the cyanide, but I swear, I'll be right there with you."

"So once the treble hits, I'll be magically transported into Ezrina's body?" I hate Ezrina's body, the version that lives in the Transfer anyway. "And what if she's tricking you, and I get stuck there?" I foresee this as more than a possibility—plus its win-win for Ezrina—play with Nev under a lavender moon, then get the added bonus of being seventeen all over again.

"Not going to happen. You won't get stuck." Logan assures. "I had her take an oath. She can't break it. It's all going to work as planned." He presses a warm kiss over the top of my head. "And I wouldn't worry about Ezrina's body, you won't be in it."

"Where will I be?"

He taps his hand over his heart. "You'll be in here with me."

29

The Note

I startle awake and find myself back on my bed in Paragon far from Ezrina and a sexed-up Nev. That must have been a *real* dream. Something must have gone awry. There was no way Logan would go along with such an insane idea, let alone formulate it.

A cool breeze stirs through the vicinity, carrying the distinct scent of Gage's cologne.

I turn on the light, and squint into the room with suspicion only to find an envelope on my nightstand with my name written in his undeniable handwriting.

A dull laugh huffs through me.

I bet he popped in to see if I was telling the truth about my "date." I'll have to ask Marshall to secure my bedroom with a thousand binding spirits to keep Gage Oliver from running in and out like he owns the place—and me.

A dull ache penetrates my chest as I pick up the envelope.

Gage. The old version still has me so completely, and I wish it wasn't so.

I press the cool paper to my cheek in one final act of humiliation, brush my lips over the seam he licked and pretend it's him. I would kiss the floor he walked on if only he would morph back into the person I thought he was.

It takes a full half hour before I have the courage to run my finger along the inside ridge of the envelope and extricate its contents. A piece of paper floats out easy as a butterfly.

Dear Skyla,
Sometimes there are no words.

I'm dying. I beg of you to give me a moment. Hear me for a minute, and then if you choose to never speak to me again, I will understand.

You are the sun and without you there is only unimaginable darkness.

I miss you so much. I miss every last detail about you. I miss the way your perfume lingered in my room hours after you went home. I miss touching you. I miss your kisses. I miss being near you, the touch of your hair against my face.

I thought we would always be together. I knew in my heart that we would be. I can be wrong about everything, but I would have sworn on my life that I would never be wrong about that.

No matter what you decide, just know that I love you. I will love you for as long as I'm spinning on this planet and then I'll love you after that, too.

Love forever,

Gage

Gage Oliver loves me?

I close my eyes and pretend it's true.

🦋 🦋 🦋

The next morning, I text Logan to make sure Gage and I are working different shifts at the bowling alley, but he doesn't text me back. I can't say that letter didn't affect me, but there's a part of me that can't believe a word Gage Oliver says. It's the kernel of doubt that Chloe planted as small as a mustard seed, and now it's blossomed into a spreading tree large enough to house every bird on the planet.

I head downstairs for breakfast, trying to push that letter out of my mind. As much as I'd like for it to be real, as much as I need it to be, I'm sure Chloe and Gage have regrouped for part two of Operation Take Down Skyla.

"Morning, sunshine." Chloe raises her mug. She sits across from Brielle at the table as Mom and Tad huddle in the corner having an all too serious powwow for this early in the day.

"So," Brielle says, holding up a butter knife. She squints into its reflection viewing her upper lip, "how long do you think I should let my girl-stache go before taking action?"

"I wouldn't know," Chloe says, "you should ask someone with experience in facial hair, like Skyla. She's practically a werewolf."

I shoot a look to Mom and Tad who so obviously missed the cutting remark.

"Oh, I don't know, Chloe." I take a seat next to Brielle. "You seem to know a lot about removing unwanted debris—*people*—from the planet."

"The same could be said about you." She beams, delighted with the fact I've personally removed a few souls myself.

"Are you working today?" I choose to ignore Chloe and pose the question directly to Brielle.

"I'm off. I thought I'd go to the mall and buy something to wear Saturday."

Saturday is the day that sausage lovers everywhere will descend on Rockaway Point to indulge in a gluttonous frenzy of pig flesh—otherwise known as the Fourth of July. Ironic how Tad has no qualms about eating pork-filled intestines and yet bacon is permanently off the menu. His hypocrisy knows no bounds.

"Aren't you due to spend some time at the Edinger estate?" Chloe purrs. "I'll be there all day, if you want to join me. I'm excavating the basement. It's full of interesting goodies—portholes." She scatters the crumbs to see if I'll follow.

"I'm busy later." Weeping in my room, but I don't tell her that.

"Girls..." Mom heads over. "I was wondering if I could get you to do me a favor."

"Anything." Chloe is quick to accommodate. She'd mop the floor with her hair, if my mother asked her to.

"I promised Mr. Dudley I would drop off print samples at his place this afternoon, but something just came up." She nods back at Tad with a scowl on her face.

"Oh," Chloe straightens, "I'm sure Skyla can. She has a little crush on him. Don't you, Skyla?"

"I do not have a crush on him." I'm quick to refute. My face burns a thousand different shades of red. I may have a little crush on Marshall, but it's only because he keeps pushing himself on me so successfully.

"He is a doll," Mom whispers before biting down on her lip.

It's like those hormones she's injecting herself with have turned her into a lust-driven lunatic. It's no wonder she's pawing all over Demetri whenever she gets the chance. His image has been warped under the lens of mega doses of estrogen. I'm sure once those erotic-shaped scales fall from her eyes, she'll eschew his company every chance she gets.

"Sure, I'll do it." I volunteer. "And I do not have a crush on my teacher." I decide to reiterate the fact just to play it safe.

"That's right," Mom corrects, "you have a crush on Gage." She says it so dreamily I suspect she might have a crush of her own on the blue-eyed sage.

"No." I shake my head. "Actually, I don't. I'm back with Logan again." Technically, I'm not, but eventually we will be, so it's really not lying—it's fast-forwarding the truth.

"What?" Mom gasps as if I had just made some egregious declaration.

"Told you she's fickle." Tad slides his coffee along the counter. "Give her another month or so, and they'll both be history."

"That's not true." Mom cuts him an icy look. "Skyla, what happened?"

"I'd rather not say." Like ever.

"Well, I'm concerned. Are you OK?" Mom rubs my back, inducing in me the strong urge to bawl like a baby. Speaking of which...

"So did you tell them the great news?" I ask Brielle, mustering all the enthusiasm I can to get the words out.

"Oh, I totally forgot." She spins her finger in her hair. "I'm bringing the baby by this week. I hope you're ready. He needs a bottle in his mouth twenty-four seven just to keep him from screaming bloody murder." She snorts into her toast.

"Yes, I'm ready!" Mom grips her chest with excitement. Little does she know, she'll have a casket permanently lining her bedroom just like Tad predicted. He also predicted I would have dumped both Logan and Gage in a month, but that's not going to come true, at least not the Logan part.

"So where are you headed this afternoon?" Chloe bats her doe eyes into my mother. "Anything else you might need help with?"

Really? It's like she's trying to steal my mother, too.

"I'll be at Detective Edinger's estate. He's donating some of his grandfather's belongings to the Paragon Community Museum along with organizing items for auction."

"He's a real saint," I grumble. Just like he's donating my blood to the Counts and organizing a win for the faction war.

"Oh, he's..." Mom looks to the ceiling in her allusive search for adjectives. "He's better than an angel."

I pin my mother with a look.

Demetri Edinger is no better than an angel—in fact, it's about time she understands what a demon he really is.

≈ 🦋 ≈

Just before I leave for work, I hear Mom coming down the hall, humming a happy tune, because *hello?* She'll be rid of Tad for a few short hours. But it just so happens I can't stand the way she's decided to fill her time.

"Can we talk for a minute?" I widen the door to my room extending the invitation.

"Of course." She strides in and takes a seat next to me on the bed. "What's going on, sweetie?" She brushes my hair behind my shoulders.

"That's what I'd like to know." I was going to ask what was going on between her and Demetri, but my vocal cords shut down on me. I just know she's going to get all defensive when I peg him for killing my father—when I tell her how he's in the process of killing me. "You know, about Gage and me." Shit. So not where I wanted to go with this.

"Oh, hon, it's going to be OK." She pulls me into a tight embrace. "I just know you and he will work things out. That other boy is just a filler."

"Logan is not a filler." I have proof positive I'll be marrying him one day—Logan, Gage, and I can all attest to the fact since we shared the vision en masse. "Anyway, I don't want to talk about me. What's going on with *you*?" Do I really expect her to burst like a dam and fill me in on all the juicy details of her affair?

"Well, I'm sort of torn right now." She sighs, looking down at the comforter.

"What?" I honestly didn't think we'd go there.

"Therapy isn't what I thought it would be. It just seems to be getting worse and worse. I think I might have to shore up the reserves and force the entire family to get on board. I could really use some support right now."

"Support you? With Demetri?" I want to gasp or scream or throw things, but it's all getting a little too real.

"Demetri?" She looks genuinely confused. "No, I was thinking more along the lines of a colon cleanse."

I give several hard blinks. I do see the connection although vague and disturbing in nature.

"Oh right." I get it. "To help with the baby. So, you're still wanting to go ahead with that whole infertility treatment thing? I mean you're a grandmother now." I shrug like it's no big deal, but secretly I'm hoping she'll change her mind about trying to add another Landon to the mix.

"I might be a grandmother but I wouldn't know it, and I certainly wouldn't know my grandchild lived right next door. Every time I go over there, they act like they're not home, even when their cars are sitting right there in the driveway. I'm not holding my breath for Brielle to bring over the baby."

"Sorry about that." I sit up, fresh with an idea. "Hey, maybe Darla is ticked off at you."

"Whatever for?" Mom says it real pissy like maybe there *is* a rift between her and Darla.

"You know," I start, "you've been spending an awful lot of time with her boyfriend." Referencing Demetri as anybody's boyfriend makes me want to gag.

"Why didn't I think of that?" Her hand flies to her mouth. "Of course—she's the jealous type." She smacks herself on the forehead. "I'll have to think of something and make it up to them. A romantic getaway, just the four of us."

I blink into her, stymied by her problematic mathematics. It's becoming clear she won't be removing herself from Demetri's equation anytime soon.

"Maybe start by inviting them to dinner," I suggest. "You can really lay it on thick with Tad—then Darla will totally get the message." So will Demetri.

"You know, Skyla, sometimes you're a real genius." She winks.

Not sure a wink is what you want after hearing those words.

"In fact," she says, clapping her hands into her epiphany, "I'll have the Oliver's over and their boys. I'll see if I can't make more than one love connection that evening. I just know Gage is the right one for you."

"No, please, don't do that."

"Are you sure?"

"I'm positive."

She leans in and hugs me a very long time. I guess I blew my chance at ratting out Demetri.

"Hey, Mom?" I pull away and look right into her bold, emerald eyes. "What would you say if I told you I thought Demetri was a really bad guy?" Like responsible-for-the-death-of-your-husband bad.

Her lips tighten in a ball, her gaze narrows into a spear. "I would never believe you."

Exactly what I thought.

30

Mad Kisses

The island transforms itself into a tropical paradise. A dark canopy of clouds lay thick over Paragon, locking in the heat from an unnaturally warm day. The pines glow verdant and supple. Their dark, corrugated trunks lie camouflaged in tawny and ebony bark, interlocked like the pieces of a puzzle.

I pull into the bowling alley parking lot and step out of the Mustang, taking in the scented brine from the ocean. I can see the whitecaps crash over the shore from across the road and the angry blue steel of the water sweltering in the heat. The boy I once loved holds that color in his eyes. Gage holds the ocean, the universe, and my heart hostage in those cobalt spheres. He had so much power over me with just one look, but now he's gone, and all that's left is an imposter taking up space in his heavenly form.

Gage's black truck is nestled next to the entrance. I knew I should have begged Brielle to cover my shift. I suppose I could hightail it over to Demetri's to knock out some more of those community service hours and lock myself at the hip with Chloe of all people.

I make my way through the dimly lit arcade. It bustles to life with robotic clicks and whistles. The bowling alley opens up like an air-conditioned haven, bright and airy, the scent of fresh popcorn thick in the air.

A voice emerges from the kitchen.

It's Gage—I know that husky laugh, that guttural moan as he shows his discontent. I miss the way his baritone would rumble through my body as he held me tight, the way it sounded in my hair.

"Skyla." He comes upon me quick, making me wonder if he teleported to spare the seconds he would be without me, but I know that's wishful thinking—the quicker to kill me, perhaps.

The sound of bowling pins being thrust off their base lights up the facility like a heartbeat. But the cacophony of sounds, the steady roll of the ball, the whir of the machines, and the techno music blaring from the arcade all seems to dissipate as Gage presses forward.

Gage bows into me and takes in the scent from my neck with a long draw. The look of ecstasy explodes over his face, as though he had just sampled the most exotic flower. Palpable angst corrupts the air as his breathing grows erratic, his hunger, his wanting skyrocket into the stratosphere.

"You look beautiful," he pants the words out. He sweeps over me with a serious gaze. "You glow, you know that?"

"I do?" I hold his gaze without wavering. There's something sobering about being this close to him—with his attention strictly focused on my person. "That's because I went out on a date last night—had some *real* fun." I shake out my hair like it was no big deal.

Gage twists his lips holding back a grin as if he knew better. "Where'd you go?" He tilts his head in anticipation of an answer that he already knows.

"None of your business where Logan and I go."

"Have you talked to him this morning? He didn't come home last night."

Crap. "Is his truck there?" I know for a fact he was home and sleeping in his bed.

"Still there." Gage takes me in almost disinterested in our chit-chat—his eyes, his soul, are having another conversation entirely.

"He spent the night at my house." I shrug, trying to act like this is the new norm in my life. "He slept with me."

Technically it's not a lie. "You know, as in *together*." God, I sound like an idiot.

Gage lets a smile slip, then retracts as if he didn't mean for it to show. He knows damn well I slept alone last night because he was probably popping in and out of my room at regular intervals.

"So," he says, with a single soft whisper, that lustful gleam in his eye elongates, sharp as an arrow, "you don't have any idea where he might be?"

"Nope." Ezrina flashes through my mind. Shit!

Gage leans in, pulling me in close with his heavy magnetic stare. His breath falls over my face, soft as feathers. He tilts his head before coming in for the kill. I can feel the heat from his neck touching me before he does.

I don't want to do it. I refuse to do it. I will hate myself if I do this. *Down* girl. But my lips draw up and ache for his with nothing but a breath between us.

"Ms. Messenger." Marshall flashes a look of dismay from the black hole of the arcade.

"Marshall," I gasp. I don't put a lot of thought into what my body does next. I run at him a million miles an hour, jump up on his waist and ravage him with a kiss so wild he can hardly stand as I writhe over him. Marshall backs us into a wall and sits me down on an animatronic pony. I know just the one—it wears a colorful fiesta hat and a sarcastic toothy smile, and to my surprise, the machine comes to life beneath me. Before I know it, my hips are forcefully grinding into his, and it most likely looks as though I'm doing my math teacher right here in front of the entire junior population of Paragon.

I needed this kiss. I was going to explode if I didn't kiss Gage—splatter over all four corners of the island if I didn't jam my tongue down his throat just to satisfy my parched affections for him.

It's me, Skyla. Do try to focus on the suitor at hand, Marshall suggests while pleasuring me with a kiss I won't soon forget.

So this is what it would be like to love Marshall—his bold affection—the intense wave of pleasure emanating from his being. It's heaven like this with him. I could more than forget my troubles if only for a little while. Maybe what I really need is to spend a few good hours under Marshall's lustful supervision, maybe that's how I'll repair my shattered heart. Marshall would never refute my efforts and make me wait until the end of the faction war like Logan. Marshall would take me right now on this vibrating donkey, if I let him.

A vision appears, a blinding pain surges throughout my body, and I bear down hard.

"You can do this," a voice calls from behind. "Push, Skyla—*push.*"

I turn ever so slightly and see the face of the man rooting me on—it's Marshall panting out the beginnings of a smile as he looks down over me and the vision fades to black.

I jump off him as though he were on fire.

Dear God. I *am* going to get knocked up by my math teacher.

"Did you see that?" Marshall braces me by the shoulders. "We're going to have a baby, Skyla." His eyes dance around my person at a million miles per hour. "Not only will you be my wife, but you'll bear me a child. This is beyond my expectations."

I'd hate to be the bearer of bad vision interpretations, but I highly doubt things will pan out the way we see them. Now that I know things aren't always what they seem, it's very possible the child I'll be bearing will be Logan's. Marshall will probably just be in the vicinity. I'll probably have my baby in the parking lot at prom just like Brielle.

A surge of heat spikes through me as I try to do the math to figure out when Logan and I will most likely do the deed.

"You are aware that I'm touching you." He sneers down at my bare arm.

"Oh, right." I give a dry smile and step away. "Thanks for listening. By the way—I've decided to call in sick. You think I can come over for a while? Maybe we can toss Nev into Demetri's mirror of horror and find out where it leads?" I think Nev totally owes me after that stunt he pulled a few months back when he almost robbed me of my virginity.

"No can do. I have a pressing meeting in less than five minutes. I came to pick up the prints."

"Oh, right. They're in the Mustang on the passenger's seat. It's unlocked, and I think the window is rolled down. Just reach in and grab it."

"My how safe and secure you must feel living on this floating rock." His jaw clenches as he mocks me.

"I know, right? It's so different than L.A. It's almost paradise." Gage catches my attention. He gives a disapproving look in our direction before pecking at the register. "Anyway, I guess this is more of a fool's paradise." And I'm the fool. "So where's your meeting? Are you coming back with that reverse tan? Maybe I'll come by later and check out your celestial glow."

"Whether or not the Master shows is not up to me. Delphinius will be there. He's going over the bullet points of what he'll be discussing at the faction meeting. I presume you'll be forced into attendance. Does all this special attention please you?"

Ellis's words come back to me.

"Attention isn't necessarily a good thing," I say, knowing full well none of the attention I've received thus far has been good. "The Counts are up in arms over the fact I've got a treble. Why the hell would they care?"

"They have ethics, Skyla—although misguided, they do try to adhere to the rules of their nefarious game. In the event you're not aware, you, my love, are breaking just about every canon they've ever bothered to instate."

"Correction, Demetri is breaking them. You're right, his lust for my mother is a powerhouse to contend with." I stop shy of mentioning Demetri was kind enough to return the third disc to me after he so unkindly had pints of my blood removed from my body in his sadistic tower of terror—not that it matters now. I'm sure forfeiting another region, whether by accident or not was all a part of his plan.

"I must leave. Shall I grace you with my lips once again?" Marshall glides into an easy grin. "I believe Jock Strap is witnessing this encounter with great interest. Oddly, he's replaying our resplendent exchange of passion, casting himself as the lead in a rather pornographic display of affection. I doubt we were so crude, and in this, a public establishment."

I glance back over at Gage. Just the thought of him reenacting that kiss I shared with Marshall makes my heart beat faster.

"Oh, for sure you can have another." I hike up on the balls of my feet and accept a quick kiss full on the lips that says I've got more where that came from, even if I don't.

He gives a causal wave to Gage before speeding out the door.

Well, I guess there's that. I'd better feign monster cramps, so I can get out of working shoulder to dysfunctional shoulder with the ex-love of my life.

I head in his direction. He's just standing there going over the books with a studious expression on his face, and my stomach bottoms out. Gage is obviously aware of the super powers he holds when it comes to his looks. God knows he's completely abused their ability to seduce me. It's so not fair.

Instead of offering some lame ass excuse as to why I'm about to leave, I want to kick him in the balls.

"You OK?" he asks, counting out the dollar bills before placing them in the register.

"Why wouldn't I be?" I can feel Gage luring me into quicksand.

"Because he was trying to resuscitate you." He presses out a bleak smile. "The next time he decides to perform CPR, would you kindly take it outside? You were scaring the kids." His affect flattens to the point of vexation.

"Is that what has you up in arms? A couple of frightened children?" Unexpected tears blur my vision and I blink them away. "Screw you, Gage Oliver," I hiss. "Unlike your fake ass, I actually had feelings for you. And, by the way, rumor has it that Chloe's vagina is the equivalent of a Chinese finger trap— once you're in, you can't get out. That would serve you right, being conjoined to that monster for the rest of your natural lives. And the next time you decide to leave a psychotic letter in my bedroom, I hope you spontaneously combust. I never want you in my room again!"

"I meant every word." It stamps out of him harsh and aggressive. His brows sharpen like Nev with his wings in flight, hovering over twin beryl globes.

"That's what makes you a good liar—even you tend to believe them. Just like you lied when you said Chloe didn't pay you. So how much did you get? A grand like Brielle? Did you get a bonus? I bet she does all kinds of nasty favors—"

He holds up his hand in defeat. "Skyla"—he gives a long blink—"let's go in the office," he pleads. "We can go anywhere. I'll take you to the moon, just let me speak to you for a minute."

My entire person wants to cave. He could take me to the morgue, the cemetery. I'd listen to every word. I could sit spellbound for hours just listening to his hypnotic voice.

A surge of anger takes hold of my heart for sympathizing with the devil.

"I think I'd better go." I struggle to get the words out as a baseball size lump settles in my throat.

"Looks like Rockaway is getting invaded tomorrow." He glances down as if replaying a memory. "You going?"

That's right—Paragon's firework spectacular is converging on our love nest. I hope the hut he built for two meets with an unfortunate demise by way of an ember. I might arrange for that little mishap myself.

"Yeah, I'll be there," I whisper.

Unfortunately, his girlfriend will be there, too.

Gage steps in close, pins me between the counter and his rock-hard chest. His lids lower as he rakes his hot breath across my neck. Volcanic levels of heat radiate from his body. I want to press myself against it, warm myself against the fire that is Gage, but he's already burned me once, and playing in the flames is never a good idea.

"You really did it, Gage?" I mean for it to sound accusatory, but it comes out childlike. "This thing with Chloe?" I can't bring myself to call him out on being the well-placed anything.

He locks his gaze over mine and takes in my hair, my eyes, and lips before flexing his dimples, no smile.

"Yes, Skyla. I did."

My heart bottoms out and I run like hell all the way to the Mustang.

31

Cellar Door

Demetri Edinger's palatial estate was supposedly handed down from his dead Fem of a grandfather. Although I seriously doubt that particular acquisition of real estate ever took place, it doesn't change the fact I need to fulfill some serious community service hours. I made the error of trying to procure some of Ellis's magically replenishing, albeit very illegal, weed—not for me of course, for Emerson Kragger.

The sky boils thick as mud over Paragon as I take in the oversized McMansion. It's an exact replica of the one in the Transfer, and this unnerves me to no end.

It's not until I come upon the stairs do I note the minivan tucked in an alcove just off the driveway. Figures. Mom must be rummaging through his grandfather's belongings herself, and I bet the belonging she's fondling just happens to be Demetri. Honestly, I don't get the appeal. Sure he's rich, handsome in a maniacal way, and he treats her like a queen, but still. Can't she see through all the trickery?

I freeze midflight on the stairs.

God—he's just like Gage. Gage was in every way the perfect boyfriend, *too* perfect. His perfection alone should have set off a dozen different sirens embedded in my stomach. Obviously said sirens are in need of recalibration. Everything about my internal warning system seems to be defunct. After all, I'm the one responsible for reanimating Chloe.

I head up to the door and give a gentle knock before letting myself in.

"Hello?" My voice echo's reminiscent of Ezrina.

"Skyla!" Demetri's voice booms with great cheer from the sitting room. I tread over and find my mother planted next to him with her skirt cut above the knee and her legs neatly crossed at the ankles. She looks attractive, far too attractive to be cradling a teacup with her pinkie out, having a tete-a-tete with the head of all demons.

"So, I was just swinging by to help. I still have some hours to kill." I say the word *hours* as faint as a whisper and over annunciate the word *kill* for kicks.

"I thought you had a shift at the bowling alley," my mother protests.

I'm not sure if she's fearing for my employment or simply highlighting the fact I've interrupted her precious one-on-one time with her toxic suitor.

"I, uh...left." I sweep my gaze over the ornately gilded furniture, the garish gold-framed mirror carved meticulously with a pattern of grapes enwreathing the glass.

"Was Gage there?" Mom asks softly as if she understands how difficult it must be for me.

"Was there a falling out?" Demetri feigns surprise. "Say it isn't so. I've never met a young couple so well paired."

"I know." My mother taps him on the wrist. "They're like Romeo and Juliet."

I'd hate to interrupt my mother's warped fantasy, but if I remember correctly, Romeo and Juliet ended in a double suicide. I doubt we go down that path anytime soon. Besides, Gage has already killed me on the inside.

"We'll have to make an effort to bring the lovebirds back together," Demetri whispers loud enough for me to hear before reverting his attention. "Back in the day, your mother and I used to set up mutual friends on blind dates."

"We had an impressive track record." Mom nods into him.

"Sounds like you should've opened a dating service." I try not to lay on the sarcasm too thick. Really, all I want is to vacate the premises. Obviously coming here was a big mistake. "Anyway, I hear Chloe is roaming around. Does she have instructions on what to do?"

"She's your boss." Demetri winks at me from over his teacup as he takes a sip. "Follow the narrow hall to the left, there's a door that leads to the cellar."

I turn to leave.

"And, Skyla?" Demetri calls out. "Don't hesitate to explore. Some of those passageways lead to a whole new world."

I bet they do.

I follow the narrow hall down for what feels like miles. The heavy carpet cushions the sound of my mother's laughter until I'm left with a welcomed silence. The last thing in the world I want to hear is my mother chortling herself into a giggle-gasm with the prince of darkness.

At the end of the hall, a mahogany door appears in lieu of a tunnel of light, and I dash the rest of the way over to it. It's unlocked, and a light emanates from the bottom of a rather steep staircase. I descend slowly, in the event Chloe is positioned with a hatchet ready to take me down Ezrina style.

Once I hit the bottom, I find a carnivorous room that breaks off into halls and a series of doorways that expand like a well-orchestrated maze. Stone floors, creamy walls, and garish, larger-than-life statues pepper the vicinity. Probably soul-stealing Fems he keeps on hand should the need arise to terrorize the residents of Paragon, so I try not to inspect them too closely.

Chloe has her back slumped over a box in the not-too-far distance.

"What's going on?" I twitch my head to the side as I pop up beside her.

Chloe jumps and gapes at me for a second before scrambling to hide whatever's in that plastic bin she's plowing through.

I *so* caught her red-handed. I can tell by the stupid look on her face I managed to scare the shit out of her in the process.

"Nothing." She swallows hard. "What are you doing here? Wasn't Gage at the bowling alley?"

"Yes." I bite the word as I say it. "You know damn well he was there. He made me so sick I had to leave." Not really, but in the event they're reporting to one another, it might make for a good jab.

Chloe springs to her feet and threads her arm through mine. "So what happened?" She begins escorting me in the other direction with a counterfeit curiosity.

"Let's see," I start, "I almost kissed Gage. Then, in a bigger fit of insanity I did kiss Marshall, and now for the grand finale, I'm confiding in you," I say, plucking free from her grasp and heading back to the box she was secretively pawing through.

She yanks me back by the wrist. "Get the hell away," she commands. "This doesn't concern you."

"Then what's it to you if I take a look?" I charge over to the plastic bin with its lid sitting off to the side. Who is she kidding? Everything Chloe sinks her claws in has to do with me. Why would this be any different? Who knows what I'll find inside. The last surprise I found at Demetri's haunted estate was a room full of decapitated Fems posing as wall trophies. I'm still hopeful Chloe will be added to the disembodied collection someday.

A layer of bubble wrap sits sloppily on top, so I pitch it to the side and peer down at the contents. Ceramic statues—of people. At least a dozen or so painted in cartoon colors, dipped in heavy gloss. I pluck one out. A man. He looks like a caricature with serious frown lines and wrinkles, but I feel like I've seen him before. He's dressed in a business suit and holds a newspaper in one hand. I pick up another, a woman, and she too looks vaguely familiar. I press my lips together while examining the rest of them. It's not until I get the last one, that of a girl, do I put together what might be happening.

"This is you," I whisper, holding the miniature troublemaker in my trembling hands. It's in every way a replica of her highness of bitchiness. "This is amazing. Who are the rest of these people? Is that your family?"

Chloe hovers above with her arms folded defensively.

"You're a genius," she says it flat. "I guess you can't get anything past Skyla the slutty sleuth. Happy now?"

"So what's this mean?" I twist the see-through container around and find the word, *discard* scrawled on the side. "Discard." I try it out on my lips.

As in discard the Bishops? I don't get it.

"Wow, looks like you've been discounted," I muse. "You think he's going to sell these on eBay or just take them out back and use 'em as target practice?"

"Shut up, Messenger." She slouches beside me and opens another sealed container to inspect its wares.

"Doesn't feel so hot having someone interfere with your life, does it?" I ask. "Looks like good ole Demetri is up to his controlling mind games, and a few pieces of the big picture are no longer necessary." I meant to let it go as a passing thought, but who am I to waste a perfectly good opportunity to offend Chloe?

"No, Skyla, it doesn't." She glares off into some invisible horizon. "I'm pretty damn sure no one is through with me or my family, especially not the Counts." Her eyes glisten thick with moisture.

Well, I'll be darned. I do believe I'm bearing witness to Chloe's nervous breakdown. And pissed at the Counts for *discarding* her family? This is too fantastic to have missed. It was almost worth the pot bust itself for landing me here.

"I have to go." She rises and heads toward the exit. "Oh and, Skyla?" She tries to hide a blooming grin. "I found your box an hour ago, smashed your entire family to bits." She plucks something out of her pocket and tosses it in my direction.

I catch a tiny decapitated head that happens to bear my effigy.

True to life, Chloe hacked me to pieces before I ever got here.

32

Wreck the Halls

Once Chloe leaves, I embark on a journey that doesn't even put a dent in the breadth and width of Demetri's cellar.

In the next room, a series of tables conjoin to create one long showcase. A miniature replica of the island stretches for an unreasonable length, decked out in a series of fake pine trees and tiny wooden houses. The schools, the library, the hospital, it's all present and accounted for. Only a smattering of houses are scattered throughout, not every home on the island litters the supersized diorama. I'm quick to find the Landon residence and bend over to pick it up. It lifts right off the base, and to my surprise, eight miniature cast-iron figures stand two inches tall on the floor of the display. I retrieve one and find Tad's distinct features staring back at me.

"Holy shit," I say, scooping up the rest of the family and scrutinizing the entire Landon clan. Chloe is numbered with us. "Huh," I whisper, setting us back down and laying the house where it belongs. I walk around the behemoth display until I hit the Oliver house. I lift the tiny home, and three figures stare back at me. There they are. Barron and Emma look impeccably like themselves. I quickly place them back and cradle Gage in the hollow of my palm. "Hello," it comes out a broken whisper as I gaze into his beautiful face.

Wait. Where's Logan?

I scan the vicinity, but there's no sign of him anywhere.

Crap. Gage did mention that Logan never came home last night.

I place the dimpled Oliver in my purse and send a text out to Logan asking him where the hell he is.

My phone goes off and it's Logan's cell.

"Hello?"

"Skyla, this is Barron. I have Logan's phone."

"Oh." I jump a little. "Is he OK?"

"I have no idea. His truck is here, his wallet, his phone—he's all but vanished into thin air."

I let out a little whimper.

"Well, he's probably just light driving," I offer. "You know, seeing the sights or doing some bizarre research that has to do with the faction war. I bet he accidentally got stuck in the future again." And, sadly, those are all viable possibilities.

"Very well. I'll try not to panic. I hope he's back before too long, or I'm afraid I don't know what I'll do."

"I'm sure he'll be fine," I assure. We exchange niceties before hanging up.

I spend the next two hours lifting every house on miniature Paragon off its base in an effort to find him. Just as I thought—he's nowhere on earth to be found.

I'll have to borrow Marshall as soon as he gets back from his meeting. It's time to pay a little visit to the Transfer, and I'm sure as hell not going there alone.

🦋 🦋 🦋

I tried to get a hold of Marshall all night. At one point, I almost accidentally answered the phone when Gage called, while on route to sending another stalker-esque text to the Sector I'm trying to locate. Anyway, that travesty was successfully averted with one simple click.

It's the morning of the not-so-great Rockaway debacle. I'm sure the planets have aligned to ensure this will be another heartbreakingly humiliating day for Skyla Laurel Messenger.

I head downstairs and find Tad hopping from leg to leg while twisting his abdomen. It looks like he's having some sort of bizarre seizure, and I might be a little concerned if it weren't for the fact both Ethan and Drake are starting to mimic his twitching maneuvers.

"What's going on?" I ask Mom while plucking a banana out of the fruit bowl.

"Tad's been studying the secrets of all the great hotdog eating champions. He's analyzed tons of Internet footage, and he claims to have picked up some great strategies," she says, holding out her coffee mug as though she were mocking his genius.

"So what's the secret?" I ask. "Making the other contestants laugh so hard they pee their pants and are thereby disqualified for lack of bladder control?"

"No, no," she corrects, "only vomiting can disqualify a person."

"Vomiting?" Dear God this is going to be entertaining beyond belief. I might have to wear a diaper myself just to witness the event. Speaking of incontinence. "You see the baby yet?" Personally, I'm shocked Brielle is hoarding her child from anyone even remotely related to Drake.

She shakes her head. "Darla and I are barely speaking. But I did arrange a double date for the four of us tomorrow. We're headed to Seattle for the day. It's all going to be very romantic." She winks into me knowingly.

"Great!" I love it when Mom and Tad distance themselves from us with an entire body of water, plus they're taking Demetri off the island, so it's made of win.

She glides her hand over my head with the tenderness only a mother could deliver and offers a mischievous smile. "It's going to be magical for all parties involved."

Oh, I'm sure there will be magic. In fact, I wouldn't be surprised if a spell or two were already in the works. Little does she know she's the victim of the sorcery in question.

🦋 🦋 🦋

After breakfast I drive over to Marshall's. I spot Nev twirling through the virgin blue sky and wave.

Summer has come upon Paragon like a newborn— glowing and beautiful after a long internment, letting out its lusty, sundrenched cry. It's obvious that either Marshall or Demetri have recalibrated the weather for the island-wide festivities today. How I wish I could share the heated splendor with the old Gage I knew and loved. I think today is as good a day as any to officially bury the old Gage and Skyla, and what better place than Rockaway? I could weep rivers just thinking about the irony.

After a series of brisk knocks, Marshall opens the door. He's wearing his unearthly glow, which clues me in on the fact the Master of universal ceremonies did, in fact, crash the meeting last night.

"You look amazing." I give him a heartfelt hug before breezing past him into the living room. He's smiling and radiating like a star and appears to be in a good mood. Suddenly, I'm hesitant to share my concerns over Logan and his possible entrapment in the Transfer. Maybe he's just working out the finer details of his arrangement with Ezrina? Marshall will probably put the kibosh on operation "let Ezrina suffer in my place," so I decide to keep my lips sealed temporarily.

"Come right in." He lays it out with a touch of sarcasm.

"Oh, please." I groan, taking in the sights through the back window. There seems to be a whole slew of new animals in the corral, and they don't resemble anything of the equestrian variety. A lama takeover has officially ensued. "We're practically family. Soon, I won't even bother knocking. I'll just walk right in."

"I'll have a key made up for you at once." Marshall doesn't miss a beat. "As 'soon-to-be lady of the manor,' I don't see any sense in you ever leaving. In fact, we should christen each of the rooms with our budding passion, if you like." He gives a mischievous smile. Marshall seems to get off on teasing me about our so-called carnal union—at least I think he's teasing.

"All in good time." I press a hand against his chest. "I suppose christening at least one room will be necessary if we're ever going to produce our lovechild." I plan on playing up the *mother of your child* angle in every capacity. Even if I'm positive that both the vision and his orator friend are extremely off base, I know for a fact it's a very good thing to have Marshall's loyalties on my side. Besides, he's always there for me. That's as good as gold.

I take in a sharp breath. The words my father said to me while I was in the tunnels comes back full throttle.

Marshall's lips hike to the side. "I'll throw in 'his and hers' towels in an effort to lure you. Anything else I can do to make you feel at home?" He glides an arm around my waist like the slither of a snake. "A warm bath while sitting on my lap?" He digs his fingers into my shoulders, and my body comes to life on a whole new level. "I've been known to give amazing full-body massages."

I give a slight moan before coming back to my senses. "Something to write with would be good," I say, rummaging through my purse. "I forgot to jot something down."

He produces a shiny gold pen, and I quickly commit to paper my father's words. *You're as pure as gold.* I draw a single line through it and correct it to read, *I'm as pure as gold.* It's not until I've dashed the words across the page do I note the dark crimson ink and glance up at Marshall with a questioning look.

"The blood of your enemy should never go to waste," he purrs, taking up my hand.

"The Counts hold the same sentiment."

"So I hear." He pauses to examine me. "Aren't you the least bit curious as to how the meet and greet went with the celestial in-crowd?"

"Dying to know," I assure him.

"You've been called to the throne, Skyla. The Master himself wants to speak with you." His features darken at the thought.

"That's fantastic! When do I go? I have so much I want to say. If anyone can help with the faction war—with the Celestra trapped in the tunnels, it's him."

"I implored him for a reprieve."

"You what?" I take back everything about Marshall being on my side. "Why would you do that? He's my only hope."

"True, but appearing in his presence is a rather permanent arrangement. You cannot see God and live, Skyla."

"Oh." I swallow hard at the thought. "What would he do with all these crazy plans He has for me? Aren't I the chosen one to win the war? Free the people?" It all sounds very political at the moment.

"He would simply find another—discard you from the task at hand."

Discard. There's that word again.

"Is that what happened to the Bishops?" I tell Marshall all about the miniature island, the houses, the people, before pulling the iron version of Gage out of my purse.

"Why would you take this?" He scoops the figure out of my hand and examines it with a disgruntled look.

"I wanted to show you."

"Nonsense. You took it because you wanted him for yourself. You still do." Marshall depresses the words out. "Nevertheless, you must put it back where it belongs. Let's not add thievery to your long list of grievances."

"Grievances? What grievances?"

"It seems your inability to win a region has more than the Faction Council asking questions. The treble was brought up. Arson Kragger and Morley Harrison aren't the only ones whose interest has been piqued over the situation."

"Arson and Morley?" I whisper mostly to myself. I'm pretty sure those are two Counts I don't want to piss off.

"You have your work cut out for you. The next region must be secured with a win. As for the faction meeting, both Delphinius and I have determined it's best if you bring up the Celestra souls that have parted and where they are now. Be sure to recount how terrible the tunnels are. Let them know emphatically that you, yourself, are willing to sacrifice everything to save them."

I give a furtive nod. Truth is, I'm scared as hell to face the Faction Council, fight the war—save those souls. I'm starting to think maybe discarding me isn't necessarily the worse idea ever.

"There is no discarding you, Skyla." Marshall gives my hand a squeeze. "We must finish what we've started. We're in too deep to turn back now."

"We need a miracle," I whisper.

"All we need is you."

33

Burn

After I leave Marshall's, I pick up my sisters and head for Rockaway Point.

The late afternoon holds true to the clear summer sky. The evergreens release their fragrant oils into the air, perfuming it with their hushed magic.

I park in the overflow parking across the street from the black sands of Rockaway. The entire island has flocked down to celebrate Independence Day together, which usually guarantees a safe combination of both drama and discord.

Still no word from Logan, which has me hysterical with worry. I'll have to do something drastic by night's end if I can't get a hold of him.

Mia and Melissa sprint from the Mustang in unison.

"Hey," I shout after them, "try to get along. Stay away from boys! Remember what I told you—they're stuck on stupid!" As if.

Both Mia and Melissa have donned baseball caps to cover their follicular setbacks. They've actually been speaking to each other lately, which I suppose is a progressive move away from the course of disaster their relationship was barreling toward.

I kick my flip-flops off and let my feet sink into the warm, familiar sand. Its ebony crystals glitter like diamonds across miles of shoreline.

I scan the vicinity for Logan.

God—where is he? My heart plummets out of my chest at the thought of never seeing him again. If he made some supreme sacrifice on my behalf, I won't be able to live with myself.

"Messenger!" Ellis shouts through the crowd while holding a bright yellow volleyball hostage. There's a makeshift net set out and a few people stand on either side. I can make out Chloe and Em on the opposing court while Michelle and some girls from East side with Ellis.

I jog on over and put down my beach bag, take off my shirt without thinking twice about revealing nothing more than my teeny bikini.

"Balance out the teams." He ticks his head over toward Chloe's side.

"No thanks." I land next to him. My feet melt into the powder-like sand, all the way to my ankles.

"We don't need her." Chloe is quick to dispense.

Two of the girls from East cross the net, and we start in on the game.

I wish I could say I was enjoying the exceptional touch of sunshine blanketing my shoulders or the fact Chloe seems to miss each ball with a comedic display of clumsiness, but I'm not. I'm scanning the area for Gage like a spy on some covert mission. I can't help but wonder if he's looking for me or if my bizarre and somewhat disturbing PDA with Marshall finally stomped out any further desire to play with my heart.

A familiar frame catches my attention next to a series of tables laden with food and beverage dispensers. Gage. His shirt is off and he's wearing dark sunglasses. His face his perfectly positioned in this direction and I can only assume he's seen me.

A heavy thump lands over my head.

"Pay attention!" Michelle barks. Her dark hair is pulled back, revealing large bruise-like rings under each eye.

I pick the ball off the sand and toss it over the net. It heads toward Chloe and she dives into the earth and eats a mouthful of sand in her failed attempt to connect with the ball.

Ha!

The best part is Emily, herself, kicked a bucket full of sand in Chloe's face as they converged. Next time, I hope to achieve a head-on collision between the two of them. A coma for Chloe would be great and perhaps some overall sense knocked into Emily would be a nice perk, too.

The game goes on for a good long while, until I start feeling prickly and tight over my sun kissed shoulders.

The ball comes my way and I manage to spike it over the net with superhuman strength. It barrels down toward Chloe with pronounced velocity and she freezes, gawking at it in disbelief as it smacks her in the face. It couldn't have been a better orchestrated play if I had planned it—dreamed it.

She doubles over and lets out a sharp cry.

"Are you OK?" I shout with my hand placed over my mouth in horror. This could have been a much more satisfying experience if I, myself, weren't solely responsible for the well-placed volleyball.

"I think it's broken," she wails, clutching at her nose.

"It's not broken," Em says, examining her swollen beak. "Get up. You'll live." Emily dispenses all of the compassion necessary for a sociopath in training.

Lexy strides over wearing a bright red bikini that glows on her already tan body. Her russet hair reflects the sun like bronze and is neatly cut right along her jaw. I should totally point out her hair to my sisters. They should make an appointment ASAP with whoever is providing Lex with a styling miracle. Apparently, no matter how many bowls you use as a template, it's really difficult to make a home-bob look decent.

"Have you seen Logan?" Lexy continues to pan the vicinity. I know for a fact she's got her hormonal sights set on him because she's clued me in on the this fact many times in the past.

Before I can answer, a heaving sob erupts from behind, and I turn to find Nat bucking with her hands plastered over her face.

"What the hell happened?" Emily barks as the bitch squad descends to comfort one of their own.

"Pierce broke up with me." She looks out at the tumbling waves with her mouth wide open, stumped by her own revelation.

Freaking Holden. I knew he'd be nothing but trouble.

A shadow covers me, and I look up startled to find a bare-chested stud standing before me.

For a second, my adrenaline surges, fully expecting that beautiful bod to belong to Gage, but it's not. It's Marshall.

"Your shoulders are pink, Ms. Messenger." A lascivious grin builds beneath his paltry concern.

I pluck a bottle of suntan lotion out of my bag and wiggle it in front of him.

Marshall and I lay our towels side by side forming one giant sheet over the charcoal colored sand. The bitch squad settles in front of us and a bunch of people from both East and West pepper our ever-expanding circle. I take a seat and nestle into the towel, forcing the sand to contour to my body.

"Hard right. He's walking with an angry gait. Don't look," Marshall says under his breath as gets on his knees behind me and begins to drain the lotion over his open palm. *Shall we put on a show?* He offers.

"Please." I tip my head back and moan into the offer.

Gage lands his towel down about a foot from my own and offers me a plate with a couple of burgers on it. I must admit, they do look good. The buns look all fluffy and soft, and the smell of fresh-off-the-grill beef is making my stomach growl like a lion.

"Would you like one?" he offers sweetly. "I got it for you."

"I'd advise against it." Marshall gently places his hands over my searing flesh, and I wince at the effort. "I had one of those hockey pucks earlier. Trust me, you'll regret ever setting eyes on the thing. Do yourself a favor, young Oliver, and eat the plate instead. Your digestive system will thank you."

Gage glances down at the Styrofoam in his hand and wisely chooses the burger. He indulges in what looks to be a hot juicy bite and moans, affirming the fact he made the right decision.

"It's delicious," he assures. "You sure you don't want one?" He reinstates the offer. "The buns came from the bakery."

I knew they looked exceptionally tantalizing, but it's the principle of the thing. I can't go around accepting rides and burgers and love letters from the enemy—although deep inside it's impossible for me to accept Gage as the enemy.

"Why don't you come by the house later," Marshall purrs as he pampers me with a fantastic massage. His ingenious smooth stroke maneuver, coupled with his feel-good vibrations, have me moaning just beneath my vocal abilities. The last thing I need is the entire island bearing witness to my quasi-sexual experience with faculty, and I use the word quasi loosely. "I promise to whip up a meal that will leave you breathless and panting for more."

"You're the only meal I'll ever need," I bleat. Dear God, I think I mean it.

Gage arches a dark brow in our direction.

"Anyway." I bat my lashes up at Marshall for a moment. "Sounds heavenly. Of course, I'll be there." Really, it's Logan I should be stoking the flames of my affection for. I wish he were here and not serving time in—

Crap.

I glance back at Marshall briefly to see if he's listening in.

"I assure you the visit will be quite sinful in nature," Marshall says to further incite Gage. *Now where exactly is the Pretty One?*

None of your business. Damn. I keep forgetting my flesh is a porthole into every thought that crosses my mind.

Often a statement like that is followed by an intense plea for my services.

Gah! He is so right.

I usually am, he quips. "I'm counting down the hours until we shut out the world and indulge in the desires of our flesh." Marshall says is with such vigor that all heads in a ten-foot radius turn in our direction.

Shit.

"Thanks for offering to tutor me over the summer," I say stupidly, trying to save what little face I have left, which, by the way, totally refutes the effort of making Gage insane with jealousy. I'm pretty sure the thought of me knocking out equations does not a jealous rage make.

A bird shatters the silence with a startled cry from above.

I scour the sky to find Nev circling the area, alerting me to the fact something is off. God—I hope Logan's OK.

Marshall sighs. *I can hardly wait to hear this one.*

Principal Rice gives a friendly wave toward him and holds up a bottle of her own *fun* tan lotion. The way she slides her hand up and down the svelte bottle elicits all sorts of awkward penile implications.

"I'd better move along before a line forms." He pats my back and ignites a sting radiating over my shoulders, welcome as an electrical current. Music cues up from a live band in the distance. "Save a dance for me," he says, moving to his feet.

"I'll save every dance for you," I shout after him as he takes off.

I glance back at Gage and catch a bleak smile quickly dissipating.

ADDISON MOORE

He sits perched on his elbows. His bare chest is cut and chiseled like a marble masterpiece. If we were still together, if that were still *Gage,* I would offer to rub him down with oil by way of my thighs, hell I'd offer to lay my entire person over him as sun block.

He takes off his sunglasses, exposing those indigo marbles that glow against his ivory face as he catches my gaze. His beauty alone should have acted as a siren. How could someone so impossibly gorgeous be so inwardly perfect as well? Those two attributes rarely go together hand in hand, with Logan being the exception.

Logan has both inner and outer beauty, that there should be two of them in the same family would be practically illegal.

"I'm going to take a nap," I say, trying to sound more annoyed by his presence than I am.

"Will you dream of me?" His dimples explode in a fit of seduction.

"God, I hope not."

God, I hope so.

34

Ready, Set, Eat

The gentle crash of waves slapping over the shore rouses me out of a comfortable slumber. A cool breeze brushes over my forearms and legs, soft as cotton. I lick the salt off my lips from the sea spray and roll my neck just enough to know I have a serious crick to contend with.

I struggle to open my eyes and observe my surroundings. The setting disorients me for a second before I realize I'm still on the beach at the Fourth of July celebration. I pull up enough to see the sun dip down over the horizon, melting into a cool sanguine puddle. A tangerine stain spreads over the ocean as it swallows down the ball of fire.

"Beautiful," Gage whispers.

Only then do I notice he's meandered onto my towel and is lying beside me like we're a couple. Does he really think I'm stupid enough to keep bending over and asking for another when he's already screwed me over so freaking well?

I muster the energy to sit up and something soft slides off my back.

"Hope you don't mind," he says, plucking away the beach towel that's pooled by my knees, "I covered you."

"Yeah, well, I do mind." I'm not entirely sure I do, but I can feel him sucking me in emotionally—physically, to places I should never venture again.

A bullhorn goes off in the distance, and the annual hot dog eating competition is announced.

"Are you in it?" I ask, dusting the soot-like sand off my pale thighs. I look far too sickly to have ever seen the sun, let alone lived on a beach a good portion of my life. A year on Paragon is the equivalent of living under a rock.

"Nope. You?"

"Tad, Ethan, and Drake." I nod. "I would have thought you'd be in it for sure."

"Why's that?" His lips curve a ruby smile.

"You seem to stomach all the bullshit Chloe dishes out pretty well without puking."

He shakes his head. "Not true. I happen to have a powerful aversion to bullshit. That's why I'm finding this whole thing hard to deal with."

"What thing is that? The pact you made with Chloe and conveniently forgot to tell me about?"

"Skyla," he says, darting a quick look around—for Chloe, I'm sure, "let's go someplace where we can be alone. I want to tell you everything."

"Words you should have used a year ago." I wipe the sand off my bottom and head over to the annual Paragon puke fest where I hope to be entertained thoroughly by Tad's foray into gluttony and regurgitation. The manner in which he chooses to bond with his spawn should set off all sorts of red flags for Mom. If she hadn't already thought twice about that whole reproducing thing, perhaps watching the three of them wretch in a bucket together will sharpen her senses on what a profoundly dangerous idea she's entertaining.

Speaking of the prospective procreator, I spot her over by Demetri and Darla. It sort of looks like he's got an arm wrapped around both Darla's waist and my mother's.

I tilt my head to get a better angle, and freaking shit, it's true. The fiend is in the process of feeling them both up. He's not even trying to hide the fact he's a pervert.

Mom caresses his hand before stroking his shoulder as she bursts out laughing. Why do I get the feeling Demetri just had more action than Tad has in a week. Eww and eww. And by the way, I'm a thousand percent sure the way to make nice with Darla is by not openly fondling her boyfriend. Not privately either, but that seems to be a different matter.

Gage pops up dutifully by my side as I make my way over to Marshall. He's already positioned in the back of the crowd ready to ogle at the sausage spectacular. If Gage wants to be a third wheel, I'll make sure to provide him with a more than an uncomfortable experience.

"Ms. Messenger," Marshall growls with his affection for me turned up to maximum capacity. "Principal Rice implored me to teach two additional courses next year, Trigonometry and Chemistry." He nods over at Gage acknowledging the fact he's within earshot. "Isn't that superb?" Marshall beams into me with his blood-stained eyes. "I'll be the focus of your attention for two hours each day. Of course, you're welcome to double up on evenings and weekends. I'd be more than happy to cater to your every whim." He cuts a glance back at Gage before dipping into me again. "As the mother of my future children, I'll be happy to supply you with nothing but the best."

"Perfect." I give a nervous laugh. I so did not think this conversation would go there, but then again, with Marshall, all roads seem to lead to my uterus. "Supply me with an A in trig. I don't plan on doing any of the work either." True story.

"Nonsense. You must do the work. How else will you grasp the material?"

"It's useless and impractical. Everybody knows that," I shout up over the announcer as the horn sounds and the contestants indulge in their wiener eating frenzy.

I watch with great interest as Tad and my stepbrothers begin their final descent into colon and artery congestion.

"What in heaven's name are you talking about?" Marshall's voice spikes as though he were genuinely surprised by my revulsion for all things mathematic. "Trigonometry is applicable in everyday life." He goes on, proliferating our first full-blown argument, right here in front of the general public and Gage, who, by the way, keeps twitching his dimples. "How will you ever understand upper level theories if you don't have a foundation to build on?"

"Oh, please, like I go around every day trying to solve for x. Let's call a spade a spade, I could care less about x and all its problems. I'll hardly *add* in real life, let alone waste my time trying to decipher relational values."

"Trust me, you'll be in need of far more than basic addition skills to navigate your way around the relational values you've embroiled yourself in." He assures, settling his hands over my shoulders.

More like my mother has embroiled me in, I say. *Get me a meeting with her, would you?*

Already with the honey-do list. He mocks a sighs before signaling for me to look up on stage.

I stand on my tiptoes to get a better view.

Oh my freaking shit.

Tad and his dancing primates are all skipping side to side, doing the worm or the snake or the *Landon* as this horrible, embarrassing stunt will be forever referred to. It wouldn't surprise me at all if both Mia and Melissa fashioned a noose out of sausage casings and have already hung themselves on the nearest palm tree. Surely death is the only practical way out of the dishonor that Tad has brought to our family.

A blond head bobs directly in front of Taddy dearest. Her cheering fists pound high in the air. It's Isis, the breast queen. And she's swiveling like a belly dancer, shouting Tad's name repeatedly in an overtly sexual manner.

"Dear God," I mouth.

I glance back at Mom as the crowd erupts with laughter. She breaks free from the stranglehold Demetri has on her and begins to maneuver through a mob, nine deep, just to get to the front.

Tad stops all movement. He's got a hotdog dangling in partial from his lips, and he's openly staring at *Izzy* and her bouncing beach balls, speechless and utterly forgetting the task at hand.

Mom wrangles her way to the front and steps directly in Tad's line of vision. She's shouting something and pointing at the stack of hotdogs getting cold in front of him.

Tad breaks free from his voluptuous trance and grabs a fist full of wieners and crams them in his mouth all at once. It's shocking how disturbingly phallic it all looks, and just as I'm about to force myself to turn away, the buzzer goes off.

"Good show." Marshall starts in on a dull applause.

"If I didn't know better, I'd swear Isis was a set up to throw Tad off."

"She is," Marshall whispers directly in my ear. "Believe me, dear Skyla, she is."

35

Nothing Lasts Forever

I was right about the puke bucket.

Turns out Ethan and Drake were capable of synchronizing their projectile vomiting, which inspired Tad to gag along and eventually join in on the fun.

Mom mentioned something about giving Mia and Melissa a ride home after the fireworks as she was leaving with the barf brigade. Personally, I think she was just trying to keep Isis from comforting Tad with her thirty-six triple E's. Mom practically needed a whip to keep her off him once he jumped off stage. It was like he was a rock star, what with all the pawing, and the way Isis pressed his face into her décolleté as a congratulatory embrace was obscene to witness. Had my mother not staged an intervention, he might have happily puked right there on her person.

The band starts up again, and people move to the sand and start dancing against the growing expanse of a deep purple night. A blanket of diamond-encrusted stars cover the heavenly vault in a display of magical delight I've never witnessed before. They wink down like lasers switching on and off, and I marvel at the jewel-tone sky.

"Shall we?" Marshall pulls me in deep into the crowd of jostling bodies—half of them being the student body, which clearly indicates, that he, as faculty, knows no shame. I like that about Marshall, not caring what anyone else might think. He controls the situation, not the other way around.

Brielle springs up beside me, and the three of us dance in a circle with Brielle mostly bopping to herself and Marshall testing out every dirty dancing maneuver known the world over and then treating the crowd to a few that I'm pretty sure are neither legal nor possible.

Marshall glides his hands over my thighs like a lover—dips in with mock passionate kisses over my neck that leaves my entire body craving the real thing. Something in me surges, and I grab a hold of his waist and sway with the rhythm until I'm panting with thirst for him. There's something about Marshall, about his hyper-vigilant desire, his indescribable zest for life that is unstoppably attractive. It's happening—that wooing effect he has on me from time to time that magnifies to an all-out volcanic level explosion—it surges me in, slow and bubbling, waiting to spew out all over the island.

The music stops abruptly, and it takes a few moments for our bodies to cease all movement. Really, I want nothing more than to run my tongue over the hills and valleys of Marshall's flesh and let him do the same to me. I could easily fall into a puddle at Marshall's feet and continue where we left off—horizontally.

Gage appears, his eyes lit up like sapphire beacons. "Great band," he says it flat with a marked pissed expression at the graphic display Marshall entertained him with. "Too bad they're having some serious technical difficulties." Gage reels me in by the hand, and I twirl into him. I can feel the power surge break from Marshall like a light switch going off.

Before I can refute Gage and his actions, the expression bleeds off Marshall's face.

"What have you done?" Marshall whispers, looking past my shoulder into the forest as if he's just been clued in on some huge misgiving I'm involved in.

"I haven't done anything." I turn to face Gage. His serene expression, those dimples that I desperately want to dive into call to me because I know for a fact I have done something, and it happens to involve temporarily misplacing Logan.

"I will see you in the morning." Marshall's tone is sharp as the tip of a blade. He stalks off toward the forest, not bothering to hide his irritation. *Be warned, we have visitors.*

I take in a sharp breath as I scan the black canvas draping over the evergreens.

"What's the matter?" Gage breathes the words over my cheek like a warm L.A. breeze.

"Nothing in particular." Everything to be exact.

A thunderous pop goes off, and a flare of light ascends into the atmosphere exploding into a luminescent bloom before sparkling like a Christmas tree on fire.

A crowd migrates toward the shore as the firework display ignites over the ocean.

"I know a place with a great view." His face lights up blue then purple, then a violet shock of white that bleaches him, pale as paper.

"Sounds like some cheesy pick up line," I say.

"Is it working?" His right dimple digs in deep. It's obvious his left one isn't sold on the idea.

"A little," I say, lowering my defenses. It's not my fault I'm caving. The heady scent of marshmallows roasting is making me delirious. Not all of us stuffed our faces with the remnants from a meat grinder. Not to mention the fact the display of light rocketing off overhead has me wishing I had a pair of strong arms to wrap around me—familiar arms that used to make me feel as though there were nothing in the world that could ever harm me.

A pink orb appears from a whisper. It holds itself in the sky for five solid seconds before a series of white shooting stars propel from its nexus. It's so achingly beautiful, and then it evaporates to dust—phosphorescent ashes that rain into the ocean, forever forgotten like Gage and his love for me.

"So where we going?" I dust his face with a look of inquisition. I've given an inch, and now I'm curious as to what it'll cost me.

"Are we going somewhere?" A twinge of hope sparks in him.

"You said you wanted to talk to me. I'm guessing in private."

His brows dive bomb into a V. "You trust me?" He's pleading with those desperate eyes.

"You've already fed me to the Counts. How much worse can it get?"

"I promise you have nothing to fear with me, Skyla." The illusion of genuine love pours from him as he melts me with a penetrative stare.

A writhing ache churns in my belly. It's as though Gage has so perfectly tricked my body into wanting him, desiring him on a cellular level. It's impossible to simply let him go.

He takes me by the hand with caution as if my fingers had the capability to ignite into flames and singe him if the situation warranted. How I wish I could hurt him so easily, although it's the emotional damage he's done to me that scalds me from the inside. I could never replicate that kind of misery and graft it over his heart. I thought I did with the DVD but those were misrepresentations of who we were—my mistakes that I deeply regret. And the idea of him in bed with Chloe, probably both figuratively and literally, was an all-out deceit birthed before I ever got here.

Gage moves us past the crowd, away from where the band is still trying to piece together the mystery of the severed power line. I think I know the origin of their misery—it was the same one that produced mine, and now I was letting him take me places.

We move deeper into the night. A familiar-looking coral tree emerges in my line of vision.

There it is, our love shack, the one he built with his own hands from palm fronds, secured with twine and his false affection, so it wouldn't blow away like we did.

It stands all of less than five feet with the soft weathered tendrils from the palms waving friendly in the breeze.

"I miss this," I whisper. I didn't mean to say it out loud. A part of me wonders if my body is working against me—letting him hold my hand, following him—what's next? Mind-numbing kisses?

God, I hope so.

Gage picks up my other hand and holds them both in the air before kissing them in tandem. He pulls us down to our knees and relaxes his warm chest against mine, his fingers reacquainting themselves with my back.

"I'm going to tell you everything," he whispers.

The sky blackens unnaturally. The fireworks fade to grey as a shiver runs through me. A glacial frost I hadn't felt before penetrates through to my bones.

"Something's happening." My voice replicates itself indefinitely.

The Tenebrous Woods appear in snatches—gnarled branches—navy sky.

One reality is fading and another is about to take over.

Paragon folds in on itself in a violent clap.

I fall through a chute of enveloping darkness so strong I breathe it, taste it—swallow it all the way down to Demetri's dark twisted tunnels.

36

Crash into You

A dark solace, a free fall into a sinister world overcomes me. The glowing embers smolder in this tubular descent. The heavy scent of smoke and ashes burns through my nostrils.

I can feel the wind licking my skin, my limbs bend the way gravity demands, but the girth of my body, the weight of my flesh feels alarmingly unfamiliar.

I try opening my mouth but seem to have lost all control. *Logan?*

I'm right here, he whispers. *You're in me now.*

Oh God. I watch as the walls ignite like a firebrand. The smell of a furnace intensifies as the ground comes upon us.

Logan lands hard on his side and we let out a solid groan in tandem.

Are you OK? I look down to survey the damage. We've landed in the hallway, the same black-and-white checked pattern on the floor—same creepy flocked wallpaper that lines the Transfer, hugs these walls.

Logan's wrist is unnaturally bent. He sits up and nurses it for a few seconds.

You feel that? He lets out a soft moan.

I feel something. It's not too bad though, no pain.

Good. I'm glad there's no pain, he says, rising.

A terrible sound comes from the left, and I'm startled to find my body lying on the ground with my blond mane tangled in a huge ball around my face.

"Skyla!" Logan tries to rouse her. *Sorry—can't call her Ezrina down here. I just want to make sure your body is still intact.*

The thought occurs to me that I might get trapped inside Logan forever, and perhaps that vision of me walking down the aisle toward him was really his wedding to Ezrina.

"Survived." Ezrina gets up and dusts herself off, still wearing my bathing suit top and shorts from Rockaway. A layer of dark sand covers my feet like glittering shoes.

"Excellent." Ellis's dad comes upon us with the requisite glowing clipboard in hand. "Your Junior Council, Wesley, is in need of a pick me up."

"Where's this Wesley guy from?" Logan asks, trying to maintain a casual air about his curiosity. I'm betting he plans on paying him a visit. Kicking a little Count ass on the side.

"He's a traveler." Morley is quick with the answer as he leads us down a long narrow hall. "Wesley is from two years in the past. That's how dry the reserves have been. We've been incredibly backlogged."

"So I heard," Logan nods. "Demetri filled me in on the treble."

Morley shakes his head. "Let's hope we don't find ourselves in a mess like this ever again." He straightens. "However, it's picked up lately. Your supplies from the faction war helped significantly." He winks into Logan.

That's because you killed those eighty-nine Celestra! I'm almost giddy over the idea that they're not really dead, although I suspect they wish they were.

Correction, Holden killed, Logan interjects. *You think they're down here?*

I know they are. Marshall said so, and Ellis senior just affirmed it. They're probably resurrecting them like they do their own. Marshall wants me to bring it up at the faction meeting, make myself look like some kind of hero or something. He thinks it'll give me some street cred, and maybe people will momentarily forget that I keep on losing.

Logan groans at the thought.

"What's the matter?" Morley pauses just shy of the lacquered double doors.

"Just hurt my hand in the landing."

"Well," he says, frowning over at Ezrina, "it'll be over soon. I've put in a request to have her instated as a permanent guest. It's not right that you're having to escort her like this."

What? What kind of request? I'm more than panicked that this older, not wiser, version of Ellis wants to lock me up and throw away the key. *He so wants my treble revoked.*

"I don't mind coming down here." Logan gives a bored smile. "Besides, this way I get to keep her around. She puts out, so it's all good."

Really, Logan? I'd roll my eyes, but I'm deficient in those at the moment.

"Can't say I blame you." He openly roves over my body. "You should consider procreation since you're close to pure yourself. Her children would be wonderful donors. Of course, the Family would pay you handsomely for such a sacrifice, and you could visit regularly."

"I don't know if I could handle my children hating me like that." Logan shrugs as if they were discussing gas prices or the brand of oil they use in their cars.

"Oh, they wouldn't hate you," he assures, "they would have the luxury tower, as would she. Once a child is born into the tunnels, they know no other way of life. It's the new model the faction is switching to. It's much easier on everyone to raise them here right from the beginning."

"I can see the logic." Logan nods.

Ezrina turns and looks into Logan's eyes, but it's me she's gazing at—holding me steady with my own steely gaze.

Ingram appears from nowhere and Morley, who, by the way, is rife with bad ideas, heads in the opposite direction.

What a freaking asshole, I say. I am so going to slash his tires first chance I get. I can totally see why Ellis feels the need to numb himself into oblivion. If Morley were my dad, I'd need more than an ample supply of narcotics to help me make it through the day. And to think I tried to encourage Ellis to quit. I think we should all be thankful Ellis hasn't taken a swan dive off Devil's Peak by now.

Morley's always been a little off. Logan shakes his head. *Now I know why.*

"Tell her to step lively." Ingram instructs without acknowledging Ezrina at all. He treats us like we're animals—cattle.

"Ingram?" Ezrina shrills, loud and sharp.

"Step inside." He all but ignores her. "Your caller has an engagement this evening."

"I have never hated you." Ezrina seethes as she steps into his face. "I have held fast that you did what was needed—but *this*?" She growls with an intensity I had no idea I was capable of.

What in the hell is she talking about? I say. God, she's going to ruin everything. If she keeps this psychotic shit up, he'll have me locked in the darkest part of the dungeon while a mob of bloodthirsty Counts ravage me all night long.

Ingram takes a cool step back and examines my body for less than a moment. "Control her, or she'll have to be restrained," he says in a soft voice with no real malfeasance behind it.

I can tell by the look on my face that he's managed to piss Ezrina sky-high with his lack of general affect.

"Restrained?" She gives a quiet laugh. "Move in my direction and see what happens."

What the hell are you doing? Logan grabs her by the wrist.

I knew it! I panic. I knew we couldn't trust her. She's going to do something stupid to ensure a free ride on the Skyla express for the next eighty years.

Ezrina seals us off from her thoughts the way Gage does when we're together. Of course, now I know why he was locking himself away from me mentally. He was just fielding me for Chloe.

Logan escorts us down the long dark path as the Tenebrous Woods encapsulates us with its spiny depraved arms. The deep navy fog comes to life with screams and moans—a subtle cry for help that sounds so faint and desperate it makes me wonder if that soul is in its final hours.

I scan the chambers for people, but the first few are empty. Eventually, we come upon two women who sit back to back. They've both been restrained at the wrists and ankles with thick oppressive chains. The woman on the right is frightfully pale, her skin sags from a lack of nutrition and her grey lips hang low as if she hadn't the strength to close her mouth.

It's nothing but one horror after another down here. It's so perverse, so twisted. Each Count responsible should rotate on a spit in hell for even thinking this is OK.

I'm sorry, Skyla, Logan says, pressing his hand in the small of Ezrina's back as he leads her to the dark pit of my former, and very present, misery. *I had no idea she was going to be such a loose cannon.*

Well, she did hack off my arm—that could have afforded you a clue, I say.

Logan's chest rolls in silent laughter. *I made sure to add a no hacking clause in the contract.*

Never mind, I say. *I'm thrilled she's offered to vet the pain for me. It's beyond brutal. So why were you missing? You scared the hell out of me. And, by the way, your uncle and aunt are beyond worried.* Gage is too, but I don't bother wasting Logan's energy on anything to do with him.

It's part of the deal. I told her I'd stick around to give her and Nevermore the honeymoon of a lifetime.

Oh my gosh, that's… eww. The visual alone puts me off.

I don't make a habit of watching. He's quick to correct. *And believe me, I wish I couldn't listen.*

So that's what you were doing?

That would be it. She put me in a chamber and induced a deep sleep.

Logan pulls Ezrina back by the fingers and nods over to the room with the giant wooden T-bar and manacles dripping from a long rusted chain. She goes over and Logan locks the bracelets over her wrists, secures her feet with the metal loops that strap into the ground. I can feel his heart breaking, his fury rising.

"Ingram," Ezrina says, dusting him with a frosty look, "come."

Ingram glances at Logan before heading over.

Ezrina doesn't speak. Instead, she hawks back all of the phlegm she can manage and showers his strange glowing skin with a fresh batch of spittle.

Shit. Logan and I espouse in unison.

Freaking Ezrina.

She was using you, I say. *And now she's ruining* me.

I've never been so afraid and yet so comforted than I am now with Logan. I can spend an eternity with him like this, wrapped in this indescribable intimacy, and with Ezrina in charge, I just might have to.

Ingram steps away and Wesley swoops in from out of the shadows.

"Boy, you're really pissed today." His eyes widen with a mixture of fear and wonder. Not only does he look like he could be Gage's brother, but his voice is a perfect match as well.

Ingram shoulders up to Logan. "As her Elysian, I suggest you instruct the caller to bleed her dry. The sooner we have a hellion like this removed, the better. Those with fresh fight in them are usually nothing but trouble for the long haul." He gives a quick nod and glares into Logan. "At once."

"Bleed her dry." Logan's voice resonates high and strong like he means it.

Am I going die?

No—but Ezrina might.

37

Triple Dose

I dream in misery. My body is submerged in the deepest part of the sea, inhaling algae by the gallon. I'm incapable of dying in this horror that's cocooned me. Gage swims toward me, his hair dances soft and buoyant. I beg for a breath from his lungs, for his lips to nurture mine, to absolve this grief I'm embedded in—but he doesn't come. He looks up and I follow his gaze to find Chloe with her perfect limbs, a black wreath of tresses framing her nefarious smile. She pours something heavy and toxic straight from a bottle, dumps it right over my head—bleach. It's sodden liquid sinks around me, envelops me in a septic cloud. I take it in through my nose—it scorches my lungs like flames.

I jolt out of the nightmare.

Snatches of stolen blinks and whispers clutter this dark new world.

The smell of smoke, the sound of laughter congests my lungs and ears. My lids are pasted shut with grit as I struggle to open my eyes.

"I've got you. You're OK." Gage depresses a wet kiss over my forehead as I begin to rouse from this aching slumber. I focus on the breeze that lingers, its cool embrace over that small token of affection he dropped. Gage picks me up and jostles us over the ebony sand of Rockaway as he shouts something indistinguishable.

Marshall appears, hovering over me, inspecting the damage. His face elongates unnaturally, and the world fades to grey.

"Open your eyes, Skyla." Marshall's voice sears my eardrums with its virulent command. "You must stay with us." His echo pulls out indefinitely. "Take her to your home at once."

The atmosphere changes. A familiar scent fills me with an intense rise of pleasure, and I'm suddenly greedy for air—taking in breaths like water in the desert.

"Skyla." Gage hums my name, rocks me in his arms like a dying child he's determined to save. A cool, damp towel pats over my cheek, and it's enough to inspire me to open my eyes.

I recognize this place—Gage's bedroom.

He pours water from a bottle over one of his stray T-shirts and presses it against my neck and forehead.

The door flies open, Dr. Oliver and Marshall burst into the room in an angry rush, and for a moment I wonder if their anger is directed at me.

"Good God!" Barron's face contorts with shock. "She's sheer alabaster."

"Two is not enough." Marshall plucks my lids apart and inspects my pupils.

"Three will kill her." Barron holds the needle in front of him as though it were a gun.

"That's always the point." Marshall takes the needle and lovingly rubs his hand along the back of my thigh. I can feel a jolt of his special brand of electricity warm me with his love. "Two more, please" he says, pushing in the needle with a forceful jab. "*Now.*"

Dr. Oliver glares at Marshall a moment before disappearing. I've never seen him so angry, so distressed. It distracts me from the shooting pain wrapping itself around my spine like tendrils reaching up from the newfound puncture.

This new reality frightens me. Ingram wants me dead for something Ezrina did. Logan is as *good* as dead stuck in the Transfer playing honeymoon suite to a couple who my mother banished apart. They're being incriminated for the same thing

Logan and I are guilty of—administering a little vigilante justice to the Counts.

There's no doubt in my mind my mother will punish Logan and I once the war is over for helping Nev and his twisted bride. I can feel it in my bones. Candace Messenger is like a bullet riding on the back of a comet, lethal in every capacity. Nothing compares to her wrath. I'll wish the Counts had sucked me dry once she gets a hold of me—I'll wish that Marshall had annihilated me with a thousand poisoned needles. At the end of the day, it will be my mother who crushes my skull with her heel. Chloe has nothing on her.

I let out a weak groan as a viral surge of pain covers my flesh. I've donned a coat soaked in kerosene, and Marshall scoured me with a blowtorch. A white-hot fire sears over me, wagering its assault along my raw exposed nerves.

Dr. Oliver appears with two more needles.

I struggle to open my mouth and beg for mercy, but the agony is too wild—too constricting in every way.

A fresh jab—a hard push of toxins burns my thigh, then another.

"Move." Marshall barks at Gage. He scoops me into his arms and reclines with me on the bed.

My entire being gasps with relief. I dig my fingernails into his flesh. There is no way in hell I'm letting go. He warms me with his magical sensations, takes the pain down to less than nothing. I can breathe again. It's so good like this with Marshall.

He presses his lips over the top of my head.

"I'll be here, Skyla. I won't let go."

"You said it would kill her if you touched her," Gage says, intolerant of the fact Marshall has taken his place in so many ways. "She needs to fight the poison, and she can't do that with you wrapped around her." Gage surges out the words like hacking through a forest.

Forgive me. I must leave. Marshall closes his eyes briefly before handing me back to Gage.

"No." I writhe toward Marshall.

Gage pulls me into his lap, and a hot poker spears from my abdomen to my temple.

Marshall and Barron exit, shutting the door behind them with a gentle click and I let out a horrific groan.

"I can make things better," Gage whispers it out in huffs.

"You've already made things worse!" My stomach clenches in pain.

"Look at me, Skyla. Focus on my eyes."

I glance up at him and immediately fall into those sweet watery pools. This is probably just some lame attempt to lure me back into his trap by way of ocular hypnosis—sadly, it's working on a rudimentary level.

"You don't love me." I hiss as a mean shiver runs through me. "You would have let me die happy in his arms if you cared anything about me. You would never want this pain for me."

"I do love you. That's exactly why I want you alive."

There's a venomous look in his eye, a general contempt for the purveyor of this intense misery.

"This pain is *killing* me," I shriek. "Marshall." His name comes out less than a whimper. "Please, bring him back. I beg of you." My muscles twist in knots. My stomach claps together like an accordion full of bile. I gag and claw at his shirt as the life slowly chokes out of me.

"Skyla." Gage presses his lips just above my ear. "Your skin is picking up color—your lips are pink. You're almost there."

I struggle in his arms for what feels like an eternity. This is a terror, an unrivaled pain that compares to nothing I've ever felt before. I would give anything to have a blade within reach, so I could slit my own throat—his throat, too, for removing Marshall from the scene.

Gage presses his lips over mine, drowns my sorrow with a spasm of his affection. All of this aching misery is extinguished with the hot pool of his mouth.

You can do this, Skyla. I need you. I need you to live for me—for us. Don't die. Just breathe—breathe.

I wake up refreshed with lids wide open and find myself alone, back in my own bedroom. A slight surge of adrenaline pushes through my veins and oddly, I feel more alive than I have in my entire seventeen years.

My room is still, quiet, with the day yet to rouse itself outside my window. A sheet lies over me and I can feel its coolness against every inch of my skin. I peer beneath it to confirm my clothing-deficient status.

Very not funny, Gage Oliver—at least he's consistent. He pulled the same crap a few months back when I passed out in his truck. It's like he has some weird fetish to strip girls naked once they're unconscious. Not that I know this as fact. The thought of Gage disrobing Chloe nauseates me, so I roll over and pick up my alarm—seven a.m.

I pull back the curtain and peer outside just in time to see the world flicker like a candle. It reaffirms the fact a storm has settled over the island. This is penance for all that nice weather Demetri furnished us with.

A raging sea of deep russet clouds moves swiftly overhead. I pull on my robe and open the window to take in the damp honeyed air of a fresh new day.

A dark winged creature descends quickly toward the ledge. His feathered plumes give off a purple hue in contrast to the strange-colored sky.

Nev squeezes in and shakes his wings out with a shiver that spans head to foot.

I plop on the bed next to him and massage him with my fingertips.

"What's the matter? Honeymoon over?" It doesn't feel quite right razzing a bird over his latest sexual adventures.

The honeymoon is very much not over. Might you forget I've a duty to attend here, but while I can manage it, I'm prone to a little afternoon tryst.

"So it's almost like your punishment is null and void. How cool is that?" Ha, we've totally outsmarted my mother and the kangaroo court she runs in the nether sphere. "You know, my mother won't even talk to me. She totally knows I've been taken by the Counts, and she still gives me the silent treatment. Baffling, right?"

Right. He twitches. *If you'll excuse me, the mere mention of that woman makes me anxious for the nearest windshield.*

"Oh, gross." I'm quick to crank open the window a little wider for him. "Choose the red sedan," I say as Nev flies off to relieve himself. Serves Chloe right to have a bird crap all over her buffed and waxed girl mobile. I should pay Nev in earthworms to follow her around all day and use her head as a target.

Speaking of heads, a dark shadow bobs through the yard. I squint and make out the shapely form of a woman, dark flowing hair—it's Chloe. She's holding a stick in her left hand, and something long and stringy drips from her right.

"What the?" I press in toward the glass and the world illuminates with a violent flash of lightning.

Then I see it—the hair—the ghastly pale face with a wash of blood at the base.

A scream gets locked in my throat.

The glint of the shovel in her other hand catches the light as she strides into the forest that borders the property.

Holy freaking shit.

Chloe Bishop just one-upped me in the decapitation department.

38

Head Hunter

I waste no time dashing downstairs in order to conduct a rather spontaneous headcount of what remains of my family.

I knew Chloe was perfectly capable of chopping us to pieces in our sleep. She probably started with Ethan because he was within hacking distance.

Mom and Tad are mulling over a bunch of packets and pills, counting them out and itemizing their cache of baby-making supplies, no doubt.

"What time did you get in?" Mom greets me with an expression that assures it was later than desired.

"I don't really remember." Honesty is the best policy.

I turn to dart back upstairs and make sure Mia and Melissa are still capable of living out another bad hair day when I smack into the guillotine girl herself.

Chloe's hair is matted on the side, mascara runs down her face creating muddied half-moons beneath each eye. She's wearing a tank top and boy shorts, both of which are loose and ill fitting.

"You're in your underwear," I hiss.

"I'm in *his* underwear," she corrects.

Disgusting.

"Skyla?" Mom calls out from the dining room. "Do you realize the girls were trying to *hitch* a ride home?"

"I'm so sorry!" I pause, trying to get my bearings on the lie I'm about to manufacture.

"You're very lucky Demetri was there," she snips. "If it were anyone else, I would have been beside myself. And, by the way"—she hustles over—"I have a very special surprise planned for you that I'm unable to cancel. Which makes me beyond livid because I don't approve of rewarding bad behavior."

"I'm really sorry," I whisper in an effort to settle her down. "I think maybe someone slipped something in my drink." More like Demetri slipped *me* into a drink.

"You know what?" Chloe's eyes widen with a farfetched innocence. "I saw three girls passed out last night—heard some kids from East spiked the lemonade."

As if my mother is going to buy that.

"It's always the lemonade." Mom tosses her hands in the air at the injustice of it all.

Chloe shakes her head. "Leave it to those yahoos from East to pervert the last piece of Americana." She slinks across the room and checks out the array of foil packets strewn across the table in a semi-organized fashion. "What's this?"

Of course, she's interested in the ovarian super booster. Chloe is interested in procreating with Gage, so why not kick-start her body with Mom's baby-in-a-bag kit? I'm sure she'll fill her fallopian tubes with an entire bushel of ripe eggs in time for some afternoon inseminating.

"It's a colon cleanse treatment." Mom heads over and shakes one of the packets before tearing it open with her teeth. "It's for the whole family. You're welcome to it."

"I hear that's so healthy." Chloe manages to assume a genuine stance on the aforementioned diarrhea enhancer.

"You should have some," Mom insists. I'll make enough smoothies for all of us. You just add yogurt and milk. It's supposed to taste like heaven." She snaps up a fistful of packets and heads toward the blender.

"So what does it do?" I ask, picking one up then and tossing it back to the table unimpressed.

"It gives you the shits," Tad quips. "It's going to turn our insides into the faucet of fire, and you won't want to be three feet away from a toilet when it hits. Makes you crap your brains out for days."

Lovely.

"Not true." Mom pauses midflight with an industrial-sized yogurt container. "And I warned you of the dangers of filling your body with those carcinogens on a stick," she reprimands Tad. "If we plan on trying again, we need to ensure a pure environment for the sake of our future child."

Yes, God forbid he produce another breeder like Drake or a dolt who would sleep with his own killer like Ethan, and don't even get me started on the twisted mind that hacks off the hair of her sister while she sleeps, which reminds me...

I pull Chloe aside by the elbow. "So what was with the early morning stroll? Needed to clear someone's head? With a shovel!"

Chloe goes over to the window and gazes out at the dense woods, draped dark as a funeral. She tilts into the glass as if she were asking herself a question.

The blender goes off like a live grenade, drilling my skull with its intrusive whine.

I step into the window alongside Chloe and watch as the sky rips open—a deluge of rain bursts over the island like the breaking of a dam.

Chloe shakes her head and brushes the dewy glass with the tip of her fingers—an apology lingers on her lips.

"Who was it, Chloe?" I forget to breathe as I await an answer.

"More like who will it be," she says it monotone into her reflection.

"You were traveling," I whisper.

Chloe proves impervious to my prodding. Instead, she jockeys for favorite daughter and chugs down a third of my mother's bowel blaster, side by side with Mom and Tad.

"Get dressed, Skyla." Mom beams with a glossy milk mustache. "We're going shopping on the mainland."

"We are?"

"Tad has some quick business to take care of, and I thought this would be a great time to catch up."

"Oh, perfect! Yes, we need to catch up on things." I'm so going to squash Demetri like road kill and expose that yellow-bellied coward for what he really is—a monster. Once my mother hears how he's been mistreating her baby—along with other people's babies—she'll be looking for the nearest millstone to tie around his neck.

"I'm heading that way to see my brother." Chloe cuts the air with the lie like a ninja. "Can I catch a ride to the ferry?"

"I don't see why not." Mom twists me around and ushers me toward the hall. "We leave in a half-hour."

"Half-hour," I repeat as I traipse up the stairs. That gives me plenty of time to light drive back to this morning and see firsthand what poor, headless soul Chloe is responsible for killing in the future.

Binding spirit.

Figures. Chloe has every dimension covered to ensure her wicked deeds can carry on undetected.

By the time we arrive at the ferry, the weather has tamed to its requisite thick layer of fog. The clouds have deposited their reserves and are ratcheting it up for an even greater display later in the day.

It's not until I hit the warm, dry cabin of the ferry do I realize what quicksand I've just meandered into.

Darla and Demetri wave up at me. To the devil's right sits Gage with his open face and pleasant smile. Crap. I totally forgot Mom mentioned she scheduled her demented double date for today. And it looks like she's decided to include me in on the misery—shopping, my ass.

Of all the stupid shit to fall for. Forget my mother throwing Demetri into the sea by way of a millstone—it's me she's drowning with her misplaced good intentions. And Chloe is here no less.

Double shit.

The horn sounds, and the boat floats away from the dock, leaving me trapped on a glorified raft with an inappropriate number of my least favorite people. I suppose there's no way out of this mess, so there's that. A perfectly good summer's day wasted in bad company and my mother.

"Surprise!" Mom rattles me by the shoulders as she pushes me down next to Gage. "I know the two of you haven't seen eye to eye as of late, but believe you me, there is nothing that a change of scenery can't cure. It's been a really rough year on us all, and I think we're just now getting the swing of things on the island." She looks over at Darla in hopes the spirit of renewal, and sharing custody of grandchildren, is alive and well. If not, I suppose there's always a legal team that will help Darla see things her way.

"You're never too young for true love." Darla gravels out the words as if she were the youth in question. She attempts to clear her throat, treating us all to a fun-filled mucus musical. "I've been up all night with that little brat." She pounds her fist into her chest as if she's trying to stop her heart—an action I might invoke upon myself in about five minutes. "He's the cutest little shit, but you'd think sleep was against his damn religion."

"We wouldn't know." Tad wastes no time in ruining the trip before we break three feet away from land.

Darla sways in her seat like she's just been cold clocked. "If you bothered to walk next door, you might get to see the little demon for yourselves."

Darla isn't one to take crap from too many people. Zero to be exact.

"Excuse me?" Mom's voice bustles to unnatural levels. "I've made repeated efforts to see that baby, and every time I knock on the door, I hear footsteps scuttling in the opposite direction."

"I'm only following my daughter's wishes." She punctuates the spontaneous confessional by jutting her head out like poultry. "Y'all got your heads tucked so far up your rears, she's petrified the kid's gonna need a shrink before he can shit in a dish."

"Speaking of which..." Tad makes a mad dash for the restroom.

You can feel the tension, the fatalistic hum of the lawyers and social workers drumming in the background as Mom and Darla start in with the death stares.

A bloom of lightning quakes through the portholes, followed by an intense growl of thunder.

"You know, I don't think it's that bad outside," I say. "I think I'll get some air." I bolt for the stairs before my mother pulls a knife on someone.

"I'll come with you." Gage offers, appearing by my side.

"I would love some air." Chloe grins her signature wicked scowl.

I can't think of a better time for Gage to explain everything than with Chloe Bishop by his side.

39

Nothing but the Truth

The sky fills in with charcoal—spastic and jagged like a picture being colored in by an angry child. Hard swirls of onyx—all-out aggression explodes on the canvas up above, leaving knife-sharp streaks as he colors outside the lines. It's a garish display carried out by the wind and the storm, both equally determined to bombard us with their pent-up frustration—like Nev bursting over Ezrina in an all-out erotic detonation, centuries in the making.

A royal blue canopy is erected on top of the ferry in hopes of keeping us free from the elements. We take seats near the back, away from a group of women huddled together sipping their morning coffee.

"So where were we?" I say to Gage. "That's right. You were going to tell me everything." I blink a quick smile at him as Chloe sits across from us.

"Oh!" Chloe squeals with delight. "I was so hoping I could be privy to this conversation. Go ahead and dish, Gage—tell her everything." Chloe's entire face glows at the prospect. "Nothing but the truth."

His jacket falls between the two of us, and he touches my hand beneath it.

I want to take you there. I want you to see for yourself what happened. He nods into me before readjusting himself as if we had never touched.

"Let's talk about Logan." Gage spears me with a look. "My dad's ready to call the police. You know anything about his disappearance?"

"Not really." It's true. I don't understand why the hell he can't leave the Transfer. He could sleep at home for God's sake. Ezrina is just being greedy. I touch the base of my neck, marveling at how well it's healed overnight. "Let's talk about Chloe running around my backyard with a shovel and a severed head." I toss the spotlight of truth in Chloe's direction and watch the smile bleed from her face.

Her cheeks turn an ashen grey. She clutches at her stomach and lurches.

"I need to use the bathroom," she croaks, evicting herself from her seat and smacking into a wall of women congesting the stairwell.

Coffee flies in the air, and two older women are flattened in Chloe's attempt to break through the bottleneck. Chloe doubles over and groans as her jeans darken down the back. She darts a horrified look to Gage and me before diving down the stairs.

Wow—who knew Chloe's kiss-ass routine would yield such impressively amazing results. I hope she craps a kidney.

A flock of pelicans sail by. Their smooth flight, their precision-like formation transforms the ever-darkening sky into a thing of beauty.

Gage lifts my hair with his finger, examines my neck for a sign of puncture.

"He looks like you," I say, gazing out into the dull grey ocean. "The boy they gave me to. He has your face, your hair, although that's where the similarities end. He really loves his girlfriend. She's all he ever thinks about." A swell of tears try to fight their way to the surface, but I won't let them win.

"You're all I ever think about. And I do love you," he says it low like a well-kept secret.

"Is that what she programmed you to say?" I turn to look at him in full. "Just answer me this. Did you have to turn in your balls when you agreed to play along with her stupid game? I did believe you, by the way, up until I was apprised of the fact we were nothing but a lie. You really went all out."

"I went all in," he says it so quick, so loud—I hold my breath a moment.

I imagine Gage sitting at some high-stakes poker game, Chloe as the deceptive dealer, shuffling cards marked to her advantage. They're a team, taking down unsuspecting players. Anyone foolish enough to sit down beside him can easily become a victim. And here I am, once again firmly seated by Gage Oliver's side. And yet I desperately want to believe him, hear him out once and for all.

Oh dear God.

I will never learn.

Once the boat docks, all of Paragon's patrons are quick to evacuate what has become a vessel plagued with unfortunate sanitation issues. I have a feeling the said plumbing debacle was not only sponsored by a faulty set of lavatories, as the ferry employees insist, but a handful of laxative-laced smoothies my mother was eager to dispense this morning.

Mom, Tad, and Chloe decide there would be nothing more curative than a shower and a change of clothes, so they opt to catch the very next boat back to the island, which actually pleases me more than the fact they've spent the last half-hour bonding with porcelain. I could use a little distance between Chloe and me. Honest to God, if I have to subject myself to another braless morning with her airbags staring me in the face, I'm going spare the next victim on her kill list and decapitate Chloe myself. Now that I know I can bury a body in the past, the fact that it's both unethical and illegal no longer holds the chain of fear it once lorded over me.

"You two have a good time." Demetri bows into me. "I hope the beauty of the city will be enough to rekindle the flame you once held for one another."

I seriously doubt that. The only flame he wants to kindle is the one under my feet once the Counts dub me a dry well. I'm sure Demetri would like nothing more than to roast marshmallows as I turn into a giant piece of Celestra toast.

"Don't do anything I wouldn't do." Darla chews her gum with the speed of windup teeth. "We've got a room to decorate with our love," she whispers pulling him toward the waterfront.

Seriously? Gross.

Demetri turns around and sharpens his evil eye on me. "Skyla, I almost forgot." He bleeds a smile that assures me, whatever he's about to spew, he most certainly never forgot. "May I speak to you alone a moment?" He steps under the shadowed awning of the fish market a few feet away and I follow.

"What?" I ask almost amused.

He pulls a giant disc out and flashes it proud like a knockoff Rolex. It's the same disc that fell out of my pocket during the faction war and cost me yet another loss.

"I want you to have this," he says, wielding it in front of me. "Accidents don't count. You have to want to forfeit the region. If anything, I want this to be a fair fight."

I stare at him a good long while before retrieving it and stuffing it into my purse. This has "I want to get into your mother's pants" written all over it, but hell if I care. I need this disc.

I don't say thank you. I don't say a word.

Demetri nods at me and joins Darla out on the wooded boardwalk just shy of the harbor. I watch as they drift off in the fog with his arm slung low on her back. I wonder if my mother wishes she were headed to some magical hotel room with Demetri instead of Darla. Mom is panting after the enemy and she doesn't even know it.

Gage crops up beside me.

"What was that about?" His dimples tremble, still insecure regarding whether or not I want him around.

"Nothing." I shake my head. "So, we're here," I say, fanning my arms out at the city. "What should we do?"

Gage steps in front of me and casts a shadow with his frame even in this dismal light. "We should go back to Paragon." He blows the words into my ear. "Two years ago—the butterfly room."

I nod and without regard for whoever might see us—we disappear.

Gage and I end up in a dank room with no light and the steady tap of rain beating over our heads.

"What version of hell is this?" I ask, as the cloying scent of dust and mildew fills the air.

"It's your house, well, Chloe's—the attic," he whispers, pulling open the door to the butterfly room just enough.

There he is, two years his junior, his hair slicked to perfection. He's wearing his dark blue football jersey with the number forty-four thick and glossy across the back. Chloe is there sitting cross-legged, content with the task at hand—cutting small paper wings out of colorful tissue paper. She looks remarkably the same, her hair and sharp features still stunningly gorgeous. A twinge of jealousy pinches through me at the sight of their heads knit together.

I know for a fact Chloe was a proficient stalker of his from before I ever set foot on the island. I read all about it in her notorious diary.

"This was from your vision," I whisper. He had seen the tiny room covered with paper butterflies in his dreams.

Yes. Gage pulls me in close, nuzzles his head into my neck and breathes in my scent.

"So"—Chloe leans back on her hands, tilts her head at the Gage sitting across from her, full with suspicion—"I guess I'll be going soon."

Gage looks up and puts down the scissors.

"I have some things lined up," she says. "You know, for later. I'm coming back." That last part bullets from her like a threat.

Gage gives a morbid nod.

"There's this girl." Chloe shakes her head. "She'll be here, living in my house, my room."

Gage looks past her shoulder, scours his eyes over the wall as though a picture were emerging.

"She'll be here taking my place." It comes from her broken, strangled as though she might cry. "I need someone to keep an eye on things. I don't trust her."

"What's her name?" Gage breaks his gaze from the wall and leans forward with a newfound interest.

"I don't want to say it," she rasps. "She's beautiful. That's all you need."

Something in me knew she was talking about the girl from my dreams. Gage rubs his thumb over my hand as we listen in on the rest of their conversation.

"She's coming after everything I own." Chloe straightens with a sense of resolve. "She wants to be me. She's got it out for me, and I'll bet good money I die at her hands." There's a look in her eye like she might know exactly why, but she'll never tell.

"Sure, I'll keep an eye on her." He shrugs, glancing up at the wall once again.

"Perfect. You can be her boy toy—break her heart like you broke mine." Chloe flourishes under the guise of their agreement.

Gage doesn't say a word, simply raises his dark brows and gets back to the task at hand.

"So that's it?" I ask, still unsure if I can trust him enough to know I'm not being manipulated.

That's it. Gage assures. *When we were reading her diary, and she mentioned the well-placed boyfriend, I wondered if that was me. It certainly wasn't some sinister plan to take you down because of my devotion to her.*

It doesn't make any sense. Why not tell me ages ago?

I take him in with the shower of golden light spraying over his beautiful face from a crack in the seam along the wall. It's as if the light magnetized in his direction, as if it yearned to grace his features and sought him out for the sole purpose of illuminating him. At one time, I believed all of creation should bow to his eminence. He was so perfect, and now I don't know what to think.

There's something else you need to see. He wraps both arms around my waist. *One more light drive?*

"One more."

We appear in the attic again, and for a second I'm unsure if we ever left, but we spot Gage in his former glory alone in the butterfly room.

This is the week before. I thought I saw something on the wall when she first dragged me up here, so I waited until she was at school and teleported over.

Gage stands in the butterfly room examining the blank walls, inspecting them with a studious interest that far exceeds the attention the chalky plaster deserves.

After I had the dream about these walls covered with tissue paper, I wondered what it meant. I knew that there was a reason I was seeing the butterflies, far beyond decorating Chloe's bedroom.

"What was it?" I look up at him.

Watch. He nods back into the orange glow of the tiny room.

The old version of himself places the flat of his hands against the wall and taps against it with a determined fervor, like patting down a thief.

The wall lights up, it pocks unnaturally as an image forms.

Then we see it, plain as day.

"Oh my, God." I breathe the words out.

"It was faint at first," he whispers. "I thought I saw your face. But then I was seeing you everywhere, in my dreams, the clouds, the trees. I was in love with you long before you ever set foot on this island."

The walls brighten under his strange command. There I am, a glowing creature with my face displaying far more beauty than it does in reality with a tiara pressed into my hair, as I gaze upward, kissed by a tangerine light.

"I've had that vision before," I say. "I distinctly remember being in awe of the peace on my face."

"The second I saw it, I knew I needed to cover it up. Whoever gave me that vision of the butterflies must have thought the same thing. This is what I was looking at the day Chloe asked me to watch over you. I was already doing it— already shielding you from her. Whatever that moment is, it's your destiny, Skyla. And someone up there has taken great pains to protect you." He picks up both of my hands. "And so have I."

40

The Vision

The stale attic air swirls around Gage and me in a cloud of dust and cobwebs. All of those old Bishop memories clotting up the air unnerve me.

So Gage was protecting me right from the beginning. He covered the walls to hide my effigy from blooming into view. Chloe was the snake in the grass, but it was Gage who was holding the gaff ready to shield me from her slithering ways. But he could have told me. We shared a thousand stolen moments in that room where he could have raked those delicate papers off the wall and revealed the prize he was motivated to hide from Chloe's toxic affections.

"I had already traveled back and met Chloe before she died," I whisper. "She knew what I looked like. Why cover my face?" Aside from the fact she'd be expressly pissed if I were mocking her from the infrastructure of the house.

Gage pulls me in, warps his fingers around my hair and kisses it. "I don't know. I think maybe I had an epiphany once I remembered those visions of you. I knew the butterfly room would exist for a reason and I know that reason was for me to protect you—to love you.

"Let's go somewhere where we can talk," I say.

"Mind if I lead the way?" Gage whispers as the gossamer languishes around him in the nonexistent breeze.

"Not at all." I let out a breath that's crowded my existence from the moment Gage Oliver was pegged as my enemy.

ꟻ ꟻ ꟻ

Gage and I appear on a white sandy beach. The sun is high overhead as a lush, searing wind, humid as a shower, blows over my skin.

"Where are we?" I marvel at the azure water. It's clear for miles before it marries the cobalt sea. It reminds me of the color of both our eyes, inextricably conjoined in this never-ending expanse.

"North shore, Kauai—Hanalei."

"Oh my gosh." I give a light bounce before plucking off my shoes and sinking my feet in the warm powder. It's bliss like this in paradise with Gage. Emerald-peaked mountains sit like silent giants behind his shoulders. The sea laps up on the shore, pulling the jealous sand down into the mouth of the water to quench it from the smothering heat.

"There's so much more I want to tell you." Gage takes up both my hands and kisses them in turn. "I need you to understand why I saved Chloe at prom."

"Yes." My voice spikes unexpectedly. "And please don't use that protective hedge as an excuse. Marshall said if her ordained time to die was in the vicinity, the Decision Council might have taken her."

Gage shakes his head. "It had nothing to do with the protective hedge, and I promise you it wasn't her time to die."

Great.

Sometimes it feels like Chloe catches all of the green lights, in this life and the next.

"The night before prom, I had a vision." Gage wraps an arm around my waist and leads us slowly down the shore. "I was going to share it with you, but life got crazy." He swallows hard as if he were reliving the memory. "But first, I want to say that, after you were taken, I immediately left Chloe. I took off about a mile down the road before I was able to teleport back to the prom where I found Dudley and asked for his

256

help. I figured since you were taken captive, that me outing him as a Sector wasn't going to affect you."

A shiver runs through me just imagining how desperate he must have felt to go to Marshall for help.

He nods as if he could read my thoughts. "He was in the middle of closing a chasm from the Transfer to get rid of 'the visitors,' as he dubbed them. He said they were floating spirits corrupting the imbalance between the living and the dead."

"The not-so-nice dead. Those were the souls from the Transfer that showed up that night."

"He dropped what he was doing and took off after Demetri. I waited for him at his house. When he got back, he said he spoke to your mother, and that the Decision Council was allowing this to happen. He mentioned Demetri had a treble open, so we would be seeing you soon. But I didn't think it would be soon enough."

"How did you know to get me?"

"I wrestled that bastard for hours before he agreed to break a rule."

"Marshall broke a rule?" I'm shocked by this.

He nods. "Said there'd be hell to pay, but you were worth it."

I take a breath at the thought. I can feel Marshall's love pour over me in the form of a floral-scented breeze. I watch the ocean lap over itself a good fifty feet from shore where the color blends a bright aqua marine.

"You wrestled for hours." The words float out of me soft and light like butterflies. "And then you rescued us." I lean into his chest and take in a deep cleansing breath. Gage pulls me in, surrounds me like an impermeable membrane with his pure intentions.

"I didn't know how long the treble would stay open. You could have been down there a year with him—ten." His jaw tightens.

I know he means Logan. Gage is openly plagued by Logan's undying devotion.

"So did you bring the baseball bat for him or Demetri?" I tug on his hand, playfully.

"In the vein of telling the truth"—he blinks a smile—"both."

"Gage." I wrap my arms around him and take in all of this knowledge, these truths that are more precious than silver or gold.

"Just before Brielle had the baby, I got a text saying Mia was in the mirror." He shrugs. "I couldn't leave, and it all started happening so fast. I couldn't do anything but help Brielle."

"You're a hero." I rock my shoulder into him.

"You know what I thought about the entire time?" He drops a kiss on top of my head as we continue our meandering stroll toward the water.

"How you'd never go to med school?" I tease.

"Nope." He pulls back to get a better look at me. The tropical sun reflects against his features with fiery glory. "You."

I'm not sure whether to be flattered or horrified. The thought of Brielle's privates warping in and out of shape makes me cringe. And that it should invoke any kind of imagery that has to do with me makes my stomach turn.

"When I held that tiny baby in my arms..." He blinks back tears. "Skyla, it really was a miracle." His dimples flex in and out as he bites down on his lip to keep his emotions in check. "I thought about the way I love you and how I can't wait for that moment to come for us. How intensely beautiful it will be just trying to get there."

A small laugh rumbles through him.

I take him in like this, soaking in the magic that surrounds us, the magic of his words. It's all so perfect in this moment. Almost too perfect and it makes me dizzy. It's like Chloe left her patina of distrust over our relationship, and now I'm afraid every moment with Gage will feel like we're tiptoeing through terrain blanketed with landmines.

I lean up and press a chaste kiss against his lips as the wind canonizes the moment with its warm resplendence. It cools the sun and its intense rays from our flesh if only for a moment.

"I see a future for us, Skyla. I can feel it."

My stomach tightens. Both Logan and Marshall expressed the same sentiment.

"Before we get too off track..." Gage pauses at the waterline and turns to me. "I want to share the vision I had of Chloe, the reason I saved her at the dance."

"Go ahead." I'd rather we focus on our future, but Chloe is a fire that needs to be stomped out long before we get there. "Tell me."

"I'm not going to tell you." He dips down into me. "I'm going to show you."

Gage seals his lips over mine. He indulges in a kiss that defies time and space and gravity. My insides cycle in hot lust-filled bites, one eternal revolution after the other, and I never want this to end.

An image appears. Gage and I are standing in a well-lit room with no walls, no floor, no ceiling. I see myself hopping up and grabbing him by the shoulders, completely overcome with excitement.

"Yes," I shout, "don't ever let Chloe Bishop die, Gage! You hear me?" I rattle him by the shoulders to annunciate my point.

I pull back from the vision and give several hard blinks.

"Gage." I bite down on a smile. "How did you do that? How did you share a vision with me?"

259

"Marshall taught me a few tricks—verbally," he's quick to add.

"Wait a minute." I shake my head. "I would never say that." I was far too eager to keep Chloe alive. "I would never *not* want Chloe Bishop dead." I try to pull his hands off my waist, but they drip down slow as honey.

"It's true." His hands float back up above my hips. "Here, let me show you another—a more recent one." Gage dips down and hesitates as he waits for permission.

I give a brief nod. A tender ache sails through me as I wait for his lips. We succumb to a kiss that feeds the hunger in me that knotted up my intestines when I thought Gage was out of my life for good. I wish I could freeze this moment— open a treble and live conjoined at the mouth for an eternity.

The vision warbles in and out until the picture comes in clear. I'm in bed with warm limbs wrapped around mine. The walls, the door, the comforter, it all looks foreign and disorienting.

"Where are we?" I flex up on my elbows, trying to adjust to the dark.

"Come here." Gage emerges in a seam of pale blue moonlight. He jostles me by the knee as if to wake me up from my slumbering stupor. *"I'll remind you."* He lands a searing kiss over my lips—wet kisses that stream on forever. His body arches over mine, his chest relaxing soft against me.

"What are you doing?" I slap my hands against his chest in an effort to keep him from sticking the landing.

A peaceable smile comes over him. His dimples dig in deep, turning into twin black pools under the anemic stream of moonlight.

"You're my wife, Skyla." He dips a quick kiss to the tender skin below my ear. *"We do this all the time."* He pushes my knees apart with his and nestles his body over my hips. He lays over me with his weight. The singe of his skin against

mine sets me ablaze, and every inch of me detonates with pleasure.

I pull back from the vision and give a little laugh. It's the same dream I had in the tunnels the first night I was there.

"Gage!" I jump up and wrap my legs around his waist in a single bound. "I have you back. That vision was real." I peck a kiss over his cheek. "Everything about you is real."

I hold him tight and revel in the moment. The sunlight behind him reflects off the water, a glare so blinding it turns the palm trees and the hills that dip their toes in the ocean into gold-dusted shadows.

Gage tucks a kiss into my neck before retracting.

"You really believe me?" He beams a sad smile from every pore of his being.

"I really believe you."

We sink into a sea of soft kisses that last forever.

41

The Haunting

The warm air wraps around us in a balmy embrace. The tropical paradise beckons us to stay, to linger on its crystalline shore if only for a moment.

"We should get back," he whispers. "If your Mom's trying to call, she might get worried." Gage walks us to a thicket of palm trees to afford us the privacy we'll need to teleport.

"Only if you promise we'll visit again." I dip my hands under his T-shirt and ride up over the warmth of his skin.

"I'll bring you back every day if you want to." He initiates one of his killer grins. "I'll take you to Paris, Rome, Egypt. I'd go anywhere with you, Skyla."

My stomach cinches when he says Rome. Logan and I went there on our Count killing spree, the one that cost us a million penalty points in the faction war. And apparently it cost nothing to the Counts we supposedly offed because they've all most likely been resurrected by now.

"Let's get back to Seattle." I graze the skin just below his shoulders soft with my nails. "But I'm holding you to Paris."

He dips in with a kiss, and the world disintegrates around us, takes the tropics, its magical breeze and hypnotic sweet air with it.

Gage blinks us into a spacious room, double beds, with an oversized patio that looks out at the Space Needle. A series of islands sit out in the distance like the disconnected pieces of a puzzle, one of which is Paragon. I step over and press my hand against the frozen glass. Nothing but an ominous expanse overhead, carbine clouds bubbling to create the perfect storm.

"Where exactly are we?" I mean, I know we're in Seattle. I'm delighted to be anywhere but the Landon attic at a time when Chloe Bishop was the queen of the scene.

"Avenue Drive Hotel—luxury suite." He gives a wicked grin.

"Gage!" I bounce with excitement. "This is so not going to be funny if we get caught."

"We won't," he assures, making his way over and wrapping his hands around my waist.

"And you know this because?" I lean into his chest. My entire body aches to crush against him.

"Because the hotel no longer rents this room out."

"Oh?" I glance around. Everything looks impossibly clean. "So why's that?" It's probably reserved for staff meetings or dignitaries.

"It's haunted," he says it as fact.

Or that.

"Shit," I say, plucking his arms off my waist. "You really must not like me. You know what I hate more than clowns? Ghosts!"

"You're the ghost, Skyla," he informs with an ever-blooming smile. "We both are. And, I swear, I don't hate you."

Crap. I knew this was a ruse. He and Chloe have finally figured out a way to off me, and now I'm forever doomed to some hotel suite in Seattle that I'll never have the privilege to haunt properly because they never freaking use it.

"Levatio has this thing," he says, gazing past me at the scenery a moment. "They wanted free stay at certain locations, so they had a little fun with people, and now pretty much every hotel has a haunted room on the thirteenth floor, except for when the builder decides to skip that number." He blooms a naughty smile.

I drop my gaze in disappointment.

"Hey..." He runs his finger under my chin and lifts me gently. "What's the matter?"

"I..." It's probably not the best time to go there, but I can feel the words rising out of me like vomit. "For a brief second, I doubted you again." I shake my head in lieu of an apology.

"It's OK." He pulls me in. I can feel his heart charging against my chest like a bull bucking its way out of the gate. "We'll get back on track, it just takes time."

"So what's the hotel room for?" I bite down on a smile that never comes.

"It's full of privacy." He plops down on the bed as his lids hood over his eyes. "Perfect place to *talk*."

"Very funny." I hop on the opposite bed. "How much more is there to say?" I can feel his love for me, his genuine feelings alive and well. Chloe tried to muzzle my affection for him, but it grew in his absence, magnified over my lust until it burned like a fire.

Gage comes over. He holds his hands out in surrender as he slides in beside me.

"I missed you." I catch one of his hands in the air and bring it to my lips. "You remember that day at Cain River when we went for a walk? You said you were jealous for me. I thought about it for a long time. It stuck in my mind." I trace his lips, the hard ridge of his cheek, before dusting the pad of my finger over his eyebrow. "I get it now. When I thought I'd never have you again. I felt that strong ache, that deep gut-wrenching heartbreak that made me wish you were who I thought you were." I pull him in until our noses almost touch. "I was jealous for you, but not with rage, with passion. I felt like we belonged. That this was our time. Chloe wanted to cheat us out of it. She'd kill for you." An image of her carrying that head quickens in me, but I force the thought away. "I won't let Chloe steal another moment of our time."

Somehow, someway, I just know we're destined to be together. Logan's words resonate in the back of my mind—even he verbalized the fact this was my time with Gage, whatever that means. Nevertheless, it justifies the actions I'm set on taking before I ever initiate them. This is our time, Gage and me. My mother doesn't make mistakes. She puts the exact people in my path that need to be there. This love—this moment—has been ordained by God himself.

I get on my knees and pull off his shirt. Even in this dim light, Gage draws an illumination. The reserve of day mists the room in a deep ethereal blue just this side of ebony.

My hands glide like a bird in flight over his bare chest. Gage pulls me down to the bed and trails blazing kisses over my mouth, my neck, my chest. My shirt flies off; the button to my jeans comes undone. We are all hands, tugging and pulling until all that's left is my bra and underwear, Gage with his jeans open in front, his hard protrusion pressed anxious against my thigh.

We come alive in a hotbed of lust. Gage and his affection move through me, radiating heat from our spontaneous combustion. He unhooks my bra, slips his hand into the back of my underwear, rounds out the curves and groans. I gasp as he holds me there, and my head rolls back with pleasure.

An urgency erupts, an explosion racks through my body. Gage runs one continuous kiss from my lips to my shoulder, moving lower and I quiver with anticipation.

I give his jeans one good yank until I can feel the bare skin of his thigh over mine.

The bed trembles.

The ceiling spins, rotates like a helicopter blade until it's replaced with a lavender sky.

The faction war—region five.

42

Field of Fire

A pale light glides through the dim night sky. It creates the illusion of a very long tail as it splices the deep velvet. The scent of sulfur fills my nostrils and lines my tongue like oil. There's a black forest to my left and a dusty clearing straight ahead, a granite hillside with a few sparse evergreens just beyond that.

It takes a moment for me to realize the fireball up above is headed right for me. I get up and run full sprint behind a pile of debris in a clearing.

The ground beneath me feels soggy and sticky—cold to the touch. I glance down at my bare feet, and take in a breath at my severe case of undress. I'm in nothing but my bikini briefs, my pink lace bra unhitched in the back. No clothes, and no shoes, and most importantly, no lifesaving disc.

Shit.

I duck down behind a pile of logs strewn on top of one another as if a giant had chopped up a small forest to ignite a bonfire. It takes me three tries to clasp my bra. I spot Ellis dashing into the woods to my left and I shrill his name out like a cat on fire.

He peers out at me from between the trunks of two noble firs as the landscape rumbles. A plume of dust explodes to my left as the ground rattles. The fresh rise of smoke infiltrates the vicinity. His eyes glint in my direction, and I wave him over.

"What the hell?" he shouts, skidding on his knees beside me. "New strategy to distract the enemy?" He gawks at my lack of clothing before emitting a dirty grin. "I like your style, Messenger."

"Give me your pants," I shout over the scorching wind. My hair flies rampant and wild like a blaze.

Ellis doesn't think twice. He jumps out of his jeans so fast you would think he were about to get lucky. He doesn't think that, right?

He whips off his T-shirt and helps pull it over me, still warm and holding the scent from his skin. I step into his jeans and roll the waistband three times to secure them.

"Thank you!" I lean up and hug him. Not only is Ellis willing to fight for me, but the fact he's doing so in his boxers is a testament of his devotion. "I owe you big time."

"I'll be sure to collect," he says, picking up my hand and glancing out into the field where a few men wander about. "Where's Gage?"

"I don't know." The last thing I remember was the heat rising in that hotel room. It was going to be *our* hotel room, the one from his vision a few months back, but my mother threw us into the faction war, securing the fact her daughter's virginity lives to see another day.

"You don't have shoes." Ellis gapes as though I were thoughtless to arrive in hostile enemy territory without the proper accouterments.

"I'm fine," I say, before he has a chance to pluck off his sneakers.

A surge of bodies infiltrate the area. My heart fills with dread as they jog up ahead, holding out long black rifles with what looks like bayonets embedded into the tips.

"Shit," I hiss, trying to pull Ellis to the side. A familiar-looking boy smiles openly at me. He breaks free from the crowd to come over, and I recognize him from the last region. It's Cooper.

He pants through a short-lived smile. "There's an enclave of Counts migrating to the west of the forest. You have about five minutes," he says out of breath. "This your friend?" He nods over at Ellis.

"Cooper, this is Ellis," I say.

"Cooper Flanders." He gives a quick nod. He examines Ellis with a puzzled look. Boxers aren't exactly the right attire for a war, especially when that's all you're wearing. "What weapons do you have?"

"What's it to you?" Ellis expands his chest like a chimp ready for an altercation.

"Relax, he's with Celestra," I say. "And, we don't have any weapons." Then it occurs to me, Gage is probably securing an entire arsenal right now.

Cooper leans in. "Let's get you something to protect yourself with." He places his hand gently on my elbow in an effort to get me to follow him, and Ellis steps between us.

"She has something to protect herself with—*me*. Get over there with your friends and we'll catch up."

Cooper winces at Ellis. I can tell he's not all that convinced of his power to protect me. "Suit yourself. We're circling around and planning an ambush. You have about two minutes before you're caught in the crossfire." He trots off and catches up with the last of the stragglers from his camp.

"Let's go." I try to yank him but he points down at the shoes he took off for me. His socks are muddied to the ankles.

"Those things are huge, Ellis. You have boat feet. I'll kill myself if I try to run in them."

An explosion rockets through the pile of tree trunks behind us. A rumble ignites, and the logs tumble violently in our direction. We turn to run just as a dark sheath of wood envelops us from behind. It crushes our backs with its violent momentum, efficiently pinning the both of us.

"Ellis?" It comes out weak, using the last reserves from my lungs.

His blond hair glows like an ember against the dark canvas splayed out around him. Two oversized trunks crisscross over his back as though they were perfectly placed to secure him.

"I'm OK," he groans. "Get Gage," he can barely get the words out. Ellis is a lot of things but OK is not one of them.

I squirm and wiggle until I free myself from under the debris.

"Give me your hand," I say, trying to push a log off him but it doesn't budge. I twist it until it rolls in the opposite direction. "There," I shout victoriously. Another trunk lies over his shoulders, and I push at it full force. Ellis lets out a groan that assures me it's a lousy idea to continue with the rescue effort.

"Shit," I seethe.

A strange light catches my attention. A flaming arrow, one, then three, then six—a multitude of them erupt over the horizon followed up by an entire throng of people—the Counts. They rain their fiery weapons over the sky and a few land in the pile of kindle that has Ellis trapped.

"No," I say, struggling to pluck off the log. I can feel the skin on my palm burn as needlelike splinters dig into my flesh—blood trickles to my elbow from the gash on my right hand.

The oversized nest we're trapped in lights up like a tinderbox. An inferno comes from nothing, and soon, the entire ethereal plane glows in an amber frenzy.

"Skyla, get out!" Ellis howls.

I glance up at the war raging in front of us. The Counts have paused from their revelry, surprised by the Celestra fighters converging on them from behind. Gage leads the assault, wielding a crossbow.

I give a labored groan as I push, channeling all of my anger toward Demetri and the Counts until the log over Ellis finally gives. An ember lands on my scalp, sending a sharp pain that begs for me to stomp it out. A wall of fire comes at the two of us—the heat sears over my flesh before the flames ever touch me.

"I got it." Ellis helps push the beam off and spins from underneath. He tackles me and rolls us over the muddied soil.

Gage comes in and swoops me up. He yanks Ellis to his feet with the strength of a lion before running us out into the open field away from the wall of flames. It's only then I notice my back was on fire, that Ellis's hair is singed on one side.

"You're bleeding." Gage pulls my hand forward. His face bleaches white at the sight of the crimson tracks running down my arm.

"It's just a cut. Where's the orator?"

"Haven't seen him."

"Hurt my fucking back." Ellis barely gets the words out as he straightens.

An arrow slices through the narrow gap between Gage and me.

We glance over at its origin and find Chloe and Nat elbow to elbow. Behind them, an entire mob of people enliven in a fury and most of those are cut and bleeding. I scan the area for Cooper.

Another arrow slices by.

Ellis pulls us to the ground, and we roll over to the giant inferno.

You know you're in deep shit when only a wall of fire can protect you. But not even the prehistoric danger of fire is enough to eliminate the threat of Chloe Bishop.

"Let's get to the woods." Gage darts a finger toward the murky shroud that lies behind the first few trees. "Ellis, go left." Gage shouts as if this were the football field.

Ellis breaks off and Gage scoops me into his arms. The fighting has dissipated, leaving the ground soaked in crimson, as injured bodies lie scattered around. How the hell are we supposed to know who's Celestra and who's not?

An explosion rockets to our left, detonating into a mushroom cloud of sulfuric gasses.

Gage jostles me through a veil of smoke so thick it strangles out any hope of taking a breath. It stings our eyes shut, rendering us blind in this heated mess. Gage trips and I sail out of his arms, landing with a thud, face-first, against a jagged rock.

"Shit," I whimper, touching the fresh cut on my cheek. I keep low to the ground where the smoke is thin and crawl until I hit the first set of pines.

I take in the frail air, choking on the fumes as I pan the vicinity for Gage or Ellis.

A hard slap ignites across my face as a stone depresses itself just below my left eye. Footsteps enliven the earth and I glance back to find Chloe thundering in this direction.

My knees buckle as I stagger to my bloodied feet. The whites of Chloe's eyes glint through the shadows. Her mouth is opened and laughing. I don't hang around for the Bishop show. Instead, I run like hell, deep in the thicket.

I have no Gage or Ellis or weaponry to help fight against the menace that is Chloe.

The only thing left is rage.

And I'm damn sure that's enough.

43

Killing Fields

Time stands still. The forest dampens with the sound of screaming, the thunder of warfare just beyond its borders. I can hear Chloe breathing as the faction war flares around us. She doesn't bother to soften her footsteps—just keeps barreling toward me.

My feet sting, my muscles ache. The air thins out. The long tendrils of smoke dissipate to nothing in this region of the woods.

"Come out, come out wherever you are," Chloe chants like a schoolgirl as if this were some innocent playground game. "I've got a treat for you." She taunts as though I were an animal. "Don't you want to know what it is?" Her voice is close enough to touch. Her breath curls in vapors around the fat trunk of a spruce.

I take a step back and trip over a branch, landing flat on my ass.

Shit.

Everything in me is on fire, my joints grind as I rise to my feet. I suck in a sharp breath as a cut pronounces itself under my right heel.

"Here you are." Chloe stains the shadows with her wicked frame. A silver chain dangles from her left hand. The protective hedge swings like a pendulum with its filigree, round as a silver dollar. The blue stone glitters in the center. "Shall we make a game of it? You can chase me, or I can toss it in the air and we'll see who catches it."

"I've already been taken by the Counts. It's no use to me."

"Oh, stupid, stupid Skyla," Chloe sings. "They can't take you anywhere, harm you, or siphon the blood out of you if you're wearing this. Don't you know any of the rules?"

I may not know the rules, but I damn well know Chloe. This is just another lasso she's luring me into.

I make my way past her, unable to take my eyes off her lunacy. Chloe and I have a history in a dark forest much like this one, and that scenario didn't end well for her in particular.

A fiery sting rakes up my leg with every step I take and I try to ignore it. Instead, I scan the landscape with my peripheral vision for Gage or Ellis but something tells me I should be looking for a stick to put Chloe's eye out with.

Chloe comes in close. She takes a step in toward me as if she's about to whisper in my ear, pinning my back against an evergreen in the process.

A line of pain rips through my thigh. I glance down to find a seam of blood erupting like a flare.

"*Oh*, I'm so sorry." A serrated knife with a curved blade takes up the space between us. "Did I knick you?" She gives it in a heated whisper as her aggression boils over. "It's sort of reminiscent of those long gashes you inflicted on me before you buried the spirit sword into my back." She steps into my chest. "Do you remember? You handed me over to Ezrina—you let the Counts have their way with me. I guess karma's a real bitch—isn't it, Skyla?"

"It should be *you* they're sucking dry." I shove her hard in the chest. "It should be you and *only* you in those tunnels. I don't get what vendetta you've had against me or my family before we ever set foot on Paragon, but I'm betting it has something to do with the fact you were rejected by more than just Gage."

Chloe winces as though I hit the "discard" nail on the head.

"Hit close to home, did I?" I hold back a laugh. "What I want to know is, who would be stupid enough to consider you in the first place."

Chloe ignites a slap across my already swollen cheek, and my lip splits down the center, leaving a seam of blood to salt my tongue.

"Maybe you should ask your mother, Skyla. Or doesn't she love you enough to let you in on all our faction-centered secrets?"

The ethereal plane shakes. The ground trembles in a violent earthquake. A loud tearing sound fills the thicket as tree roots rip straight from the soil. Chloe falls backward and sends her knife sailing to my feet.

I swipe the blade off the ground, my blood still slicked along the sides. The shaking ceases to a light rumble as I scan the area for the protective hedge.

"Right here." She waves it at me as if reading my mind.

A male voice cries out in pain from the clearing, and I recognize it distinctly as Logan.

"I could have you, Chloe." I take a step forward and jab at her stomach with the tip of the blade. "This knife could share our blood. Isn't that romantic?" I taunt while slicing a gash into the bottom of her shirt. Logan groans in the distance and splits my attention. "Right now, I'd rather save a friend," I say, speeding out of the woods.

"Skyla!" Logan shouts as I crest the edge of the tree line.

"I'm coming," I say, bolting over to him. Logan lies shirtless, his chest washed in crimson. His face is covered with soot; both his hands are cut and bleeding. "What happened?" I pant, examining the deep lacerations over his flesh. They make my wounds look like scratches from a kitten.

"Landed in a thorn bush," he says sarcastically while glancing back at a crowd of people draped with black vests as they make their way through the clearing. Heavy weaponry dangles from their hands. By the looks of their well-rationed artillery, they're most likely not Celestra.

But Logan is hurt and I doubt a thorn bush had anything to do with it. He has a hole just below his ribcage where an arrow had dug in, and a clean slice down the back of his shoulder that's gapping a good few inches, leaving the muscle exposed underneath. What hurts most is the people who inflicted these wounds were either Noster or Celestra. Everyone's bought into the fact that Logan is the enemy.

"Are you OK?" He pulls my hair back—leans in until his nose touches mine.

I nod as I bring my lips to his cheek. "You're here," I marvel.

"Are you kidding? Not even Ezrina could keep me away." He coughs. "Here, take this." He pulls a dull black gun out of his pocket. The barrel is round and fat. It looks slightly deformed, not real, like maybe he yanked it off a video game in the arcade. "Shoots darts loaded with toxins. It'll knock out an elephant for a good half hour—more than enough time to get you out of danger." *They can't see me with you,* he presses in a heated kiss against my temple. "I gotta go." He takes a step away and holds my hand as far as our fingers will allow before taking off beyond the thicket. Chloe calls after him and runs off in the same direction.

Arrows hail from the sky, dot the path thick with their long slender rods. Two opposing crowds clash in what looks like a mob scene. It looks all-out animal, a tangle of limbs, heartbreaking screams. This isn't right. None of this makes sense.

Nat catches my eye as she spears a man on the outskirts of the melee.

A frail girl, with long, stringy hair runs past me for cover in the forest. She eyes my gun and pauses.

"Don't just stand there. The Counts are killing Celestra." She pulls her words out in a strange manner, making them sound congested, contrived.

I take a breath and head over to the massive crowd. The heat of hatred lights up the landscape. I can smell the bite of perspiration, the metallic hint of blood rising in the air.

The mob pummels a pair of familiar-looking bodies to the ground.

"Oh my God."

Crap. They're beating Cooper and Flynn. A heavy-set man with steel toe boots gives the lanky boy, Flynn, a good kick in the teeth. They grind their faces into the dirt and shout for justice for their Countenance brothers. They follow their battle cry up by pounding their fists into the two of them.

If justice is what they want, that's what I'll give them.

I fire Logan's weapon into the crowd, nailing a half a dozen of them. They drop like flies, landing over one another in a satisfying heap.

I spring over and extricate Cooper first. He winces as he rises and helps up his friend.

"I owe you one," Flynn says as he tries to catch his breath. He's tall and a little gangly, but they both have gorgeous, cut features and eyes that glow against the sodden sky like polished stones.

"Yeah, well, next time," I say, heading back to the forest.

They come up alongside me as we make our way into the thicket.

"You knocked out a few of our own who were trying to help," Flynn says, dusting the dirt off his expensive looking pullover.

"Friendly fire," Cooper pats my shoulder as we move into the woods. "They'll be back on their feet in half the time as the Counts. You can't hold a good Celestra down." He winks.

"Let's hope not," I say. "I feel horrible. We should go back and pull them out."

We glance at the bodies still motionless on the ground. The fire still rages to the south where Ellis and I were pinned earlier. It congests the region with a layer of smoke, just enough singe our lungs, make us choke with every other breath.

The frail girl comes back, giving a greasy smile. She launches a missile off her shoulder, and the circle of men I put down goes up in flames.

"Shit!" I scream. "Celestra are there, too!"

"They're going to kill us anyway." Her pale eyes glare into mine with animalistic ferocity. "All of the Countenance must die."

Logan spears through my mind. Not all. Dear God, please not all.

The earth shivers, the moon and the lavender sky turn a strange ashen grey, and the ethereal plane melts into nothing.

44

Vertical Roughness

Gage and I appear back in the hotel suite locked in a rather compromising position with me wearing Ellis's clothes.

"Geez!" Gage hops off and switches on the lights. "You're cut head to foot."

"What happened? Did we win?" Hope surges in me for the first time.

"I don't know. I met up with Ellis again. He's pretty banged up. He's got a back injury for sure. I told him I'd have my dad stop by and look at him, but he needs to go the hospital." His features darken. "I saw Logan." His gives a long blink. "He told me what he was doing for you—for Ezrina."

"It wasn't my idea. I swear." Involving Ezrina in anything is like setting your roof on fire to warm the house.

Gage scoops me in his arms and winces at my wounds before brushing me with a kiss.

"There isn't anything we can't survive, Skyla. I promise you this." Gage gathers our things from around the bed. "I need to get you back to Paragon."

🦋 🦋 🦋

Gage delivers us right to my bedroom and starts the shower for me.

It stings like hell trying to clean these wounds. Just wetting them feels like a fresh laceration. I pray Dr. O doesn't have to whip out the sewing kit because my leg has been slashed straight up my thigh.

Afterward, Gage helps wrap my leg with a bandage then settles a kiss on top of the wet curls springing to life on my head.

"One day," he says, peppering my ear with kisses, "the vision we shared will come true, and there will be no one, or no war, no anything to interrupt us—just you and me, Skyla— all night long."

I give a naughty smile. My stomach tenses up at the idea of no war left to interrupt us—the war may not but Logan will. It's strange how I've accepted this season with Gage yet haven't bought into the future. I can't stand the thought of losing one of them for good. I guess that's the upside to the faction war. I have them both for a time—Logan won't accept me, and Gage won't let me go. I hate how greedy that sounds. They're both worth their weight in gold. "Hey, that reminds me." I retrieve the note I jotted down at Marshall's and tape it to the mirror above my desk.

"I'm as pure as gold." Gage reads.

"I had this dream. I think it was a vision. It was my dad. He said I needed to repeat that each day—that I should never forget it."

Gage warms me with a hug from behind as we look at the strange verse, trying to decipher what it might mean.

"I disagree with him." Gage sears a line down my neck with his lips. "You're much better than gold, Skyla."

I catch my reflection in the mirror. My eyes are swollen, my lip split in two, my right cheek rises from my skin like a red water balloon. Obviously Gage is talking about what's on the inside because, physically, there's not a whole lot I'm better than at this moment.

I spin into him and wrap my arms around his neck. "You're pure gold inside and out, Gage Oliver."

The door bursts open.

"Skyla?" Mom opens her mouth to say something then just continues to gape at the two of us as if she caught us gutting a litter of puppies. "Good *God!*"

Gage steps in front of me to cover my injuries, but it's too late. Mom makes a beeline in my direction.

"*Skyla,*" she gasps.

Tad rushes in like that's the code for all holy hell is about to break loose.

"What have you done?" Mom touches her hand to my cheek, and I wince in pain.

"Can't you tell?" Tad's entire body jerks as though the source of my injuries is painfully obvious. "He clobbered her."

"He did not." Mom doesn't hide her disgust with my step-moron.

"I would never lay a hand on Skyla." Gage refutes the accusation with a pissed off look that suggests he's not opposed to clobbering Tad.

"Nor did he." I try to emulate my mother's look of disgust, but my face finds it too painful to comply. "I fell."

"That's what they all say." Tad raises his head in suspicion.

"You fell?" Mom's eyes bulge, clearly she's not buying my version of the truth either.

"I fell down a flight of stairs as we got back on the ferry." I shrug. It seems reasonable. I mean they practically have you climbing down a ladder to get into that sardine can. It's completely plausible.

"We'll sue!" Tad's face springs to life at the prospect of a windfall.

"No—they were really nice about it." I shoot a look to Gage that suggests he should support my falsehoods with a few of his own.

"Why don't I get my dad to look at those for you?" Gage presses in a warm smile as he brushes the hair from my eyes.

"He's a mortician for crying out loud," Tad yelps. "What the hell is he going to do? Embalm her?" He whips the cell from his pocket and has me stand still while he snaps away at my swollen features. "I'll just take these pictures down to the Pacific West Boat Lines main office tomorrow and see how fast they pull out their checkbook. They hate lawsuits. It's cheaper to do a payout right there in the office. I'm betting on at least ten grand."

"Tad!" Mom looks mortified by his get-rich-quick scheme.

"We can remodel the kitchen, Lizbeth." It comes out more of a threat than a tantalizing proposition.

The idea of new cabinetry silences my mother into submission.

"I'm fine, really." God—Tad is going to cause all kinds of trouble over something that never even happened. "It was slippery. Ten different people took a tumble." That's right. I sigh. Nothing like another lie to try and rectify the first. That always works.

"Perfect!" He beams. "We just need to contact those passengers, and we'll threaten 'em with a civil action suit. They'll throw the entire safe in our direction."

"You mean class action." Gage makes the egregious error of trying to correct Tad in his moronic state of agitation.

"No, I mean *civil* action." Tad asserts the fact his legal knowledge is a force to be reckoned with. God knows he's logged enough hours to earn his YouTube degree. He's forever goofing off at his laptop—amusing himself with talking cats and crazy people who read their freshly-penned manifestos. "Say"—Tad's eyes pop with an epiphany—"why don't you come down with me as an eye witness. I'll give you kids a portion of the take. A nice crisp twenty so you can go out to dinner and a movie."

Shit. Tad is going to get Gage inadvertently thrown in jail for perjury. I can see it coming a mile away. Gage has more than served enough time thanks to me and my light driving debacles. There's no way I'm going to let him rot in a cell in this dimension, too.

"OK," I shout, slicing my arms through the air like a referee. "That's not exactly how it went down."

"Knew it." Tad grimaces like he just got a bad taste in his mouth. "The linebacker knocked her around."

"Actually..." I look to Gage. I'm certainly not going to let them think he beats me. "We were locked in one of the luggage compartments, and I tripped over a bag—head first." And this is what I opt for as a more realistic fabrication? Do they even have a luggage compartment?

"Luggage?" Mom narrows her gaze on me. "What were you two doing in a dark service closet?"

"Brushing up on their math skills," Tad says, while deleting the pictures off his phone in haste. "What do you think, Lizbeth? They were playing a game of vertical skin tag. That, Lizbeth," he says, pointing at my face, "is nothing more than the end result of rough sex."

I gasp. First, Gage would never be rough with me and second, there's a spirit in the sky that ensured the aforementioned activity did not take place.

"There was no vertical skin tag." I can't even bring myself to say the word "sex" around Mom and Tad—possibly not even Gage.

"OK, then," he barks, "vertical fiesta, vertical body planking, call it what you like. You're not leaving this house the rest of this summer."

"That's ridiculous," I balk. "Drake and Brielle practically made that baby under this roof, and Ethan has a bona fide sex slave hostage in his bedroom." Gah—I just said sex! Run and hide! Run and hide!

"Drake and Brielle are off limits, too," Tad seethes. "No more of this spending the night baloney. One invisible grandchild is enough. And, as for Ethan, he's made a very shrewd business decision and brought in a boarder." He stalks off before I can shoot down any of his claims.

I shake my head in disbelief.

"Sorry," Mom whispers. "Gage you're welcome to stay for dinner."

The only thing she should be sorry about is the vertical funeral she dared to commit twice. In fact, I'm pretty sure being married to Tad is enough to drive someone to a funeral of their own.

"Actually," Gage starts, "my parents invited Skyla to dinner. We're going over plans for Logan's birthday—it's two weeks away."

"Of course." Mom leans in and pats the skin below my eye. "Don't stay out late." She gives a distressed look from me to Gage before stepping in close. "I hope to God the two of you are using protection."

"Oh, there's no need." I shake my head furtively before the conversation lands us in that cringe-worthy place that has my mother espousing uncomfortable sexual adages.

"Making love rarely involves a bandage," Mom says it as a fact. "This isn't the football field, Gage." She glowers at him a second before leaving the room.

I'm so exhausted and mortified from the exchange, I forget to exhale.

"Is it really Logan's birthday in two weeks?" I had completely forgotten it was coming up.

"July twenty-first." Gage pushes in with a dark expression. "Will he be around to celebrate?"

I wish I knew the answer to that myself.

45

A Stitch in Time

The Oliver's home holds the heavenly scent of cinnamon and apples, an undeniable feast for the senses.

Turns out we've missed dinner, but thanks to Emma's spontaneous urge to turn the kitchen into a bakery, we'll more than make up for it with the sugar and carb fest that's about to commence.

"This is magnificent," Marshall says, after taking his first bite. He wands the fork in the air as if composing a symphony. "You must share the recipe with me."

Emma chortles. "I hardly believe a Sector of your stature has the time to play in the kitchen." She gives a coy smile, and I do believe there is some primitive form of flirting taking place.

Dr. Oliver sits beside me at the breakfast table and threads a large needle that holds the shape of a letter C.

"You should heal by morning," he assures. "But let's button you up to ensure infection doesn't set in. No reason your blood supply should have to work any harder than it already is. How have you been feeling otherwise?" he asks, jabbing the tip into my flesh, causing my skin to rise unnaturally.

I lurch alive with pain.

"Marshall?" I hold out a hand. No reason he shouldn't spare me from the torment.

"I gather Skyla is feeling vacated of any victories," Marshall answers for me as he takes up my hand. "Region five was a fail. We've just about lost half the war." His good mood dissipates as soon as the war comes to mind.

"It's not Skyla's fault." Gage folds his arms tight across his chest not bothering to hide the fact he disapproves of having a *Sector of his stature* in his presence—comforting his girlfriend no less.

"Who shall we blame?" Marshall booms. "You?"

"Blame whoever the hell felt the need to launch a war to begin with," Gage fires back. "By the way, we're all out of discs."

"I wouldn't give you a disc if you groveled and offered to lick the barn clean in an effort to retrieve one. You've squandered them, thank you very much—made me look bad." He pouts a little when he says it and just the mention of the disc has me disconnecting from Marshall's voyeuristic grip.

I slouch in my seat and tuck the smooth flat disc Demetri gave me deeper into my pocket. There is no way I'm ever going to be without it again.

"So, Logan's birthday is coming up," I say, trying to change the subject. It's not until I open my mouth do I realize I threw us out of the frying pan of one heated conversation and into the furnace of another.

"Have you seen him? Is he all right?" Emma stops kneading the dough in front of her and holds out the rolling pin with concern. The better to clobber me with, I'm sure.

"Oh, he's fine." I shoot Gage a look that threatens to slit his throat with my teeth should the truth somehow spew out. "He's taking a little vacation." God—I'm lying to the Olivers now. Obviously my dishonesty knows no bounds.

Where is he? Marshall insists, picking up my hand once again.

He's busy.

Busy? Marshall gives a disbelieving huff. *Your mother has requested your presence this evening. I suppose when I discover the origins of 'busy', it will end the mystery as to her urgency.*

"Skyla." Dr. Oliver snips the thread off and ties a knot close to my skin. "It's clear you know more than you're letting on." He softens. "You're like a daughter to Emma and me. We expect the truth from you." He looks at me from over his glasses—makes me feel two inches tall, caught in a hotbed of lies.

Something about the way he said I was like a *daughter* warms me. The Olivers have felt like family since I met them a year ago. Even Giselle, who really is their daughter and just so happens to be dead, feels very much like family.

"OK." I close my eyes a moment. "There may have been a little hiccup in an agreement he made with a certain somebody in an effort to keep me safe." There. Telling the truth isn't so bad.

"Who was this somebody, and what was the agreement?" Marshall sharpens his tone. There's a fire smoldering in his eyes like he already knows where this might be headed.

"Ezrina," I say in the smallest voice possible.

The three of them sag at once.

I make my way over to Gage, mostly for protection.

"What's the agreement?" Dr. Oliver persists.

"It may have had something to do with his dreams." I'm afraid to go on.

"Has Logan been utilizing his dream capabilities?" Emma looks astounded. "He can hardly function the next day. It zaps all his energy."

"He's letting that hag toy with the bird, isn't he?" Marshall picks up a chair, only to smash it against the floor. It splinters into a dozen angry pieces and the entire lot of us just stand there, gaping at him.

"It may have happened a couple of times," I whisper.

"Once was enough to seal his fate." Marshall zeros in on me with his steely gaze. "Say you had no part in this, Skyla."

I open my mouth to parrot back the words but they won't come. Technically, I was present the first time, and Nev did insist I declare them legally joined in matrimonial bliss so I may have played some tiny part.

"Skyla," Emma says my name in broken disappointment.

"What does this mean?" Dr. Oliver asks.

Gage secures his arms around my waist and pulls me in, and yet, it still feels like things are moving way too fast—as if I'm about to burst through the windshield of life and come out bloodied and bruised on the flesh deficient side of existence.

"It means," Marshall growls, "Skyla here has just committed a breach of faith with the Justice Alliance." Marshall pushes out a hard breath. "It makes perfect sense why they've called her to court."

"Because they're going to scold me?" Best case scenario.

"No, love," Marshall simmers, "because they're going to punish you."

"I'm going with her." Gage declares like he's not taking no for an answer.

"Very well," Marshall concedes, "we'll see you there."

He damn well knows Gage can't get there on his own.

Marshall takes up my hand, and the two of us disappear.

46

Petition for Mercy

The scenery changes. I tense up, half expecting to see my mother and the other celestial lunatics hurling brimstone in my direction, but I don't. I see Marshall's cavernous living room, and I let out a deep breath.

"Thank you," I say. I need to get on Marshall's good side and fast.

"For?" He flattens his palms against the heavily lacquered piano and stares into his rather pissed off reflection.

"You know—not taking me to my mother's. It's not like she can force me to show up."

"She can and she will."

"What's she going to do, send a clown Fem after me? A pack of wild wolves?"

"No, Skyla. She sent me. I'm to bring you. We have less than five minutes, so let's roll some ideas around before the only thing rolling is your newly severed head."

An image of Chloe and her jaunt in the forest resurrects itself in my mind. That would be the ultimate punishment, hacking off my head and giving it to Chloe to use as field practice.

"You're to tell her you knew nothing about the Pretty One's actions until it was too late," he instructs.

"Done." And true, might I add.

"Tell her you're adverse to the Transfer, and the thought of that sea hag makes your skin crawl."

"Perfectly worded." I placate him with a smile.

"Let her know you approve of whatever punishment she deems fit to give the perpetrator who dared revoke their retribution to society." He jabs his finger hard in the air. "And you demand she ban the Oliver in question from your life forever."

I shoot Marshall a look. He knows damn well I'd never say those things about Logan.

"I thought so." He breathes his discontent.

"I heard a rumor you broke a rule for me." I bite down on my lip as Marshall perks to attention. "You told Gage how to get to the tunnels."

"It was a one way ticket—one time use. He's lucky he came back alive."

The thought of Gage giving his life to rescue me lends a powerful attraction to him, but then Marshall broke a rule. That's a pearl of great price.

"So what happens? You know, to *you*." I lay my hand over his back.

"I've but three errors to make, and I've generously made my fourth on your behalf. There's a good chance she'll end my stay here on the island—or worse."

"No." I shake my head vehemently. "I won't let her. You're always there for me. You're better than she is in every way because you care about me infinitely more than she ever could."

The room swelters. Heat rises in waves, melts the walls—the furniture pulses in and out like fumes penetrating the air.

"You do realize she listens." Marshall's voice comes in clear as we begin to disintegrate.

"Good. I plan on giving her an earful," I say.

"So much for strategy."

🦋 🦋 🦋

The plush violet sky above Ahava is illuminated with a nonstop nest of lightning, slightly reminiscent of the stone of sacrifice the night Chloe arranged for the Counts to take me. The same night Gage walked through an electrical current on my behalf. I should have known then his intentions were to never hurt me.

My mother sits on her invisible throne with Rothello dutifully next to her and the Marshall twins decorating each side like a set of stunning bookends. Rothello wears his dark hair past his shoulders. He's missing one eye because my favorite Sector yanked it out of his head and gifted it to Chloe in order to impress me. It might have impressed me a little. What impresses me more is that he's broken his fourth rule for me. What in the hell is he thinking, anyway?

A hard clap of thunder explodes overhead. My mother in all of her ethereal beauty seethes in my direction. Her hair blows back dramatically as if it's trying to escape its follicular capture and sail right off her head in fright.

God—even the hair on her head is afraid of her. But it's her eyes, those cold steel lasers that burn through my skull that assure me I really fucked up good this time.

"Marshall," I whisper, "I'm afraid."

"Be afraid."

I give a wry smile. Surely he could use his seductive reasoning skills to harness her estrogen and get her off my back for a while—like a lifetime would be nice.

A bolt of lightning refracts over the sapphire floor and Logan materializes, then Ezrina and Nev in tandem, both in their altered, cursed state of being.

Shit.

This is not going to end well.

My mother looks to the left, inspiring all heads to follow suit, including mine, which, by the way is still happily attached to my neck.

It's Gage!

He comes over and takes up my hand. Giselle waves from the side and takes a seat on the grassy knoll behind me.

"Well," my mother says, picking up her chin and staring down at the lot of us. She inspects us as if a bunch of maggots just sprouted before her, "since there are so many, I don't see the harm of including one more." She lifts a finger with little effort, and my father appears from nowhere.

"*Daddy,*" I shriek as I run out to tackle him.

He lunges into me and gives me a spin, kissing the top of my head like mad.

"Skyla?" He cradles my face in his hands before dotting a kiss on my nose. "How did this happen? Why is she here?" He says it sharp to my mother.

"Calm yourself, Nathan. She's not dead—yet." She directs us back to the crowd that anticipates her wrath in acres.

"Are you in court?" My father's concern blooms like a mushroom cloud. "Skyla, no," he whispers, shaking his head. His face bleeds out all color, and I'm pretty sure it's a bad sign considering he's been dead for a good long while.

My mother sounds a ruby gavel. "Let us refresh ourselves regarding the case of Ezrina MacAtter and Heathcliff O'Hare." She sorts through a stack of velum papers with glowing letters that crawl along like an army of ants. They shift and rearrange themselves on the page as if to inform her of new things once she reads the old. "Ezrina, you fought against the wishes of the Faction Council and slaughtered two hundred forty-two Countenance soldiers. Is that correct?"

"Is." Ezrina gives a slight courtesy, as if she were proud.

I wouldn't go bragging, if I were her.

"Heathcliff." My mother licks a finger before flipping a page in the illuminated legal documents spread out before her. Nevermore flies up and lands on my shoulder, as if to afford a better view. "You assisted in this vigilante behavior

291

and added the souls of five hundred fifty-two of your own brothers."

"This too is true." Nev's voice comes from his beak, and this unnerves me.

Oh, my freaking gosh, Nev and Ezrina undertook a Countenance massacre. They're practically heroes in my book. They're like the demigods of earth-bound justice, or titans of taking out the trash—forget the Justice Alliance or the Faction Council—Ezrina, Nev, and I should team up and form the Butcher Brigade—restore a little order by way of street justice. Ezrina sounds just as ticked at the Counts as I am, and, after all, revenge is personal.

She gives a menacing looking my direction. Her burnt orange hair rises like flames against the pale blue expanse.

"We can hear you, love." Marshall dips into my mother as if he were speaking to her.

"Skyla." My mother's voice resonates throughout this strange dimensional plane. The water in the lake below vibrates in oscillating ripples. "You and Logan have already replicated their misguided depravity."

"Depravity?" I balk.

"Not now," Marshall, whispers.

"Yes, now," I say, stepping forward, causing Nev to flee from me to Gage. "Do you realize they burn my people alive as a permanent means of taking them off the planet? If I remember correctly, you were one of them. And what about the tunnels?" I spin around to look at my father. "Which, by the way, I am privy to because the Counts have *captured* me."

"What?" He looks up at my mother disbelieving. "Candace? Is this true?"

"Of course, it is," I say, "I wouldn't lie." Not to him anyway.

My mother lifts her head and takes a breath, acknowledging the malfeasance against her own flesh and blood with a solid span of silence.

"It's torment down there," I continue. "It's a living hell, and yes, *Mother,* I would most certainly say it falls under the category of depravity. Let me guess. I'm supposed to stick it out and take it up the tailpipe because you and your destination reputation are at stake." Her face puckers. "You sit up here, high and mighty, and pretend you know exactly how this is going to pan out, when in reality it's all out of your fucking control."

An eerie silence stops up my ears. The waterfalls in the distance have hushed themselves—the lake, the breeze, nothing moves.

"Are you finished?" She offers a peaceable smile.

Logan and Gage both shoot me a look that suggests I'm very much done in more ways than one.

Am I? I'm pretty sure I have a rather long list of grievances I'd love to shout in her face, in front of her henchmen and my father, but, unfortunately, nothing else comes to mind.

"For now," I say.

"Good." She folds her hands in front of her. "We dole out the punishments." She fans her hands out at those seated beside her. "We follow principles of behavior. We take verbal contracts seriously to the point of death, and we set in motion an entire list of rules for those of you dwelling on Earth to abide by, one of which is to obey authority—and for the Nephil kingdom that translates to the Faction Council. Rules are in place to enforce order. And you, Skyla and Logan—like Ezrina and Heathcliff, broke them. I've already made this clear to you once before."

I take in a breath and let it fill my chest until it feels as though my lungs might burst. It's like talking to a wall, chasing my tail. It's completely useless trying to convey to her why it's so important to stop the Counts.

"I understand the danger you're in, Skyla," she says, acknowledging my thoughts. "I understand how important it is that the Sectors rule the day and that Celestra hold the night. I did not take the task lightly when I set foot on Earth to bear you."

Marshall leans in and whispers, "By day she means the heavenly realm and by night, the Earth."

"Did you love my father, or were you using him?" I ask, never wavering my gaze from her.

A gasp is heard in the distance from where Giselle is seated.

Logan rests his hand over mine and gives a squeeze that begs me to stop.

"Please, excuse my future bride." Marshall slits the air with his attempt at moderation. "She's still reeling from a rather nasty blow to the head she procured during an altercation in region five."

"Which, by the way, was not secured." Rothello, the one-eyed tattletale, is quick to highlight my recent failure.

"Your future bride is out of control." My mother doesn't bother hiding the fact she's irritated.

Gage glances over when she refers to me as Marshall's future bride.

My father steps forward. "What's this future bride business?" Dad looks wild-eyed from me to my mother. "Marshall? The Sector?" He looks right at him. "Is that why you chose me as your mentor? Because you had some ulterior motive with my daughter?"

That's right. Marshall once mentioned that my father was his mentor. I've wondered what that was about myself.

"With heaven's sanction, I will marry your daughter." Marshall gives a nod in Dad's direction.

"Personally." My mother digs a smile into the side of her cheek. "I'm rooting for Logan."

47

Team Logan

Logan produces a grin that suggests he's the cat that ate the canary, and suddenly I'm feeling rather canary-ish.

We're standing on the sapphire floor just below the lake in Ahava while the fab four frown down on the fact my mother ever gave birth to me.

My mother—in front of my father, Gage, Logan, Marshall, Ezrina, and Nev—just openly declared herself team Logan.

"What about Gage?" I glance at his perfection. I thought my mother set them in my life as equal opportunity suitors. None of this makes sense. Besides, Gage is an ideal physical specimen who most likely just had his feelings hurt. But she wouldn't know that because apparently she has none of her own.

"What about *me*?" Marshall queries with his finger jabbed into his chest.

"Nevertheless, I know the conclusion of each of your stories," she says it banal as though at the end of the day this conversation holds no more weight than table salt. "Logan," she pauses, "do you remember me?" She tilts her head and tries to ignite in him a memory through her eyes.

"From my time in the Transfer?" Logan is clearly perplexed by my mother's head games.

"No, not then—from before." She calls him forward with the flick of her finger.

Oh, dear God, she's going to do something insane like join us in holy matrimony right here in her legal chambers, which I'm positive will involve some lifelong, binding covenant. Not that I'm opposed to marrying Logan, just not at seventeen.

"Marriage does involve a covenant, Skyla." She looks over Logan's shoulder at me. "Of which carnal relations are a very intimate, yet important factor. Do you realize that the Master has very strong feelings about sexual purity?"

I have a feeling Lizbeth Landon is about to be bested when it comes to mortifying her daughter.

"I noted on several occasions that you and *Gage*"—she says his name like it's a sexually transmitted disease—"have come very close to uniting yourselves on a spiritual level you know nothing about."

Whew! For a second there I thought we were talking about S-E-X.

"The topic at hand *is* premarital sex," she spews, "that and the fact you've just about delved into scalding waters that would have landed the two of you in a binding unity. And you didn't even have protection with you for God's sake!"

"Skyla!" My father bellows his disapproval.

Shit.

"Gage." My mother bears her fangs in his direction. "Do you love my daughter?" Her face crimps as she freezes him out with her glacial stare.

"Very much." Gage takes up my hand and kisses it.

Her eyes enlarge at his apparent audacity. "Do refrain from fondling her in the presence of myself and her father. Have a little respect," she spits out the words.

Gage drops my hand, cold, as if it were a rattlesnake.

She clears her throat. "I demand you take a proactive stance and restrain yourself when in her company. Do you understand?"

Gage gives a furtive nod.

"You're to care for her in an absolute chaste manner." My mother persists. "As though she were your sister."

I give a sorrowful look up at Gage. I can't imagine a lousier time for him to have shown up. I'm pretty sure he wasn't gunning for a new sibling when he resolved to come here.

"Like my sister." There's a note of sarcasm in his voice. "Got it."

"Good." She gives a satisfied smile. "Skyla, your father and I are coming to Paragon. Does this please you?"

"As in my dead father—?"

She cuts me off. "Yes, Skyla, the one who stands before you." She sharpens her gaze at Marshall. "You'll prepare a room for us."

A room? As in singular? Speaking of carnal relations.

"We were joined in holy matrimony." She afflicts me with a scorching look. "We can delight in our flesh all we desire," she says, honing in on my thoughts.

Um, eww? And by the way it totally feels like Dad is about to cheat on Mom, and I'm not talking about this one.

"Nonsense. We're both dead." My mother laughs. "As far as the punishment goes for assisting Heathcliff and Ezrina, it will be cast down to both you and Logan once the war concludes. Heathcliff and Ezrina, this little stunt will be held as further evidence against you once the new trial commences. Now, be gone, I've business to tend to with Logan." She flicks her fingers at the lot of us, and we all disappear.

"She is *insane*," I scream, standing in the middle of Marshall's living room.

He stabs a finger in the direction of the fireplace, and it roars to life in one giant blaze.

"Of course, she's insane. That would be your genealogy by the way." Marshall points to the ceiling, and the lights dim, music filters in through the air. He holds out a hand, and I absentmindedly take it.

"She just basically declared open season on my vagina," I say, leaning into Marshall's chest as we begin to slow dance. "I mean, one conjugal visit, and we're as good as married?"

"It needs to be consensual." He insists. "Of course, the bride price still needs to be paid, but these days, all that amounts to is a clerical fee at the county courthouse," Marshall rambles.

"That was so freaking embarrassing. What's next? Some triple-X video on how babies are made?" I seethe. "In front of my *father* no less?"

"Oh dear, I pray not. Why don't we head upstairs and I give you a step-by-step demonstration. We can avoid the entire fiasco."

"Very not funny. And, by the way, don't think for a minute I'm not onto you." I rattle his hand in the air.

"What you're saying is, you are very much aware of the fact I'm attempting to woo you," he muses.

"That I am." I sigh, closing my eyes a moment because I'm so unbelievably exhausted. "You feel good, and I'm short on fight at the moment."

"I don't believe you." His chest rumbles with a thin rail of laughter.

"OK, I like you. I like the way you make me feel. I like having you in my life. I don't know why. I haven't figured this out yet." True story.

"Perhaps because I'm so unbelievably attractive I'm fit to be tied—I have a four-poster bed should the need arise. I'm quite eager to return the favor should you feel inspired."

"Wow, that's quite an invitation." I don't bother opening my eyes. Nothing about his sexual banter surprises me anymore.

"Bored you already, have I?" He huffs. "Every day, every night would be a new experience with me by your side. I promise you consistency, my undying affection, sparkling conversations, the intimacy behind closed doors, open doors, wooded areas, bodies of water, and what I presume will be a favorite—the barn."

"The barn?" Just the thought of all that hay needling in inappropriate places assures me Marshall's perception of romance is slightly askew.

"Very well, we'll nix the barn... for now."

I slap his chest playfully. "You belong in a barn. I belong with..." I pause, thinking about what kind of mindboggling strategies my mother might be going over with Logan right this very moment. I bet she's whipping out diagrams for him like some football playbook. I can envision him trying to maneuver around Marshall and Gage with me as the ball.

"Nonsense." Marshall scoffs, giving my hand a gentle squeeze. "I'm in control of this ballgame. Delphinius has assured me as much. He's eager to speak with you at the next faction meeting."

"Excellent. I have some choice words for him as well."

"There will be no slandering of celestial beings. I've warned you on countless occasions."

"If said celestial being weren't spreading celestial rumors, perhaps I wouldn't be moved to wrench celestial balls."

"Delphinius is an orator, Skyla. Once he affirmed the fact you were to be my wife, it was etched in stone."

"Maybe he meant in the next life. You know, the *after*life?" I can almost buy that.

"Not so, there are two covenants that cease to exist in the Master's Kingdom—death and marriage."

"What an appropriate pairing," I muse.

"He thought so."

I lean my head against Marshall's chest and feel the soothing hum repair the broken blood vessels around my eyes—my bones sing a song with their marrow. I love the way this feels. Marshall is a balm, a midnight sun in the cruel world of my mother and her cohorts. If only all spiritual beings were as loving and kind as he was, I wouldn't be in half the mess I am now.

"I would spare you of all harm."

"I know you would."

"Although, the purpose of life isn't to spare yourself from pain and heartache, Skyla." He singes my cheek with a kiss. "It's who you can spare. You must live your life for the people."

"For the people." I nod, thinking of Lacey and all those souls in the tunnels, the Nephilim and Sectors counting on me to win the war. But when it comes to Logan, Gage, and Marshall, I can spare no one.

Every heart will be broken.

Including mine.

48

Summer Loving

Summer on Paragon stretches her wings like a dove in flight, an olive branch tucked in her beak as she glides through the damp, cool fog.

Gage and I have extended the olive branch. We dive into the ocean of our love and rekindle the fire that Chloe tried to extinguish with her barrage of well-plotted hatred strewn over time and memoriam.

I'll be working a shift at the bowling alley later today with both Logan and Gage, which should be interesting since Logan is finally back from his internment, first with Ezrina, then with my mother. He left a text late last night once he arrived safe and sound in his bedroom—said he loved me more than the heavens love the sun and the moon. Those words made me quiver. Made me fear for Gage. Logan still has me in a very real way.

It's almost nine in the morning as I trot downstairs to grab a banana before I leave.

Chloe is yawning into her coffee as Tad, Drake, and Ethan hunch over the counter completing the roll call of idiocracy. A stack of papers are spread out between the three nitwits, and they squint into them as if trying to decipher their hieroglyphics. It couldn't be possible that all three Landon males hold the curse of illiteracy, so this must contain confusing verbiage or perhaps it's all text and no pictures.

"What's going on?" I ask en route to grab some OJ from the fridge.

"A business opportunity came our way." Tad doesn't bother glancing up.

"Clearly, said 'business opportunity' is of the female variety. I gather it involves giant knockers." Did I just say that out loud? I'm still feeling kind of loopy from lack of sleep. I stayed up way too late wondering what life would be like with both Logan and Gage. Truth is, I'd rather be sawed in half than decide between the two of them. I guess, in a small way, I'm thankful for the war. It makes the battle for my heart a little easier to bear.

"Skyla!" Mom pops in the room like an apparition, balking at my statement. "This family needs a financial infusion if you hadn't noticed."

"Skyla is absorbed in her own world right now." Chloe tries to sound sympathetic, but she snarls at me once my mother turns her back.

Mom darts Chloe a look. "You really know, Skyla." She slashes her finger in the air at Tad "Anyway she's right, this should involve breasts."

I stop breathing.

"Breast milk is big business." My mother uses my sarcasm as a springboard for her insanity. "We should consider opening a shop that caters to the market. We can call it 'The Milk Bar' or 'Mother's Milk.'"

Good grief. And I suppose she'll be the lone supplier, or worse, enlist me in on the effort.

"Think of all the cute babies you'd have running around as customers." Chloe makes a face when Mom isn't looking. "You wouldn't even mind that you can't have one of your own."

Mom snaps her head in Chloe's direction.

Leave it to Chloe to hang herself so efficiently, flushing all her kiss-ass efforts down the toilet with one cutting remark.

Chloe straightens in the midst of her verbal faux pas.

"I love that color on you." She steps lively with the false adulation. Chloe dispenses flattery to my mother like candy at Halloween—strychnine-laced candy. My mother had better keep an eye out for razor blades if she knows what's good for her.

Ethan slaps his hand on the counter. "We can have like ice cream made from that shit." He nods into my mother, stony faced, as if he didn't just let an expletive fly. He looks over at me. "We're thinking of opening a coffee shop just a block from the high school."

I assume he means West since East has about six different coffee holes barricading it from every side, the most popular of which belongs to the Kraggers. That's where Emerson died—where Chloe killed her to be exact. I'm assuming if she came back to life, she wouldn't bother placating her executioner with niceties the way Ethan does. Then again, she doesn't have a penis, so her thinking would be a lot clearer.

"Arson Kragger is talking about franchising," Mom informs.

I spray the first luscious mouthful of my not-from-concentrate citrus pick-me-up in a three-foot radius, inadvertently giving Sprinkles a bath.

"You can't go into business with him." I charge over. Getting involved with a Kragger is the equivalent of sticking your head in a crocodile's mouth. I've dealt with enough crooked Kraggers to attest to this personally. I've killed just as many, but that's beside the point.

"The Kraggers are business savvy." Ethan says it cool like he knows this as fact. "Plus, it'll give me something to do with my time other than hanging out on the Internet all day long and amounting to nothing," he says directly to Tad, playing into the deep-seated fear he holds for his eldest offspring.

It's clear Ethan is manipulating his way into Taddy dearest's pocketbook in order to finance this java juice disaster.

"The Kraggers have invited us all over next weekend." My mother squeals like a schoolgirl at the thought of the Paragon social structure finally engineering the Landons into their private posse. Not that any social network is strong enough to endure the Landons en masse, or in partial for very long.

"Lovely," I say. Of course I'm going to go. I'm more than curious to see how the wicked half-lives. It's doubtful dungeons are involved—with exception of their secret world otherwise known as the Celestra tunnels. Although, I do find it mildly comforting my future children and I might score the luxury suite in the tower if Logan so wishes. As if.

I wonder if Candace, the celestial matchmaker, went over *that* strategy with him.

"Oh, it will be lovely." Mom's eyes bug out at the prospect of playing footsy with Demetri at the head Count's quarters.

"Will there be a dress code inflicted upon us for this joyous occasion?" As in hooded accoutrements, to be more specific.

"I'm sure it's cocktail attire." Mom gives an apprehensive nod into Chloe as if she could decipher the dress code better than my mother could. It's like she's her favorite daughter. "There's a big dedication ceremony taking place. I don't have all the details yet."

Sounds suspicious. Maybe this is some sort of ambush wedding Demetri is going to pull on Mom? No, wait, that can't be right, she's legally bound and gagged to the moron at the counter currently engrossed in a flatulence war with the offshoots of his wayward lineage. If Mom hasn't already sent a cease-and-desist letter to Tad's penis, the time would be now.

"That's sick!" Chloe isn't afraid to insult the king of the Landon porcelain throne.

"What?" Ethan pipes up with a laugh. "It's our mating call."

I don't miss the opportunity to shoulder up to Chloe.

"Isn't this great?" I whisper. "You get Ethan, and I get Gage?" I would be remiss if I didn't rub her nose into the Landon's special brand of cologne that clots the air.

Mom opens the backdoor and the screen. Usually Mom is terrified that some winged creature might buzz right in and is extra vigilant about securing the screen before we even hit the other side. Obviously occasions such as these, when she realizes what ineptness she's married into, must make her wish she could take down entire walls to help alleviate the pain.

"I agree with Chloe," she barks into Tad, "you're teaching these boys that it's OK to be disrespectful in the presence of women. I'm not impressed with you at all at the moment." She sears him with a look that could set a puddle on fire.

"I'm as big a gentleman as they get," Tad replies nonchalantly as if he believed the lie.

Mom scoffs. "I know men who would make your version of refined behavior look as appropriate as a wild boar at afternoon tea." She cinches her hands over her hips in a declaration of war.

I seriously doubt comparing your husband to a feral land mammal that appreciates the finer points of a good mud bath is ever a good idea. And, by the way, she so wishes he would magically morph into Demetri.

"Well," Tad starts off curt, "I've met *ladies* who happened to appreciate this locker room behavior and find it more than mildly attractive."

He so means Izzy look-me-in-the-boobs-I'm-a-fake-doctor Edinger.

"You know what I appreciate?" Ethan breaks the tension by tantalizing us with the recognition of his values. "A credit line to open my first chain store. Now, which one of you is coming to the bank today to co-sign for the loan?"

I sort of like the way he gets straight to his asinine point.

My mother and Tad glare at one another for an ungodly amount of time. You can practically see the divorce decree written on the wall. Their marriage has been weighed on the scales and found desperately wanting. Their days of matrimonial unity are most certainly numbered.

"Hello?" A voice calls from the entry.

Brielle appears, holding a tiny swaddled infant and a diaper bag big enough to house the space lab and suddenly all is right in our little corner of the world.

49

A Tisket a Casket

"I hope you don't mind." Brielle is quick to pass little Beau Geste to my mother. "I've got a shift at the bowling alley in less than an hour, then Emily is having this raging party I can't miss. And"—she spins into me—"we so need to plan for Logan's birthday." She plunks down the bloated diaper bag. "Anyway, Gage is helping with the rest of his stuff."

Chloe perks up at the thought of her faux suitor on the horizon.

A tall, dark, and handsome frame lights up the family room—Gage. He carries a tiny white casket in his arms, which he's quick to place on the coffee table.

"You should have the lid removed," he suggests. "It's just a few screws."

"Oh, don't do that." Brielle balks at the idea of an oxygenated environment. "He sleeps much better if you close it. You'll hardly hear him cry." Bree's alarming suggestion highlights the fact social services has fallen behind on securing the well-being of this child.

"And they let you breed?" Chloe snipes under her breath.

Same could be said of her parents. Although, I hate to admit it, I happen to agree with Chloe. Drake and Brielle are the last two people on the planet who should multiply in combination.

"He's smiling at me!" Mom bounces him in her arms like she's getting ready to hoist him through the window.

"He's just gassy." Brielle corrects.

"A genetic marker of a true Landon," I say, letting him curl his tiny perfect hand around my finger. He gives it a squeeze, and it feels like a truck just barreled over it. "Shit!" I pull back.

"He's strong, right?" Brielle looks slightly terrified.

"Right." It's all that calamitous Count blood boiling in his veins. It'll be a miracle if the island is intact by the time he's three.

"Maybe he just doesn't care for Skyla." Chloe gives an approving coo in his direction.

"Gage does," I fire back. "And that's all that matters."

Chloe cringes. She walked right into that one, and she knows it.

"Hello!" Mom shakes her head into the baby. "You are *amazing*!" She barks it out at Mach 5 as if it were a scolding.

"What in the hell was that?" Tad leaps up at attention after my mother's demonic outburst.

"It's all a part of dynamic parenting," she reasons. "It's a very progressive form of thinking. You have to affirm positive verbal statements throughout the day. It's vital in building character and confidence." She doesn't hesitate to educate us in all things ridiculous.

"Is it necessary to shout?" I ask, clasping Gage's arms around my waist like a seatbelt as I ready myself to board the insanity express.

"Oh, yes." Mom assures with hyper-vigilance. "It's important to jar the psyche. You really need to capture their attention."

"You're going to capture his attention all right," Tad quips. "He'll be crapping his pants every time you walk in the room."

Mom ignores his verbal snipe and dances around the table with the newest victim of her controversial parenting technique. She blows in the poor baby's face like a makeshift hurricane.

"You are above and beyond our every expectation!" She shouts each word like its own sentence.

The baby shudders and startles before belting out a howl that rivals my mother's.

"Have fun!" Brielle spins toward the door. "Remember—the lid works wonders," she shouts as she heads on out.

"You think she'll be back before evening?" Mom's face creases with concern.

"I think she'll visit on occasion." Like Christmas and Easter. I'm pretty sure this is a permanent arrangement.

"Dr. Edinger will be here tonight." Mom averts her eyes. "We've got couples counseling." She mouths the last words.

"What about the girls?" My sisters are dying to babysit a human. Lord knows they've dressed that dog of theirs up six ways to Sunday in only the most fashionable pink frilly pet wear they could afford. I'm sure they'll have junior here looking like a million dollar transvestite before the sun goes down.

"They leave for camp this afternoon." Mom pecks the baby with kisses in an effort to quell his tantrum.

I glance over at Chloe who's suddenly clammed up. I'd volunteer her services, but I'd like my nephew to live to see another day.

"Skyla and I can do it." Gage offers.

I look up at his dewy black hair, his open face, that smile that makes his dimples tremble. He's perfect in every way.

"It's only an hour." Mom blinks with relief.

"Great, because I really want to get to Emily's raging party." I can't wait to infiltrate Casa Morgan. It's rife with prophetic pictures and paintings. One of which includes Marshall in their dining room. Say—I should totally bring Marshall and let him check the place out. I bet he could solve a thousand cryptic mysteries.

I look up at Gage and smile. I'm glad there aren't any more mysteries revolving around him and his dimples. I press a kiss into him, and my stomach explodes with heat.

"See that, Lizbeth?" Tad crows. "I predict another casket in our future."

Chloe steps in close and glares at me. The protective hedge slices through the light with its brilliance. "I bet you're right," she says, stroking Tad's ego. "I bet there is another casket in your future."

Gage gives me a ride to the bowling alley in his truck. I missed this. I missed being by his side and trusting him infallibly and yet something in me stirs with apprehension, and I can't shake the feeling.

I rub my open palm against his dash as if it were the fur of a most beloved animal.

"You OK?" he asks, pulling into the dirt lot out back. It was here that Chloe arranged for the Mustang to mow him over in hopes to insert Holden Kragger into his body. I can't even imagine the insanity I would be going through right now if "Gage" and Chloe were running around the island secured in a lip lock. I would die. Of course, the real Gage wouldn't have been guilty of the malfeasance. But, his body, his soul— I'm greedy for them all.

"Skyla?" He waves his hand over my face before taking off his seatbelt. "What's going on?"

"Nothing." I shake my head. "I'm just zoning out. I was up late, and I found out Tad and Ethan are thinking about going into business with the Kraggers. It's been a weird morning to say the least."

Actually, Chloe's parting shot about the casket stuck with me, and the visual of her running through the woods with a severed head keeps playing on a loop in my brain, but there's no way I'm bringing up Chloe. It's bad enough I have to endure her morning breath. The last thing I want is her needling into my relationship with Gage at all hours of the day.

We climb out of the truck, and Gage leads me over by a juniper tree before entering the building. The scent of crisp morning pines infiltrates our senses.

The clouds over head expand in billows, thick as clotted cream. The sun boils just above the precipitous canopy stretched over Paragon, bathing us in humidity. We can feel the heat but are denied of the beauty the precious rays provide.

Gage wraps his arms around me, while dusting kisses over each of my lids.

"Meet me in the freezer in ten?" he hums.

"OK, but first I'll meet you in the arcade in five." I bat my lashes. Oh, that reminds me. "Hey, I'm thinking about asking Marshall to Em's party later. You OK with that?" I shrink a little when I ask.

Gage closes his eyes an inordinate amount of time. "He's annoying as hell."

"I know, but I thought if he saw those paintings, he might be able to help us in some way. It might give us the edge we need to win the war—hell, a region would be nice."

A slight frown darkens his features.

"You really don't like him, do you?" Stupid question, I know.

"Do you like Chloe?"

"That bad, huh?"

"That bad." He grazes his eyes over the dirt. "Look, bring him tonight, let him check out Emily's paintings. If it'll help us win a region—if it keeps you safe, I'm all for it." He cradles my face in his hands and bows into me with a tender kiss. A sweet strumming sensation pulses through me, not quite as strong as it does with Marshall but something far more organic, pure. It's as if our love came to life and sizzled through us, vibrant and sparkling, like a wave in the ocean. I push him in by the neck. Forget my mother and her hard-lined rules. I want all of the love Gage is willing to offer and then some. I'm greedy for his heady brand of affection. It leaves me reeling like a drunkard. Gage is the best drug, and I never want this addiction to end.

"I predict a visit to Rockaway in our future," he rumbles into my neck.

"I was thinking maybe there's a thirteenth floor that might need some haunting."

"I think you're right." The curve of a naughty smile springs to his lips.

Gage reduces me to cinders with a heated kiss.

I've always wondered what made those disembodied spirits moan so wildly.

And now, I'll discover firsthand.

50

Suspicious Minds

The bowling alley holds the scent of fresh popcorn, the thick smell of pizza dough rising in the oven, and unfortunately, the somewhat pungent odor of used shoes. Tons of people from East and West have chosen to patronize the establishment and, of course, that includes the bitch squad.

Chloe is wearing her Band-Aid inspired bathing suit top and ultra-short shorts that accentuate her long, tawny legs.

Whatever the hell happened to no shirt, no shoes, no service? Where's Logan when you need him to enforce the rules?

Chloe keeps complaining about the "shoddy equipment" and redirecting Gage to the technical difficulties by way of her scantily clad bod.

"She never quits." Brielle seethes as though it were *her* boyfriend Chloe had declared open season on.

"She's tenacious," I say. "Her jealousy should be classified as a deadly weapon."

"Totally illegal," Brielle sneers. "We should do something to her. Just me and you."

I graze over Brielle with a quick look. I'm still not sure I can trust her one hundred percent, and I really don't want to confront her about being paid a cool grand to be my friend while we're staring down the barrel of a six-hour shift.

"What did you have in mind?" I'd love to hear Brielle's unique take on exacting revenge. I'm always open to entertaining new possibilities in that arena.

"I don't know." Brielle rests her hand next to mine. "Someone like her—you almost have to hurt her ego. You know, build her up then pull the pin on the grenade and run like hell."

"I see Chloe more as a landmine." She specializes in blowing your world apart when you least expect it.

She and Gage make a beeline over to us. Much to my delight, he looks totally annoyed with the overexposed witch by his side.

"I had a great idea." Chloe presses out her chest. "Gage, here, thought I should run it by you." She curtsies into me sarcastically. "I think the bowling alley should start a recycling program. It's such a waste to toss all these bottles and cans in the trash. It could be the beginning of a green revolution right here on the island."

"Perfect." I force a smile. "We'll be sure to let Logan know once he gets in."

Chloe scowls before heading back to Emily and Lexy. What did she want? A statue erected in her honor?

"I thought I'd redirect all her inquires to you." Gage lands a sultry kiss on my lips. "That way she knows she can never have a minute of my time that doesn't involve my better half."

My stomach burns with heat when he calls me that. I wrap my arms around him and lay my head over his shoulder.

Chloe singes me with a look from across the room that could melt a glacier.

I have a feeling the recyclopath is up to her old tricks again. The only thing turning green around here is her. I'm pretty sure the only revolution she's interested in igniting is the one for Gage Oliver's heart.

Brielle is right. It's time to put her in her place once and for all. Build her up and watch her explode into a million tiny pieces.

I smile over at her.

Payback is a bitch Chloe—just like you.

It's not until almost noon that Logan walks through the door, showered and shaved, looking like his usual resplendent self.

"Logan!"

He reels me in by the hand and indulges in a very long embrace. I can feel his broad chest heave with relief. It's so good to have him back right here on Paragon. This madness we've embroiled ourselves in has got to end.

"Tell me everything," I say. "Start with the Transfer."

"Hey." Gage comes up and knocks a fist into Logan's side. "Everything OK with you?"

Logan pauses, looking from me to Gage.

"I'm great." The smile slides from his face, and that perennial sadness clouds him. He heads over and opens the register, checks to see if we need any more dollar bills. "So you guys work things out?" He washes over the two of us with a brief glance.

"Yeah." Gage nods as though he were affirming a grim diagnosis at the oncologist's office.

"You!" Brielle lunges at Logan with a big rocking hug. "Your birthday is knocking at the door. So what are we doing? The Cape?"

"What's the Cape?" I ask as Gage tries to wrap his arm around my waist, but I pretend to lose my footing and move a little out of reach. It doesn't feel right to have him holding me openly in front of Logan. I can't stand the fact that my love for Gage keeps stabbing him in the heart.

Brielle opens her mouth a moment and nods. "That's right, you weren't here."

Gage steps over and pulls me in. Obviously, Gage and I don't see things the same way when it comes to sparing Logan's feelings.

Brielle continues, "A bunch of us went out last year and camped at the north tip of the island for his birthday. It was completely wild." She looks up as though she were reliving a memory. "We should totally go to the Cape." Brielle bounces on her feet like a child pleading for a new toy.

"What do you guys think?" Logan swallows hard as he traces Gage wrapped around me—eyes him as if he were an anaconda about to swallow me whole.

"I think it sounds great." It's doubtful Mom and Tad will approve, but a girl can dream.

"Get the shifts covered and let's do it." Gage jostles me, thrilled by the prospect of losing ourselves in an overnight adventure. He tucks a kiss into my neck. "I'll get our wetsuits ready. I've been dying to take you out."

"Perfect." I reach up and cradle the back of his neck to reward him for his stroke of genius. I glance up to find Logan glaring at the counter like he's just been robbed, and there's not a damn thing he can do about it.

The main board lights up showing two different lanes with jammed pins.

"I got it." Gage jogs over without hesitating.

"I'm on Chloe patrol." Brielle declares, heading out after him.

"Chloe patrol. Some things never change," Logan says, as he tries to reprogram the machines, but it's clear his mind is elsewhere. Logan is wearing his heart on his sleeve and it's visibly broken for all to see.

"No, some things never change," I say, glancing back over at Brielle. "I think she has a transference issue with Chloe and Gage regarding Emily and Drake—something like that anyway." I step into him and lay my hand carefully over his forearm. "She's really worried about protecting what's hers but won't admit it." *I know you're hurting*, I say it telepathically because I can't find the strength to push the words through my lips.

Logan blinks a smile, still hacking away at the keyboard.

I mean, I go on, *you spent a few days with my mother. That's enough to psychologically scar just about anybody. What did she do? Lock you in the lion's den?*

He darts a quick look in my direction. *No lion's den. Turns out, she likes me.* A devilish grin breaks out on his face.

Oh, that's right. Actually, I hadn't forgotten. I was trying to make light of the situation because, in truth, I'm scared to death to find out what she might have revealed to him. *She's team Logan.* I run my fingers down his back and feel him shudder. His eyes close as if he were locked in passion, and it catches me off guard. It pulses a wave of pleasure through me uninvited.

"I heard you." He bows into his words with a bashful apprehension that I'm not used to hearing from him. "And, you're right, your mother did reveal something to me." He runs his sad orbs over me, washes me with those dark saffron eyes, slow as molasses in January.

"Really?" I try to sound freshly surprised. "OK." I sag with defeat. "Just give it to me straight because I can't handle the suspense. What is it? Is Chloe going to hack my head off? Or maybe Tad will lock me in a cellar somewhere. Oh, wait— Demetri hangs me upside down in his trophy room." I know Gage once predicted Logan and I would live very long lives, but there was never any stipulation about whose head I'd be wearing while I did it. With Dr. Oliver's handy dandy tool bag and Marshall's knowhow, I could be staring at anyone's face in the mirror before I'm officially a senior. God—what if *that's* why I demanded Gage keep Chloe alive in the future? Holy freaking shit. "I'd better not end up wearing Chloe's head like a hat."

"What?" He lets out a low rumble of laughter. Logan loosens up for the first time since he's stepped into the bowling alley. "It's nothing like that, I promise. She didn't mention anything about you accessorizing with anymore of Chloe's body parts."

"Then what is it?" I step into him, pleading with everything in me for the short and sweet synopsis that I'm hoping against hope doesn't involve mortality or eternal curses. I can't wait to hear what moronic bullshit my mother is up to now.

"I'll tell you." Logan glances behind me as Gage calls him over to assist with a sticking gutter. "Emily is having a party tonight." His eyes switch back to mine. "You going?"

"Are you kidding? And miss the artistic display of my future playing out on at least three hundred canvases? Of course, I'm going. Who knows what she's whipped out since we were last there." I leave out the detail of bringing Dudley.

"You think maybe we can hang out after?" There's a boyishness about him. A wide-eyed apprehension I don't ever remember seeing in him before.

Hanging out after a party is usually a right reserved for people who are seeing each other. The idea makes me nervous, as if Logan is trying to move the invisible boundary line of what we should and shouldn't do.

"Sure," I say. "We can all go out for a bite, hang out at Rockaway or your house."

He shakes his head just barely. "Just me and you, Skyla. You're the only person I'm going to share this with."

Just Logan and me alone after Emily's party—the idea has me flustered. I can feel the heat rising to my cheeks. An unnatural level of lust beats its way to the surface, but I submerge it as I glance back at Gage.

Logan leans in. "I think there should be a whole lot more time spent with just you and me," he whispers.

I take a quick breath at the thought. There's something powerful about the two of us together. We seem to harness all of the energy in the universe, strong enough to slice through granite boulders with precision.

Logan looks up and brands me with his wanting. Logan could drill a hole straight into the core of the Earth with all of that sexual tension bottled up inside him.

"OK." I nod into Logan. "Just you and me."

51

The Crying Game

That evening, I hang out with baby Beau in my bedroom. It's the big babysitting stint Gage volunteered us for. He's conveniently late for our nonmonetary employment, and seeing that it has the potential to involve bouts of incontinence, I really don't blame him.

It's just a few hours before Emily's big party, so I text Marshall and let him know I'll be expecting him to drop by and hang with the teen scene. To which he promptly replies.

There's not a spirit in the sky that could keep me away from you tonight. Shall I bring the wings?

NO. ~S

Figures Marshall would go there. I say hello to him these days, and he considers it a proposition. If I did marry Marshall—which I'm a thousand percent sure I'm not—I have a feeling tying me to the bedpost would be a rather permanent situation. For a second, I envision us there in his palatial bedroom—Marshall in his unclothed glory, panting over me all sweaty with that perplexingly sexy, devilish grin of his. I can practically feel his hands tugging at the haunted corset I'm sure he'd require me to wear, the hot red and black one he fashioned for the woman he thought would love him but didn't. My heart breaks a little for Marshall. Then all unholy hell breaks loose in my imagination, and I let him rip the bodice off me before I latch onto him like some sexed-up chimpanzee. I can practically feel his hands swimming over my hips, his hot breath in my hair, an entire string of hot kisses that lead all the way down to my stomach—

Baby Beau lets out a gurgle, and I snap out of my erotic-laced fantasy. He's already tucked snug in his casket sans the lid, which Tad removed after Gage's oh-so-lucid suggestion. Mom needed me to baby-Count sit so she could effectively fight Dr. *Izzy* off her husband during their sham of a couple's counseling session.

I pull outfit after outfit from the closet and settle on a pair of jean shorts and a tight white T-shirt that's perfectly see-through. It's actually freezing out, but I noticed that doesn't stop anybody on Paragon from pretending it's summer.

My phone buzzes lightly.

Almost to the door.

It's Gage. I made him promise to text me so he wouldn't interrupt the therapy session Isis is busy misconducting. Plus, the baby is sleeping, which, by the way, was totally easy to get him to do. I have no clue what Brielle was griping about. Gage and I should have a whole blissful hour to ourselves before we leave for Em's.

I head downstairs and startle at the sound of hysterical crying, only it's not coming from my bedroom.

What the hell?

I know for a fact it's not the baby. It's definitely originating from downstairs and holy shit if it's not more than one person—a woman's howls are intermingled with a man's bizarre form of shrieking.

Oh my, God. I bet Isis brainwashed Tad into slaughtering my mother. She could have easily hypnotized him with a pair of swirly pasties.

A shadow lingers on the other side of the front door, and I pull Gage in and brush him with a quick kiss.

Gage rides a low sexy smile, and for a moment I forget all about the insanity taking place in the other room.

"Did Logan say anything about his time with your mom?" He washes over me with those steel beams. His features transform with a heavy burden. Gage is as concerned as I am over the content of said conversation. He has a look on his face that suggests Logan might have been promoted in a spiritual manner—soon to be followed in the physical sense.

"He asked if he could talk to me in private after Em's party," I confess.

Gage huffs a laugh. He isn't at all amused that Logan wants alone time with me. He sees the threat, and he feels it's real, I can tell.

Another bout of hysterical weeping emits from the family room. I use Gage as a human shield and walk over to the edge of the hall. Obviously, Isis made them eat a serious shit sandwich because Mom and Tad are very fucking upset.

Gage pauses just shy of rounding out the wall and inspects the carnage.

Voices escalate, yelling ensues, then a fit of frenzied sobbing—far more intense than before.

"What the hell's going on?" Gage whispers after examining the situation.

I peer out and spot Mom and Tad bawling like babies while Isis the serpentine solicitor looks on with a content grin on her face. She's encased in a hot pink tank top with no freaking bra, as exemplified by the twin hat pegs poking from her shirt that look as if they could cut through diamonds.

"What the hell *is* going on?" I take Gage by the hand and drag him over to the tear fest with me. "Everything OK?" Obviously, everything is not OK. The breasty one here brought up a bunch of past offenses, and now Mom and Tad are just buying time before the dissolution of their marriage kicks in.

"Sky*la*," Mom drags my name out in two equal parts, "please don't interrupt. We're in the middle of something." She bows into a heavily used tissue and lets out a few good honks.

"Method acting." Tad wipes his eyes with the back of his arm in one fell swoop.

Method acting? Obviously the "method" is madness.

"That's right." Isis smiles up at me with a vacant look in her eyes. "It's a new therapeutic treatment that brings couples to the brink of distress and allows them to drain every emotion."

More like brink of disaster.

"I do feel drained." Tad nods into her genius. "You really know your stuff." His eyes venture south, and he reaches over and strokes her hand while hypnotized by the lower forty-eight. I'm sure that's not all he'd like to stroke.

"I agree." Mom continues to pinch her nose. "I'm finding this very beneficial. Skyla, you should consider a session with Dr. Edinger. She might be able to pull some things out of you that Dr. Booth couldn't."

I suck in a breath. Dr. Booth and I have a mutually satisfying professional relationship. I pretend to see him, and he collects a check. Besides, I thought we moved past my need for psychiatric attention.

"I would love to see Skyla and Gage." Isis beams. Her glittering teal eyes light up the room with anticipation. "I've long since believed young lovers could very much benefit from counseling if not more than some old married couple."

I'm not sure what's more reprehensible, the fact she referenced Gage and me as lovers in front of my mother and Tad, or the fact she collectively dismissed them as hopeless geriatrics.

Mom fumbles for words. I'm pretty sure Lizbeth Landon wasn't suggesting couples counseling for her seventeen-year-old daughter. She meant the glowworm and me going at it mano-a-mano. But now look what she's done. She's gone and dragged my perfectly good boyfriend into the picture.

"They think they're engaged," Tad balks. "Maybe you can knock some sense into them."

"A-huh." She gives a dreamy nod into Gage. "I would certainly love to knock something into—"

"I think I hear the baby," I say, grabbing Gage and leaving the room before Isis has the chance to knock any more of her perverse psychosis around.

I drag Gage all the way upstairs and shut the door, then turn off the lights.

It's time to reinstate my sanity, one kiss at a time.

Alone in the dark with Gage Oliver is quite possibly the most perfect place on the planet, in this or any other dimensional plane.

I pull him in and cover his lips. I can feel his love pulse over me, his chest palpitate in rhythm with mine. If I could relive a moment over and over, if I could choose my own treble, it would be this moment with his searing affection poured out like oil.

I love you, Skyla, he says, walking me back toward the bed.

There are still so many questions I have, like how he could even tolerate being in the same room with Chloe after what she did to us but I push the thought out of my head for now.

A thin seam of light floods over him from a crack in the blinds, and I can make out a faint smile on his lips as the inky dots on either side of his cheeks twitch in my honor. It's magic like this with Gage—watching him take me in, swallow me whole into his heart, his mind. He memorizes my features, my body as it's pieced together in shadows.

Gage lies me down. He raises my hands over my shoulders, blesses me with a river of kisses that span the distance of my lips and chest as far as my T-shirt will allow. He pulls up next to me and indulges in a sea of soft pecks before his determination increases. Those charged kisses harness an entire force field of raging passion. They're the ones that let me know there's a deep well of craving in him that can only be satisfied in a carnal manner. Gage longs to christen our love with a holy exchange of rapture that, according to my mother, will conjoin us on an unbreakable spiritual level—let no man put asunder what Gage and I fuse together with our flesh. The thought of the two of us merging our souls is amazing, a miracle I could ponder all night while feasting on the fire that races from his mouth.

A vision appears—Gage and I stand on a windy beach— it's dark. The sand moves in smooth ripples, it looks alive beneath our feet, black as a panther. I'm yelling, crying. Gage points hard in my direction with a searing expression. This is no showcase of our affection, no prognosticating of some rosy love affair.

Gage sits up and takes a breath.

A choking sound emits from the tiny casket followed by a hacking cry—a welcome distraction to that alarming vision. I switch on the light and jump over to Beau, screaming himself into what looks like a seizure.

"Hey, you." I reach in and pluck him free from that horrible crib they keep him in. Who puts a baby in a casket on purpose? Plus, it's making me feel a little like the crypt keeper. "It's OK," I whisper as he wails into my shoulder. "You're a noisy little Count, aren't you?" Cute one, too.

Gage gives a crooked smile from the bed. He rides his gaze over me as I try to calm the screaming infant by bobbing him around and petting him like a puppy.

Gage pats the bed beside him until I bop the junior Count all the way over. We sit side-by-side, staring down at the red-faced infant with his tiny balled up fists and erratic kicking legs. So this is what it would be like if Gage and I accidentally had a baby—noisy.

"He's an angry little guy." Gage picks up his hand and jostles it gently.

"His diaper feels dry." Lucky for him because I would sooner hack off my Chloe arm and eat it before I would change a dirty diaper. Yet another reason I would make a lousy teenage mother.

I pick him up and cradle him the same way I used to hold my dolls—which I'm pretty sure is entirely wrong positioning for an actual human, but instinct is kicking in and the only point of reference I happen to have comes from Mattel.

The wailing doesn't stop. Instead, he arches back before digging his face into my shirt. His head turns side to side at a million miles an hour as if he's trying to settle his hungry mouth over my boob, and he starts chewing on my shirt without the proper invitation.

"I'm guessing he gets this from his dad," I say, handing him over to Gage before things get X-rated.

"Whoa." Gage freezes, holding him out like a hot potato. "I don't know how to do this." An elevated state of panic brews in him.

"You're fine." I hop across the room and pluck the bottle Mom armed me with from off the desk. "Try this." I lay the tip over baby Beau's lips, and he shakes his head before latching on furtively.

"That's better." Gage sighs with relief. He steadies the bottle in the baby's mouth and relaxes his shoulder against mine.

My heart melts at the sight. Gage is going to be the hottest daddy on the block one day.

He glances at me and his dimples ignite.

"So..." I push into him. "What do you think happened in that vision?"

Gage lays his head over mine. The world grows still around us, and for a brief moment, I trick myself into believing that we're sitting in some distant future ten years out with our own child, on our own bed, free from the faction war and tunnels and Tad.

"Would you want this with me, Skyla?" He whispers it out like the lyrics to a very sad song.

"A family?" I pull back to look at him. "One day—very far away—but yes. I can't wait until we make it through this all." God, I hope we make it.

He sighs and gives a hesitant nod. "I wouldn't worry about the vision. Let's get through one day at a time—one *moment* at a time. Just know that I love you deeply. I would never in a million years hurt you."

I dig my fingers into the back of his hair and dust the side of his face with a kiss.

"Same here," I whisper.

But something must happen. You don't just end up on a beach in the middle of the night screaming your lungs off at the people you love best. An ax has to fall right over your heart for something of that magnitude to take place.

And if it's one thing I can't stand, it's waiting for the ax to fall.

I bet I know who's responsible for landing the guillotine right over my heart. I bet she's scheming on how to do it right this very minute.

52

Testosterone Rising

Paragon trembles. The trees sway under the hostility of the storm brewing overhead.

Gage and I drive through a dark, restless night on our way over to Emily Morgan's haunted habitat. The dirty clapboard hovel sits crooked on top of a sharp-peaked hill. It sits tucked in a far less posh neighborhood than even the humble Landon home resides.

"So Dudley's coming?" Gage furrows his brows as he kills the engine. As much as I hate making Gage miserable, there's something distinctly hot about a worked-up boyfriend.

"I swear, it's just to look at Emily's finger paintings. I have no intention of ever being alone with him. I'll die if you leave me with him for one second." That steamy fantasy I had earlier of Marshall flexing on top of me swirls through my mind, and I sink a little in my seat.

"Well," he says as his eyes saucer out, "now that your life is on the line." He relaxes his arms around my back, and blinks a quiet smile. His demeanor quickly changes. Gage grows still, altogether serious as death. "I can't stand the way he looks at you, Skyla. I don't need to read minds to know he has you ten different ways—nightly." He gives a long concerted blink at the idea of Marshall fornicating with me in his mind like some pay-per-view movie. "I take zero responsibility for how I might react if he looks at you crooked. God forbid he bumps into you." He glances out into the blank of night. "On second thought, he can bring it. I'm a bomb just waiting to go off, and trust me, he lit the fuse the minute he set foot on this island."

"Don't blow up." I dot his lips with a kiss. "Marshall Dudley is so not worth it."

Gage dips in, brushes his lips across mine soft as a butterfly before nourishing me with a lingual expression that lifts us to levels of ecstasy we have never visited before.

Let's ditch the party. Gage pulls me close as if he's about to save me from the strong arms of the sea.

"I love you," I whisper before thrusting my tongue in his mouth with a forceful kiss that falls in line with his desire to rearrange our plans for the evening. I run my hands inside his shirt and trace out his chiseled body as if it were a poem written in Braille that I'm determined to memorize. My fingers track down to his waist and I accidentally touch the hard bulge in his jeans and a groan wrings from my throat.

A spastic knock erupts on the passenger's side window.

Gage and I pull back to see the Sector of his discontent in all his youthful glory.

"Shit," Gage says, getting out of the truck. "Let's make this quick."

I take in the cool night air as Marshall seethes over at Gage. He looks like he can set off a thousand bombs with just one glance from his heavenly-ordained features. Marshall is sick of Gage, and Gage is sick of Marshall. I have a feeling they'd love to come to blows—thrash each other to pieces.

Something tells me I won't be leaving with Gage, if Marshall has anything to say about it. Then there's Logan and our "date" centered around my mother and her meddling ways.

Something tells me it's going to be a very, very long night.

"What's with the fountain of youth?" I ask Marshall as the three of us make our way up the twisted path to Em's slightly dilapidated dwelling.

"This is the new face, love. I've grown bored of the tired expression that greets me each time I look in the mirror. Speaking of which—young Oliver, are you open to adventure later in the evening?"

"I'm busy." Gage doesn't even bother glancing in Marshall's direction when he asks. "Skyla and I have plans."

We do? I thought Logan and I had plans. I thought Gage OK'd that late-night meeting with my ex, but apparently Gage isn't taking shit from anyone tonight when it comes to our relationship.

Marshall strangles out a laugh. "Too busy to investigate what might lie on the other side of the most prized engineering endeavor the Fems have to offer?" If he's trying to sweeten the pot, he's doing a lousy job.

I'll throw him in myself. Shall we take bets on whether or not he emerges in this century? Marshall lays an arm over my shoulder and gives a sly smile.

Gage flicks his arm off as if it were a swarm of bees. "Hands to your fucking self."

"Testy, are we?" Marshall's eyes glow a strange mix of tangerine and crimson. "And to think I was toying with the idea of joining you in adventureland. Who knows what hijinks and hilarity would have ensued."

"Why don't you do us all a favor and dive in on your own." Gage broadens his shoulders gazing out at the dark mouth of Emily's porch. "I could push you in if you want."

The wind stirs. The fog swirls around us erratic, signaling the fact a serious typhoon is about to hit.

Marshall scoffs. "Shall we review the carnage that unfolded the last time you and that nitwit half-breed relation of yours tried to extricate me from the planet?" Marshall is incensed that Gage would even consider a replay.

Truthfully, Marshall spared them. It was Chloe who applied her own brand of bitch squad retaliation that night and tried injecting Holden Kragger's soul into Gage's body by way of the Mustang. But in true Chloe fashion, it backfired magnificently, and the entire event was one huge mess that landed me in the future and Logan floating in a vat of Liquid Drano.

"Perhaps Skyla here will join me," Marshall purrs. "We have a lifetime of adventures to look forward to. I don't see why we should delay the inevitable any longer."

Right. Like I'm going to lose my freaking mind and hop right down the demonic bunny trail with Marshall so he can paw me every chance he gets.

"I think we're back to Nev," I whisper as we hit the stairs. Only, I'd hate to think of what might happen to him—Ezrina would be intolerable if I accidently offed Nevermore in the Fem-isphere. "We should throw Chloe in. Better yet—tell her Gage is in there, and she'll go willingly." It's ingenious.

"Doubtful Jock Strap has that capability."

"I have Skyla," Gage says, reaching for the door. "That's all I need. And I won't let anyone or anything take her away from me."

Logan blinks through my mind. *The faction war—*

Before I can finish the thought, Gage swings the door open and a blast of music washes over the three of us, pulsating through our bodies with its thumping beats and rhythm.

"Mr. Dudley?" A female voice squeals, and before long, an entire throng of enthusiastic, estrogen-laced damsels in sexual distress migrate on over.

"Ladies, ladies—I'm here with a friend," he says, riding his hand up and down my thigh before landing a molten kiss on the side of my face. *Do you know what would make a splendid early wedding gift? If you ravaged me, right here in the midst of your peers. Go ahead, Skyla—tear off my clothes. I give you full permission.* He pulls back and melts me with a smoldering look. *If you're going to have my child, we'll have to start someplace,* he adds to further entice me with his lewd request.

I highly doubt that a party at Emily Morgan's house will be the place where that carnal exchange occurs. In fact, I'm thinking the "realm of impossibilities" is a much more likely venue.

I cast a quick glance over at Gage who, thankfully, is busy panning the vicinity, probably for Logan or Ellis or a good place to set Marshall's body on fire.

"Come here," I hiss, annoyed at Marshall's inconsiderate words and impossibly handsome features. He knows I'm here with Gage. I walk him over to the painting in question and jab a finger at the long canvas stretched the length of Emily's dining room.

"Stunning." His lips twist as he takes it in.

"She's good, right?" I muse.

"I was referring to you, love. She really brought out the come-hither in your eyes and that sensual pout you seem to throw my way on occasion. I look forward to invoking many more provocative expressions from you accompanied by that aching moan of delight you exude when you press your lips against mine."

Gage bites down on his disapproval and smiles for less than a second before pulling back his arm and launching his fist in Marshall's direction.

Marshall catches him midflight and holds him steady.

"Think twice before discharging a physical assault," Marshall warns. "I have no qualms about snatching you in the night and feeding you to that perverse speculum parked in my living room." He tosses Gage back so hard he smacks into the wall just shy of the fireplace with a force that rattles the interior. "Now, if you don't mind, I need a moment alone with the woman who will grace the remainder of my time on Earth as my wife. Find someone else to coexist with. Perhaps that cousin of yours her mother prefers. I'm sure you have a squabble you'd like to proliferate with him as well, seeing that destiny has spoken out against you."

"I'm not leaving." Gage steps forward and folds his arms across his chest like a bouncer.

"Skyla?" Marshall perforates me with a harsh stare. "I can't work in this hostile environment. Do find a ball to occupy him with or another cheerleader perhaps. I hear he's partial to dark-haired beauties that play fast and loose with death."

I spot Logan headed in this direction and spin Gage around.

"Just hang out with him for a second," I whisper. Ellis walks up and strikes up a conversation with Logan. They stop abruptly and look directly at me with a DEFCON level of concern.

"You asked me not to leave." He turns and penetrates me with his gentle gaze and kindles a fire in me that only Gage and his flesh could extinguish.

"You won't be leaving me, I swear. You'll be less than twenty feet away." I give a gentle shove in Logan's direction. "You can watch the whole thing."

Gage complies begrudgingly as he makes his way over to Logan and Ellis, and now the three of them stalk us with great interest.

I scuttle over to Marshall's side. "What do you think?"

"I've seen this before. It's from the vision we shared months ago." His features transform to an ultra-serious demeanor I'm not used to. "Where are the rest?"

"The basement." I glance back to see Gage glaring in this direction. He lets a smile slide up one side, before leaning in to hear whatever Ellis is telling him.

"There's a binding spirit sealing the premises—we'll have to walk." Marshall takes up my hand and begins leading me toward the exit.

"Wait." I pull him back. "I can't go with you. Gage says you've turned him into a grenade, and he's going to explode." Nuclear bomb to be exact.

"Messy." He looks over my shoulder and shoots a look of contempt at the explosive himself.

I note Chloe, Michelle, and "Pierce," a.k.a Holden, gaping in our direction. As soon as I spot them, they dive back into conversation as if they hadn't even noticed that it looks like I'm having a lover's spat with West Paragon's most controversial faculty member. Although, on this night, he looks more teen, less faculty, and for darn sure we're not lovers.

"Yet." He raises my hand to his lips and nibbles on my fingers in a heated lusty exchange.

Gah!

I snatch it back in fear of Gage detonating into confetti-sized pieces. I'd rather wrap my hand in a bloody steak and feed it to Cerberus than reduce Gage to shrapnel.

"I'll let you know of my findings." Marshall gives a quick nod. "I gather one of your male suitors will have evacuated you from the premises by the time I return. Do stray from any carnal inclinations you might have." He digs a look of disgust over my shoulder. "Their intentions are anything but chaste. I may have to teach them a lesson."

I don't like the thought of Marshall teaching anyone a lesson.

"You don't own me." I try to control my voice to keep from going off the rails.

"Neither do they, love." He glares at them openly. "Perhaps that, my dear, is the very point that needs to be driven home."

I watch as Marshall speeds out the back. Michelle gives an icy look in my direction before trotting off after him.

Chloe steps into my line of vision. She loses herself in a gaze over my shoulder, and I look back to confirm her obsession with Gage lives on.

Chloe may not have Gage, but it doesn't seem to stop her from longing for him, dying a little daily just to linger in his direction, molest him with her eyes.

It looks as if this entire summer is going to be rife with lessons on ownership and relationships, heartache, and revenge.

Chloe catches my eye and I give a little smile.

I think some of those lessons should start tonight.

53

Steam Heat

The party at Emily Morgan's house rages at maximum hormonal capacity with the entire teen population of the island gyrating under its questionably sturdy roof.

The walls quake from drunken laughter. Wild screams erupt without rhyme or reason, followed up by ruthless cackles as girls and boys bump and grind into one another. This is quickly descending into an all-out orgy of naked limbs and faces tinged with lascivious intent.

I bump into Brielle as I maneuver my way over to Logan and Gage. Her face is twisted with venom, and for a brief second, I think she's about to unleash on Chloe for glancing in my boyfriend's direction.

"What's going on?" I ask, pulling her to the side.

"That." She nods toward a moving heap on the couch.

"Oh my God," I gasp.

My moronic stepbrother has his body draped over the mistress of ceremonies, and, holy freaking shit, I think he just pulled out a condom. Clothes start to fly, shoes are flicking off, and of course the condom in question has been launched clear across the room because dumbass Drake has no clue what to do with it.

I head over to a table laden with beverages and snatch up a two-liter soda.

"I will not let this shit fly," I grit through my teeth. Really, I mean the fact Drake is about to fertilize another unsuspecting ovum. Just the thought of him spewing forth another Landon heir who will most likely end up in a casket in my mother's cemetery-themed bedroom has me beside myself.

Brielle pulls back her chest and rides shotgun as I head over at a livened clip.

I shake the contents of the bottle using my Celestra-inspired vigor. The cap explodes off its base, and I don't hesitate showering the lovebirds with high fructose corn syrup just as Drake's bare ass makes its debut for the evening.

"What the—!" Em jumps up, dumping Drake on the floor unceremoniously.

"Thanks, girl," Brielle shouts as she thrusts a fist bump my way.

Drake springs to his feet and jumps back into his jeans before getting in my face.

"You need to stay the hell out of my business." He grabs a hold of my shoulders and gives a hard rattle. "Stay the fuck out!" His beer breath explodes over my face.

"Hey!" Logan knocks Drake off my person and keeps shoving him until he's pinned against the wall.

An eerily mounted dragon's head supervises the melee from above. Its ruby eyes glitter, while its mouth curls up in a chilling grimace.

Logan bumps his shoulder into Drake's. "Does it make you feel good to pick on girls? Shake them around for the hell of it?"

Drake plunges his hands into Logan's chest and bucks him away.

"You can stay the hell out of my way, too. I'm sick of Ms. High and Mighty judging me when, every time I turn around, she's bagging half the island. How does it feel to share your girlfriend with your brother?" Drake barks in his face.

I try to leap forward to implant a vase or the heel of my shoe in his forehead, but Gage holds me back.

"I'm not sharing my girlfriend with anybody." Logan picks Drake up and dangles him three feet off the ground before launching him over to the couch from whence he came.

"Let's go, Skyla." Logan wraps an arm around my shoulder and pulls me free from Gage. "We need to talk."

ʍ ʍ ʍ

Logan leads me right out the front door and into a palpable fog that shrouds the night with its pale splendor. I inhale its textured reserve by the lungful from the sheer rush of almost getting in an altercation with my step-monkey of all people.

Gage and Ellis appear by my side, and we follow Logan to the far end of the wraparound porch. For some reason, when Logan whisked me away, I assumed it was for our previously scheduled rat-my-mother-out session where he lays out all her deep dark secrets like a deck of useless tarot cards. I'm sure she's confided more than a few things to him now that they're besties.

"We have a problem." Logan grits the words out as if Drake were a real threat.

"Please," I balk. "I'll snap his neck in his sleep if I have to." Not that I would, but I'll keep the possibility open should the need arise.

"Not, him." Gage pulls me in and steadies me as if I were about to hear something devastating. "The Counts held a faction meeting last night. Looks like Morley and Arson are sick of Demetri's on-the-fly rulings."

I spin around to look at Ellis. "What does that mean?"

"It means they're coming after him. They're considering a petition with the Justice Alliance to have your treble revoked."

"What?" I jump a little at the thought. "Why would the Justice Alliance help those kidnapping bastards?"

"Because they have prisoners of war bylaws and shit." Ellis gives the legal breakdown with a sober expression. "You need to stay in Celestra jail, or everything goes to hell."

"I'm not going to stay in Celestra jail, *Ellis*," I sneer. "And, by the way, my mother happens to run that circus in the sky. I seriously doubt she's going to side with those lunatics and send me to never-bloody-never land just to keep this crooked game moving by the rules."

Logan clears his throat and shakes his head at me. I glance up at Gage, and he nods as if agreeing with Logan that, yes, my mother would gladly side with the Counts in the name of all things legal.

Crap.

They're right.

"So now I guess I'm screwed." I give a hard sigh, bringing my hands to my ears because I can't take much more of this.

"There is a way." Ellis comes over and drapes his arm over my shoulder. "I've got an idea."

"What's that?" I look up at him with an intense measure of hope. The fact the prospect of my future lies in the hands of Paragon's most notorious stoner makes me sway slightly on my heels.

"I talked to my dad after the meeting and asked if there was anything that would get him to change his mind." Ellis meets my gaze with a serious demeanor I've never seen in him before. "There was one thing."

A harsh wind blows through the porch. The fog spins around us like a flurry of cantankerous ghosts—as if the entire graveyard came to life and decided to join the party. Everything hinges on what Ellis says next. Everything hinges on whether or not I agree with the serpent, who is his father, and if I'm able to meet his hostile demands.

"What is it?" I blow out a breath and clasp my hand over Ellis for support.

"He said if you meant something to me, he would consider dropping the issue."

"And what did you say?" My heart rattles unharnessed inside my chest.

"I said he should spare you because we got a thing going." He swallows hard. "I said you were my girlfriend."

54

Blood Count

"So now what?" I ask, stupefied by the fact my treble depends upon whether or not I'm Ellis Harrison's new fornication station—or at least pretend to be.

A light rain starts to beat down on us sideways, infiltrating the porch at Emily's house of artistic and carnal terrors. Inside, the party rages on even though Emily, herself, is probably in the shower, trying to remove the sticky residue of corn syrup I just baptized her with—and if my gut is correct, she's not alone in the endeavor. Drake has a lot of nerve to attempt to openly buck Emily in the presence of the mother of his child. It would seem common sense isn't a genetic marker of the Landon clan, which completely disproves Darwin's theory on the survival of the fittest because obviously the unfit breed and breed prolifically.

"So." Ellis shrugs. The porch light casts a white glare off the top of his head and illuminates his high cheekbones, the crest of his greasy smile. "You wanna do it?"

I bite down on the inside of my cheek. If it were anyone else, I would seriously doubt I was just propositioned right here before God, Logan, and Gage—Marshall somewhere within earshot. But this is Ellis, which assures me the double entendre was more than intentional. And, if it were anyone other than me, it would probably land him a nice little hoebag for a solid ten minutes, ready to turn action into satisfaction.

"Yes, I want to *do* it." I over enunciate. If I'm going to fool his father, I might as well take his son for a ride, too. Not physically. Besides, sexual banter is Ellis's native language—Marshall's too. Hell, Marshall most likely invented it. "But it's going to be fake."

His entire person brightens. "Of course it's going to be fake. Right up until you fall hard for me. Then I'll have to get my mom to write up a restraining order to keep you away."

"So that's it?" I shrug. "I have to show up and watch a movie at your house? Go to dinner with you, hold your hand in public?" I'm getting off easy. Every single person in those tunnels would give anything to have a chance to live on the outside again. Hanging out with Ellis would be a small price to pay for freedom.

"Simple as that." Ellis subdues the curve of his smile like he's a used car salesmen trying to close a deal. "One more thing. My dad mentioned we might need to find a way to appease Arson. He's not one to go away quietly."

"As in what? Date Pierce?" A rise of vomit surges to the back of my throat at the thought of Holden pawing me.

"No, not that." Logan steps forward and needles me with a serious look. "He didn't have a suggestion for anything that might take Arson off your back."

"Perfect. I'm right back at ground zero." Trying to please a Kragger is a near impossibility let alone Big Daddy K who stalks around Paragon like some Albino demon. I'd have better luck surviving a pit of starving tigers while holding a can of cat food.

"There is something that might make him change his mind." Gage dips his head into his chest. "Rumor has it he visits his daughter's grave nearly every single day, twice on weekends and holidays.

"Emerson?" Chloe poisoned her after promising to super-size her bloodstream with some Celestra goodness. Of course, Chloe took her down with strychnine, something she keeps on hand for a snack. "She's in the Transfer. The Counts can bring her back anytime they want to." I saw her down there myself. Emerson was gorgeous, and now she's locked in a tube of blue keeping solution, floating like some macabre mermaid until the Counts see fit to blip her back into existence.

"They can, but it'll take a lot of reserves to do it." Logan shakes his head. "Her kidneys were destroyed, her liver is shot, and her heart was severely damaged."

"Sounds like they need a Celestra." Gage circles my waist like he's trying to protect me from the idea, which started out as his by the way.

"Why couldn't they use one from the tunnels?" Not that I'm averse from doing it, but I'm curious.

"Supplies are backlogged," Ellis offers.

"They've got the tunnels in some kind of treble of their own," I say. "Stuck on two bastardized years ago."

Logan pulls me free from Gage with a gentle tug of the hand. "Counts that require full transfusions like Emerson are on a waiting list. According to Ezrina, Emerson is ten years out."

I for sure don't like the fact Logan is buddying up to the hatchet princess. Nothing good is going to come from this. I'm betting we'll have a tomahawk missile crisis to avert sooner than later.

"Sounds like Emerson is desperate for my services." I can see it now, me in Ezrina's lair hooked up with a crimson hose pumping my blood directly into the she-Kragger. "You guys think that's enough to buy Arson's vote to keep me on the island?"

Logan bears into me with a morbid sense of heartbreak. "I'm not sure."

"I gotta get back inside." Ellis moves toward the door. "I'll call you so we can get started on operation Whipped for Ellis. My dad's in town, so maybe you can come by and we'll watch a *movie* or something." He winks because I suspect movie is code for let's get naked. "I'll surprise you with something good."

"Whipped for Ellis," I swallow a laugh. I can think of a million worse things than watching a movie with Ellis. This is going to be a cake walk, not to mention Logan and Gage live right across the street, so I can just drop by afterward.

"Let's take off." Gage wraps his arms around me. He lands a wet kiss behind my ear, and the wind licks it, enlivening my skin from head to toe in goose bumps. "I have a surprise for you, too."

"Actually—" Logan steps forward, presses into me with a solemn expression, a smile plays on his lips, but he tries to hide it. "I'd like to borrow Skyla for a little while if that's OK."

Gage doesn't bother to mask his irritation. "Is that OK with you?" He hums it into my ear.

"Um..." I look back at Gage, his sturdy open features, his strong arms still firmly planted around me. "It's fine."

"I'll catch you in the butterfly room?" Gage delivers a sultry kiss before I can reply.

"Sure." I feel uneasy with Gage's PDA in front of a very broken-hearted Logan. Something about our arrangement isn't settling well with me anymore.

A pair of heels clop along the porch and we glance over to find Chloe barreling in our direction.

"Is this where the line begins for Skyla's kissing booth?" she asks Logan, openly mocking him in the process for having to bear witness to the lingual exchange.

"Leave," I say. "I've met my drama quota for the day."

"I was just about to." She leans her cleavage into Gage as if she were trying to lure him with her.

"I'm taking off to," he says, planting a rather docile kiss on the top of my head. "Butterfly room?"

"Butterfly room," I whisper.

We watch as Gage heads over to his truck with Chloe struggling to keep up like a stray dog begging for a boner.

"Can I catch a ride?" she shouts after him.

I bet she wants a ride. She'd rob the U.S. Treasury if she thought it would get him to drop trou and give her a ride on the Gage express.

In your dreams, Chloe.

Gage would rather hang himself than tote her around on his person or in his truck.

"Butterfly room," Logan scoffs to himself. He picks up my hand and warms it with both of his.

I have a feeling he's not tolerating this after-the-war crap anymore. My relationship with Gage has never ticked him off so openly.

"You're right, Skyla," he affirms, "I just may have changed my mind."

Knew it.

I lose myself in Gage's taillights. This is all going to end in a spectacular crash, the three of us colliding at a million loving miles an hour.

The empty street startles me to attention.

Where the hell did Chloe go?

He didn't.

He couldn't.

Dear God, I think he did.

What in the hell is Gage Oliver thinking?

55

Elysian Fields

Logan and I drive the long stretch of Paragon highway with his headlights reflecting off the powder-like fog, immersing us in a God-breathed whiteout. Every now and again, Logan switches on his brights, but it reduces visibility to less than nothing as the mist lights up proficiently as the sun.

I try not to think too hard about Gage giving Chloe a ride. I wouldn't put it past her to duck for cover once he left, just to make me think he did. Instead, I lose myself in the pale, arid night—its stony calm matching the atmosphere in the car.

I press my gaze into the crystalline mist. I imagine that's what you see when you land yourself on the other side of existence, what it must be like to die. One minute you're on a ski lift, and the next you're swallowed by an exquisite illumination. It beckons you to stay, pulls you forward until you land in the Transport. Marshall showed me that jasper cave, red as lava, with angels inside ready to send you to a more permanent location.

"When is my dad coming out?" I ask, breaking the silence we filled with the comfort of being alone. That's the best part about being with Logan. Nothing is ever strange. We could be silent for a thousand years and not think anything of it. With Gage there are always reassurances that have to be made, Chloe rearing her ugly head, asking for a ride.

"Your dad?" He squints into the windshield as if he were trying to decipher who that might be—either that or he's busy trying to navigate us down the highway by memory. I know for a fact we could easily get killed on a night like tonight. One wrong turn, and a head-on collision could pole vault me to see my father a lot quicker than I ever imagined.

"I just figured my mom might have mentioned it. She said something about the two of them coming to Paragon. I suppose I'll know soon enough. They're probably coming to remind me what a disappointment I've been."

"You're not a disappointment to anyone, Skyla. You're on the right path."

"Right path to what? Losing the war?" If I do lose the war, I won't mind one bit sharing the blame with my destination-wielding mother.

Logan makes a hard left without answering the question. The headlights refract off a sign that reads *Welcome to the Falls of Virtue.*

I sink a little in my seat. Logan has a track record of stripping down to his next to nothings while here. And although the thought of Logan doing the big boxer reveal is hot, I'm pretty sure I'm back together with Gage, so major awkward will ensue should the urge arise to drop his pants. Also, I'm a little apprehensive because Logan all but declared himself back in the game before we left the party.

"Damn Kragger," Logan hisses just below his breath as he parks high on the ridge overlooking the lake.

"Is he here?" I straighten with a mild sense of panic as Logan takes up my hand. The last people I care to deal with are the Kraggers, and now it looks like I'll be doing a revival in exchange for survival with yet another from their evil brood— Emerson.

"No, he's not. And as for Emerson, I wouldn't get worked up over reviving her. Counts won't allow it. Accepting the blood of a captive in order to fulfill a bribe would be cause for a hearing. From what I hear, Arson doesn't drift too far from the Count playbook. That's exactly why he wants to hang Demetri by the balls. He's a legalist. We'll think of another way." He kills the engine and sits back dejected.

"Crap." Everything in me sags. "I have nothing outside of my blood to offer the Kraggers. Hey, maybe we can remind him that I'm sort of the reason Holden is around?" I think about it a moment. "No, that won't work. I took him off the planet to begin with, Pierce, too." Killing Kraggers is just one of those spooky things Chloe and I have in common. "Anyway, don't feel bad about what Holden tried to do to me at the lake."

"I do," he says, bringing my hand to his lips and closing his eyes. His lids tremble—a seam of liquid lines his lashes, thick with remorse. "When he was evicted from my body, I was left with the memories. All that crap he pulled will haunt me for the next fifty years."

"Holden didn't seem to have your memory," I say. Holden was clueless to life in general, which is par for the course.

"That's because Holden is a dolt and didn't know how to access it. Proof positive that he's not firing with all pistons." He pinches his eyes shut before turning to look at me. "I know what he did to you here. I'm sorry." He gives my hand a squeeze. "I would never hurt you like that. I would never even force you to look at me, let alone touch me—nor would I touch you without permission."

"Don't apologize for something you clearly didn't do. Holden is a natural born asshole. I'm just sick he lives to see another day. Did you hear he broke up with Nat? Just dumped her at the beach a few weeks back like she had the plague."

"I heard." His voice softens. Logan looks as if he's about to dive into me—like I were the exact warm pool of water he was searching for. I had become an entire ocean of desire to Logan, and he wants nothing more than one last swim. "I did bring you here to talk about someone's relationship," he rasps out the words with a sad smile. "Ours."

Everything in me freezes.

The fog presses against the windows in an effort to listen in. It permeates the small spaces and seeps into the atmosphere, becomes a part of us like it has been all along. All of nature has bent its ear in this direction. This is seismic. Everything about Gage and me—Logan and me—might hinge on this very conversation.

I pull back my hand and nod into him.

Logan is the fog circling everything Gage and I built together. He wants to permeate it, come back and claim what was rightfully his to begin with because he's a part of me. He has been all along. My heart has had a Logan-shaped hole in it ever since he cut me loose, a small secret space for him to gain his footing. I'm already so ripe for him to penetrate, saturate, reclaim, and reign over my heart again. But now he's walled in my emotions with Gage. I'd love to blame Logan for pushing us together, for making me fall impossibly in love with a dark-haired boy with the face of an angel, but that was destined to happen anyway. I can feel it in my bones. But it was Logan and me that started this wheel turning. It was our love that started the inferno that is the faction war, our love that pointed me in so many dangerous directions for all the right reasons. And life had somehow reduced him to nothing more than my Elysian—my death suitor bearing skeletal armor, a sickle in hand at the ready.

"What are you thinking about?" he whispers soft as a dream.

"Our love." I don't bother hiding the fact—just go with it. They weren't bad thoughts, nothing negative about Gage in the process, so why deny it? With Logan, there's no use pretending.

"Let's go for a walk," he offers.

Logan comes around and helps me slide to the damp soil below. The air is sweeter here at the falls than it is just about anywhere else on Paragon. And life is sweeter with Logan by my side even if Gage is in the picture.

"Can I?" He takes my hand and holds it up, asking permission after the fact.

"You never need to ask." I kiss him over the knuckles. "Now tell me everything my lunatic of a mother said while she held you captive."

"She didn't hold me captive," he says, leading me through a trail in the woods toward the back of the lake where the falls aren't drilling their lusty cry of existence into our ears. "And it turns out, she's not a lunatic."

"Sure she's not, especially after she declared you as the best man for her daughter's heart."

"Especially after that." He gives a playful tug. "She's right, though. I am the best man for your heart."

"And what about Gage?" There it is. I didn't want to go there, ever, but I knew where the train was headed long before it ever left the station.

"What about him?" Logan pulls a bleak smile before dissipating to an all-out frown.

"Doesn't he factor into the equation somehow? I saw this vision, and he was able to replicate it for me. There's something there—some kind of future."

"He replicated it?" He tucks his head back a notch. "Sounds fishy," he growls. "I don't buy it."

God, I hope he's being playful. The last thing I want is to play suspicious minds with Gage again.

"Forget it," I whisper. My heart lets out a few vagrant thumps and fills my ears with the sound of its percussion. Gage and I had moved past deception, hadn't we? And now, Logan had stirred the pot again. With everything in me I want to believe in Gage, believe that he knows things and that not a cell in his body could ever be deceptive. But a warning siren is going off inside me. It sits in my chest like a brick that Chloe cast there herself.

We come upon a steep hill with a slick, muddy path. The scent of the eucalyptus perfumes the air.

Logan wraps an arm around my waist and helps steady me until we get to the bottom. It's a miracle I didn't end up on the seat of my pants.

"So let's talk about us," I offer, lifting my head to see the barely visible lake. The quiet hush of the falls whispers "Logan and Skyla" from the distal end of the hillside. I'm betting it's more *mother* than *nature* procuring the strange phenomenon.

"I'd like to think we're getting back on track." He leads us to shore, to a small water cavity that hangs from the edge of the lake like a hot tub.

I peer inside the black cauldron. This is no heated whirlpool. This small body of water is capable of freezing your fingers and toes off before you realize what's happened—might land you a permanent residency in the cemetery on an unlucky night. Barron will probably give Tad a price break on the burial if I kick the bucket.

Logan taps the water twice with the bottom of his shoe, and the deep well lights up a bright glacial blue.

"Wanna go for a swim?" He gives a smile laced with a bite of lust, but the trappings of eternal sadness remain locked behind his eyes.

"I'm not wearing my thermal bathing suit." I give his hand a squeeze, affirming the fact we should abandon the hypothermia-inducing idea. "Plus, we'll freeze to death," I say, sticking to the more practical part of my argument.

"It's warm. I promise." He reels me in like a fish. "And you can go in fully clothed, if you like." Logan wraps his arms around me tight as if he were saving me from taking a flying leap off a very tall building. "Can I take you somewhere, Skyla?"

"Not until after you fill in a few blanks." I don't know whether to struggle free or succumb to Logan's healing touch, so much of me cries out for him—to love him just a little while longer. I'm so afraid I'm going to lose him—that in some way I already have. Sometimes I think just putting up a wall and pretending that I never had feelings for Logan would be easier than living in this crazy world without him. Even with Gage by my side, something lingers in my spirit for Logan—howls for him like a child lost in the woods on an Ezrina-filled night.

"You make me feel safe," I mouth the words.

"Let's jump in, and I'll fill in all the blanks for you." He moves us a step over toward the rim of the glowing pool of water. "I promise I'll always keep you safe."

Logan pulls me in tight, latches onto me with a bionic force and leaps us into the tiny offshoot of the lake. He lays his cheek over mine as we plunge deep into the Caribbean-blue waters, warm as a tropical sunset.

A rush of bubbles explodes around us. Streams of evanescence float their way to some nebulous surface as we drop through a tunnel of liquid so beautiful I never want to leave.

It's magic like this with Logan. A lifetime with him would be nothing short of a miracle.

We spring to the surface, gasping for the honeyed air only to discover the surroundings have transformed themselves. A well-lit world awaits us with the blush of a lavender sky. The touch of a tangerine glow kisses the horizon and an emerald lawn sprawls for miles in every direction.

Everything about this mysterious place feels so richly familiar. I've been here before in my dreams with my father. He told me to go back, that I was pure as gold.

"Where are we?" I ask as Logan spins me slow in the water.

"Elysian Fields." He lands a soft kiss on my cheek as if all he sees is me.

I take in a quick breath. "Does that mean—?"

"Yes, Skyla—we're dead."

56

An Afterlife Kind of Love

"Dead?" I say, startled.

I take in the beauty, the majesty of the landscape as the sweetened air fills me with far more than my olfactory senses can handle. This place, it touches me, cradles me in its perfect loving arms. I throw my head back, and an unexpected laugh bubbles out.

"You like this, don't you?" Logan lovingly caresses my hips. He pulls me underwater with him and steals a kiss, as if such corporal displays of affection weren't allowed in this strange, new universe.

"Logan." I pant as we reach the surface. A smooth vibration tunes through me. It feels like Marshall in every way, just richer, more refined.

"Come on." He lifts himself out of the warm pool and gives me a hand, landing us both on the cushioned grass.

The sky shifts a pale vanilla. Soft overtones of pink outline the hard ridge where the trees meet the sky, and the dark rich lawn rolls out into a viridian horizon.

"What are we doing? We need to explore," I say, pulling Logan up as we set in on a walk. Both my clothes and my hair, dry in seconds. A perfumed breeze sweeps through the air, intoxicating me with its floral welcome. "This is bliss. I'm not afraid at all. So are we really dead?"

"Mostly dead." Logan glances back as if he were looking for someone. "I happen to have scored a day pass—one for you, too." He rocks into me before nuzzling a kiss in my hair.

"From my mother." Of course it's from my mother. Death totally falls in line with the kinds of gifts she would give. "So we're in the Soullennium? Marshall took me on the guided tour. Didn't look like this though."

"Nope, not the Soullennium. I was a guest there for a while, remember?" He jiggles my hand. "This is the other side of Ahava, past the lake. It's the real deal." He points over toward a mighty body of water with a two tiered waterfall on its outer banks. "It's gorgeous. Earth could only hope to have such peace and beauty. I was hoping your mother would let me bring you."

"Sort of gives two tickets to Paradise a whole new meaning."

"You got that right." He drops a kiss just shy of my lips before beaming a fantastical smile.

In the distance the waterfall glows a warm shade of crimson.

"Logan," I say, stopping him in his tracks, "that's where the sword of the Master is. We should use this and try to get it. We can end the war right now."

"No. There's a chasm." He pulls me in by the waist, rides his hands up my body, slow, like he's familiar with my curves, like he dreams about them nightly. "I asked to bring you here today. I wanted to show you that it wasn't so bad. That it feels good—that we're still alive in every single way."

"It's better, it's richer," I add to his sentiments. "I feel more alive here than I do down there." Instinctually, I know the Earth is somewhere below us, a footstool to the throne of this exotic locale. There is not one ounce of illogic to fight me on the matter.

Just past the lake, a soft wave sweeps up from the ground and wobbles through the air like radiating heat.

"So that's the chasm," I say, looking out at it, inspecting it. It looks penetrable. I can see clear to the other side. "I love it here, Logan." Powerful feelings of joy pulse through me. "I never want to leave."

Logan cradles my face in his hands and pulls me in. I can feel his ache to kiss me deeply. His entire being draws me in and I give. There's not one cell in my body that suggests otherwise, just the sweet anticipation of his precious lips as I wait for them to fall over mine.

Our passion explodes into flames like gunpowder.

I had waited so long, denied the both of us of this spectacular splendor, and now, here we were on the other side of death. There were no rules, and no doubt, and no one else to stop us.

Logan pushes me in by the small of my back as he caves into his desire. His soft lips against mine, his hungry tongue— Logan gifts me with all of his willful affection. For the first time in a long while, he's unafraid to love me.

I miss this. I miss Logan with an indescribable urgency. I hate my mother for making me choose. She did this. Let all of the penalties lie with her because she force fed me two great loves.

Logan pulls away. Gone is the perennial sadness in his eyes, replaced with inexpressible joy.

"It's this place, Skyla. It's coloring your feelings." He smiles as though it didn't offend him in the least.

"Not true. I love you. I've always loved you."

"You love Gage, too. I didn't bring you here to take you physically or ask you to erase him like a bad memory."

"Take me." I push into him with a laugh. "You can bark out orders, and I will obey every single one." It streams from my lips with lust-filled passion.

"Skyla..." His demeanor softens. "I needed to show you this place. I knew you had feelings for me," he whispers soft as tears, "that you held a place for me in your heart." He swallows hard. "Look." He nods behind me.

A beautiful little girl with butter-colored hair strides by. She glances up at the two of us and offers a shy smile.

"Hey..." I look back at Logan. "I think I know her. I've seen her someplace or..." I rack my brains trying to figure it out. I turn around and she's disappeared. "She's gone."

"That was a vision," he whispers it so low it was almost impossible to hear. Logan pulls me in and holds me for a very long time. I can feel his warm breath as he sinks a kiss over my neck. His body trembles slightly as though he were on the verge of tears.

"What's happening?" I whisper, almost afraid to ask.

"I just needed you to see this place—to know that people who come here are going to be all right."

"Is this all there is? I mean it's quiet and peaceful but..." There's something off and I just can't put my finger on it.

"No, this is just the beginning, the entrance to Paradise. This is where your mom brought me. She wanted me to see it, and I couldn't stand the thought of not sharing it with you."

"Why did she bring you here?" Oh my God, we're going to die. Gage's visions were nothing but a hoax to get in my pants.

"I don't know." Logan pulls me down to the grass and cradles me in his arms as we look out at the lake. "I figured since she was giving me the tour that it was a strong possibility I would soon be a resident. And"—he sighs into the back of my neck—"if I am, I want you to know I'll be OK. That I'll be here waiting for you."

I don't like this conversation. And suddenly, I'm not so hot on this magical mystical death portal, either.

"What did she want?" I ask.

"She wanted to know if I remembered her, and when I said no, she filled me in. She put her hand on my forehead, and then it was like watching a movie." He gives an impish smile. "I remembered everything."

"What happened? When did you meet my mother?"

He takes in a lungful of air. "When I was alive, in the time after my parents died, I met her. She was working at a research and development hospital on the outskirts of L.A., and I had been down there recovering after another one of my surgeries."

"You knew my mom!" I twist in his arms. That hurt look on his face lies buried below his smile.

"Sort of, we met in passing a few times. She was interning for a doctor who had my case. We got to talking, and I told her my story. I told her my parents died in a fire, that I was badly burned in the process."

"Oh, Logan." I wrap my arms around his neck, sniffing back the tears. Logan and I rock slow and steady to the beating of our hearts, right here in the eternal city. "I'm so sorry you had to go through that." Tears roll down my cheeks.

"It's OK." Logan warms my back with his hands. It's typical Logan to comfort me when he was the one who lived through the harrowing trauma. "Your mom was very sweet. She said she knew who I was, that there was much hope for me. She said I was chosen to live out another life, one that would cost me my own, but I needed to leave that life to come to this one."

"I wish you were born here to begin with." Leave it to good old Candy to take the hard road to get where she's going. And why drag Gage into this? Why dangle me in front of Marshall like some matrimonial prize? God—I bet she's in bed with Delphinius and perhaps in more ways than one. "I don't see why she couldn't have arranged a different time and place for you to begin with."

"I asked the same thing. She said I needed my genetic code, that it was worth more than gold."

"What did she say?" I pull back and examine him.

"She said my genetic code was worth more than gold."

"That's sort of what my father told me in this weird vision or dream I had when we first fell from the stone. He said for me to write it down—repeat it to myself."

"Really?" He studies me a moment. I can see the thoughts shifting in his mind like a landslide, the movement of something big coming up from underneath. "This means something, Skyla."

"What else did she say?"

"When I knew her back in L.A., she came every day. She listened and spoke with me. I had very few friends and no family out there, so it was a welcome reprieve from the loneliness. I was in pain, and she touched me—she healed my affliction."

I wonder if I was an infant at that time? Knowing my mother, she could have just as easily morphed to Earth and pretended to be an intern. Her ulterior motives know no bounds.

"I thought the past didn't change." I pull my eyes along Logan's precious face. I wish this moment would stretch out forever, but I can feel it closing in on us, coming to an end like a rubber band ready to retract. "But it changed for you."

"Your mother changed it," he says, swallowing his excitement. "She said I made an impression on her and that she wouldn't let me go to waste, that I wouldn't have to worry about being lonely again." Logan holds my eyes with a heavy gaze. "She said her daughter needed me. That we were meant to be together right from the beginning, but we were on different paths."

"That's me." I breathe the words like a dream.

"She said our paths would converge, then disperse for a short time." His expression dims. The light in his soul goes out completely before starting in on an incandescent flicker. "Then we would be back. We would find our way together again." His lips bloom into a smile. "She said our love would be strong, Skyla—that we had a spiritual covenant."

I take in a breath and blink back fresh tears, this time they were all for Gage. A slow boiling anger stirs in me.

"Did she tell you why she shoved another perfectly good Oliver in my direction?" I want to strangle her for breaking my heart, for breaking Gage's heart—for toying with us like we were kittens. It makes me want to claw out her perfect, sparkling eyes.

"It's OK, Skyla." Logan shakes his head. His brows crease as the world starts to wobble like a stiff piece of plastic, bending and flexing violently in the breeze. "Believe me—there is a time for us. And we will love deeply."

The world snaps into darkness.

Logan and I appear back at the Falls of Virtue in a pool of illuminated water.

"Logan!" I pull him in and hold on tight. I have just as many questions as I did when we started, only now, I'm afraid to ask them. Every good feeling has washed away and the stale air of Paragon infiltrates my marrow with a destitute misery.

"I love you, Skyla Messenger," Logan whispers, brushing his lips against my ear like painting a picture. "It will all work out in the end. I promise."

"I love you, too," I say, and wonder what he really means by "the end."

Thank you for reading **TOXIC Part One** (Celestra Series Book 7). If you enjoyed this book, please consider leaving a review at Amazon, Barnes and Noble, or your point of purchase. Look for **TOXIC Part Two**, (Celestra Series Book 8) available now!

Acknowledgements

To my family: thank you from the bottom of my heart. A special thanks to my husband who graciously does all of the cover art for the books and never bats a lash when I tell him to start from scratch. To my four awesome children, who are all so much more emotionally mature than I will ever be.

To my wonderful, spectacular, awesome, fantastic, out of this world editors, Amy Eye and Sarah Oaklief (and no, I won't reduce my adjectives in that sentence). I am so happy to have you both overlooking the wellbeing of my novels. Thank you for talking me down from a few grammar ledges.

Thank you to Rachelle Gardner, the world's best literary agent, who lets me do whatever the heck I want. For that, I will always be grateful. Rachelle, you are the best cheerleader ever!

To my wonderful readers who make my adventures in Paragon a whole lot sweeter knowing that I can share them with you. You bless me far beyond words.

To Him who holds the world in the palm of His hands. To your name be the glory, and power, and honor, forever. I owe you everything.

About The Author

Addison Moore is a *New York Times, USA Today,* and *Wall Street Journal* bestselling author who writes contemporary and paranormal romance. Her work has been featured in *Cosmopolitan* Magazine. Previously she worked as a therapist on a locked psychiatric unit for nearly a decade. She resides on the West Coast with her husband, four wonderful children, and two dogs where she eats too much chocolate and stays up way too late. When she's not writing, she's reading.

Feel free to visit her at:

http://addisonmoorewrites.blogspot.com
Facebook: Addison Moore Author
Twitter: @AddisonMoore
Instagram: @authorAddisonMoore

CPSIA information can be obtained at www.ICGtesting.com
Printed in the USA
LVOW08s1902210616

493516LV00005B/506/P